General Preston Belvale: From giving FDR the real story of an Allied "friendly fire" tragedy in Italy to preparing a POW rescue in Burma, the old general fought a stateside battle of planning—in a war that wouldn't go according to plan . . .

General "Crusty" Carlisle: Holed up on a nameless Pacific atoll with a handful of courageous Marines, Crusty Carlisle got a chance to fight again. And so he did what he was born to do: go on the attack . . .

Sergeant Eddie Donnely: He challenged Crusty Carlisle when he asked permission to marry the general's granddaughter. But even though he had married into the Carlisle clan, he was already wed to the army. He knew he had to get back into the fight—and into a war of jungle ambushes and murderous deception . . .

Penny Belvale: As a Women's Auxiliary Service Pilot, she was officially a civilian. But as a POW she was singled out by the Japanese camp commander for a special shame and horror. And when a hired band of Burmese bandits ignited an escape attempt, she channeled her rage into a fierce fight for freedom . . .

Captain Owen Belvale: The war in Sicily was bogged down with logistical snafus and bitter German resistance. In bullet-whipped dirt and blood, Owen would come to terms with what it meant to be a Belvale, and what it meant to be his father's son . . .

Books by Con Sellers

Brothers in Battle
The Gathering Storm
The Flames of War
A World Ablaze

Published by POCKET BOOKS

Most Pocket Books are available at special quantity discounts for bulk purchases for sales promotions, premiums or fund raising. Special books or book excerpts can also be created to fit specific needs.

For details write the office of the Vice President of Special Markets, Pocket Books, 1230 Avenue of the Americas, New York, New York 10020.

MEN AT ARMS

BOOK 3

A WORLD ABLAZE

CON SELLERS

POCKET BOOKS

New York   London   Toronto   Sydney   Tokyo   Singapore

This book is a work of fiction. Names, characters, places and incidents are either the product of the author's imagination or are used fictitiously. Any resemblance to actual events or locales or persons, living or dead, is entirely coincidental.

An *Original* Publication of POCKET BOOKS

POCKET BOOKS, a division of Simon & Schuster Inc.
1230 Avenue of the Americas, New York, NY 10020

Copyright © 1992 by Con Sellers

All rights reserved, including the right to reproduce this book or portions thereof in any form whatsoever. For information address Pocket Books, 1230 Avenue of the Americas, New York, NY 10020

ISBN: 0-671-66767-X

First Pocket Books printing April 1992

10 9 8 7 6 5 4 3 2 1

POCKET and colophon are registered trademarks of Simon & Schuster Inc.

Cover design by Todd Radom

Printed in the U.S.A.

To Marvin Wilson Bailey, H. Co.,
16th Inf. of the Big Red One.
My friend,
I know that all battle wounds do not show.

A WORLD ABLAZE

CHAPTER 1

The New York Times—Allied Headquarters in North Africa, July 10, 1943: Allied infantry landed at 0300 on the Sicilian coast today under a blazing canopy of naval gunfire as the long awaited invasion of Europe began. For six days preceding the landings, bombers hammered enemy air bases, communication centers and factories around the clock. More than a million pounds of high explosives were dropped on the town of Catania alone.

Resistance is "fierce," according to war correspondents on the spot. An estimated 12 Axis divisions are committed to the defense of the rocky island, backed by a strong force of tanks and dive bombers.

In blackness lit only by gunfire, Colonel Chad Belvale plunged off the ramp of the Landing Craft, Personnel and into chill water over his knees. Carbine held high, he waded ashore behind the attack company of his 16th Regimental Combat Team. Enemy tracers snapped and sparked overhead, green and pink comet trails of phosphorus; Kraut and Wop. GI tracers fired a bright red, and he saw no blinking of those yet. Other 9mm slugs kicked vicious geysers in the water.

Splashing on, he ducked instinctively when the freight train rumble of big shells thundered in from the combat

1

support ships at sea behind the landing force. They blew up inland with great, deafening slams that shook the earth, but fire control had to be delicate now. Advance jumps of GI and British paratroops were scattered inland, too.

Earlier salvos of those giant shells had paved the way. Recon reported bodies hanging in trees and defense positions obliterated. But infantry dug in and determined to hold was seldom shaken loose by bombing, naval guns or land based artillery. Their opposite numbers had to go in and dig them out of their holes, infantry to infantry. Nobody ever said the job was easy or glamorous. It wasn't fully appreciated except by the dogfaces themselves.

And even the infantry called their crossed-rifle insignia the "idiot sticks."

"Left front—pillbox!" somebody in Fox Company yelled, loud enough to be heard over the rattle of small arms fire and the thump of enemy mortar shells.

Gela beach; the coast of Sicily and the second seaborne invasion within a year for the 1st Infantry Division. Survivors were left from the relatively easy walkover in Algeria and the hard fought Tunisian campaign where the outfit was truly bloodied. They remembered the bitter taste of defeat and the heady draught of victory; now they were capable of handling both.

The hard core of this outfit was professional, the old soldiers of the Regular Army, their casualty-depleted ranks brought up to strength by draftees they called handcuff volunteers. They didn't dwell on how long their luck would hold out. They came to do a job; they soldiered for their pay, such as it was, and for honor, although they would laugh at anybody who tried to put that into words.

"Take that damned pillbox under fire!" Captain Goldstein's tenor voice shrilled, pitched higher by strain. "Where are the 60s? Goddamnit—mortar section, get with it!"

A man screamed, but it wasn't in answer.

Ten yards up the slant of sandy beach and scattered rocks; fifteen, his hightop shoes sloshing, soaked leggins grating his shins, Chad pumped deep for breath. He was getting old for this kind of thing; not too old yet, but close to it. And given the chance, the commanding officer of this second battalion would tell him that any regimental CO playing head-on combat games was a beaucoup damned fool, him.

Major Lucien J. Langlois could turn a Cajun phrase, and he was right. No point arguing that it was in the blood, a rioting within the genes that pushed the Belvales and Carlisles to their destiny in battle. They were the holy warriors whose ancestors embarked on the Crusades, the samurai of the west; they fought for both the Blue and the Gray. Sallying forth from ancestral lands in England and later from their American fortresses turned mansions at Kill Devil Hill and Sandhurst Keep, untold generations of the intermarried family had made war their business and they were good at it. If any of the family's many generals were on the spot, they wouldn't be back on the floating headquarters ships, either.

Brrrttt! Brrrttt!

It was the magnified ripped cloth sound of a *Schmeisser* machine pistol too damned close by. Highly efficient as most Kraut weapons, the weapon's cyclic rate of fire was 900 rounds per minute. The U.S. had nothing to match it; the Thompson was too heavy and expensive; the 45 caliber grease gun much slower.

Chad hit the dirt with a dive that jolted a grunt out of him. Holy warrior, shit; the damned fool appellation was closer to the truth. Every ragged ass doughfoot ducking bullets and sizzling mortar fragments on this misbegotten beach earned the title of warrior. And now they were giving it back to the defenders, spreading out and leapfrogging to higher ground, firing cover as they went. The distinctive *ka-chung* of the M-1 rifle picked up that special kettle drum roll of a firelight coming under control.

Turning onto his right side, Chad squinted through swirling smoke for a clear target. There couldn't be many Jerries out of their holes; the prelanding shelling and bombing had been too fierce, but cunning landsers would slip out of their fortified positions to set small ambushes on the flanks. Nobody could say that the Jerries were stupid, and they were

3

experienced. Their survivors had been at war for five years, longer than most of Chad's regiment had been in uniform.

Jerry: the nickname originated from some ancient Limey with a warped sense of humor. Originally, a jerry meant a pot placed under an English bed for night use, a stateside thunder mug, a chamber pot. But these Jerries weren't crappy; they were tough, mean sons of bitches with a ton of combat know-how and discipline out the gazoo.

Cough! Cough! those blessed hollow belches of Fox Company's 60mm mortars sounded as they spat their finned shells into a haphazard pattern that would at least keep enemy heads down.

Brrrtttt!!

Not that son of a bitch's head. He should be hauling ass inland as fast as he could. Instead, he was lying out here to kill off a few GIs before he got his own brains scattered. That was not the stuff of heroes; it was the blind stupidity of dryland crawfish rearing up at a steam engine. That kind of bravery was merely a messy suicide.

Brrttt! Brttt!

This time the muzzle flashes gave the guy away, but not soon enough. One of the laboring mortar men loosed a choked yell and pitched onto his back. Chad figured the burp gunner to be tucked flat into a camouflaged hole just a hair to the right of the thick-walled concrete pillbox: one of the interlocking defensive positions that was raising so much hell with the advance, pinning down Fox Company's skirmish line.

Guesstimating the line of sight of his M-2 carbine, the redesigned 30 caliber whose killing power was limited to close work, Chad was glad for the new banana clip. The trouble was that its 30 rounds would not penetrate even light metal, like the armor-piercing rounds of the M-1 rifle. They had little killing shock, but the long curved clips doubled the short range firepower.

Propped on his elbows in the dark, Chad aimed at the spot where he'd picked up the muzzle flashes. Flexing his trigger finger, he fired three rounds center, then moved his muzzle an inch right and then left for two more short bursts. A pair of rounds up and two below his imaginary bullseye, and the target was covered. Chad waited, lying motionless and with his nerves drawn tight. Nothing moved there in the blackness, and the burp gunner didn't return fire.

Got the bastard.

Bullets kicked sand over Chad. He rolled right, seeking cover that wasn't there. These rounds were higher velocity stuff, probably from a Maxim 08. That water-cooled gun fired a 7:29, and being near obsolete didn't put a brake on its effectiveness.

He had to roll left when the gunner walked a string of sand geysers past him. One GI yelped; another shouted, "medic!" and his curses followed in rapid fire. Chad tasted powder smoke and dirt, and the thin, brassy flavor of fear. Every soldier was scared or crazy; the good soldiers used their fear and overcame it; the crazies got caught in the middle and blew up. The others just crapped out, and worse than losing their guts, let their buddies down.

Spinning left, Chad came up cutting a burst in the general direction of the heavy machine gun. Then GIs lifted from the ground before him and zigzagged forward, screening his field of fire. His right hand throbbed and he realized that he must have scraped it against a rock.

He settled back to thumb out the empty clip and feed in a fresh one. He would do well to wait here until the regiment closed in upon its primary objective, the high ground of Ponte Lupo. Hearing the stacatto banging of the battalion's heavy weapons start up, Chad thought of his son in H Company.

Following family tradition, Captain Owen Belvale went through the Academy at West Point to infantry platoon leader to company commander so far. And so far he had been lucky. In the same outfit was more family blood, a maverick who didn't give a damn about his field commission or decorations earned back in Africa.

Lying upon damp and chilly sand, waiting for battalion headquarters to catch up, Chad thought of what soldiers inevitably said to each other in parting: good luck. Stateside that meant hope your new outfit is what you want; that your transfer comes through, have a good reenlistment furlough, make it through the service school, all those things. In combat it meant try not to get killed. Good luck, Owen; good luck, Farley, my son, soldiering on the other side of the world.

To you also, Kirstin, mother of those sons and once my wife.

Now the 81mm mortars belched, and their heavier shells blasted the set of pillboxes; popcorn strings of red from the Browning machine guns worked over the area, four invisible AP rounds slamming in between every tracer. The gunners had been issued antiaircraft ammunition and were zeroing in with it on any target of opportunity.

A plane roared low and Chad rolled onto his back, ready to fire. But even if it were light, the thing zipped past too blurred to call friend or enemy. If the Krauts had been faked into believing the primary invasion would be on Sardinia or Corsica, they would still have plenty of combat aircraft available to strike here from the Italian mainland, from fields in Calabria. And come daylight, they would be over the beach in force. The troops would have to depend upon AA fire from the ships bobbing close in to beat off the *Luftwaffe*.

Men from support companies came to earth beside Chad, and in a moment got up and passed on. But they didn't get far; the enemy defenses were holding and troops piled up.

"Medic!" shouts chorused, "medic over here!" Closer by, a bullet *chunked!* into meat and a kid moaned oh shit, oh shit.

Climbing up, Chad moved through the gray-black morning, making his way back to the beach proper. Regimental headquarters would soon be setting up there and he was needed. Since Langlois the Cajun had been moved from Chad's right hand man to battalion CO, a new major carried the weight at regiment when Chad was gone.

As the firing increased behind him, Chad knew one thing for certain. The regiment's objective would not be taken before daylight, and after the sun came up things were going to get a hell of a lot tougher.

TWX, SECRET to Kill Devil Hill, July 10, 1943: High winds broke formations of transports carrying 3,400 paratroopers from North Africa, causing them to approach targets from several directions, and in the dark. Facing heavy antiaircraft fire, they were shot down and/or scattered their jumpers all over southern Sicily.

British glider troops fared worse. Of 144 gliders that took off from bases in Tunisia, 70 were released prematurely and fell into the sea. Early reports suggest that less than 100 English soldiers have reached only one of their objectives. These troops are under heavy attack.

Maj. Gen. Charles Carlisle snorted. "There's both god-damn sets of flyboys for you. Put poor bastard infantry up in those goddamn kites and then throw them away. Can't find their own asses with both hands."

Lt. Gen. Preston Belvale poured bourbon for them both. The family war room circled them, situation maps with over-lays, a bank of direct line telephones, short wave radios and teletype machines. On a smaller scale, it was as well equipped as the War Department's command center. Belvale glanced around it and lifted his glass.

"Here's to the poor bastards."

"Yeah, but not to the fuckups who sent them out."

Belvale's cigar had gone out. He got it going with his Ronson, fingertips touching the engraved motto: WE SERVE BY DEFENDING. A phone buzzed and he said into it, "Got it and thank you."

Turning, he made a mark on a celluloid overlay. "Crusty, at least some good is coming out of the blunders. Reports of so many landings have the defenders running in circles. Radio intercepts say not only the Italians, but also the Germans swear that twenty thousand of our paratroopers are ranging around behind their lines."

Crusty Carlisle grunted. "Goddamn Air Force peanuts will claim that's what they had in mind."

"The way it goes." Belvale tried to stare through the map of Sicily and see instead the lush and rolling fields of Kill Devil Hill, its stables and fine thoroughbreds. Imaging like that could usually calm him, but it was difficult today. Chad and Owen were in the middle of that landing, and that great–something kin of Crusty's—the Travis boy, a soldier in spite of himself.

And that was only on one side of the world.

Crusty must have sensed his feeling, for he said, "It's what we do, Preston. You know we wouldn't have it any other way and neither would our people. You going to roadblock that bottle? My arthritis is acting up."

Belvale passed over the bourbon. "It's always acting up. One of these days both your arms will fall off, or your knees will lock and you'll take a nosedive. You have no business leaving the country, the shape you're in."

"Don't start up. You got your feet wet in Africa and—"

"Found just how old and tired I am. You're a lot worse off."

"Worse, my money-making ass. Besides, the tropics will help my arthritis. I felt pretty good in Hawaii."

Belvale sighed. "Just because you were raising hell and fixing blame for FDR's investigation of Pearl Harbor. You know damned well that—"

"You wouldn't screw up my TDY orders to the Pacific? Goddamnit, Preston—Sicily ain't the only war, and as many of our people are out in the islands."

Belvale took back the whiskey bottle and poured for himself. A teletype bell clinged twice: nothing top priority coming in. "No, I wouldn't try to stop it, you bullheaded old bastard. Just remember you swore to me that the trip would be *Temporary* Duty, only a *short* TDY and you come home. While you're off playing cowboys and Indians, we can't slow up here. There are still priorities to push, legislation to ride herd on, ridding ourselves of military dead wood—"

Rubbing his right shoulder, Crusty Carlisle said, "You have enough help for now—my granddaughter, if she can turn loose that goddamn sergeant long enough, and Ben Alexander, and—I may not have another war left in me, and it's my turn. Hell, after this fracas, the world may not have another war left."

Belvale thumbnailed his moustache and nodded. "There shall be wars and rumors of wars—"

"Don't go holy joe on me. One sky pilot in this family is already too fucking many. Just tell me it's my turn now."

"Your turn, Charles."

"I've got your *Charles* swinging. Go answer the phones."

CHAPTER 2

INS FEATURE SERVICES—Gela, Sicily, July 10, 1943: All men on this gory beach face waves of enemy armored assaults, fire from infantry in well-prepared defense positions, and hourly attacks from the air.

Gela is a short round trip for *Luftwaffe* dive bombers based in nearby Calabria. The sea is at the Allies' backs and there can be no retreat. Neither can they move forward against such desperate and powerful resistance. Grimly they dig in, fight back and hold on.

Soldiers less proud than this core of Regular Army troopers might consider surrender, but here is where the U.S. 1st Infantry Division begins to earn its new nickname—The Big Red One. War correspondents already claim that this division is writing the book.

One reporter pinned down in rocky sand asked the assistant division commander, Brig. Gen. Theodore Roosevelt, Jr., if another Dunkirk is possible.

"Little Teddy," propped upon the mortar aiming stake that he uses as a walking stick, said, "Hell no! We're not in trouble. Our artillery hasn't been overrun yet."

Captain Owen Belvale used his SCR-300 to call for artillery support. Fox Company's radio was knocked out and a runner had panted up to Owen's CP to ask help from his.

"Goldstein knows that he already has all my 81s, but tell him that artillery is short," Owen said to the rifleman. "Most of it is still on the ships, but there's an LST coming in with some 105s now. Unloading the guns will take a—"

!!WHHAAMM!!

The explosion knocked Owen down. Eyes blurred and ears ringing, he spat sand as he struggled up to his knees. The Fox Company rifleman fumbled around to find his helmet that had been blown off.

"Jesus, sir—what the hell was that?"

Owen's eyes cleared and he saw it—the Landing Ship Tank coming in just off shore and blown all to hell by a direct hit. Torn and gutted, it was a smoking wreck going swiftly down with its vital load of artillery pieces.

Going down among wounded men struggling in the sea.

One shoe off before he reached the water, Owen had to hop in the surf and fight off the other one. When he splashed out, big Emmet Strong belly flopped right beside him. Matching Owen stroke for stroke, the corporal swam into the choppy waves. He reached out for a bloody, floundering soldier before Owen got to his man.

Hooking his left arm into the pack webbing of a sinking man, Owen fought to turn for the beach. Farther out, men screamed in agony and terror. The stern of the LST hung dripping into the air for a long moment before plunging beneath the surface.

Owen pumped for air and coughed salt water. The man he dragged was heavy, a dead weight threatening to pull them both under. Owen kicked hard and jerked with his free hand, bobbing under and up, under and up again as he choked. Heart drumming and lungs burning, he thanked God when his feet scraped bottom. Other men waded out to help; other hands drew his burden from him, but first they had to pry open his stiff fingers.

Crawling out of the surf, Owen rocked on his hands and knees before he threw up.

Dimly, he heard voices yelling at Corporal Strong. "Let go, soldier. Goddamnit, turn him loose—we got him now!"

Somebody helped Owen to his feet. He swayed and

wiped at his mouth. Emmet Strong; who'd think the kid would stick his neck out like that? A back country Virginian, Strong was quiet and withdrawn, with few friends beyond his country boy clique. There was an aura about him that said: keep to yourself and don't fuck with me.

And he'd risked death to swim out and bring back a stranger.

Another voice then: "Too bad, mack; the guy was all torn up. He's dead."

Strong said, "Knowed it halfway back."

"Then why the hell did you drag a dead man all the—"

"Ocean ain't no place to die. A man gets born on land, he deserves to lie down on land."

"Son of a bitch; if that isn't the damnedest thing you ever heard?"

Coughing up a last bitterness, Owen said, "It's a fine thing." He turned to look to the sea, where no more heads bobbed in the water, where only two more swimmers were helped ashore. He walked unsteadily over to Strong and said, "Thank you, corporal."

"No need, captain."

No thanks necessary because the man was a good soldier doing his duty, doing his job and a little more. Owen shook hands anyway and sloshed back up the slope to his radio man and the company CP. At least his man hadn't died—yet.

Big Mike Donelly said, "Panzers, captain—those 26-ton Mark Fours; we could sure use Cannon Company about now."

"They're off-loading now—if they don't catch another shell." He hand-cupped water from his clothes and realized he had no shoes and leggins.

His radio man said, "I'll go get them, captain."

"Stay on that radio. I may get to run barefoot through hell. Bazookas, get on those goddamn tanks!"

The launcher teams were already zeroed in. The lead tank staggered as a rocket slammed just below the turret. It slewed left and another 3.5 round blew off a track. The

12

panzer's machine guns fired long, blind bursts at the sky and sand; blue smoke corkscrewed from its opening hatch.

The tank commander fell crawling onto the deck and a burst from the 5th Squad gun knocked him off. Two other Germans escaped the burning tank only to die in a hail of bullets that ripped them up and squalled off the steel plates.

First Platoon heavy machine guns and the mortars were backing up Fox Company in attack; Owen had Second Platoon's four guns and they were all set up to sweep the company front. Finding his carbine, Owen didn't get a chance to use it. Another panzer swung around the dead leader and rumbled on. Its 88mm blasted and the hot breath of hell seared Owen's face as the shell zipped by to explode in the sea.

Second Platoon's guns hammered, bright red tracers and invisible AP axing Kraut infantry off the tanks and chopping down those who tried to follow behind the armor. Bazooka men finished the job and nobody climbed out of this wreck as its inside ammunition exploded.

Big Mike Donnely pointed. "Holy mother of God! Will you look at that big son of a bitch? That's a *Tiger* tank!"

A Tiger, indeed, a mammoth sixty tons of steel and guns blazing in every direction, the cannon blowing graves in the sand and filling them with new dead. It was the biggest tank in the world and damned near indestructible.

Leaping from his hole, Big Mike raced across the open space to the rolling dunes where his mortars were in support of F Company. A linen of sand spouts kicked up by one of the Tiger's machine guns followed him but didn't quite catch up.

Grabbing the radio handset, Owen yelled into it: "Sea power, sea power! This is Red Dog One. Can you register on that Tiger to my front? Yeah—I know he's close, so cut it fine."

"Oh shit," the radio operator said. "I knew I didn't dig this hole deep enough. Those five- and six-inch destroyer shells are liable to chop us up into hamburgers."

"If not them, that fucking 88. Stay low everyone! Make like moles!"

But the two bazooka teams hung tough, and their rockets flashed out to slam into the Tiger's bogie wheels. A long steel tread twisted off, flopping like a snake with a broken back.

Cupping his hands, Owen yelled, "Oh, you beautiful bastards!"

Then the panzer swung its gun muzzle and fired. One bazooka team disappeared in a geyser of dirt, metal and chunks of flesh. Machine guns raked the other position and a man shrieked in agony.

Second Platoon's 30s homed in on the turret and viewing slits of the huge tank with a fiery hail of tracer and AP, four guns firing close to their cyclic rate of 600 rounds a minute. The crew was blinded for the moment, long enough to give a GI time to race out and meet the tank head on, bent low and arms pumping. For a split second he thought it might be Sloan Travis, the regiment's reluctant hero, but Sloan's guns were up on line. What the hell did he think one man could do? Owen's hands tightened hard upon his useless carbine.

Leaping onto the riveted front plates of the Tiger, the man slammed something against the driver's viewing slit, and fell back to roll away. A flash of searing brightness candled the nose of the tank—white phosphorus, the hottest liquid flame known to man; Willy Peter splashing into the narrow slot where the driver and assistant sat.

In seconds, the panzer stopped firing and the hatch flew open. The water-cooled heavies didn't let up, and now some of the steel APs made riccochets down inside the turret.

They yelled then, the bastards, and in desperation the blind driver kicked the tank around on its good tread. But then the Willy Peter fingered a fiery trail into the ammunition supply for the 88, and fire blasted high from the open hatch. The tower of light showed a pair of Mark IVs revving up behind the destroyed Tiger.

Carumph! Carumph! Two direct hits on the tank turrets. Those blasts ripped jagged shards of steel loose inside the panzers and threw them around like so many great, bloody razors. Men couldn't last in that brutal storm. Scratch two more tanks.

"Big Mike's mortars," Owen breathed. "The crazy bastard about faced some of them from behind Fox Company. There never was a mortar man like him!"

Corporal Didyk cradled the radio phone. "Battalion says a lot more tanks building up. We can't keep lucking out."

Now Sea Power answered the distress call; 5-inch shells screamed in and ripped open the stalled tanks. Both hands over his ears, Owen yelled: "Tell them to lift the fire, up ten but no more. Our rifle companies are still pinned down by those pillboxes."

The destroyer fire control people were good. Two salvos plastered the area where panzers were trying to build up. No short rounds fell among Owen's men and none strayed into company positions; they just sent Kraut tankers to hell in their gutted, burning machines.

Chad Bevale rang off an EE8 field phone and said to his exec: "Hear that real big stuff sounding off behind us? That's a British cruiser laying 10-inch shells into an Italian regiment our spotters caught marching down the beach road, right out in the open. Forward Observation reports hundreds of them are dead and hundreds more are punch drunk, wandering around dazed without their weapons. It's going to work, major—the goddamn landing is going to work!"

At the radio, Bobby Cullis rubbed a hand over his face. "Enemy pillboxes are still holding out. Fox and George companies are taking casualties and Division says the whole damned Hermann Goering Division is on the move. So is a Wop regiment, the outfit that wears feathers in their helmets."

"The Bersaglieri," Owen said, "the best the Italians have. They're not the running kind. See if you can reach that weird Limey ship—"

"The *Ambercrombie?*"

"That's it. My grandfather would say it looks like the *Monitor,* that Yankee cheesebox on a raft. The English call

15

it an experimental ship, a floating gun platform. They haven't fired their 15-inchers yet; maybe the recoil will sink her. Ask the captain to concentrate on the pillboxes first, please."

"Will do."

Turning, Chad looked back at the sea, at the flotilla bobbing at anchor, gunboats cruising up and down, LSTs and LCPs bustling ashore to disgorge their loads of men, machinery and supplies, a bridge of British and American warships and freighters that stretched all the way back to Tunisia. The Allies had a toehold on this beach, and given any luck, they would stay and move inland. The longer they held on, the better chance of success. If the enemy didn't drive the invading forces into the sea, or at least contain them on the beaches where they could be bled, the assault would not be stopped.

He breathed deeply of risen sun and salt air, and tasted gunsmoke. Gun thunder rose and fell, and the continuous rattle of small arms fire was comforting.

Then the *Ambercrombie*'s 15-inchers went off.

"Jesus!" Sergeant Jellicoe muttered. "I think my eardrums busted."

Shaking his head to clear it and lifting his binoculars, Chad focused on a German pillbox in time to see it leap into the air on a gout of flame. "Direct hit! No more pillbox!"

The next giant shells ripped the corner off another Kraut position and created sandstorms. Chad turned back to put his glasses on the *Ambercrombie*. When the big guns fired, the front of the ship lifted from the water and the stern went awash. As floating artillery, it was doing a hell of a job.

"Message from the ship, colonel." Bobby Cullis held out the handset.

The voice was definitely British and for an unsettling moment, pushed a sharp memory at Chad, that of Leftenant Stephanie Bartlett, of love in Scotland and London, of a rare closeness. He shook those things away; this was the time and place for calculated hate, not memories of a love that might be already dead.

Stephanie, Stephanie—you were noble, standing by your husband stationed in Singapore. You swore you loved me, you showed me how much, and I believe you still do, but your goddamned British sense of honor would not let us remain together. Stay alive despite the Japs, darling; stay alive for me.

"Sir," the Britisher repeated, "I say, is the mission accomplished? I am receiving emergency calls for another fire mission."

"Exceptional job, captain; thank you."

Blinking through the glasses, Chad saw the *Ambercrombie* crew climbing busily around the bow as the ship huffed almost onto the beach proper. Men lowered themselves into the shallow water and did things Chad couldn't make out. But within minutes the bow raised and the ship's stern dropped.

Bobby. Cullis said, "Ballast tanks; they're emptying water from the bow tanks and filling those in the stern. I'm guessing that the captain is trying to get far more range than his guns normally have. That mission must be a long way inland."

The angled turret loosed both guns; although fired at one time, some trick of sound made a double boom. "Like a double barreled shotgun," Chad said.

The radio man said, "Attack companies moving up; direct resistance fading, but division says a shitpot full of Krauts and tanks are on the road."

The *Ambercrombie* fired again and again, sending smoke rings into the air and making big circles in the water as her platform jumped up and down. Chad stopped watching and said, "Maybe that column is her target. What's with that Bersaglieri regiment?"

"G Company came up from reserve and took First Platoon's guns with them. They set up grazing fire and beat the holy shit out of those Wops." Sergeant Jellicoe grinned and lit a cigarette. "But my ears still hurt."

The phone buzzed and Chad took it. "Red Dog Six here. What's the—oh hell. Hang on and pray we can get more heavy guns on them."

He replaced the handset and said to his CP crew: "That was 1st Battalion. They report the Hermann Goering Division is taking hits but not even slowing up. The Kraut commander is General Conrath, and he's plenty tough. He'll force his troops to keep coming and a spearhead like that could punch a big hole in us."

"Damn," the sergeant said, "and I can't swim a lick."

CHAPTER 3

REUTERS NEWS AGENCY—Allied Headquarters for the Southwest Pacific, July 11, 1943: American planes loosed the heaviest raid yet on Japanese positions on New Georgia Island yesterday. More than a hundred bombers hammered Munda and Bairoko Harbor while U.S. destroyers also shelled Munda. Four Zero fighters were shot down, and on land, a determined allied attack by Americans, British and Australians gained much ground against battered Japanese hidden in the jungle.

Major Keenan Carlisle pissed on his hands and wiped them across his cracked lips. Any Chindit knew that drinking urine would kill a man, but nobody had tasted water for far too long, and a touch of moisture of any sort was refreshing. The blazing sun had no mercy and they were so deep in Japanese territory that they must keep moving, losing sweat and salt as they hurried.

Brigadier Orde Wingate himself moved ahead of the column, pith helmet still riding jauntily upon his shaggy head. Pushing himself, Keenan caught up with the commander of this special group of behind the lines raiders, this mix of Burmese bandits, volunteer English Tommies, tough, stubby Gurkhas and—oh yes, one bedraggled American.

In passing, Keenan heard the Burmese whispering about

He Who Will Not Die, and hoped this time they were right. Superstitous natives gave the name to him when he roamed the jungle alone for some seven months, killing Japs. He was the only survivor of a Chinese communist seaborne patrol. Officially an observer, he had been carried as Missing in Action back home, and there were moments when he wished himself dead with the men—and the woman—he had fought beside over a good part of China.

There didn't seem much use to staying alive after gutty Major Hong and sweet old Grandfather Lim died among feeding sharks; after nurse Chang Yen Ling was blown apart or drowned unseen. Chang Yen Ling, so much beauty and compassion and a fighting heart, the women he loved. But to revenge her, he lived and went out to kill Japs. He had beaten a slow and painful path to the Indian border from China, searching out Japs to ambush along the way. He learned to live with the jungle and its creatures, for a man who didn't left his bones among the creepers to be stripped by hungry things. His torturous route zigzagged him at last to British lines and a field hospital. Food and drink, and with some of the malaria washed out of his scrawny, insect ravaged body, he refused to go home. Instead he joined with Wingate's Chindits because he wasn't through with the Japanese.

The Japs called him something else: *yonsei,* the ghost that eats heads. His brand of psywar had been to hide the heads of the emperor's soldiers he killed. Right now he'd trade every slope head he'd taken for one long swallow of cold spring water from Sandhurst Keep, the family home in upstate New York. It snowed there, and the thought of that made his stomach twist. Had it ever really snowed anywhere? There was so damned much jungle that by now it might have spread across the whole world, humid and buzzing and deadly.

"I say, Yank—a good-o party, eh?" Wingate's piercing eyes and beaked nose stood out above his matted beard.

Glancing down, Keenan saw that the man carried books of Aristotle and Plato under one arm, in this heat and on this forced march. The son of a bitch was crazy, no doubt of that. He was also an offbeat military genius and a rebel who stood orthodox British commanders on their ears. Best of all, he hunted out Japs to kill. That was what Keenan was doing here.

Keenan's grin hurt his lips. "If this is a party, where's my beer?"

"Never mind, lad. We're heading for a Jap watering hole the Burmese found for us. A great storage tank, they say. Perhaps we'll all have a swim, eh?"

Keenan shifted the weight of the Sten gun he carried slung on his right shoulder. The weight would have been negligible under other conditions; now it felt like a great iron cannon. He wasn't alone in his fatigue and misery; every man jack of the Chindits was in poor condition, ground hollow by forced marches, sucked dry by leeches and gray spiders, snake bitten and hungry.

Here on New Georgia they were hanging on; once they reached water and had time to scavenge the jungle for edible roots and greens and grub worms, they would perk right up. Closing his eyes for a moment, Keenan thought how good a python steak would taste right now. Maybe they'd find one of the big, juicy bastards around the water hole, or a few frogs and a handful of crunchy grasshoppers.

Mechanically dragging one foot ahead of the other, he noticed that his hightop British shoes were rotting away. Enemy troop movements and building typhoon weather promised no more supply drops by Colonel Flip Cochran's American flyboys. Fully half of the earlier airborne packets had parachuted into territory held by the fucking Nips and some were lost in deep jungle.

Pursued by vengeanceful Jap troops angered by blown bridges and the lone rail line ripped in a hundred places, now the Chindits had to run for home. If they were blocked, the only choice was to dig in and grab their left nuts in communal prayer. They were tired out and scared shitless, ready to latch on to hope rationed to them by radio static, trying to believe that it was possible to cut their way through five battalions of Japs.

They who so believeth in army bullshit shall never die

more than once. Sure. And who are the Japs believing in—their bucktoothed little emperor who puts himself a grade higher than the round-eyed God?

The Gurkha scout's trot was half a stagger, but he braced straight as he reported to Wingate. "Sir—only fifty kilometers to the tank."

Wingate nodded. "Very good. How many Japanese?"

"I think one hundred, sir. Not alert."

"Jolly good; enough for everyone then. Major Carlisle, will you disperse the men as skirmishers and lead the advance party?"

"Yes, sir." Cool as if Wingate was strolling Piccadilly Circus, as if he wasn't burned out of body liquid and on the verge of dying of thirst. Crazy son of a bitch, and Keenan loved him.

Water; they would load up on captured water and make it to the Chindwin River; once across, they would be home free.

Keenan followed closely behind the Gurkha and a pair of Burmese scouts. Backing him was half a dozen men so shaggy, ragged and sun baked that only the Englishmen's height set them apart. Experienced jungle fighters, they slid along the path with no sound until the Gurkha dropped to one knee and signalled them to low cover. Crouched, Keenan moved up to check the enemy layout.

Big tank, hell. Rusted and with weeds growing around it, the iron container looked like the upper part of a locomotive. But it must hold water for the Japs quartered beneath palm frond shelters, the Japs asleep in the day's heat. Gently tapping his Sten gun twice, Keenan signalled the patrol to spread out, signalled the getaway man to drop back and bring up the main party.

It seemed weird, gearing up to fight a pitched battle over water, but firefights had erupted for less cause—land that would grow nothing useful, or a sagging bridge, or a swamp that nobody really wanted.

Waiting until Wingate eased up beside him. Keenan waved his men forward along an unguarded path that wound through elephant grass higher than their heads.

When it opened upon the camp clearing, he stood up and lined his Sten on a Jap sentry dozing in the shade of a thorny tree. The three-round burst tore off half his head with the soft peaked cap.

The attack was fierce—Enfield rifles and Sten submachine guns pouring heavy fire upon the unsuspecting Japs. Still some of the bastards fought back, especially a Nambu machine gun on the other side of the tank.

"Flankers!" Keenan yelled, and hammered a clip at the Nambu position, guided only by wisps of blue muzzle smoke.

Running low and catlike to the earth, the Burmese scouts circled the tank, firing as they went. One went down, then another—small brown men with big hearts. Keenan leaped up and waved his men forward.

Whack-whack-whack! went the Nambu.

Until Keenan overhanded a grenade that cleared the low water tank and bounced into the treeline shadows beyond. As it exploded, he poured another clip into the flame and smoke.

The silence came suddenly, a quietness of no gunfire and no screaming, and not even the creak and rattle of equipment. For a long moment nobody coughed, nobody said anything. Sharp and bloody, the fight was over.

Wingate approached the water tank and twisted off its center cap to look inside. "A bit short, lads; only a few inches in the bottom. They must have been waiting delivery of a fresh supply."

"Damn, general," Keenan said. "Is there enough?"

"Has to be, old chap. We have a fair walk to the Chindwin River."

That's when the Jap slithered from beneath the old tank with a pistol and shot Keenan.

It was a hammer blow to his chest, a blow that drove him backward where he tripped and fell down. Head sagging, he muttered "Yen Ling, Yen Ling—"

He heard the guns that chopped the Jap into little pieces, but when he listened hard, Keenan couldn't hear the beating of his own heart.

The British medic crouched over him, ripping away the rotten shirt.

"Back luck," Wingate said. "How bad is it, sergeant—and what is he trying to say?"

"He's hit center, sir," the medic answered. "Can't tell what's done to his lung unless he can be got out to hospital. As for his talking—can't understand a ruddy word; sounds foreign like."

Penny Belvale pretended she didn't hear the women hiss when they had to stand aside so she could go into the camp commander's private *benjo*. Toilet, damnit—toilet! Too many Jap words were creeping into her vocabulary, more so than the pidgin other prisoners needed to get through the day. Bits of Japanese were handy with her captors, but she'd be damned if she started thinking that way.

The guards refused to learn English, the main language of the women rounded up when Singapore fell. A few Dutch and Oriental women had been caught in the trap, but the great majority was British. Then there was Penny Colvin-Belvale, Women's Auxiliary Service Pilot, technically the assistant leader of the prisoners because the Japs wouldn't believe a WASP was civilian. But no woman would ever pretend to listen to her now. She was a lousy Jap lover and therefore a traitor, not only to the Allied nations, but to all women everywhere.

Squatted over the Japanese-style toilet, Penny was ever thankful that she still had a friend who understood her problem. Leftenant Stephanie Bartlett knew that Penny had no choice but to be Major Watanabe's mistress. And as military leader for the camp population, Stephanie was in a position to protect Penny from the bitterest and most resentful women, those who had lost husbands and lovers to the hated Japanese.

Leaving the unusual privacy of the frond-enclosed toilet, Penny walked calmly with her head high, ignoring the glares and the occasional "bitch" aimed at her. If they only knew—but then her carefully balanced house of cards would come tumbling down. Crackdowns would eliminate black market food transactions, and covert visits to the men's compound down the road would certainly be cut short by executions, or at the least, terrible beatings. No advance warning would be given on "surprise" inspections so any contraband could be spirited away.

Only Stephanie knew that the inside information came from Penny, and it had to remain that way. If more people came in on the secret, Major "Wobbly" Watanabe's violent anger would flash out to sear everyone in camp, including the two surviving children.

She slowly climbed the steps to the high bamboo porch of the camp headquarters building and made the obligatory bow to the sentry there. Watanabe sounded his announcements from this porch, standing high above the defeated, tapping his riding crop against his booted and crippled leg. From there he looked down upon his own little world, the unquestioned god of all he surveyed.

How she hated the shiny, strutting, little bastard; how she dared not show her true feelings. Some day, she told herself, some day she would be given the chance to kill him. She would look directly into his slant eyes and smile as he died.

If for no other reason than he was a goddamned Jap like the ones who blew up her C-46 transport on the tarmac at Singapore, and blew up sweet, faithful Theresa Menasco, who'd never hurt anyone in her life. If not for Theresa, then for the memory of women and children who died on the march to this camp, for the studied brutalities forced upon the living.

With Theresa her copilot, Penny had brought the American transport plane in to lift out women and kids and maybe a few of the seriously wounded. The city was about to fall, but nobody had told them that. And there was Stephanie, commanding the last battery of antiaircraft guns at the airport.

After they reached camp, they discovered they had something more in common—Stephanie was in love with Colonel Chad Belvale and Penny was married to his nephew. To add to the small/vicious/world department, Watanabe had also known one of the Belvales in China. That was not too surprising among professionals of many armies, since the Belvales and Carlisles were such an extended military family and spread all over the world.

A family of samurai, Watanabe called them, and took a special delight in humiliating one of its daughters by making her his mistress. She had to admit that sometimes he was not all Jap. He had come to respect her intelligence, even if she was only a woman. And during certain nights in bed when he had drunk much *sake,* he called her beautiful.

She hated him most for her rare orgasms, for making her own body turn traitor.

"Ah so," Hideo Watanabe sat at his desk beneath the palm frond fan that swung back and forth above his close-cropped scalp, the rope tugged by a native boy. His smile was poisonous as a copperhead sliding through the grass back home in Virginia.

She bowed because it was required, hating it, hating him. She smiled back. "Do you wish anything of me?"

"You may press my uniforms and polish my other boots. I will dine after sundown."

His English held only the barest accent. It should be good, she thought; the bastard had studied at UCLA and often reminded her of his superior grades. He was so goddamned smart that he went back to Japan to become a warlord for his holy emperor. But he would reach no higher rank; some Chinese or Russian had shot up his leg, and since he was unfit for combat, he was assigned to a women's prisoner of war camp. Since women were nothing in the Japanese consciousness, that made him a step lower than Major Yamaguchi, who ran the camp down the road because those POWs were men.

That was something never mentioned.

"Yes," she said.

He frowned. "What, woman?"

Oh shit. *"Hai, hai, arrigato gozaimas."*

Yes, thank you. Some day, you arrogant bastard.

Passing through into his quarters—she still refused to call it theirs in her mind—Penny saw that the charcoal brazier had already been prepared, that the pressing irons heated upon it. Watanabe was fastidious about his uniforms; they must be spotless and fit just so. His boots must be black mirrors, and she took care of those things. She was not allowed to touch his samurai sword.

As if she wanted to. Her image of those long blades was too recent; she saw them as they butchered the fallen, the piteous sick who could not travel.

Somebody scratched on the palm leaf wall. Penny went to the window. Outside, the sky was dark and threatening. She hoped the rains would hold off because the camp turned gloomier then. Kneeling, she looked out and down into Stephanie's anxious face.

"Haven't seen you for days except at roll call," Stephanie whispered and held up a small, dented can for a dollop of *sake* which would be used as a disinfectant. "I made it to the men's camp last night. Bribed a bloody guard and finally saw my husband. Dacey looks terrible."

Penny poured just enough *sake* into the can so that it would not be missed. She knew that Stephanie's husband had been wounded and captured in the siege of Singapore, that the wound was a bad one.

"But he'll pull out of it? I can smuggle a little more food and some aspirin—"

Stephanie held the can close to her chest. "That's good, you ken, but it will nae help to grow legs. He's lost them both. Now if we all last through this bloody war, I can never leave Dacey for Chad."

CHAPTER 4

REUTERS NEWS AGENCY—Allied Headquarters, North Africa, July 11, 1943: British paratroop units jumped yesterday to attack Syracuse in Italy, specifically to take and hold the bridge at Ponte Grande. Fierce counter attacks by determined German troops cut them to ribbons. Only 47 men and officers even reached the bridge. When American infantry and tank support broke through to them, only 19 survived.

The New York Times—Detroit, July 11, 1943: Vice President Henry A. Wallace called upon America today to take the lead and plan a war-proof, postwar world pledged to the enlightenment of all peoples. He said that full employment, full production and cooperation with other nations is needed to enforce international justice and security.

Urging America to heed a destiny that "calls us to world leadership," he attacked power groups that put money first and people last, and declared that nothing will prevail against the common man's peace in a common man's world.

Night came down, and Lieutenant Sloan Travis hadn't been sure he would live to welcome it again. It had been a day of concentrated hell—no, two days of fire and fury that should have the devil taking notes on improvements. Refined brimstone still strung out over the harbor like bloody pearls as comet trails of tracers crisscrossed themselves, and inland the devil's obsolete sulphur had been transformed into flares white and bright, poison blossoms unfolding in the dark skies.

"Not bad," he muttered, hunched over a canteen cup of oatmeal not completely dissolved. It was heating over waxed K-ration boxes in the bottom of a hole, so the flame couldn't be seen. "A purple tint to the prose, but not bad."

He'd forget the lines before morning, even if the Krauts didn't try another attack tonight, but it kept the best part of him working and cleared the rust from his mind. Some day, somewhere, if he made it through this insanity, he would write again. But he would not write about war; sulphur and brimstone should be ferried back across the Styx to stay.

> . . . and there'll be bluebirds over
> the white cliffs of Dover,
> tomorrow, just you wait and see . . .

Maybe he'd get to see those white cliffs and yell back at the circling gulls . . . *tomorrow, when the world is free* . . .

Sloan poured canteen water into the cup and stirred. The spoon was his only utensil; knife and fork had been discarded long ago. (Drop the joker from your deck of cards; you're packing too much weight.)

"Lieutenant?"

"Guilty as charged. The guns dug in, Pelkey?"

"Two on the flanks, two in Fox Company's center, plenty of backup ammo. The gunners went underground when the first panzers showed. If they dig any deeper you'll have to charge them with desertion."

"I didn't know you made jokes, sergeant; that is, besides that lousy Donald Duck you do. Want some oatmeal?"

"Now you're joking. Radios are out again and the phone wire's blown up. The Old Man sent a runner to say come see him when you can. Company CP is just this side of the water. Line up on a beached LST and you can't miss it."

"Nose count?" Sloan wrapped his handkerchief around the folding handle of the aluminum cup. It took military engineering to design a cup with a handle and rolled rim that would blister hand and lip while its contents were only luke warm. He couldn't remember when he'd last eaten anything.

"Macera and Andralovitch bought it when that tank broke through; Ryan and Slayter got hit in the dive bombing; nothing serious, just a few fragments. Lucky bastards are probably on the hospital ship by now. Come to think on it, the way the Kraut planes go after those ships, they might wish they were back on the beach."

"Four casualties; not too bad." If he hadn't mixed in three packets of hoarded sugar, the oatmeal would taste like glue. Two more dead men from his platoon; did death taste like it smelled, left out in the hot Sicilian sun? Only four down—not too bad. Acceptable losses; what the hell was he turning into, a professional soldier?

Spooning the sludgy cereal, he stood up, M-1 rifle slung over his left shoulder, straps hanging loose from his tin pot. With all this frigging equipment hanging on him, just trying to grab a bite to eat was a bitch.

"Hold the fort, sergeant. After the walloping the Krauts got the last time they ran at us, we ought to be clear until daylight. You get the lines repaired and I'll see to the radios, liberate a couple if I have to. I'll be back ASAP, quicker if I hear a firefight start up here."

"Okay. And lieutenant—"

"Yeah?"

Pelkey squatted next to the fire hole. "I had you pegged as a Class A prick, and I was right, back then."

Sloan swallowed thick oatmeal; now the flavor was closer to wallpaper paste. "So?"

"So now I'm damned glad you're my platoon leader."

Hesitating, Sloan bent to put down his cup with the spoon in it. "I'm glad, too. Guard that for me."

Then he went off in the dark poisoned by deadly fireflies to see what Owen Belvale wanted.

*   *   *

Kirstin Belvale-Shelby put a knee into the Morgan gelding's side and drew up the cinch two more inches. Laddie Simbo was a school horse, an old pro who would use all his personal comfort and loafing tricks if she didn't watch him. Lowering the stirrup, she reached for the horn and shook the saddle. Now it was solid and wouldn't roll under Harlan's weight. He had been in the hospital riding program long enough to handle an accident without spooking, but most of the military patients were still jumpy around horses and she didn't want to take chances.

If she wasn't a Senator's widow and had no history with the Carlisle-Belvale family, the administrator of the Harmon General Hospital wouldn't have gone along with her program in the first place. A single bad accident would drive the amputees back to making wallets in Recreational Therapy. Kids who had left parts of themselves on desert sands or Pacific islands didn't need to learn how to pound and lace leather. They needed confidence, to know they could make it in the world again, and that they would be accepted as men, not pitied as cripples.

Leading Laddie Simbo from the portable stalls to the show ring, she looked across to where Harlan waited in his wheelchair. Buck sergeant Harlan Edgerton, born in Shubuta, Mississippi and lately of Faid Pass in Tunisia and the 18th Infantry Regiment.

She could not see the chrome clamp that acted as his left hand and the missing right leg without thinking of husbands and sons—Jim Shelby killed on Guadalcanal last year, Chad Belvale still alive the last she heard, playing the Crusader until he was also KIA or wound up with missing parts like the man in the wheelchair. And her sons, who of course followed the great family's men at arms traditions, leading their pikemen into gory battle: Owen in Sicily, Farley on the other side of the world.

Farley hurt now where the breakage didn't show, perhaps wounded more than Harlan Edgerton's amputations and maybe as permanently. At least he was out of any more danger in the Hawaii hospital, but Chad and Owen—

Suppose the family had not been aristocratic men at

31

arms, but churchmen, high priests? She smiled at the concept: bless me, Father Chad, for I have sinned? Who gave absolution to the confessor?

"Morning, Miz Belvale." He was even younger than Farley, but no boy should wear eyes so old and tired.

"Good morning, Harlan. Laddie Simbo's ready for you."

"But the world ain't."

She crossed the arena, the horse plodding behind, accepting his fate. Harlan had good hands—hand—on the reins, so Laddie Simbo wouldn't give him any trouble. He wouldn't expose any show ring fire, either; that wasn't his job now, and the old gelding knew it.

"Sure it is."

"Maybe I ain't ready for the world, then."

Although it was early in the day, the East Texas sun already burned off last night's dew and the air was humid. Kirstin lifted the braided reins over the horse's head and rested her fist on the saddle horn as she held them. She knew better than to help any amputee from his chair and onto the horse, especially not Harlan. He pushed from the chair and balanced a moment on one foot, then reached for the saddle and pulled up to get the foot into the near stirrup. He swung up and sat looking down at her.

Keeping it light, she said, "Hey, if you can handle this slick old horse, you're ready for anything."

"Yeah; I can walk new ground behind a turning plow, just like always. You ever see a pegleg farmer?"

"When the shop finished your prosthetic, it won't be a crude wooden gadget."

"Course not. Might work good as this clamp—open, shut; open, shut. Hell, you think they might keep me in morphine to deaden the stump?"

"Harlan," she said, "you're young and strong and—and—good looking. You can't retire from life just because—"

He picked up the reins but didn't cluck to the horse, his way of starting Laddie Simbo off, since he couldn't really leg him. "Retire; that's pretty good. I meant to stay twenty years in the army and retire. I was Regular Army before this war started, ma'am. Never cared much about staring at the wrong end of a mule the rest of my life. Ain't nothing else I can do now, and I won't be able to farm worth a damn, so—''

She was about to say the standard things, how he'd have a pension, and in time the prosthetics would work almost as well as his real parts, that losing a hand and a leg didn't make him any less, that real manhood came from inside. For him it didn't seem right, so Kirstin didn't say them.

He clucked and the Morgan walked off. Turning in the saddle he looked back at her. "Did you mean that, Miz Belvale?"

"Mean what?"

"That you think I'm good looking."

She didn't have to lie. "Yes."

CHAPTER 5

TWX, SECRET to Kill Devil Hill—July 11, 1943: Commanding officer of Sicily defense forces is Italian General Alfredo
Guzzoni, not seen as nominal head. G-2 lists him as one
of few top rank Facist military leaders. German commander
on scene known to be Maj. Gen. Paul Conrath, who brought
the Hermann Goering Division down through the Brenner
Pass under direct orders from OKW, the combined German
general staff, as directed by Hitler.

Theater Commander in Chief, Rome, is still Field Marshal
Albert Kesselring.

Feldwebel Arno Hindemit spat an olive seed, chewed on
stringy cheese and helped it down with sour red wine. With
his captain of this patched together group of *landsers* who
had escaped from Tunisia, he had searched out a hoard of
food and wine in the root cellar of an abandoned house.

Tucked into a freshly dug two-man hole, he thought that
discovering the food was the best thing that happened to
them since they barely made it to land in that *verdammt*
rubber raft. Lucky for them that the *Ami* and *Tommi* pilots
who came strafing were driven off by antiaircraft. In the
beginning they sank most of the rafts and the men in them.

The second best thing was listening to the racing motors
of Tiger Panzers as they tried to get free of the tough trees

of a thick olive grove. The *dummkopfs* thought their clumsy iron turtles could crawl over anything, but a tangle of little trees stopped them.

"Best they had looked to those faulty steering mechanisms," he said, and bit off more yellow-white cheese.

Hauptmann Franz Witzelei chewed an olive. "Those must be some of the early models."

Arno passed the wine bottle. "Schoolmaster, you tend to give passing grades to fools."

"In civilian life, I have been accused of that. But if a student has really tried to approach his potential—"

"Those *panzer truppen* have gone beyond their limits. Listen to them curse and whine; it is such beautiful music.

Witzelei said, "If the *Ami* land their own armor, you will hope to hear a different song."

Shrugging, Arno used his knife to work the cork out of a new bottle. Nothing like the Rhine wines, it was still welcome. What food these Italians had was good, but they needed something to make up for being so unsoldierly, and for bringing heaven's curse upon all infantry. Arno firmly believed that the Roman legionnaire who thrust the spear into Christ's side eternally damned the foot soldier to misery.

Look at the Italians of the Livorno Division who had taken the advance this day after the first thrust of the panzers was driven back. About six hundred of the idiots marched down the road toward Gela as if they were on the parade ground. The *Amis* waited until they were close before cutting them down with mortars and small arms fire. Not one of them lived to see Gela.

"It is pleasant to be in reserve," Witzelei murmured. "We will not be needed after the Hermann Goering Division moves to the attack."

"Ah, *mien hauptmann;* we are left out of it because there are no papers on us, no number of officialdom. But we will not be forgotten in the retreat of Fat Meier's division. Someone will have to stand as the rear guard."

Arno sipped wine and finished his cheese. *Reichmarshall*

Goering had promised that if a single bomb fell on Germany, he could be called Meier.

The captain's voice hardened slightly, but Arno was used to that. Despite his rank, Witzelei was a good man even if he still half believed in the *Führerprinzip*. "The Hermann Goering Division will not retreat, sergeant. it is famous for its gallantry."

"True, but where our famous *flieger* grows fatter, the unit has shrunk beyond its replacements, and it is tired from the long trip, tired of fighting. *Ami* strength increases by the hour, and they will break the attack."

"You are a pessimist. We were beaten in Africa because the supply lines stretched too far and—"

"The Führer was too busy at Stalingrad to look our way. I am an old *landser,* captain, which means I am a live realist."

Rising to his knees, he poked his head above the foxhole. Heavy firing broke out at the Gela beachhead, panzer cannon and heavy machine guns; rifles and *Schmeissers* peppering through any lapse of louder sounds. The fight was growing intense and he was glad to be out of it, even if only for the moment.

His company would be called upon soon enough, this band of survivors, walking wounded and stragglers rounded up by the Chain Dogs, the *ketten und hund* of the busy Military Police. And they would fight, the old soldiers because it was their job, the young graduates of *Deutches Jungvolk* out of desperation.

"The battle swelled in intensity, and American planes wheeled and darted above the beach. Their many ships loosed salvo after thundering salvo of big guns. Arno eyed the wine bottle and lifted it, then shook his head and corked it again. Enough for now; he would soon need a clear head, or a final toast.

Witzelei raised up beside him, helmet askew and eyeglasses smeared. One lens had been cracked in the battle for the Kasserine Pass in Africa, and although he had tried on several pairs taken from dead men, none suited his eyes. "What is happening?"

Arno lit his last *Ami* cigarette and stared over it. "Panic. The entire Hermann Goering Division has broken under fire and is fleeing to the rear."

"Impossible! General Conrath would never allow such—"

A big shell exploded nearby; the earth leaped and steel fragments zipped through the grove, ripping at olive trees and whining off the stalled panzers.

Arno shared the cigarette with Witz and said, *"Scheissen!* That is what caused the panic—those ship cannons. How many six inchers can anyone stand? I also heard something much bigger pass overhead to search out our staging area."

Witzelei shouted, "You there!" at the five men running in a pack; *"Kommen Sie!"*

The soldiers did not stop and only two had hung on to their weapons. More frightened men trotted past and more rode on tanks grinding to the rear. It really was impossible; that unit was mostly veterans hardened in every major campaign since the conquest of Poland. Now he could smell their wild terror, the sweat of unreasoning fear mixed with the panzer exhausts.

The cover of dark was fast coming on, a blessing for the disorganized troops. But military tactics taught that the only place to halt a seaborne invasion was on the beaches before the enemy gathered the strength and supplies to drive inland. The *Ami* landing place was not only secure, but building rapidly under cover of their warships. It would be a long hard night for the *Wehrmacht* and if tomorrow came, all men would not see it.

Preston Belvale straightened his tie and glanced down at the alignment of fruit salad on the left breast of his uniform blouse. Gleaming behind the old ones from another war, the new issue ribbons looked good there—American Defense, American Theater and European Theater of Operations with a battle star, the last earned by his short tour in North Africa. Normally he wouldn't think about his decorations, but today he had a highest level meeting in the White House.

Chief of Staff George Marshall would be there, Secretary of the Navy Frank Knox and Henry Wallace; a gold plated circle of admirals and generals gathered to make reports and offer suggestions to the President of the United States. Roosevelt rarely listened worth a damn to anyone but Marshall, and sometimes not even to him. FDR could charm the entire War Department into going his way; he could also get loose of lip around the press and go mule stubborn. Today Belvale would see which face the President showed when he got the bad news with the good.

Past the Secret Service guards and then returning the snap-to salutes of the Marine sentries, Belvale headed into the conference room. He shook hands with his cousin Ben Alexander and a few others. Stopping in place, he stared at the two most brown-nosing politicians in the army, and one of the bastards was blood kin.

Major General Thomas Skelton had sneaked home from a posh assignment in England, which meant some anti-Churchill group of Limeys had flattered him into presenting their case. And Chaplain (Colonel) Luther Farrand was supposed to be off in the far Pacific, seeing to soldiers' religious needs. Instead, he was back here on some personal mission; polishing his halo? Belvale sighed; he supposed that every family had their black sheep, but no other suffered one who bleated from behind the bell, book and candle.

Ignoring the pair, Belvale took his briefcase to his assigned seat beside Ben Alexander at the long, polished table. When Roosevelt was wheeled in, everyone stood at attention until waved down. There was another short wait until the President lit the cigarette in his long holder; then protocol declared that others could smoke. Cigar in hand, Belvale thought the process was like the court waiting until the king and his partner took the floor before joining the dance.

The angle of FDR's cigarette holder was a tipoff to his mood. If it was angled high, he was jaunty; if it sagged, he was either ill or had gotten news he didn't want to hear. This morning it pointed about half mast, and someone must have passed word to him before the meeting because he cut across tradition and aimed his cigarette at Belvale.

"General, I understand you have a special report on the Sicily fighting."

Belvale slid papers from his briefcase and stood up. "Yes, sir. This came direct to me—"

Across the table, General Skelton muttered something and the President frowned at him.

Belvale put on his glasses. "Last night, after attacking our convoy off Gela during the day, the *Luftwaffe* returned over the fleet anchorage. Their bombers dropped strings of parachute flares, lighting the ships in brilliant white."

Clearing his throat, he went on, wishing he didn't have to. "Gun crews fought back as best they could, although the German planes were invisible through the flares. Shortly after 2230, it appeared the enemy had made a mistake; the planes came in only a few hundred feet above the water, so low their exhaust flames showed. More than 5,000 guns of all kinds opened fire. Planes crashed into the water and on the beachhead while the gunners cheered."

Belvale took a deep breath. "Mister President, the planes were American. 144 of them were C-46s carrying two thousand paratroopers of the 82nd Airborne. We count 23 planes destroyed and many more damaged. Airborne casualties are estimated at 229 killed, wounded or missing."

FDR's cigarette holder tilted low. "What went wrong?"

"Sir, when General Patton brought in the troopers to strengthen the beachhead, he ordered that all units be notified. Division commander General Ridgway had assurances from the navy that if his planes flew through a narrow corridor they would not be fired on. Some ships didn't get the word. Even if they had, after being bombed day and night, the gun crews would probably have reacted the same way."

The room was silent, waiting for Roosevelt. He said, "Thank you, General Belvale. There will, of course, be a thorough investigation. There will also be no word of this tragedy even hinted to the press. Is that understood by everyone?" The holder became a rifle barrel.

A murmur of agreement circled the table; somebody

coughed, someone else shuffled his feet. Skelton and Farrand both were staring at Belvale. The bastards smiled, as if the fiasco in Sicily was his fault.

War News Summary, *The New York Times*—July 11, 1943: The 14th U.S. Air Force in China beat off four waves of more than 100 planes when the Japanese attacked advance American bases in Hunan Province. Damage to the bases was slight, while 44 enemy planes were destroyed.

More than 200 Allied aircraft gave the battered Japanese base at Munda in the Solomon Islands its heaviest bombing of the South Pacific War.

There is U.S. Marine and Army movement among certain islands, but all information is at the moment classified.

Staff Sergeant Eddie Donnely had never felt at ease in the great stone-and-log pile of Sandhurst Keep, with servants being discreet around every corner. If the payoff for remaining here was anything but Gloria, he'd have done a rear march and doubletimed out of here a week ago. Now that Crusty Carlisle himself was in residence, Eddie was doubly uncomfortable. The sprawling old fort crawled with gold braid and the polished stars of generals. The great hall with its ancient pennants and shields, its swords and dented combat armor from wars so old he couldn't name them, made you walk tiptoe and hold your breath. A sergeant in such hallowed precincts could be only a dog robber, shining shoes and polishing brass, not holding hands with the general's granddaughter.

Damn, suppose Crusty caught him sneaking into Gloria's bedroom? No matter what, that was one risk he had to take. He needed to be with this woman, not for a quick lay or an overnight bivouac, but every chance he got. Gloria swam in his blood and throbbed in the marrow of his bones. Because of her, he had crossed that barrier into officer country, and not just company or field grade officers, either; Christ—generals!

This general was one hardnosed, down and dirty son of a bitch. He was also a hell of a man; driving his staff car in Hawaii, Eddie had learned to respect him, and seen the results of pissing him off. Then the guy turned into a Sherman tank on the roll with all guns firing.

And this—a sergeant and Crusty's granddaughter—look what had happened to Eddie's old man for screwing a field grade officer's kid away back when all she had to do was whisper rape and it was ten years in Castle Williams. Mike said he'd divorce his wife and be with golden Freida Thornton forever. She laughed. The bitch had hurt Big Mike Donnely worse than a general court and time in that tough guardhouse.

Taught me what I already knew, he said: we stay on our side of the line and make sure the fucking officers stay on their side.

(Barracks talk: don't call me sir; I work for a living.)

From the start, if Eddie had known who she was, it would have been different. Maybe he would have laid her since she belonged to brass and was Off Limits; he always set his sights on brass, zeroing in on their women to pay back for his father's lasting hurt. Funny thing, though; he could never hurt them back, and he always fell temporarily in love. But with Gloria Carlisle temporary wasn't in it.

It was a good thing that Crusty was upstairs throwing last-minute things into a Val-pac for a quick trip overseas; otherwise the facedown would have started earlier and lasted longer. If an argument really came to a head, he'd just have to tell the general to kiss off, because he meant to marry Gloria if it cost him his front seat in hell or got him shanghaied to walk sentry duty around the North Pole.

Sure, an old guy like that was getting ready to ship out, and Big Mike Donnely, with one war already behind him, had fought through the African campaign and was now in Sicily. And here a young sergeant sat around being a candy ass. The wound he'd picked up on the Canal was healed and he should rejoin his outfit in the Pacific, even though the Americal Division had stacked arms in the Solomons for months now. It would move back into combat soon and his place was with it.

If it wasn't for Gloria—but Gloria was here to touch and smell and taste. She was more important to him than any woman had ever been. Was she more important than his soldiering, than the war itself?

He heard the general stomping down the long flight of stairs and Gloria's sturdy hand tightened upon his. "Don't let him scare you, Eddie."

"He already has."

"Oh, I know everyone thinks he's so gruff—"

"And tough, and everybody is right. Why don't we just run off and get married?"

"Because it would hurt him and the family. We are really traditional about events like weddings and funerals. If he yells at you when you ask for my hand . . ."

"Jesus—do I have to ask his permission? What if he says no?"

". . . just remember that he pushed me into my first marriage and still feels guilty because his choice for my husband was such a bastard."

Eddie automatically snapped to attention when the general bore down on them. For an old man supposedly crippled by arthritis, he moved right along.

"At ease," Crusty said, and Gloria said, "Oh for God's sake, grandfather; this isn't a military formation. What will you put on the invitations—Reply by Endorsement instead of RSVP?" She squeezed Eddie's hand hard and then let go, putting him on his own.

"Sir," Eddie said, slipping into the old army's third-person form of an enlisted man addressing an officer, "Sergeant Donnely requests permission to marry the general's granddaughter, sir."

Crusty stood with feet wide apart, and fists on his hips. "Why?"

"W-why?—I don't understand the general."

"It's a simple word, sergeant. *Why*, goddamnit? Why do you want to marry Gloria? To get out of Soapsuds Row and pin some bars on your collar? To stick it to another officer, your practice at Schofield Barracks, as I remember? Maybe you think that by marrying her you can homestead in the States for the rest of the war. Gloria—get the hell out of here so I can talk plain."

Clamping one hand upon Eddie's arm, she said, "I'm staying; do your damnedest."

Eddie said, "Goddamnit—"

"Must be something like that, for a cocksman like Eddie Donnely to come sniffing around. By a long shot, Gloria's not one of your married playgirls—and she's not all that beautiful."

Shoving her hand off his arm, Eddie took a step forward. "The hell she's not! I respect you, general, but only so goddamn far. I'm a line soldier, not a desk jockey, and you can shove lieutenant bars up your ass. I sure as hell don't want them. I've been in combat and I'm going back. And if you can't see that Gloria is a fine and beautiful woman, then you're a blind old bastard as well as pretty goddamn stupid—sir!"

Was the old bastard grinning? It was hard to tell.

"Son of a bitch," Crusty said. " 'Scuse me, Gloria. Damn if I don't think you found yourself a man with eyes. His mouth works, too."

"You brought it on yourself, granddad. But you haven't answered Eddie."

"Oh. Yeah. Yes, sergeant, you have my blessing, and I hope you know how lucky you are."

"I know, general."

Gloria went into Crusty Carlisle's arms and held him close. "Will you have time to stay for the wedding? We'll keep it simple."

Eddie looked down at his fists and unclenched them. Christ, a few more words and he might have punched out a two-star general. Gloria wouldn't have gone for that.

"I have forty-eight hours," Crusty said. "Get Preston and the Kill Devil Hill group up here by 0900 tomorrow. They're not the only bunch that can put on a wedding—"

"I'll set it up with Minerva. She'll want to bring the family minister."

"That old bat? Oh Christ; I guess she'll have to stick her nose into everything."

Turning, he stuck out his hand and Eddie took it. Crusty's palm was callused and the twisted fingers strong; his long and steady grip wasn't so much a welcome as a warning.

CHAPTER 6

Captured enemy document, evaluated by 8th Army G-2 as genuine—Aboard Flagship, Allied flotilla off Sicily, July 13, 1943: Document reads as follows: *Panzerdivision* Hermann Goering: acts of hysteria in this unit were committed by not only the youngest soldiers, but by NCOs and warrant officers. Withdrawal without orders and cowardice are to be punished on the spot, and if necessary, by the use of weapons.

I shall apply the severest measures against such saboteurs of the fight for the freedom of our nation, and I shall not hesitate to give the death sentence. Signed: CONRATH, Commanding General, Hermann Goering Division.

Owen Belvale sent his Second Platoon forward in support of George Company and asked for a casualty report from the First Platoon, withdrawn from the line with battered Fox Company. Regimental losses were already heavier than he wanted to think about, and he hoped his company was better off.

His 81mm mortars had to stay up where they were, and he was grateful for the fresh supply of ammunition just off-loaded on the beach. Maybe a few replacements would follow, and they would be green and jumpy, but warm bodies with rifles.

Turning from the radio, he called out, "Sergeant Russamano—get that mortar ammo loaded onto two jeeps and run it up to Big Mike's people. They're scraping bottom by now. Be sure the drivers punch it, Russ; this whole area is under daylight observation."

A cocky product of New York's East Side and an old soldier, Russamano grinned. "Can't tell them that, captain. I already have to make them drive sideways to keep those jeeps from flying."

Owen's smile-back relief was short. A panzer shell whipped by just overhead to explode at the edge of sea and scatter workers in the beach party. By now he could recognize the *slap-whine* of the 76mm flat trajectory gun and hated it. All of the German tanks had not pulled out, and more tough fighting lay ahead before the 16th Infantry would reach its objective by dark—the village of Niscemi.

From the divisional briefing that had been passed down to him by his father, Owen knew that today's toughest assignment belonged to a sister regiment, the 26th. It was ordered to keep a battalion front in attack with another battalion in immediate backup in case the Krauts turned and struck back. Grabbing the airfield at Ponte Olivo was a must, but before it could fall there were Mt. Canolotti and Mt. Gibilscemi to be taken. The 33rd Field Artillery was in support, and CG Terry Allen's order was simple: *push!*

Fishing a bent K-ration cigarette from his shirt pocket, Owen gave himself a few minutes to sit down and smoke, to plan ahead and adjust his thoughts. He knew damned well that his father had gone ashore with the lead elements on the landing. It was an illogical thing for a regimental CO to play at being a rifleman just to taste the powder smoke. But that was so like his father, his grandfather and God only knew how many great-greats before them. They had to meet combat head-on, or they didn't feel they were truly soldiers. In antiquity the call to arms had been the clash of sword on shield; now it was the sounds of a firefight.

Possibly Owen understood, but that didn't mean he would emulate his ancestors; the Academy had taught him better, whose place was where in war. If all commanders were line troopers, who would command the troops and get them supplied and see to strategy?

Perhaps he also understood why his mother had filed for divorce: his father's bullheaded attitude; the army's forced separations, the unbending creed of the military families at southern Kill Devil Hill and northern Sandhurst Keep. It must have all piled up.

That didn't mean he would ever approve or that he blamed Kirstin any more than Chad Belvale, or that it didn't bother him when she remarried almost right away. There had been several divorces in the immediate family, proving what—that the women weren't up to the problems of soldiering as well as their men? Where in Army Regulations did it say they were supposed to be?

On the opposite side there was Pretty Penny née Colvin, who had married Walt Belvale, killed as an observer in Poland before the U.S. got into the war. Then she married Owen's brother Farley, and he had always felt it was more to become a part of the family than for overwhelming love. And where did that leave Pretty Penny? Suffering hell in a Jap prison camp, if she was still alive.

He brushed the butt of his cigarette into the scuffed sand. Maybe he didn't understand any of it, after all. He had better stay with tactics he knew and men he believed in.

"Captain?" The radio operator worked his arms into the straps of the heavy SCR-300 and stood up. "Captain, headquarters says the whole regiment is moving out."

"Is the Old Man back from the line?"

"That was the colonel himself on the horn."

And Colonel Belvale hadn't asked to speak to Owen; he hadn't even said the traditional good luck. Christ, every time he thought he knew his old man, whenever he thought they were getting close—

Owen raised his voice. "Saddle up, H Company!"

Lieutenant Nancy Carlisle didn't pull away, although the sweaty clamp of Farley Belvale's hand was painful. "It's all right," she murmured. "You're here in Tripler General

Hospital with me, Farley. This is Hawaii, not the jungle on Guadalcanal, and you know me."

Slowly, his fingers loosened and he stared into her face, frowning. "I . . . I . . . know . . . you . . ."

"Yes; I'm Nancy; Nancy Carlisle. I was married to Keenan, to your uncle."

For a moment, his eyes cleared. "Carlisle?"

She glanced up at the ward boy standing by, in case. "See? He recognizes a family name. He's coming out of it."

Sergeant Fitzgerald Kaole DiGama smiled. "Score another big screwup for the shrinks. They said he was wiped out."

"Carlisle," Farley repeated, staring down at his hands. At least he had stopped counting his fingers over and over.

Nancy rose from the bed and brushed her hand lightly over his cheek. "I'll be back, Farley. Hold on."

And outside the padded room that the sergeant locked behind them, she said, "Fitz, he's not violent; he should be on the open ward."

"They don't want to take chances. The first couple of battle rattle cases that came in here went ape and hurt some nurses."

"And you?"

He shrugged, his shoulders wide and heavy inside the white jacket. "A punch in the mouth. What the hell."

What the hell, the philosophy of Hawaii itself, embodied in this man of mixed races—Irish, Hawaiian and Portuguese. She had asked the first time she heard his full name. Live and let live; the islanders didn't just pay lip service to the credo; they practiced it.

She marched for the nurses' station, her starched uniform rustling, rubber soled shoes making tiny squeaks on the waxed floor. "The NP staff has to learn that no two of these cases are alike. The trauma is severe, more so than in civilian life, because damned few civilians are forced into a kill-or-be-killed situation. These guys aren't cowards, they're wounded, as much as if they had been hit by shrapnel."

He stayed close at her shoulder, big and dark and good looking. "Ain't been no shrapnel since World War I, *malihini*. Shrapnel was like a big shotgun shell full of steel balls that aimed down and went off in the air. Now only the shell casing blows apart and scatters fragments of itself."

"*Mahalo*—thank you. But I'm not all that much a newcomer to the islands, and you know a lot about artillery for a medic." She turned into the office whose ward-side wall was practically all glass so the nut cases could be watched.

"I was an artillery redleg for two hitches," he said, "but at Pearl I took one of those fragments just over my tail bone. The army says my back is no good for combat, and I wouldn't take the discharge they offered me, so now I'm a pretty fair medic. No *ohumu*—I don't complain."

"Sorry, Fitz. I didn't know."

The head nurse looked up from her record keeping. Captain Flora Harris flinched, as she had been doing ever since General Crusty Carlisle flew in to kick ass and take names. That was his specialty, and the hospital CO, the neuropyschiatric doctors and Flora Harris still hadn't gotten over the reaming they took. Still, being medical people, they were slow to change Standard Operating Procedure. Tech/5 Paul (No Middle Initial) Morrison, who started the uproar by mistreating a patient, had been reassigned to the infantry with orders to have him carry an 81mm mortar base plate. It was heavy and the most awkward load that the line outfits could inflict on a man, and those first soldiers delighted in receiving shanghaied eight balls, those losers shipped to the line to get rid of them.

Nancy still believed that the bastard had it coming.

Chubby faced, the corners of her over-lipsticked mouth quivering, Flora Harris said, "Can I help you, lieutenant?"

"You can put Lieutenant Belvale on the open ward."

"But he's fresh from the jungle fighting and therefore dangerous and—Belvale, you said? Is he related to—"

Nancy thought she heard Sergeant Fitz smother a chuckle.

"Yes," she said, "he's close kin to General Belvale, and to General Carlisle, but that's not the reason you should let him out of isolation. He's ready; he has probably always been ready. The treatment of battle fatigue cases has to change; it's not only inhuman, but downright stupid to put those men in isolation."

The head nurse's swallow was audible. "But the doctors say—and Captain Zimmerman's orders are specific—"

Leading over the woman, Nancy said, "Zimmerman hasn't been in uniform as long as me, and I figure he's still operating on precepts based upon his civilian practice. And he will go back to that cushy, big city office when the war is over. But you're Regular Army, are't you, captain? You'll still be around."

She put an edge on her voice. Flora Harris probably didn't realize that she would never pin on the major's oak leaves she coveted so. Once an officer fouled up enough to get his name and service record on Crusty's shit list, he might as well resign his commission or plan on reaching retirement in his present grade. Unless, of course, he redeemed himself in combat. Nancy couldn't see Flora Harris under fire in a forward aid station.

"I-I'll put in a call for Captain Zimmerman, right away."

"Thank you—nurse." Using no address of rank put the woman in her place. Damn, but it was good to have all the weight of the family behind her, even though she wasn't married into it anymore. Once the family stamp was on you, they never forgot, although some of them had come down on her hard in the beginning because she didn't belong and they thought she never could. And because after aborting, she was unable to give Keenan, and the holy family, an heir.

Keenan; she thought of her ex-husband, Major Keenan Carlisle for a long time carried as Missing in Action. He had lucked out on that one, but he was still a volunteer in the China-Burma-India Theater, mixed up in the guerilla fighting he liked so well. She hoped he had found the Chinese woman he had gone back for. Keenan loved that woman as he had never been able to care for his wife. He had shown it to her when he came back stateside for a short while, in every muscle of his face and every change in his eyes, the thickening of his voice as he remembered her. For a moment back there, she had been just a touch jealous, but that passed quickly. Whatever they once had was a long time gone, buried unmourned by the people who helped cause their divorce.

Only helped, she admitted; the basic fault had been her own, and Keenan's, but there could be no going back. She had no bitterness left for him now, and Nancy hoped that his present involvement wouldn't end in a hurtful mess like her affair in Washington. Representative Marshal Bailey from Georgia had never loved her; he just used her for the family connections. Looking back, she realized she had never been in love with him, either. She had only been in heat and Marshal was exceptional at taking care of that.

Conscious of the bulk of Fitz walking beside her, the maleness of him, she wondered if Marshal Bailey had ever recovered from the family pressure that broke his political back and cost him his seat in Congress. As if she gave a damn.

What kind of shaving lotion did Fitz use? It smelled like pineapples, like frangipani and the flowered scent of Hawaii itself. Maybe it was the special aroma of his sweat. It was happening again, and this time she recognized her mood, her needs. The trouble here was—even if Sergeant Fitzgerald Kaole DiGama had the hots for her, too—he was an enlisted man and she was an officer. The army frowned on such liasons, and said so plainly in regulations. Captain Flora Harris would give half her future pension to get hold of any scandal like that.

Perhaps by chance, her hand brushed Fitz's and a shock raced through her. She stopped in that bare hallway lined by isolation rooms with steel doors and looked up into his black, black eyes.

He murmured, "What the hell—I'll say it anyhow. You are much *nonohe*."

"Meaning?"

"You are beautiful to me."

"You are beautiful, too."

CHAPTER 7

War summary, *The New York Times*—July 16, 1943: British and American air forces struck their heaviest blow yet against Germany with around the clock strikes. The RAF rocked Hamburg at night with 2,500 tons of bombs. Daylight brought Flying Fortresses which hit the port again, and spread their attack to Keil.

The Red Army captured another 30 villages, halted incessant German counterattacks and encircled the enemy base at Orel.

More than 200 Allied planes battered Japanese bases in the Solomons in what was described as the largest and most damaging raids of the South Pacific war.

Sloan Travis was no longer a platoon leader of heavy machine guns, but only a rifleman pinned down like the rest. Digging his fingers into the dirt, he tried to make himself flat, to crawl right down into the earth. But he couldn't hide from the *nebelwerfers*.

BLAMM! BLAMM! BLAMM!— BLAMM! BLAMM! BLAMM!

They came in vicious groups, in air-splitting, dirt-throwing bursts of six, big and heavy—150mm and 21mm rockets. The explosions ripped great holes in the earth and made the ground buck in successive earthquakes that had him hanging on to keep from being thrown off the world.

How many of the frigging multi-barreled launchers were emplaced around the town? Too damn many for certain, and in the biggest concentrations the outfit had ever faced. They had been introduced to *nebelwerfers* in Tunisia, but never in such a pack as this display of raw and deadly firepower.

BLAMM! BLAMM! BLAMM!

In the acrid smoke of that echo, two badly wounded men shrieked in a duet of agony; *medic . . . medic!!*

Rockets: what the hell else would the engineers invent to make the infantryman's short life more hellish? Sure, the British had used them as far back as the battle of New Orleans, but they hadn't worked very well. Now some industrious son of a bitch had refined rockets until they were murderously effective; some frigging civilian who didn't have to face them, of course.

Some civilian? What was Sloan Travis but a civilian dragged kicking and cursing into uniform? It would take more than one war to force him into the family's rigid military mold, rockets and *nebelwerfers* be damned. His relatives would always be pissed at him for being the only draftee in a century of family history, and screw them, too.

BLAMM! BLAMM! BLAMM!

Jesus, his ears throbbed and his head ached. Where the hell was the counter-battery response? Some FO had to be calling back to Divarty for the 105s to register on target and stop this killing fire. If the forward observers hadn't been blown all to hell along with their radios by now. If those guns could even range in the launchers. All of combat was a series of ifs and maybes and goddamns: the best laid plans of mice and generals . . .

Don't think of the next salvo, the next rocket that might find him and make a jellied mess out of what used to be a man. He had never felt more naked, more exposed. How do you write this paralyzing fear, this quivering nakedness of expectant skin and tender flesh so easily punctured, this delicate lacework of bones? How to explain this blind retaliatory hate for the faceless bastards who were firing the rocket launchers?

Kill them all: kill them quick so they would stop.

He was learning to think like a soldier; there were no abstractions at a gun muzzle. The problem might come in getting rid of that thinking after the war. If there was an after.

Overhead, torn air freight trained by; outgoing mail. Divarty was replying. His fingers eased their burrowing into the ground, but not for long. The rockets kept coming, massive explosions that left men screaming in their echoes, that left behind some men who would never scream again. What was wrong with the frigging artillery? Couldn't they find the range?

Sergeant Pelkey skidded belly-down beside him, his sharp face dirty and strained. "Travis! Oh shit, I mean, lieutenant—the artillery can't reach them. The bastards are out of range of the 105s, but battalion says they're bringing up the Long Toms of the 5th Field; they'll zero in."

No doubt the 155 howitzers would plaster the enemy positions; they could reach out for five miles. But given time, the Krauts would eliminate this attack. Waiting out the next barrage, he said, "How nice of battalion. We'll have to send them a thank you card."

"What?"

"Nothing. If you're going to stay here, make sure you're between me and the next rockets."

"Horseshit—sir."

Medic! they cried, *medic!* But there were never enough medics, for men with the red cross on their brassard fell to the rockets, too. Death did not respect the Geneva Convention.

And finally, finally, the Long Toms reached far out to drop their big shells among the launch sites, among the goddamn Krauts who worked them. Kill the bastards and scatter their remains to the wind. Then the attack on the high ground guarding the village of Pietraperzia could continue. George Company would move on, what was left of it, and Second Platoon guns would move along in support. Up on those mountain ridges, they could send plunging fire down into the town, overhead fire to make the Krauts keep their heads down and so protect the skirmishing riflemen. Big Mike Donnelly's mortars were already looping shells over the mountain. The attack would move forward, and the cost would not be questioned. Acceptable losses.

Sloan thought about being a private again; no responsibility, no heavy thinking, just protect your ass. The trouble was, he hadn't been able to let it alone. To keep his skin whole, he'd had to do some stupid things, like going head-on with a machine gun. That brought him a medal and a set of gold bars, neither of which he wanted, but accepted because he had no choice. Colonel great uncle or whatever Chad Belvale made that clear enough. Sloan could never keep track of family relationships and hadn't really cared, until they had been forced upon him.

Silence; blessed silence, so quiet for a moment that his mind ached. The *nebelwerfers* had been stopped. The moment ended with the rattle of small arms and automatic weapons fire.

"Let's get with it," he said to Pelkey, as bullets kicked a line of dirt directly in front of them.

Schmeisser; machine pistol up close! Where had he been during the rocket barrage? Where was the bastard now? The Kraut fired again, a long, rolling burst.

Eddie Donnelly lay glowing and spent beside her in the little motel room. She was Gloria Donnelly now, the union more or less blessed by the preacher that old bat Minerva had brought up from Virginia. He was a prissy bastard who acted like he was doing Eddie the greatest favor by binding him into the family. Screw that; the favor was in binding him to Gloria.

That line about until death do you part was sobering, reminding him of the oath of enlistment, not by the wording, but the solemn intent. From the first time he raised his hand and swore to defend the Constitution of the United States against all its enemies whomsoever, foreign and domestic, he knew the commitment was for life, or until death did him part.

There in the great hall, where the high balconies were

sentineled by suits of polished armor, and beneath the rows of tattered banners older than America itself, Eddie said the vows he had thought never to say, and was glad for the promises.

Eddie stood tall in his issue suntans and his stripes, three up and a rocker, while a circle of brass and the women of brass outnumbering them shone in their dress uniforms and jewels. A small gathering that Crusty apologized for, since most of the family was scattered across the world and there hadn't been much time to gather them. Apologized to Gloria, of course; the old man wasn't used to talking to sergeants on the same level.

General Belvale was first to shake Eddie's hand while Crusty kissed the bride. "Congratulations, son. You have a fine young woman, and she has a good man."

The goblets were scrolled silver, time-worn and heavy to the hand, filled with golden champagne. Eddie held his touching Gloria's, waiting for the wedding toast, wanting to run away with his wife and the hell with the ceremony.

Belvale lifted his goblet. "To this new bonding, to our family. *Defende Vinco!*"

They drank, and a squad of waiters refilled the goblets as Gloria whispered to Eddie: "The Belvale motto: I conquer by defending."

Crusty Carlisle raised his cup high. "*Oderint Dum Metuant*—let them hate, so long as they fear. History is but the clash of arms!"

"Oh Jesus," Gloria whispered. "Let's get out of here before they go into every battle of every Crusade. I do love grandfather, but he can be so damned—"

"Crusty? My family has no motto, but when my old man gets into his second pitcher of beer he usually has a toast: Nothing's too good for the troops—and that's what they get—nothing!"

She laughed and took his arm to guide him through the relatives. The other handshakes and remarks were perfunctory. Old lady Minerva offered a wrinkled cheek for him to kiss; smelling lavender powder, he deliberately missed and pecked air.

Grinning, Eddie wondered what the stiff-necked mistress of Kill Devil Hill would think of what Gloria had just done in their wedding bed. If Minerva could possibly conceive of such an act of sex, of love. If she could accept the reality of flesh, she would sniff that Eddie had corrupted the girl. It was to be expected if a Tidewater lady allowed herself to become involved with a white trash Yankee, an enlisted man.

She had just sneaked in the most sensual trick he had ever known a woman to use, and he thought he knew them all. Sweet, quiet little Gloria, born to the purple, had shaken him up. After their first married sex, she had reached down and touched his glans with gentle fingertips, then she drew a slow, damp line up from her mound to her belly button, and up again to roll each of her nipples. Finally she touched those fingers to her lips and kissed him, only slightly sticky.

Face snugged to his chest then, one sleek leg over him, she whispered, "I never learned that anywhere. I just now invented it. I never wanted to do it before."

Stroking her hair, he held her close, this woman who had reached him more than all women, this descendant of generals whose natural home was the castle of Sandhurst Keep. He sure as hell wouldn't honeymoon in that gloomy old pile. Down the road they went in her car to the nearest motel, leaving the wedding party to champagne it by themselves. They had only half promised to be back for goodbyes before Crusty was ready to ship out tomorrow, but probably would. If the house was still overrun, they'd go right back to the motel.

Crusty's overseas travel orders were the reason the wedding had been hurried and short on guests. Despite his age and sometimes crippling arthritis, the old man had bucked his way to a tour in the South Pacific. Crusty was tough, but Eddie wondered if he knew what he was getting into.

General Carlisle, General Belvale, General Ben Alexander, stars and bars everywhere you looked. If Eddie had known in the beginning, he would have placed Gloria Carlisle off limits, but she had used her ex-husband's name,

Johnson. As a doughnut dolly at Walter Reed Hospital she caught his eye right off, and not because he'd been without a woman for so long. He saw something the other guys didn't, because they didn't whistle or try to play grabass and acted as if she were another plain jane.

She wore no makeup, just a touch of lipstick, and her brown hair swung free. When he met her unflinching eyes he saw the startling warmth and hidden promises of passion. Then he was twice glad the army had shipped him to Walter Reed in D.C. where a hotshot specialist patched the hole in Eddie's lung and stopped the whistling noise that irritated him so. A thousand times, he had cursed that Jap who shot him on Guadalcanal, but now he might have to credit the little bastard for Gloria.

(Barracks talk: it's all jawbone—PX checks, barber ticket, show book; the army runs on credit, on jawbone.)

He didn't know she was in any way connected to high brass. Sure, he always planned carefully to seduce the wives and daughters of brass. It was a thing developed since childhood, since he discovered what that major's daughter did to his father.

And Gloria? The surprise of his life. She had electrified him from the moment she came to work as a Red Cross volunteer. She said okay to a date and on his first three day pass from the ward, she had driven him up to Sandhurst Keep and told him who she was. By then he was too tied into her quiet and sensual power to care.

And after they made that long, deep loving on the floor in front of the big stone fireplace, Eddie forgot that he was already married for life—to the goddamned army where there was no divorce in wartime. He forgot that gold braid and ODs didn't mix, or even that there was a war on, a war he was duty bound to return to. He only remembered Gloria.

"Eddie," she said, her warm breath tickling the base of his throat, "I know how you feel about going back. I'm RA too, remember. But I hope you don't want to. You don't have anything to prove, not to yourself and certainly not to the family. Please, darling—don't ever worry about them. I'm the family for you."

She smelled of soap and sex, clean and honeyed odors, the special scent of Gloria, a golden sweat. Gloria naked was a radiation of scent—a rain forest humid and fecund, a sweatiness of lubrication, a state of readiness that made her impossible to resist. And who would want to?

"You're all the future I want," he said, "all the now I need."

Snuggling closer, she sighed. "But you're thinking of shipping out. Damn it, you're no different from the rest of them."

"Good lord, all those generations of knights and ladies, the coats of arms, the battle flags—would you *want* me to be different?"

Lifting her face, she kissed him lightly, a taste of geraniums and a hint of need. "I guess not. But promise me you'll wait until your lung is completely healed and you're in shape for fighting."

"If you promise not to have the family block my orders or slip me into some rear echelon outfit."

She didn't hesitate for long. "Okay, it's a deal. They wouldn't like me to ask, anyway. Just come back to me, Eddie Donnely, and not on your shield; always come back to me."

"Yes," he said, and meant it.

This time her kiss was not light, but full, drawing him into her.

TWX, coded and scrambled TOP SECRET, to Kill Devil Hill, Lt. Gen. Preston Belvale, Your Eyes Only. Rome—0600, July 17, 1943: Office of Strategic Services operatives on scene report Benito Mussolini's position shaky since defeat in Africa and invasion of Sicily. Possible ouster of his entire cabinet imminent. Replacement expected by either King Victor Emmanuel or Marshal Pietro Badoglio. OSS estimates this move to be crack in Axis and preparation for Italy to back out of war, if Hitler allows.

Captain Gavin Scott met with the escape committee, a pair of dusty looking majors and the ranking POW, a Limey Leftenant Colonel with a castrated face, any strength it might have had cut out of it by getting his ass kicked in Libya.

"Yes, captain?" Colonel Sanderman tapped a chewed pencil upon the ration box that served as a table.

Damned if Gavin would salute or stand at attention; he was in a better army. He said, "The camp radio says we're ramming deep into Sicily. You can look around and see how the Krauts are rushing troops south. The Wops are going crazy and clogging the roads. It's a good time for a break."

Goddamn, he had to get out; he urgently needed to get back into the air and add to his record. More, he owed the fucking Krauts; not only for shooting him down twice, and leaving him with half a face. They owed a tab for beating and kicking him on the ground; for all this prisoner bullshit, the stink of mud and fear.

"And go where, captain?" The colonel's voice was dry as the desert where he had lost his command. "Even if your scars and lack of civilian clothing didn't make you stand out, where would you go?"

"South; mingle with the refugees and head south."

One of the majors said, "Refugees are heading away from the port cities, going north and east." The other major sucked on an empty pipe.

"Get off the road, then. Take to the mountains and hide out until our troops land and move up the boot."

The colonel tapped his pencil. "That could take years, if ever it happens, and . . ."

Fists on his hips, Gavin cut in: "The American army doesn't drag ass. *We* get things done. Sicily falls, then Italy."

Unblinking, Colonel Sanderman continued, ". . . the camp commandant has just informed me that we are all being hurried farther north. All escape plans and permissions must be placed on hold."

"Within two hours, at nightfall to avoid the bombings," the talky major added. "Perhaps you'll pass the word to your group."

"Permission, shit!" Gavin said, and stamped out of the ragged canvas cover. He always had trouble with Limeys, especially the little bitch in uniform who had given him such a hard time. After he made his break and got back into the air, he'd get a line on the whereabouts of Leftenant Stephanie Bartlett, if he had to buy half the personnel clerks in the British army. The Carlisle-Belvale money was meant for things like that, at least Gavin's share of it.

First things first, though. He scrounged an extra piece of tattered blanket to wear like a poncho over his shirt. Turning his flight jacket inside out, he rolled his few belongings into it, tied and made shoulder strings from blanket strips. He saved the issue dinner of olives and black bread and when he climbed into the converted Italian bus that evening, he figured he looked ratty enough to be just another Wop on the run.

The PW trucks and buses crawled forward, a clumsy inchworm stopped again and again in the dark by breakdowns and traffic jams, by the precedence of German troop convoys and clattering tanks. Once some night bombers worked the road over a mile up the line and jittery guards bailed out of his bus to take cover in the ditches.

Hunched over in the chaotic blackness, he scuttled for the open door. Somebody caught at his arm and he slapped the hand away. Stumbling over the ditch, he ran a few yards before falling to lie flat. Permission from the Limeys, hell; Gavin Scott was out and on the first leg to home.

Roaring low, a night fighter raked the road with machine guns and a 20mm cannon. Up the road, a truck burst into flame and men yelled. From where he lay he couldn't tell if they were Krauts or POWs. Maybe Eye-ties, the cute name used by the English; their terminology was real cute—the Wogs, the ruddy Jerries, and aren't all Yanks crackers? Well, Gavin wasn't cute; he felt pretty damn good, so relaxed that after the strafing stopped and the convoy rolled on again, he nodded off.

It was daylight when he woke, a little chilly, dew beading his blanket poncho. Climbing to his feet, he stretched, yawned and rubbed his eyes. Just as they cleared, the SS trooper smashed him in the mouth with the butt of a rifle.

CHAPTER 8

INTERNATIONAL NEWS SERVICE—Somewhere in Sicily, July 18, 1943: A small task force here was dubbed the Rough Riders today because they are led by Brig. Gen. Theodore Roosevelt, Jr. Patched together from Division Headquarters personnel and based on the 70th Tank Battalion, the 1st Reconnaissance Troop and part of the 1st Engineers, the Rough Riders passed through the outpost line and drove furiously north. It took and secured a critical road junction about five miles east of Barrafranca, and from there, scouted in three directions for enemy buildups.

Chad Belvale rode in the back seat of a Recon jeep beside the gunner. The 30 caliber air cooled was mounted on a tall swivel bolted to the floor so the gunner, by draping himself around, could kneel and fire a full 360 degrees. Up front, even ahead of the lead tank, Little Teddy's jeep bounced along the dusty road.

The Recon lieutenant turned in the front seat and yelled it: "Ain't he a crazy little bastard? General Roosevelt just don't give a doodly squat how many Krauts may be out there. I expect to see him gallop by on a horse, hollering charge, charge!"

"If he did it," Chad yelled back, hanging on to the side of the jeep, "the whole division would jump up and follow him."

Bambambambam! The gunner rapped out a short burst.

The jeep swerved and the lieutenant shouted, "What the hell?"

"Thought I saw something move on that ridge."

Good reaction, Chad thought, or bad nerves; either way it was better to shoot first. Not expecting the unexpected had almost caused Owen to buy the farm the other day. It happened right after the Long Toms and some ship to shore fire ranged in and blasted the concentration of *nebelwerfers* that had held up the attack.

Battalion aid station flashed Chad word that his son was being treated, and Chad trotted there. It was a flesh wound across the left bicep, a raw gouge that didn't get a tendon or much muscle. Chad nodded at the doctor and let out his breath.

Burp gunner playing possum, Owen said. Lousy shot or he'd have caught us cold.

Bought yourself a vacation in Tunis or maybe even England. Chad held his voice steady.

No dice, dad—ah, colonel. Look at Sergeant Pelkey's wound; it's nastier and he refuses evacuation. So do I—sir. We can make it okay."

Your choice, son. One thing.

Yes, sir?

Be careful of possums?

It had been good, those few minutes where they actually communicated without animosity. Word had come that his other son was out of the Pacific action with battle fatigue. It could happen to anybody, for even the finest Toldeo blade had a snapping point and Farley had always been an imaginative and sensitive kid. He was safe now, and that counted for something.

Thinking on family made him think of Kirstin, of her cold anger and the helplessness he'd known when she caught him in bed with that hooker. It hadn't been his being with the woman so much as the steady decline of Kristin's and his caring for each other. Part of it was the army, but she knew to expect the separations, if she didn't want to move with him because of her horses.

And their drifting apart couldn't be blamed upon family pressure. Kirstin not only stood firm against family tradition, she defied them when she felt rebellion was called for. As with the horses; the family fortune was based upon thoroughbreds that won Derbys and auctioned for millions. No racehorses for Kirstin; she raised show and working horse Morgans.

So it had been mostly his fault; the shrinks were at least partially right about the formative years. His trauma came a bit later, but it was no less deep and lasting, after Aunt Minerva caught him masturbating. She had never approved of him since, and even now he rarely glanced at her without shameful remembering.

After that, sex had always seemed somewhat dirty to him, and if whiskey didn't make it any less embarrassing, it was made numbly acceptable. Chad might have gone on sliding downhill if he hadn't met Leftenant Stephanie Bartlett in a London bomb shelter. Because of her, he learned to laugh in bed, to be open and honest. He made love with Stephanie, real and hearty and poetic and fun. She freed him sexually and he could not help falling in love with her.

Ba-rramm! The tank following Roosevelt's jeep fired its cannon to the left front.

"Shit," said the lieutenant. "I wish the army would issue ear plugs."

The machine gunner said: "That ain't the kind of plug I need. Every time one of them big guns go off, I have to shake my leg."

They came up on the crossroads fast, Recon jeeps zigzagging out in front of the tanks and spraying their 30 calibers. The tanks fanned out, churning the rocky dirt, their hatches buttoned down. With Little Teddy on hand, nobody took chances; the tanks slammed HE rounds into every suspicious gulley and chugged their 50 calibers along the ridgelines.

"Wops!" the gunner hollered. "There on the right front! I'll get those sons of—"

"Hold fire," Chad said. "They're coming out."

Hands stretched high overhead, a few dirty handkerchiefs fluttering, a dozen or so grimy Italian soldiers filtered out of a low stone hut that blended into the ground so well that it could easily be overlooked.

"No weapons in sight," the lieutenant said. "What'd they leave behind in that hut?"

Chad climbed down, carbine at the ready, watching the Italian faces—fearful, bloodied and dirty; most of the eyes had that thousand yard stare of infantrymen who have seen too much and lost track of the world. They should be no trouble, but one of them didn't slouch; he marched stiffly as if a bayonet nudged his back.

M-1s at the ready, a pair of GIs herded the prisoners to a shallow gulley and motioned them to sit. Chad said to the lieutenant, "Best we check out that hut before the general heads that way."

Roosevelt was his usual exuberant, grinning self, helmet tilted back on his balding head, chin straps swinging. In rumpled ODs and leggins, he strode to the center of the crossroads and stopped there to lean upon the mortar aiming stake that was a walking stick and his trademark.

Shaking his head, Chad followed the Recon officer to the shack, conscious of the jeep gunner kneeling on the seat and alert to lay covering fire.

Riflemen approached from another angle. Two of the Shermans from the 70th Armored pulled out, clattering away from the crossroads and off to scout the rolling countryside.

From across the road, one of the Italians yelled something high pitched and desperate. The Recon officer had neared the hut door when a man dashed from behind the shack and ran for cover, firing a machine pistol from the hip. He ran crooked, staggering as he was hit again and again by the jeep gunner. Going down in a heap and spasming, he triggered his final shots into the earth.

"Kraut!" Chad shouted. "Goddamn SS trooper! Lieutenant, don't go—"

The hut blew up with a tremendous explosion of blinding flash and a thunderclap that smashed Chad flat. His helmet flew off and his carbine spun away; he tasted dirt and gunpowder.

Swaying and dizzy, he climbed to one knee and shook his head, trying to clear his ears, trying to wipe the shock from his eyes and bring them into focus. His teeth grated and he spat dirt.

The hut was gone and so was the Recon lieutenant. Small pieces of both were scattered all the way to the crossroads. Two men shrieked in turn for a medic; on the left flank, a tank fired its cannon twice.

The SS, Hitler's fanatical elite, goddamned *Schutzstaffel* outlaws. This particular bastard had the shack loaded with what?—probably antitank mines, and set with a time fuse. After disarming the passive Italians, he'd driven them out to surrender as bait, setting the trap. If that one Wop soldier hadn't yelled and made him cut the fuse short, he'd have gotten more than the poor bastard from Recon, possibly General Roosevelt himself.

Chad didn't even know the lieutenant's name, and Graves Registration might never find his dogtags.

Be careful of possums, he'd told his son. Be doubly watchful for assholes wearing the double lightning strikes of the SS on their collars.

Coded radio message from Convoy B-114, enroute Bougainville to CINCPAC—July 19, 1943, 1900 hrs: Victory ships *General Pope* and *General Hardee* torpedoed and sunk by Japanese submarines 1800 hours this date. Possible hit upon one submarine. Troopship casualty reports as yet incomplete but heavy; number of survivors picked up by destroyers. High ranking officer missing; name withheld pending notification next of kin. Further search called off at sundown under threat of additional attacks upon convoy.

The tropical water wasn't cold, but piss-warm. Damned good thing, Crusty thought; if the cold had stiffened his arthritic joints, he couldn't swim and would already be shark bait. Blown off deck and slapped into the sea, he never lost consciousness and managed to dog-paddle to the nearest raft. In thickening twilight, the oil soaked uniforms told him that one swabbie and two soldiers huddled inside. They made grudging room for him. He was thankful that no lake of oil burned around them, and thankful just to breathe. The water stank of diesel and some kind of rot.

He wondered where the hell they were, which way they might drift and how far they were from land. As if it made a difference right away and maybe never. There would be no rescue; the destroyers were herding the frightened convoy away from here. This dinky little rubber boat floated in Jap waters, and a feeding shark would be more merciful. Crusty grunted; either way, he would give a tiger shark or a chickenshit Jap a bellyache.

"Jesus," a GI said, "you must be the ship captain. Ain't nobody else that fucking old."

"I'm a goddamn soldier," Crusty said, and nearly gagged on oily water he had swallowed. "More soldier than you babyshit recruits ever saw. I got to be older than grass because I'm so fucking tough."

The sailor pushed up to rest the back of his head on the rim of the raft. Blood seeped from his broken nose. "Ain't this a bitch? Highest ranking officer in the whole convoy and he crawls into our boat. This old bigmouth is a general, name of Carlisle."

"Bet your money-making ass. And I'm here to tell you we're going to make it. Head count—who the hell are you and how bad are you hurt?"

The swabbie said, "Sullivan, Seaman First; nose and a couple of fingers broke, that's all."

The little soldier vomited over the side. The other one mumbled, "Thornton—corporal; busted leg, I reckon. Real son of a bitch."

The little guy choked it out: "Something's fucked up inside me—sir. Name's Woodall; just—just a private." Turning his head, he threw up again.

Crusty's stomach bobbed with the motion of the raft, but

he forced it steady. "You're a soldier, Woodall. That's not *just* any goddamn thing, and you remember it. Come daylight, we'll see what we can do for you. Sailor, any emergency rations and water on this floating condom?"

"Let me feel around for—yeah, the packet is still here. Two gallons of water and dry biscuits; three signal flares; line and fish hooks with lures; folding canvas bucket to catch rain water. A half ass first aid kit. No folding mast or sail; they're for the big rafts; no paddles, either. There's supposed to be a compass—wait one; can't make out what shape it's in—so damn dark . . ."

Wiping his face, Crusty propped himself erect and stared around. Of course he couldn't see a light; the convoy was running blacked out, hauling ass from this spot of ambush by Jap subs. That was SOP. The crews and troops had heard the lectures: man overboard is on his own; we can't circle back for him. In case a ship is torpedoed, the destroyer escorts will do what they can for survivors, but not for long. The existence of the convoy must be held more important than its individual parts.

"In other words," Crusty said to the featureless night, to the ships that had left them behind, "tough shit."

"What?" the sailor asked. "This damned compass is smashed."

"Like I said, tough shit. But we aren't planning any complicated trips. Let's see—the last I heard in the ward room was that our ship was moving close to a bunch of islands—Choiseul, past Munda, I think, and heading for Bougainville."

"Holy shit," the big soldier—Thornton—said. "That narrows it down to about half the Pacific Ocean."

The little guy puked softly over the side.

Seaman Sullivan grunted, "There's a bunch of little islands around, some two-bit atolls scattered off Bougainville, most of them not important enough to get named."

Thornton whimpered that his leg hurt like hell, then added: "Most of them little islands are held by Japs, ain't they? Goddamn; come morning they're going to have our asses. Planes and subs . . ."

Crusty rubbed dry lips. "I don't figure they'll be looking for small rafts, if they search at all. The little shits will be sweating out our invasion landings at Bougainville. Hell, if they did come looking, this little rubber duck is as hard to find as one pimple on a fat lady's ass."

"Goddamn, Woodall—don't bump my leg again," Thornton said. "General. I could sure use some water."

"So could sinners in hell," Crusty said. "Tomorrow's sun will make it a lot harder on us. We'll sweat it out until then, and go on rations. Sailor, your job is to guard what we have."

"That won't be hard. The way we're jammed in here, can't anybody wiggle without wiggling somebody else. Best we scrape off as much oil as we can; this goddamn diesel will eat you up. When we float out of the area, we ought to wash off our uniforms. Salt itch isn't as bad as oil rash."

"Thanks," Crusty said. "Appreciate your know-how, son. We'll depend on it." He went to work palming the greasy stuff off his body.

Thornton bitched about water, then said, "Reckon it's a good thing we got a bigshot officer with us. They'll come back for him. They'd kiss off us poor old enlisted men, but they can't afford to lose no bigshot general."

"Son," Crusty said, conscious now of bruised ribs and a sore shoulder, "that must be your ass talking; your mouth knows better. In this situation I'm not worth a damned bit more than the lowest yardbird, so don't hope for rescue. Now I suggest that everybody get as comfortable as we can and rest. Come daylight, we'll take a reading on what we have and what we can do."

Head propped on the rounded support of the raft, Crusty closed tired eyes and heard Woodall softly vomiting. The kid would get the first issue of water in the morning, if he was still alive.

If any of them were still alive. Water was seeping into the raft.

CHAPTER 9

UNITED PRESS, Delayed—Somewhere in the South Pacific, July 19, 1943: Primarily American, Allied forces have landed on Bougainville and gained a solid foothold. A volunteer regiment of Fijian Infantry joined the Americal Division and strong Australian units to fight their way inland against well prepared positions dug in and fortified by coconut logs and sandbags. Some pillboxes are reported to be thick concrete reinforced by iron bars. These are situated so that they can protect each other with interlocking crossfire from machine guns. Fanatic Japanese banzai counterattacks led by sword-waving officers slowed, but did not stop, the forward movement of the fresh Allied troops.

Major Dan Belvale sweated. Stewing in his own juices was more like it, and he might run out of liquid at any time. Humid jungle heat was like no other; the air was a hot blotter that sucked the sweat through every pore of your body. The rain forest fogged the mind, too.

Holding the map so droplets of sweat wouldn't fade spots on the folded paper, Dan stared at the antique map brought up to·date by hit and miss, and by bloody confrontations with Japs who had popped up where they weren't supposed to be.

And popped up was correct terminology. The hard way,

71

the outfit had discovered spider holes. Jap snipers burrowed into the earth, making narrow holes just wide enough for their bodies and their weapons. They made sturdy and well camouflaged lids for these holes, covers that blended with the jungle floor and could be walked upon. Like the trapdoor spiders, they rose silently from behind to kill their prey. These slant-eyed spiders rose and fired, then like yoyos, slid back underground.

The mason spider, Dan thought, or the *Cleniza California nica,* and was surprised that the identification returned so easily to mind. West Point instructors made certain that cadets received a well rounded education in the sciences as well as military subjects, but didn't exactly concentrate upon entomology. That had been Dan's idea; if a career was left up to him, he might have found a satisfying life in the study of fascinating insects. But there was the family, and the Academy and the natural order of things.

Which had cost him his only son, Lieutenant Walton Belvale, KIA in Poland, 1939.

"Looks mean, doesn't it?"

Blinking at his executive officer, Dan said, "It's even meaner than it looks. Coming up the Numa-Numa trail was bad, but this," he pointed to the area they had to take, "all ridges and sharp peaks split by deep ravines. Good God—Recon reports that the sides climb almost straight up from the muddy valley floor."

Captain Sands let pipe smoke drift from the corner of his mouth. "And of course the vegetation is all rain forest and matted undergrowth. Sure glad we have a bunch of native bearers for the heavy work."

"Never enough, and they can't haul the weapons; that responsibility is ours. No matter how heavy the mortar base plates get, or what a bitch the ammo is to carry, I don't want to see a single native carrier toting arms."

Sands's pipe made bubbling noises. "Yes, sir, and something new controlled by regiment. We just had six dogs brought in—four messengers and two scouts from that Quartermaster War Dog Platoon."

"What do they eat—K-9 rations?"

"I hear they really enjoy Japanese ass, raw."

Dan wiped his hand across his face. "No accounting for taste. Okay—this battalion moves out; have our radio notify regiment that we're jumping off as of now. When we reach the—shit! who can pronounce all this?—Kariana-Igiaru-Magerikopaia area, we'll call for artillery support. And henceforth this area will be known as the K.I.M.—KIM."

Rot; the air smelled of rotted vegetation, of moldy bones, putrefied flesh and great beetles melted into the sticky black soil. A man shot here and not found would swiftly be stripped of his meat, his guts reconnoitered by lizards and spiders, gnawed upon by whatever slimy, scaly or hairy things that slithered through this underbrush.

Good God; an entomologist could spend a lifetime here and never catalog the insects already known, while finding a hundred new species that the books had yet to list. He might become famous and have a beetle named after him, the *Scarabaedae Belvale*. Dripping sweat, he planted his feet hard against the slope and took a handhold on a curly vine to help him higher up the trail. His whole body itched, not in just the places where jungle rot had taken hold.

Any scarab called Belvale would of course be heavily armored, wield strong, sharp mandibles and probably possess a chemical warfare weapon. He wished the air corps would send in crop dusters to saturate the enemy held high ground with any kind of poison gas, the stuff out of World War I—phosgene, mustard, even tear gas. He could not understand Geneva Convention agreements—that the Japanese had never signed, anyway—that allowed the use of flame throwers and white phosphorus, but not gas. And what of the Japs boobytrapping American wounded, the slow torture and brutal beheading of prisoners?

Damnit, like General Carlisle said, the object of warfare was to kill the enemy, as swiftly and efficiently as possible. And that, Crusty added, went for any son of a bitch who helped to feed, clothe or supply him. There are no civilians in a combat zone.

A sharp rattle of gunfire from above told him that his

rifleman had run into trouble, an ambush along the steep trail, a hidden pillbox. The M-1s answered the flatter cracks of the Jap 25s, the Arisakas and Nambus. The company's air-cooled 30s couldn't be brought into play on a cliffside, but the Browning automatic rifles pounded back with short bursts. Panting, he braced carefully against a sapling whose fanned leaves hid ragged thorns. He signalled for the radio handset. "This is KIM six—K-I-M, damnit! You don't expect me to go through all those stupid map names? Fire mission for the 245th."

Staring at his map, he wiped sweat from his eyes, gave coordinates and repeated them. "Battery B, don't fuck it up. This is steep territory and my people are close. A short round can raise hell. Over and out."

Then: "Easy Company! This is Battalion Six. Hold where you are. I repeat, hold your ground and do not advance. Divarty is giving us a fire mission. Out."

Turning to Sands a yard below him on the precipitous trail, he said, "Pass word to the 81s. They're to fire over—repeat, over—the high ground, extreme range. Drop an extra handful of increments down the tube if they have to, but keep Easy Company safe."

The mortars held machined slots between their fins for little flat bags of powder; the more powder, the farther the projectile flew. Oldtime gunners knew that extra increments in the tube before the shell was dropped would throw it away the hell and gone beyond the official range limits. It was a practice frowned upon in peacetime as damaging to the tubes and disconcerting to firing range officers.

Dan couldn't actually sit; he half-lay, half-propped in supporting brush beside the narrow trail. Outgoing mail *whooshed!* overhead, shell after 105mm shell wailing high and zeroing in to explode to the rear of and among the blockading Japs. Immediately behind came the throaty hiss of the mortars. The riflemen were being helped, and in terrain like this, they needed all the support they could get, and all the prayers that profane dogfaces could slip past any angels dumb enough to hang around battlefields.

"Artillery is lifting," Sands said, radio handset at his ear.

"Easy Company is stopped cold. Word from our scouts up on Nip Hill says trying to buck through the automatic weapons crossfire is suicide. They also said about halfway up this pisser of a ridge, another trail cuts around the left flank. They don't know how far it goes or exactly where. Might run out in a few hundred yards."

"Might not." Dan fumbled out the map. "This shows a village to the north, just a few shacks, enough for Japs to use as a dump or just to hole up in."

"How far north?"

Dan considered. "I make it about three thousand yards."

"Oh shit; considering that hillside and the jungle, it's no farther than from here to Denver."

Folding the map, Dan passed it to his exec. "I have a hunch. You take it from here, while I round up some spare parts troopers and work us around Nip Hill on that new path. If we can get in behind those bastards up top—"

"If you make it all the way, major; if you don't run into a shitstorm of Japs back there."

"It's the way the dice bounce, Sandy. What the hell."

"Yes, sir. I'll hold the artillery and mortars. Good luck."

The path was barely more than a game trail, snaking along the side of Nip Hill, overhung with unfriendly brush. Ticks lurked on the leaves, waiting to drop on clothing and work their way to skin. Fatigue jacket sticking to his shoulder blades, Dan paused near the head of his struggling column to pump damp air into his heaving chest.

Ticks; a thousand varieties of flat, oval bodies, six legged, eight legged, equipped with anesthetic to deaden skin so they could insert their heads and suck your blood. When they were sated, swollen to great size, they dropped off and left an open infection. Then they laid a hundred or so eggs to hatch and wait around for the next chow call.

A pace beside Dan, a soldier twisted a tick out of his arm and said, "Shit—what do these fuckers eat when they're not eating me?"

"Nothing," Dan said over his shoulder. "Entomologists knocked off their lab tests after ten years because there had been no change. Ticks remain in stasis at least that long, not even alive as we know life. Animal body heat wakes them and they drop on their host to feed."

"Jesus, major—I was scared of the fuckers before. Now you tell me they're some kind of zombie; oh shit."

Somewhere ahead, Corporal Thorson held the point, an exceptional scout who could smell Japs from a distance. A three-man connecting file spread behind him; then came Dan and the platoon sergeant of his composite group, Dutch Schneider. Two BAR teams, gunners and ammo bearers, were the only automatic weapons firepower; rifles and carbines were the other armament. The going was too tough for anything heavier, and hard on the men whatever they had to carry.

"Long way to haul," Dan said to his sergeant, "let's get on the road."

For some reason, he saw the winding white road on Kill Devil Hill, that wide and smoothed road of crushed oyster shells that led back to the family memorial grove. Many Bevales and a few Carlisles lay there beneath simple headstones, and some of the monuments were only symbolic, marking pseudo graves that would never be dug, the memorials of family members Missing In Action, whose bodies would never be found.

A stone gleamed there for 1st Lieutenant Walton Belvale, vanished in the fall of Warsaw to the Nazis. Dan had stood beside it through the ceremony, through the traditional firing of the honor guard, the mournful echoes of Taps and the presentation of the folded flag to his wife. Adria, after her moment of hysteria in the house before the funeral, stood the ceremony as expected, the family woman/soldier calm and brave. Daughter Joann broke down once; she had been close to her brother.

And Pretty Penny Colvin, Walt's bride—tall and straight, she looked out of the past and into the future with deep eyes. Dan didn't fault her for marrying Walt's cousin later. From the first, Penny had belonged in the family; it was a shame Walt didn't share it with her.

Twice more, Dan halted the column for rest breaks. The rain forest heat and humidity sapped men's strength before they realized it. Some stumbled into thorny vines; some went face down onto the path and were helped up by their buddies. Dan was proud of the way they tried to keep the noise down, to avoid the clang of a rifle barrel or rattle of a helmet.

They lucked out all the way, never seeing a Jap or running into a booby trap. The Emperor's G-2 unit had screwed up, not covering this trial, but Dan hoped to save them the trouble of *seppuku*. A 30 caliber ball ammo would do a neater job than a *hara-kiri* knife.

The forced march was the prime enemy of the troops, and the jungle, the ever present insects, the heat. Then the foliage thinned, and Dan figured they had reached the backside of the knob, and climbed high enough to be about on a level with the Jap defense lines on the face of Nip Hill.

Corporal Thorson came eeling back through the brush, silent as a good hound on a faint scent. "The village, sir— couple of hundred yards. Six shacks, a pig pen and the town well. We're coming up on the ass end of it; didn't see any natives or Jap sentries out, but the little turds are there."

Dan slapped his chest and crushed a stinging ant. They were everywhere, big, medium and little, black and white and red; some bit and some stung. The biters usually attacked in swarms; the stingers shot formic acid into skin openings.

The common ant: *Hymenoptera;* another goddamn enemy, no matter the name.

"Take the connecting file and pick a good observation point. Everybody is out of gas and we need about a twenty minute break before we go barreling in like a bunch of wild ass Indians. If they spot you and start firing, we'll be there on the double."

"You got it, major."

Dutch Schneider passed the whisper down the line: rest and check your weapons; no smoking and be sure your equipment doesn't rattle.

Dan wanted a cigarette, but in the jungle, the smoke

could be picked up from twenty yards. Sitting in the trail, carbine across his thighs, he lifted his knees and rested his forehead on them.

Adria and Joann back home in Virginia, pitching in to help run the information center at Kill Devil Hill. They were still his close family, which gave him an edge over Chad Belvale and Keenan Carlisle, both divorced. Things had been doubly tough on Chad's wife; Kirstin's second husband was KIA on the Canal. And Nancy Carlisle, now doing okay as an NP nurse in Hawaii, a job that had made her bloom. She had never looked better when they had drinks in the Schofield Barracks Officers Club. In fact, she looked tempting as hell.

Lifting his head, he licked his lips and grinned. Like any soldier far from home he might stray, given the proper time and opportunity, the right woman. Nancy might have been the right woman for the moment, but she'd given off no signal, and thinking back, he was glad. Mostly.

He blinked and pushed himself erect when Dutch Schneider said, "All right—off your dead asses and on your dying feet. Time's up and we're moving out."

Easing out of the bush and bellied down to reach a higher bump in the ground, Dan found Thorson and the three other men. They had spaced themselves and peeped through a line of weeds to watch the huts below. Dan joined them and hand signalled Dutch Schneider to have the troops stay down and fan out. He saw a raggedy Jap soldier bowleg it out to the well and drink from a gourd dipper.

On his side, Dan looked up and down his line. It was a semicircle of eager men who looked down the enemy's throats. He could wish for a couple of 60mm mortars and some machine guns, but hauling all that extra weight they would never have reached here before dark, if at all. He checked again, and the BARs were in position to his left and right.

Two more Japs came out of the near hut and joined the one at the well. One of them giggled. Dan sighted his carbine in on that one and triggered a short burst. The little shit finished laughing in hell, and a crescent of fire thundered out around the village; lightning struck into it.

Japs scattered from the huts, going down before they ran more than a few steps. Dan could see a dozen down, and one of the nipa palm huts caught fire. The BARs raked the others, back and forth. A rifleman yelled as his target went down.

A bullet snapped past Dan's head. They hadn't nailed down all the Japs. Some must have made it into the treeline beyond the shacks and were firing back.

He leaped up. "As skirmishers—forward!"

Catch the little bastards before they make it to the others holding the face of the hill; catch them and kill them.

The central hut exploded with a blast that hurled flame and smoke high into the wet air. Ammo dump! That made the whole torturous flanking movement worth the effort it had taken.

He raced with his men, firing again at a scuttling shadow that might have been a man or might have been a pig. He was a few yards from the town well when something happened to his ears; he couldn't hear the gunfire; couldn't see his men, either.

Dan had no idea how he got flat on his back or why his legs refused to work. Then his hearing came back but not clear enough to understand what Dutch Schneider was mumbling—something about a mine? And he could see very clearly, so that he had a fine view of the beetle on his belly. Scarab-something; he couldn't remember the name just now. Funny that it should be on its back and not trying frantically to turn over, not waving its legs.

Then he stared down past the shiny green beetle and could not find his own legs.

CHAPTER 10

Daily Variety—Detroit, Michigan, July 19, 1943: Because of so many defense industry workers, this is the town where the play "Dear Public" drew $32,000 on opening week. It's where you stand in line for a beer and can't get a good steak even on the black market. A night spot here spends $10,000 a week for floor shows, and more dames wear slacks than in Hollywood. This is where the sidewalk madonnas get too much opposition from amateur talent, the patriotic V-Girls.

ASSOCIATED PRESS—Aberdeen Proving Grounds, Maryland, July 20, 1943: Recently women were taken on here, after a good deal of resistance, to perform traditionally male tasks ranging from loading shells to cleaning and firing big guns. The commanding officer seriously pondered the hazards involved: would women faint when a big gun went off? Would they be afraid to handle gun powder? Could they stick to the recipe and not do kitchen experiments while loading a shell? Would they resist getting very dirty and greasy?

Penny Belvale hated performing as a Japanese woman. Screwing Hideo Watanabe was about as bad as things could get, because he kept all things his way. On those rare nights when she desperately swallowed too much *sake*, she wasn't allowed to seek her own pleasure. If she forgot where she was and who he was, he slapped her. Everything she did, everything that was forced upon her, must be only for him.

Once he took time to explain that was the fashion of the geisha, the professional trained from childhood to flatter, entertain and bring sexual joy to men.

And she had said, Oh yes, the poor girls sold into slavery by their own parents. In America, we have heard of the barbaric practice.

You do not understand, he said. Otherwise, girl babies of poor farmers are less than worthless; they will grow and demand food, therefore endangering the entire family. If they cannot be sold, they must be left out in the paddies to die. This is economic reality.

That is barbarism, she said, and I am not a slave trained to be a whore, but a prisoner of war.

Because he was in a good humor and his wound did not pain him, Watanabe didn't slap her for her impertinence. He was just rougher than usual when he took her, just a little more demanding.

This day, she had asked him for help in cleaning his quarters, his uniforms and boots. He did not often deny her now, since he considered her properly humbled. And by hanging his drawers out the back window, that strip of white, twisted rag that looked more like a loose jockstrap, she signaled Stephanie Bartlett to volunteer.

And after Stephanie bowed her way past the porch guards, Penny wrapped her arms around her friend and drew her close. She badly needed to hug someone and made a soft noise in her throat.

Stephanie said, "Wheest—has it been that bad, lass?"

Taking a step back, Penny continued to hold only to one hand. "Only at times. I just get so—so—"

"Sickened?"

"Yes, but any nausea is mixed with hate and shame." Penny let go and tucked both hands over her stomach. "Nausea—morning sickness; oh my God! I always wash out after, but—oh God! What if I get pregnant? So far it's

been luck and—and maybe the diet, but if I get pregnant—
Stephanie—Stevie—I'll kill myself."

"Dinnae fash yourself; don't worry so. If it happens,
we'll see it's taken care of. There are two native midwives
among us, and they're knowledgeable about such things.
They've been caring for the children, and nursing as they
can. Besides, you would not be the only pregnancy."

"There've been others, and abortions? Of course, rape
and—"

"Not so much rape as trading off. Teat for treat, you
might say. The midwives are good; they've lost no women
yet."

Abortion; the image scared Penny, sharp cutting things
and bloody spoons. But if she got caught there would be
no other choice. If she were forced to bear Watanabe's
bastard, she would kill it herself.

"Here's to abortion, then. I'll take any chance to avoid
carrying that son of a bitch's child to term. He'd make me
care for it, anyway, if the goddamn war lasts so long. He
already told me that impure blood—impure!—is not accepted in Japan, that mixed race babies are nonpersons.
Like descendants of the Korean artists kidnapped and
brought to Japan, they can only grow up as whores or
criminals."

Stephanie crossed the room. "You seem to be learning
much bloody Nip culture, if it can be called that."

"As camp commander, his rank demands that he can
speak only with another officer, and that means Lieutenant
Hidori. Talking *to* is a better phrase; that ass kissing little
bastard only answers with bows and goes *hai, hai.*"

Lifting a *sake* bottle from the bamboo table, Stephanie
took a small swallow. "Ahh; if only I didn't feel guilty for
not saving this as antiseptic. So Major Wobbly pours out
his heart to you?"

Sweat gathered under Penny's arms and in her belly button. She took Watanabe's underwear off the windowsill,
and thought a moment. Then she threw it aside. "I'd rather
melt than wipe with this. Him pouring out his heart? Difficult, since he doesn't have one. But he does talk to me,

and I have to listen, if only to find out what's going on with our jailors and pass along the information. Have another drink; I have more *sake* put aside for the hospital shack and I saved you a piece of dried fish from supper."

"I need this," Stephanie said. "I truly need to become roaring drunk and remain so for the rest of the war. To even think of sex as you must, with puir Dacey lying that flat and hopeless, but half a man with his legs gone—it upsets and shames me. For to remember sex is to remember Chad Belvale, both but another name for love. Is it so terrible for me to wish my own husband had been killed fighting, instead of being crippled like this? It's punished I'll be for thinking the rest of him should die."

Penny took her hands. "If this damned war goes on much longer, he'll have to be lucky not to die in that camp, and it certainly wouldn't be your fault, but because of no medical treatment from the lousy Japs. You do get to visit Dacey once in a while, and he has to be grateful for that."

"Thanks be to you finding a sentry to bribe. And for so many good things you've done for all in camp."

"So they can call me bitch and Wobbly's whore."

Stephanie squeezed her hands. "They'll know the truth in time and bless you for being a martyr."

"Martyr, hell; I didn't have much choice, but I live fat and sassy like any practicing whore. Is there any good news from the men's camp radio?"

"Somewhat; the Allies are landing on this wee island and that. It will take forever to defeat the bloody Nips at that rate, but at least we're nae backing up these days."

Penny kneeled to remove the cover from the *futon*, the thinly padded sleeping mattress on the floor. She moved the log-shaped pillow filled with dry rice. The hard Jap pillow might be worse; Watanabe could insist upon using the wooden kind with side by side hollows for their goddamn slope heads. Her hands trembled, and she didn't know if it was because of the attacks of malaria growing closer as the months dragged by and the supply of quinine lessened or because her fingers had just brushed a starchy dried spot on the *futon*.

"A right bloody toff, isn't he?" Stephanie asked. "Look how polished his gear is. All things cleaned, shined and pressed and set in their proper place."

"To include me; I'm allowed to bathe in hot water, but only after he has used it. Another delightful Jap custom of the bath, the master first, sons next and then the lowly wife. Christ knows when or if any little girls get a shot at the gooey water. But then, women aren't worth much and girls practically nothing! Oh, thinking of kids and before I forget, here's some extra quinine."

Stephanie tucked the tablets into her pocket. "Your own ration, of course."

"Nobody else gets a regular ration and the children need it more."

"Does Major Wobbly pay any attention when you get the chills and sweats?"

He did, and if supplies were on hand, he either doubled her quinine or almost apologized for not being able to get more medicines. At certain moments like that, he was solicitous, even tender, and she hated that more than his cruelty. Penny did not want to believe that he could be that near to human.

Preston Belvale threw the Secretary of War a deserved highball and took his place at the table in the smaller meeting room that George Marshall kept for more intimate briefings. Preston's cousin, Maj. Gen. Ben Alexander was present, with two vice admirals and a buck general of the air corps.

No Congressmen on the scene, and no hint of the President to arrive, which meant that this meeting was top secret. FDR and some of his legislators had a tendency to talk at the wrong time and place. Preston thumbnailed his moustache and bit the end off a cigar, but waited to light it.

"Gentlemen," Marshall said, "it's about to hit the fan in Rome. It's now definite that Mussolini will go out and Badoglio come in. For how long is anybody's guess. The Germans will just as definitely not allow Italy to surrender, which we expect Badoglio or the king to announce. The German Kesselring will fill the country with emergency troops direct from Berlin and will probably hold some Italian divisions on line by force."

One of the navy men lit up, so Preston did, too, and the smoke tasted good. He pictured reluctant Italian troops caught between granite and grabass, GIs coming at them from the front and Krauts threatening at the rear. But first, those GIs had to finish the job in Sicily, which was proving to be no walkover. The mountains there were steeper and rougher than those in Tunisia, and the Germans were hanging tough on every ridge, their supply lines only the short jump from Calabria across the Strait of Messina. Airfields in Italy afforded the *Luftwaffe* dive bombers quick round trips.

Marshall uncovered a situation map and picked up a pointer. He touched upon Italy. "After Sicily falls, landings will be made upon the mainland. Maybe that will stop Joe Stalin's bitching about a second front; he considers Sicily a mere island hop."

Ben Alexander muttered, "He would; in his goddamned moustache."

"The exact targets are still under discussion," Marshall went on, "but I do know that some battle weary troops will be withdrawn to England, those who fought through Africa and Sicily. There they will rest and receive further amphibious training for another place and another time."

What remained of the 1st Infantry and 1st Armored, Preston thought, those hardened units of RA veterans where draftee replacements took on the skill and attitude of the surviving old timers, or died quickly. Eisenhower had already called the Big Red One his Praetorian Guard. Chad and Owen had made it safely so far, and Sloan Travis had become a good soldier in spite of his attitude. Another family member was a POW somewhere in Italy, or had possibly been shipped into Germany by now. News out of PW camps was scarce.

The family was doing all right in the European Theater of Operations, but not so well in the Pacific. Kee-rist!

Crusty the indestructible gone missing and presumed dead in the torpedoing of a troopship, and Dan Belvale killed on Bougainville.

Preston wasn't sure how well Adria was taking it. Losing first a son in Poland and now her husband, she had gone into seclusion at Kill Devil Hill, speaking only to her daughter, Joann, and once in a while to Minerva. It was true that the family was good to horses they raised and hell on the women born into, or married into, the Carlisle-Belvales. No amount of family tradition could prepare a woman for losses of the heart, but Adria and Joanna were both solid army. They would snap back in time.

Preston wasn't sure he would ever get over the death of Crusty Carlisle. At every turn, he missed the old bastard. Who would head the clan Carlisle?

Marshall changed maps. "Some of you already know that we broke the Japanese secret code early in the war. Recently our advance information cost Admiral Yamamoto his life while he was on a flying visit to take a direct look at the fighting on Bougainville. His replacement as C-in-C of the Jap fleet is Admiral Koga, not nearly so formidable. So much for the victor of Pearl Harbor and Midway."

Ben Alexander leaned close to Preston. "Ambushed his plane and splashed his ass. We would have hung him, anyway. There's a strong movement underway in the War Department, and oddly enough, much approval in Congress to bring all the warlords to trial as criminals. That includes Hitler's bunch. The new feeling is: start a war and end on a rope."

George Marshall moved his pointer across the map. "Our offensive of two weeks ago went well, generally. General Krueger's army forces hit the Trobriand Island Group with two landings. Mainly Australian, General Herring's people landed in the Huon Gulf and Admiral Halsey's bunch drew New Georgia.

"Six thousand enemy troops are holding up Herring's attack; ten thousand more are dug in on New Georgia's mountains where the heat and rain are brutal. A surrounding belt of reefs on the north-east and little islands on the south and west make backup landings and supply difficult. Again, knowledge of the Imperial code tells us that Tokyo has ordered no retreat."

Preston drew upon his cigar. Usually the little bastards fought to the death without specific orders, but now, under directions from the lord high god of the Imperial Palace, they would banzai themselves into bushido heaven, if they took the enemy into death with them. The New Georgia campaign was going to be a bitch and a half. To men on the spot, all campaigns were.

"Any suggestions will go through the usual channels," Marshall said, "unless you have something unusually hot; bring that directly to me. That is all for today, gentlemen; thank you."

Rising with the others, Preston watched the Secretary of War out. To Ben Alexander he said, "Coffee?"

Ben shook his head. "Sorry, no time, but I'll make the dinner next week. Preston—I haven't given up hope for Crusty. He's too damned mean to die until he decides it's time."

"He never could swim worth a damn. But the family is marking time; no symbolic grave in the Carlisle grove at Sandhurst Keep for him. Not until the end of the war, anyway. And we voted to wait on the others for the time, if and when, their bodies are returned after the war. Congress is looking ahead to that, also, pushed by their sorrowing constituent moms."

Ben frowned. "Too bad the dead can't vote. I'm sure a lot of them would prefer to remain where they fell with their buddies, beside men who understood. What the hell do civilians know?"

"Heartache has nothing to do with understanding; Adria is family, but I think she'd want Walt and Dan brought back."

"I guess," Ben said, "if Walt is ever found. Speaking of Walt always brings me to Pretty Penny. And?"

"And she was alive at last report from the POW camp, as was Chad's girlfriend, the English girl."

"The married one that caused a stir in the London press when they saved that kid?"

"Leftenant Bartlett; antiaircraft. We're considering bringing her out with Penny. It won't be any tougher for two women."

Ben swung around, clutching his briefcase close. "Then you're going to do it at last? Payoffs to Japs and locals, use the Burmese bandit trails and the seagoing pirates? A million dollars in gold, I'd say, but what the hell, that's only money—*if* they deliver their end."

"More honor among bandits and pirates than ordinary thieves, and far more guts. Besides, payments are dependent upon delivery at each checkpoint."

"It's time we did something for our own. I realize that getting Gavin Scott out of Italy is well nigh impossible, and PWs in German stalags are better treated. But the goddamned Japs are such murderers—"

"Which is why we're gambling on bringing her—them—out. Every time we land on another Pacific island, every time the halfway sensible Japs feel the cold breath of inexorable fate, they come down harder on the prisoners. I just hope we're in time."

CHAPTER 11

UNITED PRESS—Somewhere in Sicily, July 21, 1943: General George S. "Blood and Guts" Patton clashed with British General Sir Bernard Montgomery today, demanding a more aggressive role for his 7th Army men and armor. The American units had been assigned the job of protecting the English rear. Montgomery, surprised by Patton's vehemence, agreed to let Patton lead the drive to capture Palermo.

Elsewhere on the island, the mountain fighting was fierce and progress slow. German troops seem determined to hold every foot of this bare and ravaged countryside.

The 16th Regiment was in constant movement, companies detailed on odd jobs here, a detached platoon there. Owen Belvale thought that the Old Man—his and the regiment's being the same—was probably chewing holes in his helmet liner. Word came down that the 36th Field, up near Villarmosa, needed protection, and off went a rifle platoon of Easy Company, supported only by its light machine guns.

The Sicilian sun hammered down, making Owen's steel pot an oven. He separated it from the liner. Early on in combat, everybody tried to crawl up inside their metal womb, seeking the ultimate safety from shell fragments and bullets. There were jokes about men getting their shoulders jammed in their helmets, but for all its weight, its protection was nominal and psychological. Deflection by shape was its best feature, for just about any direct hit by a slug or a shell fragment much bigger than a grain of sand popped a hole through both sides of the helmet and both sides of the skull and kept right on going.

Opening a can of meat and vegetable hash, only by markings in any way distinguishable from greasy meat and vegetable stew, Owen cursed the rear echelon troops who stole the only other choice of C-rations, the meat and beans. Latrine rumor had it that enough of the newer K-rations were coming in before the jumpoff tonight. Owen hoped so; they'd be a welcome change. Better yet, maybe the troops would get a chance to liberate some vino, honest-to-God civilian bread and cheese when they took Villapriolo. It was too much to hope for dried sausages or leggy *calamari,* or even *bacala,* whose heavy salting didn't hide the odor.

About the only good thing about being point outfit in an attack was the opportunity to loot chow and booze before anybody else got a grab at it. Sicily was too damned poor for any other loot. A bad thing about being attack company was the booby traps; the Krauts were masters at hiding death and enticing you to find it.

Back in Tunisia, low-flying planes dropped whistles, binoculars and fountain pens behind the lines. To blow on a whistle was to lose teeth and a good part of your face; to put the glasses to your eyes and adjust them was to go blind; unscrewing the pen cost fingers, even a hand. And never, never pick up an enemy weapon or open the breech of an 88mm gun.

A severely wounded man was worth more to the Krauts than a dead man; it took at least three others to care for and transport a wounded GI. Of course, there were exceptions.

Even earlier in Algeria, when the troops were freshly warned, a departing and diabolical German antitank and mine expert blew hell out of a cautious GI at Tafaroui Airport. Abandoned openly upon a table, the Luger pistol gleamed irresistibly, but the GI was suspicious. Carefully, he attached a cord to the Luger, then backed off several yards to the lip of a fresh foxhole also abandoned in the rush of the German Armistice Commission to get out of Algeria. He tugged the cord and jumped into the foxhole.

Which had a mine hidden in its bottom and blew him all to hell.

Whoosh!

Owen didn't duck deeper into his rocky hole. The incoming shell was too high and traveling too far to affect his reflexes. Strange how the body geared to the distances of danger, adjusting because it could not remain in a state of high tension without destroying some part of itself—the vulnerable section that brought on battle rattle. The mind tightened and stretched and trembled with the strain. Finally it let go so it could back into a secret place and say screw any more of this. The trouble was, that didn't happen to enough Krauts to end the war.

At least half a mile to the rear, the shell exploded.

Pebbles dripped into Owen's hole and Sloan Travis slid in after them. The company CP was in a good position, its holes scooped into the side of a rocky gulley, and hidden overall behind a series of huge boulders.

"*Buon giorno,*" Sloan said. "Although it's not morning, it's about all the Italian I know, besides certain generally obscene hand signals. Sergeant Pelkey has the guys catching up on cleaning the guns and their personal weapons. Any new poop from troop?"

Propping his feet on the side of the gulley, Owen said, "At about 2000, we become foot cavalry when battalion moves out, less Fox Company, which stays at Enna to guard ammo dumps. Objective: Villapriolo, and if we don't get stopped cold, on to Villadoro."

Whoosh!

Sloan didn't flinch, either. "Must be the ammo dump that gun's after. It must be Italian; doesn't sound like an 88 and because it's not hitting close. A night hike—rougher on heavy weapons people than riflemen. Full combat loads, I imagine."

The shell blew up, even farther away.

Owen offered a cigarette. "Right; I'll load the company

jeep with 30 calibers and 81s. K-rations are due; if they get here before we saddle up, they'll be passed out right away. If not, soon as the Ks arrive, the kitchen crew has orders for full speed ahead, damning the torpedoes, 88s and Kraut panzers."

Whoosh!

"Damn that Wop gun, too." Sloan grinned. "But not its gunners; bless them for their inaccuracy."

KA-WHAMM!!

Owen had just ground out his cigarette when the blast knocked him ass over mess kit down the gulley and slammed him into something hard. Sitting up in a daze, he felt over his numb face and found blood, with the splinters of rock that caused it. He coughed dust and burned powder, then fingertipped carefully over his eyelids. Thank God he could see.

"Sloan?" He couldn't hear himself well, so he yelled louder: "Sloan—are you okay?"

His radioman—where was Corporal Cazazza?

There, but with his head missing above the eyes, neat as if it had been sawed off; inside the skull was empty. Then Owen saw the gray-green jelly smeared lumpy over the radio.

"Oh shit! Sloan—"

"Okay, boss—but I'm going to have a hell of a headache. Will the radio work? We'll need that tonight, and—" He clanged his helmet to the ground. "Listen to me! A man here with his skull ripped in half and I worry about a goddamn radio. I'm a frigging Carlisle, all right. It's in the frigging blood. And you—blood all over. How bad is it? I'll get the medics."

Shakily, Owen climbed up and leaned against the guardian boulder, that huge rock wearing raw new scars. He felt over his web belt and brought out the first aid packet. "Just surface wounds. Anybody else hit?"

"Not that I can tell. What was I saying about Wop gunners? The bastards dropped a short round on us. Here— let me fix your face."

Owen winced when Sloan pulled a needle of rock from

his left cheekbone. Others had just torn gashes that Sloan powdered with sulfanilamide and pressed hard with the flat packet of gauze.

"Now," he said, "I'll tug aside that poor bastard and see if we still have a radio. Cold, efficient son of a bitch, ain't I?"

Owen took the bandage and pressed. "Efficient."

"Captain, captain? Lieutenant Travis?" Doc Tozar's face was tense. Every medic was called doc, Owen thought, but Pfc. Tozar took his duties as seriously as any surgeon. He kneeled at the lip of the gulley. "Anybody hit bad? Oh Jesus—that's Cazazza."

"Was," Owen said. "Check on down the line, doc. I haven't heard anybody yelling medic, but you never know."

"Nobody else touched but you guys, sir. I mean, Big Mike and me were down behind that other boulder when the thing hit, and—"

"Sergeant Donnely? Has he been wounded?"

Tozar squatted, his aid pack in both hands. "I ain't supposed to say anything, but I figure he's sicker than he thinks. He hustled me for some pain killers, just APCs that don't seem to do much good. I mean, he won't let me give him any morphine because some wounded guy might really need it, he says. Captain, I can stop that bleeding and paste you up like a halfass mummy or maybe you better report to the aid station."

"I'm not badly hurt."

"But you got hit a spell back, too. And it'll get you a cluster on your Purple Heart."

"Doc, up your purple ass."

Sloan Travis looked up from the radio. He had wiped the handset clean. "No damage. I'll send Weintraub up as your new man, if that's okay. He was a commo man before he fucked up and got shanghaied from battalion. He'll be more useful here than carrying ammo."

"Okay, and Sloan—"

"Yeah?"

"You were right. A dead man is out of it; the radio remains important."

Spitting, Sloan turned and trotted away.

Owen said to the medic, "Doc—where's Sergeant Donnely now?"

"Beats me, sir; probably back with his mortars."

"Sick how?"

"His guts, sir. I mean, it has to be something deep in his guts since he don't have an appendix and I checked his ribs."

Moving back a step, Owen took a long swallow from his canteen. Big Mike was more than the nominal first soldier of H Company; he was the best mortar man in the regiment, if not the whole division. More than that, he had helped break in young Preston Belvale back in that other war. He was that kind, one of the true sergeants that were called the backbone of the army.

"Doc, pass the word. Sergeant Donnely is to report to me, right bigod now." Owen blinked; he sounded more like Crusty Carlisle than Preston Belvale.

By the time Mike Donnely climbed down into the gulley, Owen's face hurt like crazy and a cut on his lower lip forced him to smoke carefully. He offered a Phillip Morris.

"No thanks, sir; they just don't taste right lately."

Owen hesitated. "What's it look like for tonight? S-2 assumes that taking Villadora will be a walkover."

"With the captain's permission, sir—assumption is the mother of all fuckups."

Even under combat conditions, Donnely stuck to the old-old army EM to officer address in the third person. Owen's grin hurt his mouth. "That sounds like something General Carlisle would say."

"He did, sir; a long time back. And S-2 ought to know that the only thing that can walk into Villadora over the paths is a he mountain goat. It's too straight up for a pregnant nanny. No road exists for any vehicle to get into that bird's nest village, and that includes tanks. They'll turn turtle if they try."

Owen didn't ask about the information. Old line noncoms

had their private sources and a special inbred sense of warning that sometimes amounted to extrasensory perception. He watched Donnely's sweaty face, pale beneath the tan of malaria-fighting Atabrine and a streaked layer of Sicilian dust.

Donnely said, "The captain didn't invite me here for a recon report, now did he, sir?"

"No, sergeant. I wanted a close look."

"Somebody has a big mouth, sir."

It still made Owen uneasy to be sirred constantly by a man who had served long and honorably with his grandfather and his father, but he knew Donnely would resent his crossing the line into familiarity.

"It's a long hike and a tough climb under fire at the end of it."

A muscle twitched along Donnely's jaw. "I can make it, captain."

"How about the next mountain, and the one after that? This damned country never runs out of mountains. The company needs you, but we can get by one firefight without you. I'd rather skip just one than lose you altogether."

"But sir—it's probably these fucking C-rations—begging the captain's pardon, or I twisted a gut jumping in and out of foxholes."

Drawing on his cigarette, Owen said, "Then let the medics check you out. Who's capable of taking over the mortar platoon?"

"Captain—"

"*Who*, sergeant?"

"Goddamnit, sir; dropping shells on a target that high up is tricky. Frank Dymond don't have that kind of experience."

"But he *is* the platoon sergeant and you're supposed to be the topkick. Corporal Solomon takes your place okay with the morning reports and such, and Sergeant Dymond can run his mortars until you get back."

Donnely tried to hold a poker face, but Owen saw the pain hit. Donnely hooked thumbs into his web belt and held on. When he fought to pull in a deep breath, his eyes needed time to focus.

"The c-captain will allow me to come back? Sir, I can't—I'm just not cut out to be a garritrooper: too far forward for spit shines but too far in the rear to fight. The captain will take me back?"

"My word on it, Mike—ah, sergeant."

Donnely stood up. "Then the sergeant is dismissed, sir?"

"To report to the battalion aid station. Doc Tozar will take you there."

Straight-backed, Big Mike Donnely climbed from the gulley and practically marched to the rear. Owen wanted to call good luck after him, that standard so long, *au revoir*, good-bye of the army, said too often when you didn't really hope to see the man again. Maybe the doctors could give him pills or patch him up for return to duty, but Owen suspected that something was seriously wrong with Donnely, something that reached deeper than age and normal fatigue.

Two stretcher bearers parked their litter atop the gulley lip. "Holy shit, what a mess. Okay to haul it out of here, cap?"

"*It* was a good man. I'll take one of Corporal Cazazza's dogtags."

After they wrestled the radioman's corpse onto the stretcher, they looked around for the rest of him and found the helmet with some of Cazazza cupped in it. Owen didn't watch where they put the helmet when they moved off.

The replacement dropped into the hole, yellow hair sticking from beneath his helmet, blue eyes of shiny and shallow innocence. "Weintraub, cap'n."

"Are you good with this radio, soldier?"

"Pretty good . . . sir. I've fixed up a couple that took hits . . . sir."

Lighting another mildewed cigarette, Owen drew smoke deep. He caught the deliberate delay before the sirs. "Why'd you get shanghaied from battalion?"

Weintraub grunted and watched the cigarette. "Got caught with some vino back in Tunis."

"Vino? Everybody liberated vino in Tunis."

"Not a deuce-and-a-half full, cap'n."

Owen raised an eyebrow. "A truckload of wine? What were you doing with it?"

"Like you said, liberating it from the fucking MPs; they was hiding it out for the provost marshal. Figured GIs would appreciate it more, and time I got done trading off cases of *vin rouge* for chickens and goat meat and such, I figured the boys could use some genuine whorehouse ass, even if it was A-rab. So I swapped the truck for all the pussy the company could catch up on, and throwed in the extra gas cans. The provost got some upset and wanted my balls for his dogtag chain. So the major helped bust me out and hid me in your line company. I'd hid my dogtags and gave the MPs the wrong name, you see, and the major, he figured them bastards wouldn't never come up to the line looking for me."

Staring, Owen said, "Son of a bitch! I just inherited the regiment's most notorious scrounger."

"Reckon so, cap'n. But I'm pretty good with a radio, too."

Owen grinned and hurt his torn lip. "Have a cigarette, soldier. What this outfit needs is a damned good scrounger—and a pretty good radioman."

CHAPTER 12

CINPAC, TWX scrambled—TOP SECRET; refer Japanese code message intercepts, Rec. 0400, 22 July, 1943: GHQ Imperial Japan formulating new operational policy based on minimum area essential for war aims. Quote: absolute national defense sphere unquote Burma along Malay barrier to Western New Guinea; to Carolines, Marianas up to Kuriles. This contraction of defense means most of New Guinea, all the Bismarcks to include Rabaul, Solomons, Gilberts and Marshall islands now classed nonessential.

G-2 estimates piecemeal withdrawal from enemy held areas over period of four to six months. On home grounds Japan attempting to triple aircraft production and step up rebuilding of Combined Fleet in order to challenge U.S. Pacific fleet in open battle once again.

Crusty fought to hang on to the man's wrist, but his shoulder arthritis fought back, and slowly his fingers loosened.

"Going back home," Corporal Thornton said as he pushed off from the raft. "All I got to do is swim the Tombigbee River and walk on to Grove Hill. I'm going home."

He slid away in the ocean and swam with clumsy, floundering strokes toward his mirage.

"Tried to keep the stupid bastard from drinking sea

water," the sailor muttered. "We only been out four days, but big mouth couldn't take it, so he kept sneaking sips of salt water and went nuts. Look how his broken leg drags; can't swim worth a shit anyhow."

Gasping, Crusty leaned back. "Even Johnny Weismuller couldn't swim to Alabama. That's where Thornton's heading."

The kid Woodall said, "I always figured Tarzan could do anything—outswim crocodiles, beat up lions and outclimb the great apes."

"In the movies," Sullivan said. "Hell, in the movies Weismuller's jungle is clean and pretty and has Jane in it. How far you think he'd get swinging on a vine on Guadalcanal? If the vine didn't break and drop him in a shitty swamp, then some fucking Jap would pop him; or he'd get malaria and have to skin Cheetah and use his hide for a blanket."

"Be nice to climb a tree now," Woodall said. Normally pale skinned, his face was blistered red and black, and his lips swollen to twice their size. "Be nice to sit back in the shade of a mulberry tree. I never saw shade any deeper and cooler than under a big old mulberry."

Crusty glanced at the bake-oven sky and quickly away. "Thornton shucked out of his shirt. Prop up that oar and spread the shirt to make shade."

"Sir—I don't need special attention."

"Never said special. We'll take turns, but you first." The boy had plenty of guts, but something was physically wrong with them, something busted up from torpedoing. He had stopped vomiting blood, but he'd thrown up far too long and lost more body liquids than the rest of them.

They were almost out of water; one careful spoonful each in the morning, one more to celebrate the going down of the sun, and they might last three more days. Concentrated fishing had brought them only two bony fish about hand size, and the skins had to be saved for bait. The juices were worth more than the thin meat.

The sun, Crusty thought; the fucking sun was beating them to death, sledging them through the long, long days, cooking their hides and sucking the moisture from their aching bodies. It was strange how cooler nights affected sunburned skin, bringing on miserable shivers instead of relief. And the salt; rubbed into nostrils and eyes, caking their mouths. When he made the next barbecue party at the Hill, be damned if he'd sprinkle salt on his corn on the cob. There'd still be plenty in his system.

He'd never go outside again without wearing a hat, either—a big goddamned campaign hat to keep off the sun.

How far were they from land? The smartass swabbies on the troopship were glad to tell green-faced GIs—we're only three miles from land, mac—straight down. Now Crusty had no idea, but he'd trade his end of the family fortune to stop bobbing up and down and sideways on this goddamn ocean; especially if somebody would throw in a cold beer or a handful of fresh snow scooped from the lawn at Sandhurst Keep.

Closing swollen eyelids that itched, he could almost smell the high pines and brittle air of upstate New York in the winter. To him and most of the Carlisles, that was much better than the soft, warm air of Virginia and Kill Devil Hill, where the clan Belvale gathered. The family command post was there for its proximity to Washington and the political peanuts who had to be steered in the right direction for the country's sake.

A drift of wind sawed his face and he closed his eyes against it, feeling for a test grip on the fish line. It jerked, or he thought it did; it might have been the motion of the raft. Eyes open, he tugged on the line and it tugged back.

"Fish!" he croaked. "Got us a big goddamn fish!"

They didn't have it yet, but it was sure hooked solid, and it was something big enough to keep them alive for days. If he could land it. If, hell; he *had* to bring this big bastard into the raft, or go in after it. Some low ranking god assigned to watch over soldiers had just sounded chow call, but he wouldn't bring it to the barracks on a silver tray.

If Mohammed wouldn't go to the mess hall, then the mess hall had to be brought to him. Bracing his knees against the rolled side of the raft, Crusty set himself and pulled.

"I can help," Woodall said.

"You'll get dragged over—Sullivan!"

"With you, general. Play him a little—he could break the line."

Crusty reared back and grunted. "Shit—he's playing *me*. But wait—wait; he's coming my way. Come on, you beautiful, blessed son of a bitch—come to Crusty!"

The raft rocked and the water beside it fountained violently. The grey head broke water first, and the forked tail slapped harder. "Hit him!" Crusty yelled. "Hit him with the oar!"

Woodall knelt there, swinging weakly at the wicked marble eyes. Bellied down, Sullivan reached to stab with the survival knife, and the flat head rolled. A flash of pointed teeth barely raked his forearm and left quick trails of blood.

"Shark—not that big, but shit—!"

With a mighty effort, Crusty heaved the shark into the raft and got hold of its dorsal fin, got one leg over the thrashing body. The thing must be hooked deep in its gut, or it would have spit out bait, hook and all. Damn; its skin was wet sandpaper grinding his flesh.

Sullivan shouted: "Bastard! Bastard!" and rammed the knife blade into a gill and sawed hard, pulling to him. He kept at it while the shark twisted and snapped. He kept at it as watery blood ran down his arm and finally he sawed the head off. Crusty battled to keep the body pinned until it stopped jerking, and that hurt like billy hell.

How big was it—maybe four feet long, but all muscle and power. Relaxing bit by exhausted bit, Crusty sagged upon the flat-bellied thing. It was solid meat, too; they'd drink its juices and chew its flesh and suck its guts. No bones, he remembered; a shark had a cartilage spine, a nonvertebrate. Made no difference; they'd chew it anyhow.

Flat belly?

"Hey, Sullivan! What kind of shark is this flat?"

Licking his lips, Sullivan lowered the chunk of meat. "Ain't no expert, general, but I'd say a sand shark. Seen them around the docks at Dago—holy shit! That means the water's turning shallow, and that means we're close to land. Holy shit!''

Woodall said, "Holy something or somebody," and sucked at raw fish.

Crusty still worked at his own beautiful, blessed food and drink when the kid threw up over the side. "Slow," he said to Woodall. "Take it slow and easy, son."

"Sorry, sir."

"Goddamnit, don't apologize. You're wounded, in a combat zone, and you're a good soldier."

Woodall swallowed. "Am I, sir? I wanted to be, but here I am all messed up and I never got to fire a shot."

"Soldiering doesn't always mean shoving a bayonet up the other's guy's ass, son." Crusty chewed thoroughly, glad that his teeth had always fit well; one of the virtues of money. He got all the fluid out of the meat before swallowing it. "Most times being a soldier means toughing it out on a hike when your legs say fall out, going right on through mountain and desert and walking your post even when nobody's looking.

"It means poor pay and fancy restaurants with signs reading SOLDIERS AND DOGS KEEP OFF THE GRASS. It means putting your life on the line for the same shit heel who painted the sign, and being bigod proud of a uniform that doesn't fit and is colored like dirt. Proud because you know it's not dirt and that you can stand tall forever because you're not a shit heel, but a bigod soldier."

Sullivan grunted as he ate. Head back, Woodall squeezed fish and let the juice drip into his mouth. When it didn't come right back up, he said, "Kind of like poetry, sir—I mean like Kipling or Dryden."

"Poetry?" Sullivan chuckled with his mouth full and dropped the shark's stripped head over the side. "Bet the old man's never been accused of that before. Poets don't whip up on a shark's ass."

A little more bloody water and a small bite, and Woodall said, "I think sometimes it may go together, being a soldier and a certain kind of poetry." Eyes closed, he rested his head on the raft and recited softly, "John Dryden wrote it this way:

> "I'm a little wounded,
> But I am not slain;
> I will lay me down
> For to bleed awhile,
> Then I'll rise
> And fight with you again."

"You got it, soldier," Crusty said, and Sullivan started to add something.

That was the moment when the great tiger shark slammed into the little raft with such force that it spun like a rubber duck in a bath tub.

Variety—Hollywood, Calif., July 22, 1943: The popularity of the jitterbug dance, first asserted in the thirties, continues unabated, especially among the young. To them, it is a separate world with a life style and language of its own, as in the extreme, the zoot-suiters demonstrate. The basic step is the lindy hop, but variations are more strenuous—the Jersey bounce, shagging, trucking and the Susy-Q. All over this town, indeed, across this country, saddle-shoed, bobby-soxed, skirt-swinging girls and long coated, peg panted youths are out to "cut a rug."

Scientific observers contend that the dance phenomenon is a healthy release for tensions induced by the war: for boys the ever present probability of military service; for girls, the looming possibility of parting forever. For night clubs, it means bigger dance floors.

Kirstin wondered if she had made a mistake. She didn't doubt that it was good for Harlan Edgerton to get away from the hospital, even for a night. But she might have thought more about where to take him, the first time out.

A drive around the countryside to show Kilgore's steadily pumping oil wells, to amuse this despondent Mississippi boy by pointing out the well in the schoolyard and where the bank had been torn down to drill another. Then they would return to Longview for a quiet dinner in surroundings nothing like a mess hall, she'd thought. Harlan coped nicely with eating out, and people didn't seem to stare at his hook, even when he used it to pin a steak so he could use a knife to cut his meat. These Texans never forgot the big army hospital just out of town, and they appreciated the sacrifices of its patients.

She just hadn't expected the music that appeared with their dessert. The quartet no sooner showed up on the little bandstand than laughing dancers swarmed out onto what floor there was. The trumpet blared the first notes of "Milkman, Keep Those Bottles Quiet," the clarinet picked it up and the piano and drums came in behind. Kirstin reached across the table to cover Harlan's good hand with hers.

His face tightened, and she had to lean close to hear him say, "You think I'll be able to do that after I get my wooden leg?"

"You know it won't be wooden, and yes—I think you can do whatever you want to. So long as you really want to."

Holding to her hand, he waited; an air corps lieutenant twirled a girl past the table, her skirt spinning high around slender thighs. Kirstin didn't take back her hand and his fingers were warm and strong about it. The song ended to applause; then he said, "Oh lord, Miz Shelby—nobody knows what crippled up guys like me really want."

"I think I do."

He squeezed harder. "Reckon you're one of the few who might. But it's more than riding a horse and looking forward to walking with a cane instead of crutches. At the hospital they're fixing me a clamp that'll work almost good as a real hand, and I'm getting a hollow screw-on clamp that looks almost like a real hand. Might be I can even work the farm some, but that still ain't enough."

When he stopped squeezing, she recovered her hand. "Did you dance much, before?"

"Never learned how. There was this girl back home, but my folks never had two dimes to rub together and we never went nowhere. Be nice to know I *could* dance, if I got around to it. Not that kind of jumping around or square dancing, but nice and slow."

Kirstin spooned fruit cocktail with a dab of whipped cream. Even in a tasteful place, the omnipresent War Department signs were posted: USE LESS SUGAR AND STIR LIKE HELL; LOOSE LIPS SINK SHIPS; KEEP IT UNDER YOUR STETSON.

"I like slow music, too. I'm too old for that strenuous stuff."

"Old? I swony, ma'am—you ain't much older than me. And it does seem like we care about the same things. I mean—slow dancing and horses and all."

She smiled. "You call me Miz Shelby and ma'am, and—"

"Just out of respect, ma'am—I mean I looked up your full name, but—"

"—and I have sons older than you, Harlan; two of them." Owen in combat in the European Theater, and Farley still fighting inside his own hurt mind. She would go to him soon, whether the army held him in Hawaii or sent him to San Francisco. And Chad Belvale, their father and her ex-husband, pushing his regiment through the deadly Sicilian mountains; she hoped he would consider their son's safety. No more than any other of his soldiers, she admitted.

Of course, thinking of Chad brought Jim Shelby freshly to her mind, that sweet and gentle man who was never meant to be military, never meant to walk the jungle where he died needlessly, senselessly.

She said, "I'm old enough to be divorced from one man and widowed by another. An old widow woman, that's me."

This time he caught her hand. It was strange that the

music should be the Beer Barrel Polka while he shifted his chair so that he could speak softly into her ear. His breath tickled. "No such thing, Kirstin Shelby. There—I said it: Kirstin, a name near about as beautiful as you are your ownself."

Stopping abruptly, the music caught them off guard. Harlan looked down and his face went red as he backed his chair. "Sorry, ma'am. I—I clean forgot who you are and—and what I am, not but a goddamn half a man."

"Harlan—"

"Please ma'am, on the ward they make jokes about half a loaf being better than none. That ain't so, and it ain't funny." He slowed a waitress and ordered two bourbons.

"I wasn't thinking straight when I asked the Tex-Mexes that work for you if you drink and what; they said yellow roses are your favorite and you like steak medium rare. For somebody like me, that was sure dumb."

She watched his eyes. "I wouldn't say so."

He looked away. "Yonder comes our whiskey. I don't even know a toast, so I'll be beholden if you just drink with me and then carry me back to the hospital."

"And waste a whole weekend pass?"

He shook his head and stared into his shot glass. "I don't belong out with people no more; not whole people. Best I stay with my own kind and make jokes that ain't funny, but we laugh anyhow about one-arm paperhangers and seeing eye dogs and such."

"I know a toast," Kirstin said. "Here's to weekend passes."

Frowning, he muttered, "I reckon," and drank with her.

She didn't help him with the crutches; all the hurt boys hated being fussed over, hated appearing helpless. And she allowed him to pay the cashier with some of his saved-up pay; otherwise he would have felt even less of a man.

Harlan had it worked out to slide sideways into a car and angle his crutches into the back seat. She turned on the car radio and they rode without talking while Harry James's trumpet lead muted so Helen Forrest could begin softly with I don't want to walk without you . . . walk without my arms about you, baby . . .

He changed the station and the Mills Brothers sang: I'm gonna' buy a paper doll that I can call my own . . .

"More like it," Harlan said. "A paper doll won't see the difference. Miz Shelby. I don't see the hospital; you sure you're on the right road?"

"I know just where I'm going," she said, and pulled up behind the little house she'd rented when her horse riding course was first presented to the Harmon General Hospital commander.

When she turned off the motor he said, "Ma'am—"

"Ma'am? You said you liked my name."

"Kirstin, I'm glad you don't push and pull on me. I never need any goddamn help, or pity, neither."

Putting her back to him, she went up the three short steps to the back door and opened the lock. When she turned on the kitchen light she heard the car door slam and him come bumping up the steps. She walked on through the tiny parlor without touching a lamp and into the only bedroom where she did.

"Miz Shelby—Kirstin—damnit—"

Her back still to him, she eased the taffeta dress over her head, the dress she thought she had worn special because he had only seen her in Levi's. Now she really knew why. It wasn't to be charitable, but to prove to Harlan that he was still a man where it counted most to him.

Unfastening the hooks on her bra, she admitted she wasn't doing this solely for the sake of a boy on the brink of dark desperation. She had been too long alone, too long a teacher, nurse and widow. Kirstin was also a woman. She hipped slowly from her panties, dropped them and lay upon the bed.

If only he wasn't so very young.

He said thick in his throat, "Would you turn off the light?"

"Am I so wrinkled?"

"Oh my god—you're so—you're beautiful; it's the hook and my ugly—"

She held up her arms. "You're beautiful to me, too."

He didn't mind her helping remove his shirt as he sat awkwardly on the bed, and only hesitated a moment before working out of his pants with the one pinned-up leg. His stump was shiny red, and to ease him, she ran her palm gently over it before urging him to her.

He even tasted young, his boy mouth searching hers so eagerly, his good hand gently exploring her breasts, her hips and thighs. Harlan's skin was slicked with quick and heady sweat, a delight to her fingertips. When he groaned and entered her abruptly, she was ready and took him into her body, into her deepest and secret places.

Of course he was too quick, but she locked him close and soothed him with murmurings, brought him back with breathy kisses and tongue tippings. And this time she moved with him and then beyond him into only herself. It was rare and wondrous. It was needed.

"I love you, Kirstin," he whispered.

Cheek pressed against the soft curling hairs of his chest, she answered, "Love you, too," and for the moment, she meant it.

CHAPTER 13

Press Pool Release, all wire services and individual accred-
ited correspondents—Army Hq, Sicily, July 28, 1943: Units
of the 1st Infantry Division pushed forward to Hill 1333,
north of the Petralia-Gangi road. The enemy pulled off the
eastern slopes of Hill 397 because he was pocketed between two U.S. battalions. However, his artillery interdicted
the road north with salvos of 88mm all night long, at 10
minute intervals.

The 16th Infantry Regiment reported capture of 32 Germans and 8 Italians, but were driven back to their original
jumpoff positions by extremely heavy enfilading fire from the
north. Forward elements were also strafed and divebombed
by the *Luftwaffe*.

When the last Stuka peeled up and away, Chad Belvale
rolled over and damned the *Luftwaffe* for helping screw up
the regiment's attack. He spat dirt and said, "Our own
flyboys aren't flying cover, of course."

And he thought of the tough and cocky Englishman he'd
soldiered with across France, Johnny Merriman and the
bloody raid on Dieppe; how Merriman blamed his RAF for
every problem and was often right. He'd run into his old
friend back in Tunis, still a hell of a soldier, although his
right hand had been replaced by a steel clamp.

109

Then Chad yelled for casualties and damage reports and got on the radio to his battalions, telling himself it was only chance that he first reached the 2nd battalion commander.

"Doing okay, us," Major Langlois said. "Nobody dancing *fais do-do;* but the Krauts, they're keeping their heads down, too."

Chad heard heavy weapons fire and muted explosions. "Langlois?"

"A la bas! Just friendly greetings, man. H Company's guns talking back, and your boy's all right, except ugly as you since he got a face full of rocks."

"Let me know if you need anything."

"You got some gumbo on the stove? Hey—one something, my friend. You know Big Mike Donnely is back up here?"

Chad frowned. "Thought he got shipped to Limey land."

"For sure it was him came through looking for H Company—*merde!* Here come another goddamn Stuka!"

Sloan Travis had two guns ready for an air attack this time, a section of water cooled 30s set high on hillsides to fire for AA, hard-hitting armor piercing ammo spaced by guiding tracers. When the Stuka shrieked down to lay its egg in mid-air and then climbed for height to come back and work over the little valley with its guns, the 30s caught him in an accurate, planned crossfire.

The bomb hit with a blast that shook the earth, but the stream of tracers had already stuck bright red fireflies into the plane like a camouflaged butterfly being pinned for a specimen. But this one wouldn't be saved. The pilot had brought it in low and slow enough to be caught by ground fire, and when the Stuka hung faltering, frustrated GIs emptied their M-1s and carbines at it. Sloan could see why pilots hated ground fire worse than regular AA; the shots were not patterned, but each was aimed directly at their heads, and somebody was bound to get lucky.

Rolling wing over wing, its fixed and hooded landing gear

spinning, the dive bomber clawed on above the ridgetops, trailing wisps of gray smoke.

"Got his Kraut ass!" Sergeant Pelkey shouted.

Owen Belvale locked a new clip into his carbine and grinned as the roar of the German plane exploding reached him. It was rare when ground troops got to hit back at enemy air, and it was a good feeling. A handful of enemy machine gun bullets, high, but close enough for a warning, whined overhead. They reminded Owen that work remained to be done on the ground, dirty work uphill against troops well dug in and looking down the battalion's throat.

Waiting for orders to move out behind the rifle companies, Owen used the sound power phone to check on his platoons. Sloan Travis was in reserve, remaining in place for the chance to put more deadly crossfire on any other dive bomber. The other guns were in support of Easy Company, and the 81mm mortars were always ready in their backup position.

"Damned steep climb," Owen's radioman said. "I figure they ought to fly over and drop paratroops up yonder; give us a break." Weintraub peeled the wrapper from a good cigar and sniffed the tobacco. "Them troopers get paid extra for jumping out of airplanes, don't they? Course, I figure anybody that jumps out of a plane that ain't on fire is crazy as a bedbug and needs extra pay for the funeral."

Owen stared. "Winey, I'll bet that's the only cigar within fifty miles; makes me glad I don't smoke them."

"You lose, cap'n; mess sergeant's got a box to pass out to them as wants a good smoke."

"I won't ask what he had to trade for them."

"I'd lie, anyhow." Weintraub thumbed the radio handset. "Yeah—okay, major. I'll tell Red Six."

"Very military radio discipline."

"Saves time. Major says the line companies move out in ten minutes."

Owen put on his web belt and settled the canteen on one hip. That's when First Sergeant Donnely squatted at the edge of the CP hole. "Captain?"

"Big Mike? What the hell—you're supposed to be evacuated."

"Chancre mechanics changed their mind, sir; said I just had a bellyache." His face was pale and strained.

"You don't look that good."

"They kept draining blood samples and stuffing pills down me, and the captain knows that any aid station chow is C-rations screwed up worse than usual. The mortars up ahead a little?"

"Sergeant, are you sure—"

But Mike Donnely was gone, crouched low and moving along the rocky ground lithe as any youngster. Owen looked at Weintraub; the man shrugged, then strapped himself into the heavy radio.

Owen passed word for Sloan Travis's 2nd Platoon to lay overhead fire on the clifftops; at least part of the beaten zone—that bullet striking pattern of known width and length that varied at different ranges—would hammer Kraut positions; part of it would pass over. It might be enough to keep down some square heads, and the more ducking meant less of them aiming down the slope at the attacking troops.

Looking up, he saw mortar bursts walking the lip of the ridge with Big Mike's uncanny accuracy. There were good mortar sergeants and excellent ones, but Mike Donnely was in a class by himself. Within minutes, the shells would march back on the flat, ten yards at a time, their flying fragments and explosive wallops playing hell with even well dug in enemy.

Slam-whizz-BANG!

Only the dreaded, flat trajectory 88 made that doorslam-blowup sound, and the American artillery as yet had nothing to match its triple threat: ground fire, antitank and antiaircraft.

Slam-whizz-BANG!

The son of a bitch was laid in too close to battalion CP, and working back toward the rear of the attacking troops. Where the hell was it? Where was its forward observer?

He said to Weintraub: "Tell Big Mike to counterfire that damned gun."

"If he can find it."

"He'll spot the gun. He has a special talent and can smell out his target."

Weintraub spoke into the handset, then looked back at Owen. "He ain't there. Went busting off up the hill with Easy Company."

"What the hell!" Owen snatched the handset. "Who's this—Dymond? What's the matter with Donnely? Has he got battle rattle?"

The answer sounded tinny: "Beats me, sir. He just said fuck it and took off with his carbine. That hill is some hot, too. Looks like the attack is pinned down and we're still lobbing the shells where Mike wanted them, in high."

"Shit! Sergeant—can you send a couple of guys after him? The man is sick."

"Sir, every man is serving the tubes. It's mighty hot out there and he's halfway up the hill by now, but if you want—"

"Never mind. Just let me know the minute you see the old bastard again. I mean ASAP, understand?"

"Roger, captain."

Weintraub took back the handset. "He went AWOL from the hospital, you know."

Owen stared. "I didn't know. Goddamnit, why didn't you—"

"Couldn't of stopped him, cap'n, and for certain you know that. Nobody fucks with Big Mike when his head is set; more hammer headed than a stripey back mule and got just as mean a kick."

"But there's something wrong with his guts—"

Weintraub shook his head. "Not his guts, just his stomach. Medic I know back yonder passed the word that the docs figure it's cancer all the way, eating his belly out and no way to stop it. When they got ready to ship him back home, Mike took off like a big ass bird. I mean, there's different ways to check out, and even if some ain't hallelujah time, like the preachers claim, some ways got to be better than others. You blame him, cap'n?"

Owen didn't, but the understanding stabbed him low in his own belly. Big Mike Donnely, being who and what he was, had chosen the time and place to retire from his beloved army. Owen could only pray that it would be quick and painless.

INS—New York, N.Y., July 30, 1943: Canned beer has disappeared because of the tin shortage, and the supply of real whiskey is very short, so the highjackers and bootleggers flourish. Racketeers grab empty whiskey bottles and refill them with alcohol cut four and five times with water. People of this city are warned of imitation whiskey on the market, made of water, flavoring, inferior cane spirits and sediment from whiskey casks.

One such formula is half whiskey, one quarter orange juice and one quarter antifreeze. In Brooklyn recently, 14 people died from drinking wood alcohol bought at their neighborhood grocery.

Eddie Donnely had a buzz on, and it wasn't a happy one. He wanted to cry and he wanted to break things, and since infantry sergeants don't cry, at least in public, he was inches away from smashing something, from tearing up anything or anybody. He needed something to fight, something to hurt him worse than the pain he had. Goddamn; because he was now officially a member of the holy military clan, the news had reached him much faster than going through channels. Rank hath its privileges, even for EM attached.

Thanks, you thoughtful sons of bitches. I needed to know in a hurry. I couldn't go one more day without knowing that my old man bought it in Sicily. KIA in his second war and after soldiering for twenty-eight years at every armpit and asshole post in the goddamn army. Just another dumb enlisted man. Jesus Christ—hashmarks clear to his elbow and still out playing infantry noncom instead of stacking arms behind some training desk like any sensible short-timer.

(Barracks talk: he's been in the army since Caesar was a roadguard.)

What did all that time buy him but a handful of Kraut bullets? The notification said . . . killed in action while leading a successful assault upon a strongly held enemy position . . .

First soldiers and mortar sergeants didn't lead infantry attacks. What the hell pushed Mike into it?

And here I am, marking time at a fucking general officer's castle because I married the daughter of high brass. Well, that's bullshit.

"Bullshit!"

"What did you say, sergeant?"

Eddie looked up from his shot glass with water chaser. He'd never been in this cutesy little bar before, hadn't sought out ranks of bottles dressed right and covered down against a blue mirror since he married. Because of Gloria, he hadn't needed to bar hop. He didn't remember finding this one. Blindly, he'd rushed out of Sandhurst Keep, balling and throwing the TWX and not answering Gloria's startled cry behind him.

The West Point cadet stood an elbow away, spit shined and knife-creased, with his head skinned and brass buttoned to the chin. He held two mixed drinks to carry to the booth where his date sat. She was just as correct, Standard Operating Procedure blond and blue-eyed, uniformed with just the proper touch of lipstick. She sat at attention, as if her ass was cake and she was afraid to crack the icing. Not the kind of woman Eddie could fully appreciate.

Upperclassman on a short pass from the Academy a few miles away, Eddie thought, like the four harmonizing on Poor Little Lambs and beering it up in another booth and a genuine U.S. Army captain at the far end of the bar, a cadet coach or keeper wearing only stateside ribbons to pretty up his blouse.

(Barracks talk: play it cool in the motor pool.)

Eddie held up a middle finger. "Even you kay-dets must have heard of rotation, so jump up and rotate on this."

"There's a lady present, sergeant. Clean up your language or leave."

Eddie tossed off his bourbon. "You don't have any rank to pull, yet. Get the hell away from me."

The cadet put down one drink and placed a hand on Eddie's shoulder. Eddie dropped his right foot back, pivoted on his left sole and whipped across a left hook that gashed the guy's eyebrow and hurled him back into the booth atop his girlfriend. Even her scream, actually a moderate yip, was proper.

"Damnit—what—come on, cadets!"

When they leaped from the other booth, he met them more than halfway, glorying in the vicious shots he landed, glorying as well in the punches he took. But PE in the boxing ring at the U.S. Military Academy hadn't taught these officers-and-gentlemen-to-be a course in barroom brawling. Tight in among them, Eddie tucked his head and used elbows and knees when he couldn't get off a solid punch, and he butted one bastard stupid. The genuine captain was a little better, but not much. He missed with the beer bottle before Eddie hit him broadside with the spidery metal barstool. The kids were tough; they kept climbing off the floor and coming at him until the barkeep put in a hurry call. it brought civilian cops and MPs through the bar doors together.

Still blinded by incoherent fury and pain so deep down that he couldn't reach it, Eddie played the fool and gutted one MP. By the book, the other slammed his club into the base of Eddie's neck, paralyzing shots on both sides. Eddie's arms went numb and useless. They dumped him bloody into a paddy wagon and wheeled him off.

REUTERS NEWS AGENCY—London, July 30, 1943: German radio announced today that a "National Fascist government has been set up in Italy and functions in the name of Benito Mussolini."

The announcement, called a "proclamation by the National Fascist Government of Italy," said the Badoglio betrayal will not be accepted. The National Fascist Government will punish traitors severely.

The broadcast in Italian said nothing about the whereabouts of Mussolini, who has been reported under arrest. It was preceded by the playing of Giovinezza, the Fascist anthem.

Tired to the bone, Feldwebel Arno Hindemit was grateful for the overhang of rock that protected him. The ground was too *verdammt* hard to chip out a hole, and he blessed this shallow indentation a hundred years of dripping water had designed to protect him and the captain. It was always him and Hauptmann Franz Witzelei and more than just the militarily correct position for them both.

He supposed it was only natural for survivors to stay close together, as if one was the lucky piece for the other. And lucky they were, to be the only soldiers left over from the original company of *landsers* that had gone proudly into Poland. Many had come and gone since then, the replacements becoming younger and younger.

"Soon they will be sending us *kinder* carrying specially made rifles; they will not be tall enough to fire regulation Mausers. Ah-hah! That is the Führer's proclaimed secret weapon—undersized weapons for midget soldiers. A stroke of genius; this will save on lower calibers of ammunition and the little boys will drink less ersatz coffee, to say nothing of wearing much smaller Iron Crosses."

A mortar round's chilling hiss preceded the blast that rocked the earth but not their solid shelter. Arno coughed bitter smoke and pressed fingertips against his earholes to clear the channels again.

Witzelei spat and muttered. "Always the cheery optimist, sergeant."

Arno rubbed his eyes. "And you? I have noticed a change in the proper schoolmaster's political attitude since the Wermacht's glorious beginnings in Poland and France. But then, true *landsers* are not political or educated; being eternally cursed, they can afford neither luxury."

"I am an infantryman; if not me, after so long, who?"

Arno squinted down the hill. Two MG34s were left to him, and they stayed quiet until the *Amis* offered closer targets, for when they swept the slope with automatic fire, the enemy mortar shells immediately came searching, and the *Amis* had become excellent mortarmen.

"*Mein hauptmann,* when this war is over—which should not take too long—and if you remain lucky, you will return to your books and students. Providing those students have not been used up, that is, and all the books burned. The true *landser* will be ordered to other miserable places where he will fight other miserable wars."

Witzelei wiped his glasses with a dirty rag, extra careful with the cracked lens. "There will be no government left to order ex-soldiers anywhere. And the victors will not be kindly disposed. This time, we may all be hanged."

Fingering his jacket pocket, Arno found a cigarette butt put by in richer times. Covering the match flare with his helmet, he lighted it and took two drags before passing it to his captain. The taste was mildewed.

"There will always be work for *landsers,* and employers to hire them. The job market is not exactly overcrowded. Why should the *Amis*—or any other ordinary soldier—think of hanging other simple soldiers? We all do as we are told. One side loses, one side wins; that is all."

Witzelei returned the butt, grown so small that Arno had to pinch it in his fingernails for one more inhalation. One of the company's machine guns fired a rolling burst. "Too long," the captain said. "The mortars will find him."

Then he added: "The ending of this war will be different, I fear. The French and Belgians especially will be vengeanceful. We have, within the space of only a few years, overrun their countries twice. It would be better to give ourselves up to the *Amis* before the end. Their wars have been too far apart for them to seek blood for blood."

Arno lifted field glasses. "Their tanks come, and I have not seen our mighty panzers all day, nor the *Luftwaffe*. Always the *landsers* left behind to catch the *scheissen*. If only that *verdammt* legionnaire had run his spear up his own ass that day."

Crummpp!!

The rock outcropping shuddered this time; jagged steel whined the air and chewed up the ground right in front of the shallow hole.

"Tank fire," Arno said.

"Enough," Hauptmann Witzelei said. "Signal the machine guns to retreat first. Men with *Schmeissers* can fire cover until they are over the crest. And then we all pull out."

"Without orders from on high?"

"Screw orders; we save our men."

Arno grinned. "I believe you are a *landser*, my captain. But if you do not mind, I will remain here only long enough to get off these two rounds left for the *Panzerfurst*, should the *Ami* tank come close. *Gott!* I hate armor."

Witzelei smiled back. "Do not delay, *feldwebel*."

"You just don't want to be left with all these children."

"Exactly."

CHAPTER 14

War Department July 31, 1943, TWX Special to Kill Devil Hill, marked SECRET: Slow progress in the New Georgia campaign has led the Chief of Staff to change policy in the Pacific. There will be no more step-by-step advances. Instead, beginning with the island of Kolombangara, its garrison of 10,000 Japanese will be sealed off and left to wither on the vine. Our forces move on to attack the lightly defended (250 enemy troops) island of Vella Lavella.

Moreover, establishment of an airfield on Vella Lavella will bring our planes within 100 miles of Bougainville, the most westerly island of the Solomons.

Penny Colvin-Belvale couldn't move with the snaky ease of the short dark men around her, but she stayed quiet and close to the ground as best she could. She halted when they did, warned by the touch of a callused hand to hold her breath and pray. In turn, she touched Stephanie Bartlett, and tried not to think of what reprisals would be taken upon the rest of the prisoners because of this escape.

If they got away with it. She still couldn't quite believe that these silent little men had infiltrated the camp like so many wraiths, and that they had given her and Stephanie no choice. It was crawl with them or be dragged unconscious and endanger the entire group. The scowling leader had made that plain with abrupt hand signs, his eyes like black diamond slits beneath the rag knotted around his greasy hair.

"Mostly Malays and Burmese, and I'll wager that some bloody Japs have been bribed to look the other way," Stephanie had whispered, "but I see a pair of Dyaks—those squatty, nearly black ones. They're murderous little sea devils far from home, honest to God pirates out of Borneo, but why did they travel all the way here for us?"

Penny didn't have time to whisper back. She would have said, "The Belvales and Carlisles, the family taking care of its own—and somebody else that one of them loves." But the leader pushed her through the quarters window and she hurt her knees on the hardpacked earth below.

Pausing now, she stared up at the north sentry tower, and over at the long bamboo and barbed wire gate secured across the double path. The moon was only just threatening to rise beyond the Nipa palms, and deep shadows overlay the compound. The only lights were candles flickering in the Jap barracks, and the gasoline lantern going in Major Watanabe's quarters. She wondered when that bastard would get enough of his nightly soaking and climb from his steaming tub to call for her to come dry and polish his dripping body.

Not now; please, not now. She wasn't all that sure that at least the nervous Dyak pirates wouldn't kill them both if any alarms went off. Money was no good to dead men and it would be easier for them to fight their way out without the burden of two unarmed women.

A match flared at the gate and she saw the flat planes of Sergeant Katana's face as the sentry held a light for his cigarette. Around her, caught out in the open, the little men went flat and Penny pressed her sweaty cheek against the dirt.

Stephanie's lips were at her ear: "That effing bastard; he's standing guard while he sends the sentry to fetch him the woman he chose for the night. He takes them on the ground right there beneath the guard tower, and all the bloody little shits know when it's going on. They climb up there for the night guard shift just after she arrives. Katana calls out something and you can hear them giggle overhead. Maybe they peer down and watch in the moonlight."

Oh lord; Stephanie hadn't said a word about it before, but it was evident that she had been one of the unfortunates Katana had raped. Of course; his major had the second ranking white woman as mistress; it would give Katana face among his friends to take the PW leader, to outreach even Lieutenant Hidori. And Stephanie couldn't have complained to the camp commander. All the prisoners learned the graphic lesson shown them by Watanabe when Penny reported her own attempted rape. She had baked for a tortured eternity in the blazing sun strapped to a post. It was her punishment for "lying about and daring to attack a faithful soldier of the Imperial Japanese Army."

Poor, proud Stephanie, having to put up with that brutal, degrading son of a bitch. And poor Penny? One son of a bitch is about like another. One of the Dyaks hissed and tapped Penny's shoulder. He eeled off for the shelter of dark puddling beneath the guard tower, not knowing that would be the most dangerous spot within the compound in just a few minutes. She reached for his leg to warn him, but he was gone.

Stephanie held to the second Dyak, murmuring beside his cheek, struggling with him. A turbaned Malay slid alongside them and whispered something. The Dyak let go a short knife with a wavy blade, but held tight to his long sword.

"No!" Penny whispered. "Stevie, don't—oh, please don't—"

But Stephanie stood up and walked straight for the compound gate, the dagger tucked hidden behind her right thigh. Penny did not move, could not move. Somewhere in the dark behind them, a night being slowly lightened by the hint of moonshine, a Jap soldier was dragging some frightened woman from her sleeping quarters.

And right here, Leftenant Stephanie Bartlett offered herself as bait to Sergeant Katana, so that the rest of them could pass by without notice. She would probably kill herself with that knife rather than go through the hell that Katana and Major Watanabe would prepare for her when the breakout was discovered.

No, Stevie, no! The family has set up an elaborate escape route so that you can get away, too. The family wants you out because Chad Belvale wants you free; he must love you very much.

She heard Stephanie speak quietly, and heard the arrogant chuckle that Katana made in his throat. Then he grunted, loud and breathy like a hog surprised by the farmer's blade.

"Aahhh!" Katana gurgled then, and Stephanie stepped back from him as the Jap clutched at her, stepped back just as the moon rise topped the Nipa palms to show a quick wink of crimsoned steel in her hand. She had cut his throat.

"There," she said, and Penny had a sudden flash of herself doing the same thing to Hideo Watanabe.

Katana fell to his knees, both hands working at his neck, trying to stop the great leap of blood from his slashed jugular. She took the Nambu pistol from his holster. He fell forward on his face and kicked twice.

Swinging open the gate, Stephanie motioned them through, and the little men ran out swift and low. She closed the gate behind Penny.

"Bad enough what that sod forced on me. He had to build on it; straight away, he sent the news to the men's camp—sent every detail right to me puir legless husband and told him what a good fuck am I. Where all Dacey's mates could hear, of course."

Penny gasped. "I thought—I thought you were sacrificing yourself for the rest of us."

"Never so noble as all that, lass. I just couldn't leave that bastard alive behind me."

As she trotted into the dark, the Dyak's wavy dagger in one hand and the Jap's pistol in the other, Stephanie Bartlett made a sound.

Following into the black and steamy jungle along the hidden path that the Malays sniffed out like ranging hounds, Penny thought that Stephanie's choked noise was supposed to be a laugh. It didn't sound like one.

Intercept, marked RESTRICTED—Japanese field report, the Solomon Islands, 1 Aug., 1943: Because of food shortages, some companies have taken to eating the flesh of Australian soldiers. The taste is said to be good . . . Senior Lieutenant Sakamoto Ikeda.

International News Service—Washington, D.C., Aug. 1, 1943: Although some 100,000 Japanese-Americans living in sensitive areas on the west coast were moved to isolated desert camps, recently Niseis were allowed to enlist. Today, Mrs. Hisako Tanouye of the Wyoming relocation camp was honored today at a Gold Star mothers banquet. Mrs. Tanouye had six sons in the army. One has been killed in action.

Crusty Carlisle unshipped the hollow, folding mast as the raft skittered over the water. Stepping over Woodall, he kneeled wide and jerked the top section of the mast forward. When the tiger shark came in again, he braced as best he could and gave it the pointed end. The raft lurched and Crusty went over onto his ass.

Woodall propped him up. "I can hang on to it with you."

"Sullivan!" Crusty yelled. "Stay up front and keep us level with the oar."

"I'll try . . ."

"Try, hell! *Do* it or we'll be playing Jonah in this bastard's belly."

The shark circled in green water beneath the hot sun. Sweating, burned skin itched by salt water, Crusty watched its dorsal fin cut the water slowly at first. He unfolded the thin mast to full length and snapped the sections into place.

"Maybe we pissed him off when we ate his young relative. This big fucking sardine doesn't realize that we can feed on him for a month."

"Jesus Christ," Sullivan said. "Who's talking about eating who?"

"Here he comes again," Crusty said, and took dead aim at the great slash of mouth as the monster rolled onto its side. The power of its foaming strike rammed the end of the mast deep into its throat. Shaking his head, the shark broke off a long piece of the metal and came close to flipping Crusty over the side.

"Holy mother," Woodall said.

Crusty grunted, feeling the shock in his shoulders. He shoved his feet against the narrow floor braces of the raft, against the cup designed for the foot of the mast. "He's not done yet, but he left us a sharper lance. Come on, you stupid son of a bitch—see if you can make it come out your ass end!"

Slowly, the great fin circled at a distance, and Sullivan called out, "I see something dark forward. I can just make it out this side of the horizon—but it might be land. I don't give a damn if it's Jap land. I just want to get there."

Not as fast this time, and shaking its flat head side to side, the shark came at them and Crusty stuck the jagged end of metal deep into its gaping mouth. Water boiled furiously around the raft and it was all Crusty could do to hang on, despite Woodall's help.

Then the mast wouldn't pull free.

Bucking, great tail slapping the surface, the shark lunged straight ahead again and again. The raft sped over choppy, sunbright waves.

"Got us a motor!" Crusty shouted. "If we can just—hold—the—bastard back."

"Hang on, sir," Woodall said, and coughed wet onto Crusty's shoulder, "unless he sounds."

"Oh shit. Maybe he won't dive—he lives in the water. so maybe he's dumb as any swabby and will just keep butting his head."

"Jesus Christ," Sullivan said. "The fucking army. It is land, by God!"

Blood flowed from the shark's throat, from the shaft of metal embedded there, and Crusty bore down on its head, grinding the sharp point deeper. Blindly, stupidly, the shark kept struggling to reach out and feed. Its pushes weakened, but it kept trying.

"Let go!" Woodall shouted. "It's about to dive!"

It was more than just his letting go, Crusty thought, but a surrender as the killer fish drifted backward and sank, still trying to shake loose the thing caught in its maw. The rest of the broken mast tilted and waved like a flagpole in a storm before going under with the dying shark.

"Bit off more than he could chew," Crusty said. "Now his buddies will come chew on him." He sagged back into the raft, his shoulder aching, breathing hard from the exertion. He noticed a seepage of blood from Woodall's mouth.

"You all right, kid?"

"Sure, general. Hell of a fishing trip, isn't it?"

Sullivan called back, "Shark carried us a long way; breakers ahead. Sailing that way if the drift holds. Might make a landing on coral, so hold on tight. That stuff'll chop your feet to ribbons."

Turning, Crusty stared at the atoll they approached. It was low and tree greened and from where he sat, not very big. If they hadn't used up all their luck, the little island might have fresh water and edible flora to round out the fish and shellfish that would keep them until and if somebody found them. If they were really lucky, they wouldn't be discovered by the Japanese and might live another day.

The New Republic, movie critic Manny Farber—Aug. 2, 1943: The central character, by the end of the picture, has become a war hero, no matter how he started, as a skulker, brother of the captain's hated rival, or an idiot. He has one personality, on the handsome side, friendly, short on ideas and emotions and capable of trading wisecracks.

The United States Armed Forces may have prima donnas in the upper echelons and goldbricks in the lower, but if they're like the movie characters, it's doubtful if they can take Central Park, much less Tokyo.

Weintraub fiddled with knobs on the SCR-300. "Reception ain't for doodly squat. It's the bounce in these damned mountains, cap'n, and this low battery don't exactly help none. Messages get through, but I have to listen hard."

Owen Belvale propped his spine against a stack of machine gun ammo boxes. "We got the main poop okay: we get to take a break and let the 39th Infantry regiment secure Troina."

Grunting, Weintraub shook his head. "Hell—they ain't even First Division troops, and you taken a good look at that setup? Even the map scares me. That regiment ain't about to flap up no 3600-foot mountain like a big ass bird. Where the hell are them paratroops when we need them?"

Warmed by the sun, Owen closed his eyes. "Second Corps ought to consult with you before they move a muscle. General Omar Bradley could sure use your input."

"I always knowed just when to haul ass. Nothing ever got a bite of mine; out of my whole family, I got the only whole skin. You hear all that 88 fire? The Krauts got guns up yonder thicker than fleas on a coon dog's belly. Even them mean-ass little Goums got pinned down. They was supposed to lead the way up. And when *they* get stopped cold, it's just too damned wet to plow."

Moroccan Goumiers; when they first went into combat in Tunisia, their regular pay stopped. From then on, they were paid bounty for each pair of enemy ears they brought off the line later. It hadn't been unusual to see a Goum drying a string of withered ears across his chest or around his waist like bandoliers of ammo.

"Maybe they ain't the fighters they used to be, unless they're chopping off them ears," Wientraub said. "Reckon that kind of payday had to come to a squealing halt, though. Besides all ears looking alike, sort of, I figure they taken to digging up dead GIs and whosoever, seeing as how dead guys don't need theirs no more."

The radio handset made noises and Weintraub said into it: "Yeah—you got Red Six; what you all want? Okay; sure, I got it. Hey now, sergeant—you don't like my radio discipline, who gives a constipated shit? What you going to do, send me to the front?''

Turning to Owen, he said, "Told you so. The 39th is reorganizing First Battalion into one reinforced company. Got their asses whipped.''

"And?" The sun felt good on Owen's face and the sounds of war far away, although he could hear the sharp whacks of the 88s and the peppering of small arms fire.

"And the 26th Infantry gets to move out about 0500, supposed to take Hill 872; that's northeast of Troina, battalion says. Something about that'll cut the road from there to Caesro. Damn these here Italian names; man'll play billy hell keeping them all straight. You ready for a swallow of that dago red I found?''

Nodding, Owen held out his hand for the bottle. Given 20 minutes out of line of direct fire, and Winey Weintraub could find enough drink for the whole thirsty company. The sour wine slid down Owen's throat, its dark odor filling his nostrils.

"Better the 26th than us. I could sleep until Thanksgiving.''

"Back in Mississippi," Weintraub said, "we celebrated Turkey Day and the Fourth of July like everybody else. Christmas time was the different thing.''

Owen took another lazy drink. "I had you down as being of German descent.''

"Yeah, my old man got into it with his landlord and carried mama home from Dusseldorf. Since he'd been a sharecropper, like, he didn't go up north where some of his folks worked in factories. He went south and made us the only Jews in Clark County, Mississippi, and probably the onliest ones past the Mason-Dixon line that didn't own a store. I got born on a red dirt farm best for growing pine stumps and stump whiskey.''

A plane whirred high overhead. Owen kept his eyes closed, even when the enemy artillery picked up its pace on the far right flank. He wondered if he would ever truly sleep again, if some part of him would not be on constant alert.

"Course, the old man didn't know nothing about the

stump whiskey. Me and my brother Jake ran the still ourselfs. But if we didn't run off a batch of white lightning once in a while for cash money, taxes would of took the place. The old man believed in that earth, the holy soil, the promised land of milk and honey. Just owning a little bitty piece of land was more than he'd ever hoped for. He never thought much on snakes in Eden until a cottonmouth moccasin bit mama.

"Then he didn't eat much and got a heap more religious. He'd keep the high holidays and skipped hog killing time and like that. Come Chanukah, he'd travel to temple down in New Orleans, but when he looked for us, me and Jake would run off in the woods. We never wore a *yarmulka* or prayer shawl in our lives. The other younguns, town and country alike, knowed us for Jews, but they left us be after we knocked some in the head with lighterd knots. I mean, we was careful not to act different, and talked like the old man wasn't right in the head. Hell, sometimes me and Jake would put on shoes and sit in a pew out in Hepzibah Church just like we belonged."

Wheeeesh!

"Away the hell high," Weintraub said, "some Kraut is hiding down in his observation post hole, lying back to the guns."

After another swallow, Owen passed back the bottle. He kept expecting Big Mike Donnely's voice to come over the radio; it was difficult to remember he was dead. The man had seemed indestructible. But Owen had seen the body, and the faces of H Company men as they watched the sergeant's litter placed across the back of the medical company jeep. Corporal Tozar rode with it. That was the first long, silent moment of group mourning Owen had ever known. Then the men passed on, nobody saying anything, nobody doing anything beyond that long look and shaking their heads.

Big Mike Donnely's requiem. He would have said it was enough.

"Okay," Weintraub said into the handset. "I'll tell him. Hey, cap'n—enemy troop report, if you can believe anything G-2 says. Whole damn German Battle Group up on that mountain with orders to stay until Hitler eats kosher. And dug in north of the highway there's 1st Battalion, Panzer Grenadier Regiment of the 15th Panzer Division, and somewhere behind them the 382nd Infantry Regiment. See how easy them Kraut names roll out my mouth. You figure it's in the blood?"

Owen sat up, blinking. "Nothing about us?"

"We ain't just lucking out. They're keeping us for the down and dirty. That bunch up yonder ain't about to turn loose Troina without one hell of a shitstorm."

Owen said, "I've seen your serial number, Winey; it's not draftee. You enlisted before the war. How about your brother?"

Weintraub tilted the wine bottle high and drained it. "Some turd backshot him and hauled off eighty gallons of real fine whiskey. Finding out about the still hurt the old man near about as much as Jake dying. I couldn't look him in the eye no more, so I joined up. Worthless as it is, the land's still there, but daddy ain't. When he kind of give up and died, kinfolks come down from New York and carried him to their kind of graveyard. We was in Tunisia then and there wasn't no way I could tell them he ought to be put down in his own ground, his promised land."

"I'm sorry, Winey."

"Me, too." Weintraub looked off at the mountain where Troina loomed. "When I think about it, I mean."

CHAPTER 15

UNITED PRESS—Los Angeles, Calif., Aug. 2, 1943: At least
two expressions have been added to the language by the
recent acquittal of movie actor Errol Flynn in a combined
statutory rape case. District Attorney John Dockwiler charged
that Flynn had his wicked way with two young girls, 17-
year-old aspiring actress Betty Hansen and 17-year-old
Peggy Satterlee. One act was alleged to have occurred in a
friend's apartment, the other aboard Flynn's luxury yacht
Sirrocco.

Conviction for sexual relations with an underage girl could
have resulted in a five-year sentence in San Quentin prison,
hence the term "San Quentin quail."

The other expression, needing no explanation, is "In like
Flynn."

During the trial, Errol Flynn consoled himself by flirting
with a counter girl in the courthouse lobby, Nora Eddington,
age 18.

Gavin Scott's breath hissed through the gap in his teeth.
That lousy Kraut had knocked out two uppers and one
lower. Starting out with his half a face, he was even uglier
now and didn't gave a damn. After the war, the finest plastic surgeons in the world could build him a new face, if he
wanted one. When he wanted one, after women got through
feeling sorry of him.

131

Glancing across the yard at the British officers lounging in the shade of a battered farmhouse, he straightened up and propped himself up on his shovel. "Kilroy was here, you bastards!" It was a thing chalked on walls and fences across half the world, often accompanied by a rough sketch of a little guy with a long nose peeping over a fence. It was off the wall and purely GI.

The guard poked the rifle muzzle hard between Gavin's shoulders. He went back to work. Digging steadily, he dripped sweat and his lower back ached, but he couldn't slow up. Next time, the cretin guard would hammer him with the butt of the Mauser and maybe break his head. The goddamn Limeys would probably applaud and insist that he get on with digging the ruddy loo.

Damn; a member of the Belvale-Carlisle family shoveling out a shithouse hole by any other name. Nothing like this had happened since the southern branch lost Kill Devil Hill and the Civil War. And somebody, somewhere, would sure as hell pay for this kind of crap, the Krauts and the Limeys both.

Hear that, Leftenant Stevie Bartlett? Listen to the wind and look up at the clouds, because I'll be coming through them to rub this Halloween face into yours and see if you laugh this time. When I jam it up you this time, you'd better not laugh, bitch.

The Limey POWs were upset because he'd tried to get away on his own, without obtaining permission from the official escape committee, the stiff-necked bastards. It was the duty of any soldier of the United States Army to escape; it said so in the Articles of War. They could go screw themselves, if they thought he would go meekly along to a German stalag. First chance he got, he would rabbit again. They'd told him how bloody lucky he was not to have been shot, especially since the SS had caught him.

That might spook the rest of them, but not Gavin Kilroy Scott.

Sweat dripped into his eyes. He shook his head and continued to work, correcting himself. He wouldn't make another blind and unprepared break. This time he had a plan.

132

The PW convoy had crawled north by fits and starts; it was holed up now, waiting for word that the roads were clear of Jerry reinforcements being poured down into the Italian boot.

More and more of them came since the Wops hung it up; they didn't mean to let the Allies hike up the Italian boot and on into Fortress Europe by the back door. But somewhere along the way, before the prisoners and their guards reached the Brenner Pass, the Jerries would have recently built some airstrips. That's why Gavin waited—to see or hear of a nearby airfield.

Jerries; Eye-ties, tea time; being around the English so much, some of their cute jargon rubbed off on him. He'd forget all about that after he reached an airstrip and a plane. That was the edge he had on most of the PWs; he could fly. He was a hot pilot, a goddamned ace. Put him in anything with wings and he'd soar back into the sky to kick ass and build his string of victories, to set a record. The world would ring with the name of Gavin Scott.

The Krauts had brought a new plane into Italy, at least a model he had never seen until lately. It looked faster than the Messerschmitt 109 and 110 and of course the Stuka. British Colonel Sanderman had called it a Focke-Wulf, and Sanderman should know everything, right, chaps? He was senior officer and the head of the escape committee.

Gavin badly wanted a Focke-Wulfe. He would grab any fighter plane he could crawl into, but a Focke-Wulfe would be especially nice. He'd take off and come roaring back for a strafing pass along the strip to delay pursuit, and then shag ass for Sicily. If he came across any Kraut planes in the air, the pilots might have a moment of surprise before he blew them apart.

And if he met American P-38s or British Spitfires? Go through the radio frequencies yelling who he was and asking everybody to back off so he could deliver this nice new fighter plane. Run like hell if he had to, stay low on the deck and hedge-hop until he could safely put down the Focke-Wulf, a present for the air corps command to examine.

Kiss my undisciplined Yank ass, escape committee. *"Eilen! Eilen!*—hurry!"

The rifle barrel slapped him atop the head and spun off his hat. He went to his knees in the fresh turned earth.

Using the shovel handle, Gavin pulled himself up. "Kilroy is still here, you blockheaded son of a sausage dog bitch."

Because he said it smiling and bowing, the goddamned Kraut didn't hit him again.

ASSOCIATED PRESS—Hawaiian Command, Aug. 2, 1943: Less than two years after the sneak attack on Pearl Harbor, this area is as beautiful as ever, although it bristles with antiaircraft guns that no Jap plane would dare. A stopping off place for servicemen going to the embattled islands of the Pacific and for those wounded returning for treatment, it is a welcome slice of home. A bit exotic, with its frangipani blossoms, wild orchids and hula girls, but home nevertheless, with cold milk and hamburgers and swing music on the radio.

These islands have sprouted giant shops for the expert repair of damaged ships and planes, and a huge shopping center has bloomed where all service Quartermasters come with their orders for vital war equipment, arms and ammunition.

And for the fighting men on their way back to California and points east, the U.S. Army's Tripler General Hospital has its own staff of experts, highly qualified specialists, surgeons and nurses who take wonderful care of our wounded boys until they can be shipped to the mainland for additional treatment or honorable medical discharges.

Since Farley Belvale had appeared on her NP ward without warning, Nancy Carlisle made a habit of checking the incoming patient lists at Admissions. While she had been a member of the family at the Hill, so many military men and their wives and kids brushed against her life. Some she remembered very well; some had already forgotten her and that was all right, too.

Moving around behind the counter in the rustling of her crisp whites, she said hi to the admissions clerk, one of the new WAACs, and lifted a clipboard from its hook. These were hospital ship patients, and she recognized no names. The other clipboard listed wounded flown in, the critical ones lucky enough to catch an outgoing cargo plane fitted with litters, and a few high ranking wounded coming in for better treatment simply because they were VIPS.

"Oh God," she said, as the floor tilted beneath her feet. With both hands, she clung to the counter to keep from falling off the world.

"Ma'am?" the enlisted woman said.

Nancy forced her eyes to focus on the typed sheet. There it was: Carlisle, Keenan W., Major, Inf.

Keenan, the man she had married and lost his child and divorced to have an affair with a sleazy congressman.

How badly wounded was he? Where was he, which ward was he on—yes, there: surgery. She swayed again and the WAAC corporal said, "Can I get you something, lieutenant? Are you okay?"

Nancy shook her head and wished she hadn't; it made her nauseous. "I—I'll be all right in a second. I know somebody on that list, and I have to go see . . ."

She didn't know how the other man managed to appear just when she needed him, but Sergeant Fitzgerald Kaole DiGama's hand cupped her elbow with warm and firm strength. The smell of the islands themselves was always with him, flowers, the sun and the sea, and something more personal.

"Fitz; I have to get over to the surgical wards. It's—it's—"

He steered her along the hallway. "I know; I saw the sheets. It's Major Carlisle. Related to you?"

"My—I was married to him." She wasn't tracking properly. She hadn't anticipated this. Of course men of the family were killed or wounded in action; it was an accepted occupational hazard, and Keenan had gone Missing in Action before. Already, young Farley Belvale waited for his stateside transportation on an open NP ward, but he was resilient and his mental injuries would probably heal soon. But Keenan had been fighting in some other faroff part of the world, not on one of the Jap-held island chains; to know he was here, in her own hospital . . .

"Eha!, a husband hurts. I think maybe it's *pau hana* for this beach boy—quitting time. I felt it was much too good to be true, that you wouldn't turn out to be real for me."

Leaning against him for support and not giving a damn who saw them, Nancy said, "I said I used to be married to him; he's the ex-husband. I divorced him, but he's not all that bad a guy and naturally I'm worried about him, but that doesn't mean—Fitz, you and I haven't even started anything yet."

His hand tightened on her arm. "Good; that means we were about to?"

"I—I don't—"

"Only *haoles* try to make hurry on the islands, pretty lady, and you're no longer a newcomer. No need to turn on speed. Just so you're not *kapu* for me because your man came back. I don't care about this other *kapu* because you're an officer."

"He hasn't been my man for so long—here's the ward. Nurse, where can I find Major Carlisle? What's his condition? May I see his chart?"

The nurse's name tag read: 1st Lt. Rowan; she was short and wide and sweaty. "Unless I know you real good, you don't peep that chart without a doctor's okay, and you already know that. But I can tell you that he's shot through the lung and draining. He's also carrying every known disease the Pacific has to offer and probably a few ugly parasites we haven't gotten round to naming yet. When he's delerious he speaks Chinese. They say he was shipped all the way from the China-Burma-India theater and damned lucky to have made it this far."

"He's tough; Keenan has been carried MIA before this. Everybody thought him dead for more than a year, but he walked into the British lines one day and—" she was prattling.

Behind thick glasses, Nurse Rowan's eyes softened. "Carlisle? Carlisle—you wouldn't be related?"

"I used to be. May I see him now?"

"Room 302; he's sharing it with a light colonel, head wound. Look, nurse, I'm sorry about the chart, but I told you everything except his current vital signs—"

"And I thank you. Sergeant, if you don't have anything urgent laid on—"

Fitz settled onto a folding chair. "I'll be right here, in case you need me. For anything."

Keenan's roommate's face was turned to the wall. Keenan lay flat upon his back, a flattened scarecrow with tubes in his arms and up his nose. He was yellowed by malaria and aged far beyond his years, and all the jungle rot smells, the suppurating odors hadn't been scrubbed from him. She pulled the standard issue metal chair up close to his bed.

"Keenan? Keenan—it's Nancy."

His eyelids fluttered, lids drawn taut against eyeballs sunken in dark, ringed pits. His cracked lips moved, and she gave him a sip of water through the bent glass tube.

"I am *yonsei*," he muttered. "I am the ghost who eats heads."

Not looking at her, but at the ceiling, he said clearly, "Chang Yen Ling?" And followed with a string of softly chanted Chinese. Then: "How did you get here, my darling?"

She gave him more water and then leaned back. Why should his saying darling bother her in the slightest? "No, I'm Nancy; Nancy Carlisle. I used to be your wife, remember?"

Slowly, his eyes rolled her way, eyes brightened by the running lights of fever, but also dulled in pain. "Not Yen Ling. Of course not; she was eaten by sharks; fed to the sharks by bastardly Japanese. But for that, I ate their goddamn slope heads. Oh, they're willing enough to die for their little four-eyed emperor, but the *yonsei* scares them out of their chickenshit minds. Without a head they can't get admitted to samurai heaven.''

She waited in silence, seeing Keenan as he used to be, strong and bright and stubborn. Chang Yen Ling was—had been—the Chinese girl he loved so much he couldn't wait to get back to the CBI. Oh good Christ, eaten by sharks, that was horrible. But this *yonsei* fixation, this ghost who devoured Japanese heads—if Keenan got well in surgery, he could end up on her NP ward. She didn't know how she could handle that; it wouldn't be like working with poor Farley.

"Nancy."

She popped erect. "Y-yes! Oh, Keenan—you *know* me."

"How long have you been a nurse?"

"Keenan, I'm so glad—not long. I work on the psychiatric ward here."

"Here; Tripler General on Oahu? Seems as if somebody said that we were heading there."

"We thought you were lost."

"Not—not lost. I was with Wingate."

"We thought Wingate was lost, too."

She reached for his hand, his dry and bony hand. "I'm so glad you made it back. The family worried—me, too. I mean, how many times can you disappear in the jungle and get away with it?"

His smile showed stained teeth, one incisor broken. "You were always more family than the rest of them realized. Preston Belvale knew, and I guess I did. I just didn't show it." He drew a careful breath of pure oxygen. "What shape am I in? Who's still alive in the family?"

"I don't really know much on either. I came as soon as I knew you were here, but I haven't talked with your doctors or heard from the family, besides—" She decided not to tell him about Farley just yet. "You look like hell, though."

He chuckled and said, "Oh shit; trying to laugh hurts. I see you've learned to be honest. Alone in the jungle, so did I. So you'll tell me anything you find out? I don't want to be shipped home, Nancy. Don't let them ship me back before the war's over. Get in touch with Preston and Crusty, pull all the strings. I'll get well if they give me a little time; I'll get well, damnit."

She stroked his hand before letting it go. "I'm sure you will, Keenan."

Then Nancy Carlisle left the room and went up the hallway to the nurses station where Fitz waited, the sergeant she fully intended to make love with, a very deep and intense love.

NORTH AMERICAN NEWS ALLIANCE—New York, N.Y., Aug. 2, 1943: Copywriters here are finding the war gives them ample scope for their talents. Here are some of the slogans that have rolled from their typewriters recently:

Can you pass the mail box with a clear conscience? (A pitch for V-mail)

I freed a Marine to fight. You can, too! (Recruiting for women Marines)

GI Joe wants the long distance lines tonight. (Cut down on civilian calls)

The food you save can help win the war.

You've done your bit; now do your best.

Although it bothered him, Preston Belvale looked Gloria Carlisle Donnely in the eye. "He brought it on himself, girl. The best thing for all concerned is to get him out of the country ASAP."

Eddie Donnely said, "That's fine with me, sir."

"Nobody asked you, sergeant. And be damned glad you're still called sergeant."

Stiffly at parade rest in the great hall of Sandhurst Keep, Eddie said, "I didn't ask for special treatment, either. Those goddamn cadets—"

"And the captain, and the MP, and Christ knows how many of those goddamn cadets you hurt. Did you have to hit the captain with a barstool? I know why you did it, sergeant. I just can't understand how you were so stupid as to pick those particular opponents on their own ground. Damnit, I loved Big Mike, too, but I didn't run out and punch everybody in sight because he got killed and his death hurt me."

"He wasn't your father, and the time was, you might have, general."

"At ease, goddamnit! We're not talking about me, but about protecting you and your wife from your stupidity."

He'd felt like punching everyone, or using his riding crop, or maybe just swinging into a saddle and riding off into the blue Virgina mountains until he ran out of mountains, out of horse or the sorrow wore off. What did these kids think—that you got so old that you couldn't miss other old bastards? Kee-rist; losing Crusty had hit him as hard as his losing his wife. Crusty, goddamnit, who couldn't swim worth a damn before arthritis took his shoulders and who hated the ocean. Preston never should have let him ship out like that.

Gloria took a step toward him. "Please, uncle—"

"*You* put a lid on it, too. Your wild-eyed groom has already had a special court and has been found guilty of assault, insubordination, drunk and disorderly and conduct unbecoming a soldier. As president of the board I fined him fifty dollars and allowed him to keep his rank, and that was no goddamn favor to you, boy. The army's better off with you as a platoon sergeant instead of a rifleman.

"You can't be tried again on the same charges; the Uniform Code of Military Justice has that much in common with civilian courts. Everyone at the Academy, the entire staff and cadet corps alike, wants your Irish ass drawn and quartered, and some of them don't give a damn about the Belvale and Carlisle name.

"Before I flew up here in that little eggbeater, I had orders cut returning Sergeant Donnely to the Americal Division in the Pacific, and any dedicated avenger from West Point will play hell finding copies in War Department files.

Besides the court martial result, everything else got lost, including the original investigation charges.

"That's it; that is bigod *it,* and neither of you have a word to say. Donnely, you have two hours to lock and load. I will allow Gloria to drive you to the New York Port of Embarkation, where your troopship awaits with green replacements. You might have time to make facsimile soldiers out of them before landing wherever the hell you will land."

Eddie Donnely said, "Yes, sir; thank you, sir."

Preston looked at Gloria again. She lifted her chin and refused to cry, but then he hadn't really expected her to.

CHAPTER 16

Special to *The New York Times*—Allied Headquarters, Sicily, Aug. 2, 1943: Troina is an ancient military town that seems to grow out of a choppy ridge atop a threatening mountain. It has been fortified since the first bloody Punic War fought between Carthage and Rome, taken and retaken many times. Now it is under attack again by determined and powerful modern forces, and defended by the toughest, most fanatic troops Germany has left to offer.

All roads leading to the foothills of Troina wind through country open but for a few patches of gnarled trees, hand-picked rock piles and scattered stone farmhouses. These roads are under constant enemy artillery observation, thickly mined and heavily protected by a legion of German anti-tank weapons. The island itself lies within easy reach of enemy planes based on the mainland of Italy. Bombers must fly across only the narrow Straits of Messina to hammer at Allied positions.

Earlier on, field commanders here assumed the taking of Troina would cost little time and effort. They sent only a unit of Moroccan Goumiers and a single American infantry battalion against the frowning heights. Both were stopped cold by accurate artillery and mortar fire, and headquarters sources now believe the battle building up may enter history as the roughest fight the Yanks have had on this side of the Atlantic.

Chard Belvale listened to small arms fire riding the hot wind, and heard the kettle-drumming of artillery. The battalion CP used a stretched kitchen fly for tentage; it guarded his three-man staff from the sun, helped by the loose sand spread over it as camouflage from marauding dive bombers. Sicily itself blew right through beneath the cover, heavy with gritty dust and the stench of death. There was also that indefinable, but to combat veterans, all too familiar smell of major trouble on the way.

He stared at the situation map. "Division says the Krauts brought a bunch of reinforcements into the town, including our old friends, the Hermann Goering Division."

Major Lucien Langlois sipped wine from a dented canteen cup. "They should have fat bellies like that big *cochon*, no? Then they couldn't dig in worth a damn; one side or the other bound to stick out. Ain't that the outfit what rabbited back at Gela, hauling ass with both hands?"

"They got stopped and convicted by Luger court martial, and some were strung up and left dangling for show, so that kind of panic won't break Hermann the German's pet outfit again. This time they'll stay put until we bury them in Troina."

"That's all right. I piss on their graves. If somebody else digs them; if not, let the crows pick them clean. But this Troina, she's going to be one bitch to take."

"Now they're not so sure that the whole division can do it; the Ninth Division is coming up in full strength." Backing away from the map, Chad sat down on a water can and held his Zippo to a mildewed Old Gold. "We'll wait the word."

If the orders to attack brought anything like the word that had come in from the Hill, he didn't want to hear them. Crusty Carlisle gone MIA and considered dead; Dan Belvale killed in the Pacific, such a short time after his son Walt bought it in Poland; Keenan Missing in Action in the CBI—again. Maybe the family's luck was at last running out.

And damn, Big Mike Donnely had been the next thing to family. The army wouldn't be the same without him.

Luckier or more determined than most, Mike had chosen his own time and place to die. There was something to be said for that. It beat lingering painfully along the way.

Here there were still one little, two little, three little Indians: Chad and Owen and Sloan Travis. Tomorrow all the little Indians could be gone, and the family would have to send more. But in time they just couldn't produce enough holy warriors to keep up with the wars that ate them. One after another, the Crusades had bled the Belvales and Carlisles, and all the dirty little European fights without names that took place between ocean trips to plant the Cross among the heathens.

Then there had been all the bigger, less personal wars that came after. Remembered names like Murfreesboro and Shiloh in that brotherly love fight; Belleau Wood in that war to end all wars; Pearl Harbor, Guadalcanal, and Kasserine Pass already staining the bloody pages of history; what would the books say of Gela and Troina?

The family had also kept busy with unofficial wars, border squabbles and political shifts. Its men hired out their lances so they could follow a flag, any flag that allowed them to ply their trade and hone their skills. And back then, they hadn't been adverse to a little looting. The women, technically the nonprofessionals, had it just as tough.

Until modern times, they might wait years for their men to come riding home, for word that they were widows, or worse, for the wrong troops to approach the castle. Now the women were in the lines; Penny Belvale flew her bomber into a hot spot, family by more than marriage. Stevie Bartlett fought her AA guns, and wasn't family yet only because she had refused to leave her PW husband and marry Chad. Those women had been swept up by the Japs and were either dead or in a POW camp wishing they were. Chad didn't know which fate he'd choose for them. Life, of course, at any cost. And he felt guilty for projecting the death of Dacey Bartlett.

And the women left at home this time—Gloria grieving deep over her grandfather Crusty, Dan Belvale's sorrowing wife and daughter hanging another Gold Star banner in a window at Kill Devil Hill. Would they wait for the body before holding a ceremony in the memorial grove? Would either of their men's remains ever come home?

He thought of his ex-wife, of Kirstin recently widowed. She would have taken that news with her chin up, hurting but not showing it to the world. Kirstin had pride, which was why she had left Chad. Odd that she should keep coming to mind even now. Maybe because she was still so much family, even though that had added to the strain of their marriage, the separations and his playing around; his other guilt, the sexual shame that Stephanie had eliminated.

But what the hell else could Chad do and still belong to the world he knew? He saw the dark side and bitched, like any old soldier, but there was nothing else he really wanted to do, no other trade for which he would be worth a damn. The dark side was often balanced by the pride.

"Want some of this sour-ass wine?" Langlois asked. "Tastes like turtle shit on the bottom of a mud bayou, but it does the job, yeah. And you look like you can use a lift."

Chad drank a swallow. "You sound like you've savored turtle shit. I guess I've been thinking too much."

"Thinking is bad for a soldier; hurts his head. Damn right I been close up to turtle *ca-ca,* and muskrat and alligator, too. I'm a coonass Cajun, me, and Cajuns had to learn to eat anything what didn't bite them first and worse."

Chad grinned. *"Ca-ca?"*

"Ethnic stuff you wouldn't understand. Now—the Krauts, they got to hold tight to Troina; it's the door to the road to Messina and the whole Mount Etna line. Kick them off that mountain and they got to run like hell and then swim for it. Hey, colonel—you think we got to jump in after them and play grabass all over Italy? I been a shrimper, remember. Flat water and flat land makes good sense. I ain't crazy about oceans or mountains, me; they got too many mountains in Italy, and for sure, too goddamn many *Boche.*"

"What the hell do I know?"

Finishing the wine, Langlois said, "Supposed to know more than me; you got the big rank."

Kaa-whamm!

Ears ringing, Chad shook his head to clear it and reached for the radio handset. "Get me Divarty. Divarty, this is Green Six. An 88 has our range. What are you doing about it?"

Then he gave back the phone and picked his cigarette butt off the ground to puff it alive.

Langlois rubbed his head. "What they say?"

"They said good luck. They're catching hell from a pair of 88s zeroed in on their own CP."

NORTH AMERICAN NEWS ALLIANCE—New York, N.Y., Aug. 3, 1943: The book was published late last year, and has already turned into a phenomenon. *See Here, Private Hargrove,* by Marion Hargrove, is reaching toward a million sales. It tells of the misadventures of a civilian-soldier generally sincere in his desire to serve his country, but one who is always at odds with military authority.

Actually a collection of letters Hargrove sent to his hometown newspaper, their warmth has humor and a reportorial quality on the life of the ordinary American GI, rather than heroic tales of foreign soldiers. The publishers expect sales to break the two million mark.

Partway up the slope, Sloan Travis had turned from heavy weapons platoon leader to basic rifleman. The 6th Squad's gun was blown to steel rags mixed with the blood of two of its men; the 8th Squad was pinned down in a shallow gully constantly traversed by small arms and machine guns. Although the other two guns still tried to lay down overhead fire for the attacking riflemen, it was sporadic since the defenders kept the gunners ducking. Nobody was going anywhere so long as Kraut artillery and mortars swept the mountainside, so long as the heavy Maxims and lighter MG 34s chopped up the slope.

Carefully lifting his head, he peered up at the military crest and lucked out; he caught a smoky glimpse of the Kraut machine gun positions, the heavy on his left, one or two lights dug in and laid to interlock a hellish crossfire upon the skirmish line.

Raprapraprap!

Sloan pulled in his head. One of the gunners had either spotted him, or was just checking the area. Tucked into only a half circle of small rocks, Sloan felt naked. The gun fired another short burst and chipped granite stung his face, hot and jagged bits of stone flaked off by whining bullets Around the left flank of his porous little barricade, he could see sprawled bodies of GIs, some of them down and unmistakable in that peculiar flatness of death; a few men clawing frantically at the hard earth to make a bit of cover.

The sun beat down, beat down, and Sloan's mouth had already turned to dusty cotton, but he saved the tepid, swimming-pool-tasting water in his canteen. If he lived until nightfall, he would need a drink worse then. Where was Gunga Din and his goatskin water bag? Where was the glory that Kipling wrote of redcoats and India's sunny clime? No glory here, just poor bastards dead and those praying not to die.

Raprapraprap!

The Kraut gunner on his left flank probed for him, and Sloan gave thanks that the bastard had only caught a flash of him and didn't know exactly where he was. When he found out for sure, the thin protection of Sloan's castle walls would vanish in a concentrated battering ram of 9mm bullets.

Sneaking another peep at the other position. Sloan made out a shadow movement, and no more. The gun hammered again, working across the slope this time, but ending with another close stab at Sloan. That gunner was just too frigging good.

He snugged the M-1 closer, glad that he'd traded off his officer's carbine. The Garand had range and a wallop that the carbine could never match, especially with the armor piercing ammunition carried in its clips. The normal load was 30 caliber ball, with a muzzle velocity of 2,800 feet per second; the AP moved at 3,600 feet, and its core was a pointed machining of hardened steel.

What would General Carlisle advise in this situation? He'd hunted with the old man in the thick, hard climbing woods at Sandhurst Keep, if by a stretch of the imagination it could be called hunting. Crusty didn't believe in killing anything that couldn't shoot back, but he taught Sloan the pure deadly beauty of the careful stalk, showed him the ways of deer and small game and the clumsiness of men caught out of their city element.

Make them curious; wait them out and they will come to you. Wait, boy; don't breathe and don't even think. And sure as hell don't move; just pull deep into yourself and wait.

Neither Kraut gunner would be coming down the slope, so they had to be made impatient or curious. He didn't know how to make them curious. Sloan had never quite believed that Sergeant York story of WW I, that the eagle-eyed rifleman gobbled like a wild turkey so Kraut soldiers lifted their heads to look. One after another they got popped and never caught on. For one thing, he kept seeing Gary Copper in the movie, bird-legged in those goofy wrap leggings. Sloan did identify with York in one way—neither of them had volunteered to jam their tails in a crack. But once caught, even draftees had to do something to pry that sore tail out.

Anyway, a whole flock of wild turkeys couldn't be heard on this violent mountain . . . larks still bravely singing fly, scarce heard amid the guns below . . . that had been another war, too—in fields where poppies blow.

Raprapraprap—zingg!

Sloan spat rock dust. "You son of a bitch."

The ricochet gave him an idea. He chanced a quick look at the left gun position. Yes, it sat under cover of a rock slab, fairly well protected from overhanded grenades. But the angle of the slab—

Carefully, he pushed the M-1 muzzle through his rock pile and sighted an angle; he popped two shots, then pulled in his head. Bank shots, he thought, as the Kraut's return fire searched blindly for him, and remembered the pool table in the raw wooden dayroom back at Fort Devens. He eased a few inches of muzzle out again and fired three quick ones at a slightly different angle. The AP slugs had to be slashing around that damned gun, bouncing down and around off that hard rock slab like a hatful of mad hornets.

The gun didn't answer right away, so he cut loose the rest of the clip. "Side pocket, kiss off the eight ball," he said. Thumbing a fresh clip into the rifle, Sloan heeled the bolt handle and took off his helmet to peer through a hole in his thin wall. He saw the machine gun barrel slanted at the hot sky.

"Damn if it didn't work," he said.

No rock hung over the other enemy gun, but somebody had a line on it. Red streaks of tracers kicked around the position, zipping off stony earth; one of H Company's guns zeroed in, duelling with the Kraut to protect the bellied-down GIs.

"Frigging-A right!" Sloan yelled, and stood up to empty his clip at the enemy's flank. "Take the bastard out!"

One man came to his knees, firing; then another and another, a few of them moving uphill at a dogged walk, blasting away as they went. Somebody got off a rifle grenade that went wild; somebody pitched a hand grenade that landed close. Sloan sprinted forward, firing from the hip. Any Kraut who raised his head into this hail of metal had to be suicidal.

Karummpp! A 50mm mortar shell blew just behind the advancing line and knocked over a soldier. The man wobbled upright and kept going. Sloan reached the gun position a step behind panting riflemen who pumped round after round into the hole, into a gun crew already sprawled dead.

These GIs were beautiful; the grimy, grunting bastards were nothing less than beautiful—the poor bloody infantry. They got up and went against any kind of fire the enemy laid on them.

And what the hell was happening to the guy who didn't want any part of the family traditions, no part of the uniform, much less a war?

A temporary change, Sloan thought; he'd get over it. When this frigging, dehumanizing war was history, he'd burn the uniform and kiss off the family and go off somewhere to get his writing started.

If he could remember anything good to write, or even how to write.

ASSOCIATED PRESS—Allied Headquarters, South Pacific, Aug. 3, 1943: Filthy conditions in the jungle are causing more casualties than Japanese action, according to medical officers here. Diseases unfamiliar to American doctors are surfacing almost daily: elephantiasis, beri-beri, the incurable fungus of jungle rot that attacks all parts of the body, but is a special threat to the ear canals.

Then there is the ever present malaria and dengue fever, better known as "breakbone fever" for its excruciating pain, and also the onslaughts of intestinal parasites that bring on bloody flux.

But they keep fighting, these GIs and Marines. They find some kind of treatment at front line aid stations and they return to the battle as soon as possible. The Japs are in worse shape, they say, and the quicker they're put out of their misery, the sooner our troops can go home.

Preston Belvale added the press release to files that already threatened to outgrow the war room. It was a wonder the story had been passed by MacArthur's censors. They wanted nothing but magazine-type pap to reach the American public—the soldiers fighting for mom and apple pie, and if by some chance one was killed, he died quick and unbloodied, as in the glamorous war movies pouring out of Hollywood. Kee-rist; in the last war, influenza had killed thousands of men who never got out of stateside camps. No studio ever made films about that.

Gloria Carlisle—Donnely now—moved from teletype to short wave radio to the phones, keeping her back to him whenever possible. She was angry for the way he'd chewed out Eddie.

I understand why he had to be shipped out, she said, glaring at him. He was getting edgy even before his father was killed, for some ungodly reason wanting to get back into that miserable jungle. Maybe I understand that in part, too; I knew when I married him that he's another god-damned bred in the bone soldier. It's *how* you humiliated him, and in front of me, goddamnit.

He saw Crusty in her, heard Crusty in the way she hurled the words, and turned away before she saw the dampness in his eyes. Gloria would soon get over her anger; it would take much longer for her to mask the hurt for her grandfather.

"I'll send Joann up to help," he said, and went out, knowing she wouldn't answer.

Minerva met him at the foot of the stairs. "Preston, I declare—if that side of beef doesn't arrive soon, I just don't know how I'm going to have a proper dinner prepared for all our guests. It will probably have to be tenderized, and—"

He braced upon his cane. "What side of beef? And where did you order it?"

Her colorless mouth tightened. "You know very well that important guests cannot dine on just anything, on—on cornpone and fatback. Besides, we need those silly ration points for pork, as well. I just do not comprehend—"

"Damnit, Minerva! Where are you getting black market beef?"

"Preston, how dare you—" she stared into his face and lowered her voice. "From the same man who delivers to Senator Whatley."

"That mindless, arrogant son of a—listen: Kill Devil Hill does not, I repeat *not,* deal on the black market. These generals and politicians can find out what it's like to eat like common folk. Give them field peas and cornbread and molasses.''

Her lips quivered. "This family has a reputation to uphold. It will be impossible for me to—"

He eased off. "A reputation, yes; an image of honor and honesty. How did we make out during the War between the States? We fed our workers first and set an example ourselves. The Hill made its own candles and soap, patched old clothes and sewed new things out of sheets and drapes.''

"Since you put it that way—but during that war there simply wasn't food or goods to be had, especially after those Yankees stripped us of every little thing they could carry off.''

That war was more real to Minerva Carlisle than this one; she still lived its history. He said, "I'm sure you'll work it out," and headed for the back porch, his bum leg aching.

If he thought it would do any good, he would report Senator Whatley's supplier, but the honorable gentleman from Massachusetts would squash any punitive action, to protect his own good name.

Kee-rist! Some men had to fight the wars that other men started, and that some didn't even realize were going on, or just didn't give a damn.

CHAPTER 17

INTERNATIONAL NEWS SERVICE—Allied Headquarters, South Pacific, Aug. 3, 1943: As island campaigns here progress from one bloody coral atoll to another brutal jungle, we are learning more about our fanatic enemy. It is often difficult to separate his bravery from sheer stupidity, and too often his tenacity is without point; the celebrated Banzai charges never achieve any important strategic results.

In his willingness to die, he often lets death become an end, forgetting that by dying he is supposed to do some good for his country, not just earn a one way ticket to that weird Oriental Valhalla reserved for men killed in combat. So fixated on death does he sometimes become that he does not wait to be killed. High ranking officers, as well as men in the ranks, are following the example of defeated Colonel Ichiki who committed suicide on Guadalcanal, and take their own lives rather than go down fighting.

Whether the Jap war gods allow credit for this kind of exit has never been established, but a Marine sergeant said it this way: "Hell, they ain't supermen; they're just a bunch of tricky little bastards."

Crusty Carlisle thought of cousin Ben Alexander's gassed lungs. A hell of a time for thinking at all while he tried to save his own ass in the surf that slammed cursing into the reef. Ben's lungs wouldn't take him far in this kind of pucker time, but how about the lousy arthritis in Crusty's shoulders?

"What goddamned arthritis?" he grunted and got another mouthful of salty bubbles.

Sharp, hard things tore at his knees and ripped his hands; fucking coral. Blinded by the sea, he rolled across the ledge and into water that wasn't trying to kill him—not right away, anyhow.

Bicycling slow feet, he wiped at his eyes and looked around for the others. The sailor might make it, but wounded as badly as he was, the kid Woodall wouldn't have much chance, unless—there he was, bobbing close by!

Crusty bellied toward him as more white water foamed over the reef. The kid was fighting; he saw an arm rise and fall, and then he had him, gripped him by the slippery collar of the fatigue jacket. They both went under when a wave slapped Crusty hard.

This time his feet scraped bottom, and he pushed up, went down, pushed up until his knees skidded along wet sand. Gasping, choking, he tugged at the boy's dead weight and fell on his face, lifted along by the rolling sea. He didn't dare shift his grip; if he turned loose now, he'd never get a hold again.

"Too—t—too goddamn much for—for an old bastard—oh shit!" His shoulder tried to twist out of its socket, and this time the wave broke him away from Woodall. They were just beyond the surf line.

Spitting sand and about to throw up, Crusty struggled to get a knee under his weight and found the kid before the sea snatched him back out. Chest heaving, eyes burned, Crusty took him by both thin wrists and pulled. A few inches, a few more. . . .

The sound broke through sea noises, a high, thin whistle that wasn't a whine, goddamnit; it was much closer to the keening of the Celts, the gut-deep mourning of Culloden forever lost.

"Hang on, son! I don't know where the hell we are, but we won't drown. Hang on and I'll find—"

Woodall's face was whiter than the sea had scrubbed it, the few boy hairs of unshaven cheeks glistening in the sun. Those poor torn guts, the cracked ribs; this boy had enough sand in his craw to build a beach of his own. Crusty slid them both higher and Woodall's lips worked, but the keening didn't force itself through clamped teeth. Crusty leaned over and put his ear to the boy's mouth.

A bubble broke against his ear lobe: "Not—not much use, sir. Been a fine thing—s—serving with you, general. I wish—I wish—"

Sitting back, Crusty pried Woodall over onto his back and closed the blue staring eyes that never had a chance to see much. "I wish, too, son."

Head sagged, his chest pumping for breath and his bum shoulders giving him holy hell, Crusty pulled into himself for strength. Keep your crotch dry, he remembered; nothing makes a soldier lose interest quicker than wet balls. Fat chance of getting dry for awhile, if ever; he had no idea what kind of land he was on. It could be a bare coral strip washed over by the murderous sea in bad weather, but he wasn't bitching; it was solid and didn't pitch and sway.

What else was it about balls? He retched, salty saliva mixing with salty water. Spitting, he breathed deeper as his memory showed him obsolete blue fatigues and beat-up campaign hats, flat tin helmets that jarred over his eyes and banged his nose at every shoulder wallop of the 03 Springfield.

Oh yeah, balls—the creed of the old soldier: keep your belly full and your balls empty. If he wasn't crowding his luck, he might find things to eat. He spat again; no hula girls, though, and what the hell would he do with them, anyway?

"Hey, general!"

Raising his head, Crusty saw the sailor kneeled at the other side of Woodall's body.

Sullivan wore an angry red slash across his left cheekbone and didn't have much uniform left. "Damn—the kid didn't make it."

"He tried. That boy never stopped trying."

Sullivan moved fingertips tenderly along his cheek. "Wonder where we are."

"Alive, but only for now if it's Jap country. You see any trees, or only coral?" He was more tired than he could remember and had trouble staying in focus.

"Good treeline comes down pretty close to the beach—it looks kind of like jungle, but not anywhere near as thick as on the Canal. I can just about see both ends of this side where the beach curves back. It ain't little but I figure it ain't all that big, either. We got to find water."

Crusty sighed. "Can you make out any wreckage of the raft? If we're among Japs, we'd better hide it. Either way, we'll need any usable scraps. First let's drag this boy out of sight. We can bury him in the sand later."

Sullivan hesitated, then said, "Yeah, I guess that's only right. I'm so beat just now, I only want to crap out, but no chance, right?"

Climbing to his other sore knee with a grunt, Crusty balanced a moment and the green smells of fetid jungle wafted to him, dying on a puff of clean air swirling in over the sea. Now he was conscious of the late afternoon sun working him over, sucking moisture from his tattered clothing and leaving bumps of salt behind to itch his sunbaked skin.

Now he also felt the coral cuts sting his hands and knees, and wondered about infection. In this unwiped ass end of the world, evil microorganisms thrived even in the sea. It used to be, an open wound washed in sea water stood a good chance of healing. Not now; not here; every scratch would get infected. Hell, sea horses were probably already hatching in his torn knees.

Sea horses were dumber than swabbies, he remembered, at least the males were. Mama popped a few hundred eggs in the male's pouch where he fertilized them. Then he got to swell up yay big until all those little bastard sea horses broke out. Where was mama, out screwing around some other racetrack? No wonder the seahorse was the only male, flesh, fish or fowl to give birth. Any more, and all the biological lines would die out.

"Take hold of his wrists and we'll skid him up into the trees. Kick sand over any marks we leave."

"Looks so flat now, and he's so damned little."

"Big as most soldiers, bigger than some."

"Yeah, I guess."

In the dappled shadows of Nipa palm trees, Crusty rested. The sand was deep here and soft, offering sleep and rest. He rubbed his face. It wouldn't be difficult to dig, as soon as he got some gas back in his tank. Dig with what? Their hands, if they had to, if they couldn't find chunks of loose coral or broken tree limbs, anything so they could scoop out a shallow grave. The kid had that much coming.

"Hang in, general. I'll check on that wreckage."

"It's good to be young."

Sullivan caressed his cut cheek. "Hell, it's good just to *be*."

Eyes closing, Crusty put his back carefully against the hairy trunk of a palm. Find water; if he remembered right, some kind of long cabbage might grow around here, a little juice in its heart. Or in tree trunks where branches spread to find more room—that kind might have cups to capture rain water.

A spring; good lord, a cool clear spring bubbling up in green shade. He could taste that kind of Sandhurst Keep water sliding down to ease his dry throat. In the raft they had been dehydrating fast, wringing every drop of moisture from the tough flesh of their prize shark. Now their bodies would need some catching up.

Coconuts, he thought; where palms grew, there would be coconuts, and sand crabs and some kind of mussels clinging to rocks, unwary minnows and maybe an octopus. Goddamn sand crabs smelled like roasted shit when smashed, but a starving man could hold his nose. They were all things that would furnish the vital juices of life for bigger, stronger things to feed upon. The law of the jungle; the way of the world.

His eyes snapped open when the rifle fired from deeper

in the trees, a vicious whiplash of deadly sound, and Crusty hunched in reflex, tired muscles drawing tight.

Down on the beach, Sullivan yelled in shock. "Goddamn!"

The New York Times—New York, N.Y., Aug. 5, 1943: Teenagers rioted at the Paramount here today, as Harry James and his orchestra opened to 5,500 screaming fans. They broke windows, fought each other, jitterbugged on stage and in the aisles until dragged off. No one left after the first performance, which was followed by a showing of *China*, starring Alan Ladd. Harry James got them to leave by promising autographs at the stage door. When he didn't show up, another riot ensued.

Keenan Carlisle clamped both hands around a thick, warm mug, holding to its stability. The hospital coffee shop was crowded and noisy, peopled with strangers. The place itself was strange—chrome and glass and impossibly rich food smells; the unreal brightness overwhelmed him, and that goddamned juke box. He was uncomfortable with all of it, with the scrubbed and laughing kids. It had been a mistake, letting Nancy drag him off the ward and down here. He wasn't ready to accept this kind of surface civilization; maybe he would never be ready again.

He belonged back in the jungle, more of him became the ghostly *yonsei* than an American officer.

"That jukebox is so loud—"

She leaned from behind his wheelchair; goddamn baby buggy. Nancy didn't wear the antiseptic scents of a nurse, green soap and starch, but a floating odor of powder and lipstick and gardenias. He didn't remember his ex-wife smelling like that. There were moments even now when he didn't remember much about her. Once they must have been close, but their worlds split, and even though she was at his shoulder now, he was much farther away.

"Just a minute, Keenan. I have to go on duty, so another

nurse will take you back when I call." She left a trail of gardenias.

Gardenias. Somewhere in a vast and hungry land, in the endless chains of dark mountains and the burned dry plains of China, perhaps there lingered an echo of another perfume. Sandalwood meant Chang Yen Ling, heightened by her own golden sweat. Oh Jesus, Yen Ling in the water, the water bloody with sharks.

His hands tightened on the cup and he fought the hard chill that shook him, a grinding of bones that might be the onset of a vicious attack of dengue fever or the lesser pains of malaria.

It passed. The roaring in his ears died away.

". . . though it would do you good to mix with people. You've been so long away. When I come off shift, I'll bring telegrams from the family, those who could be reached. And tonight you can expect calls from the mainland. Keenan . . ."

Swallowing as the chill subsided, he looked up at her.

"Keenan, I'm so glad you're back."

His voice sounded odd in his ears, as if jungle rot had gotten inside, thickened and pained it with tendrils. "I don't know how I feel. Maybe I'm glad."

She touched his cheek. "I—oh hell. Everybody still cares about you. I was so shocked at finding your name, and seeing you like—I mean, you've been carried MIA, and I din't really believe—oh, here she is. Hi, Susie; this is Major Carlisle; his first time off the ward. I'll see you later, Keenan."

He didn't look at her or at the other woman who touched the back of his chair. "Ready to go back now, major?" A softer, less assured voice than Nancy's. That too was strange; Nancy had never been that certain of herself before. But neither had he expected to see her in uniform. Nancy a nurse? "Wherever it's quiet."

He raised his head only high enough to make out the name tag: LOKOMAIKAI; a Hawaiian.

How could he explain his ears so long attuned to the slightest sound that didn't belong? The howling of monkeys and the shriek of rainbowed birds didn't register, no more than the scuttling of hardshell insect or slinking animal, because they were part of the jungle. A faint clink of metal, a careless slap at a bug, a bush whispering where there was no wind—these were sounds that made you a survivor, or made you dead.

Softly beneath the hard rubber tires of the wheelchair, inlaid tiles clicked. He watched them blur, focusing upon simplicity and shutting out the raw noises, closing off the too-bright lights and too-clean odors. When the nurse turned him around a corner of the corridor, he smelled flowers again; not Nancy's gardenias, but more delicate.

His private room, maybe assigned to him more through doctors worrying what exotic diseases he might spread, rather than Rank Hath Its Privileges. What the hell was rank, these days? With Mao's troops, nobody wore insignia, yet the leaders were known to the ranks.

The room was a white and green box that shut him in, and he halfway expected to hear the click of a lock. They hadn't gotten around to that. If he didn't watch himself, they might.

"If there's anything you need, major—"

Nice voice, throaty; the light flower perfume. Small hands but strong, helping him to the bed. Lying back in a sudden weak sweat, he looked up at her.

"Jesus Christ!"

She flinched back from the bed, a slim, sun-golden woman with midnight hair drawn up under her nurse's cap, dark eyes wide at the moment, but cast in that special shape, that certain slant. An Oriental woman.

Not Yen Ling. Nobody could be Yen Ling, but this smaller woman might have been her sister. He said it again: "Oh Christ."

"Are you in pain?"

She was afraid of him, this woman of medicine, as Yen Ling had been of medicine and compassion.

"Yes, but nothing anybody can help. My—Nancy called you Susie?"

The alert stiffness went out of her. "You're in the is-

160

lands, major. Everybody here got a little mixed in the whirl-pool, the *mimilo*. It doesn't matter much—names, races, religion, it all goes around in the whirlpool. Sueko is just as easy to say, and easier than Lokomaikai, but Susie works all right. *Ohana*—all in the family."

She was different, but somehow little glowing parts of her were Yen Ling, or maybe he was so damned tired that his fuzzy mind wrapped her in old dreams.

He felt her new easiness with him, still tentative, but warming. "Lie back, major. I'll take your vital signs, and then I'll bring you some ice cold pineapple juice. If you don't like pineapple, you better learn."

Sticking a thermometer in his mouth, she moved around the foot of the bed for the blood pressure kit higher up. He heard the chart holder rattle. She said, "Same name as Lieutenant Carlisle; are you related to—"

"Used to be married to her," he said around the glass tube.

Susie gasped. "That is *hana pau*, man!"

Rolling the thermometer under his tongue, eyes closed and the sweats slicking his entire body now, Keenan waited.

"Pau," she repeated, "like quitting time." She took back the thermometer.

Eyes still closed against light and the growing number of things he couldn't handle, Keenan whispered to the shades of good men, to the memory of a woman, to himself: "Nobody quits. The Japs still owe."

Did he hear a catch in the nurse's voice? "Not what I meant, major. And sometimes its more better to quit before you start."

CHAPTER 18

UNITED PRESS—The Sicilian Front, Aug. 5, 1943: Determined
U.S. troops battered at German defense lines burrowed
deeply into these rugged mountains. Enemy resistance
has stiffened hour by hour, and heavy artillery on both
sides keeps this end of the island shuddering with the
cannonading.

American planes generally control the skies, but they must
fight for it and arrow down upon Messerschmitts, Focke-
Wulfs and Stukas that scream in to dive bomb and strafe
the attacking infantry and supporting redlegs.

Armor rumbles in to strike where it can, but these primitive
and exposed approaches to the beleagured city of Troina
were not designed for easy movement of tanks. German
armor has been decimated, but is still capable of attack,
and the panzer survivors tend to break suddenly from careful
cover.

Often, when our tanks can be used, they become mobile
artillery, in reality gun platforms that move in support of rifle
companies needing help. More so than usual, the outcome
of this battle will be determined by the not so ordinary foot
soldier, courageous, cynical and tough. He expects no fa-
vors and will certainly not extend any.

Chad Belvale snatched the handset and yelled into it. "Lift
your fire, goddamnit! Lift it! You're too close to my people.

Up two hundred yards—two hundred, I said. If one more short round lands anywhere near my lead companies, I'm coming back there and kick some asses."

Handing back the phone, he told his operator to alternate contact with Fox and George companies. "Langlois? Get back there and pinpoint our forward positions for the artillery."

"On my way, colonel. If I have to chew out anybody at the 33rd Field, it'll take a few minutes. Then I got to find our companies. They're about to get knocked off that hill, yeah. So I expect we got to climb back up."

Passing a hand over his unshaven face, Chad said, "It's not all the fault of the guns; the lines are too tight for a division artillery shoot, and each regiment calls for its own fire support. Bound to be some screw ups."

He slumped to sit on a water can as Langlois ducked out of the CP hole freshly dug in a ratty hillside. Patting his pockets, he found a bent cigarette and dangled it unlighted between his lips. Damn, if he was this tired, what about the poor bastards on the line, gone sleepless for days but for uneasy, edge of consciousness catnaps?

What about his son? Hang in, boy; just hang in, Owen.

Chad used three paper matches to get the cigarette lighted. The enemy still held the high ground north of Troina, from Mount Acuto along the ridge east of Elia to the heights of Rene Purrazo. South of the target city and Highway 120, the Germans held the ridgelines from Hill 1033 to Hill 816, and then southwest to Mount Gregorio and Mount Salici. G-2 said that the 1st Battalion of the Panzer Grenadier Regiment III, 15th Panzer Division and the 1st Battalion of the 15th Motorized Infantry, 29th Division, held strongpoints south and west of Troina. The efficient 88s and automatic weapons were well sited, and scout planes reported prime movers dug in, ready to haul out the big guns to fight another day. Even when high ground was lost, the enemy launched immediate counterattacks. The Krauts had no intention of giving up Sicily and their fresh replacements still crossed the Straits of Messina in the dead of night to avoid interdiction by air.

When this campaign was at last wrapped, where on the boot of the mainland would the next landings be? Chad had little doubt what outfit would go in with the first wave— the experienced troops, the combat hardened survivors, the lucky few. Six little, five little, four little Indians—

What the hell. That's what they pay us for.

Special to *The New York Times*—Allied Headquarters, Sicily, Aug. 5: One of war's regrettable accidents occurred near here today. Reports from a battered battalion of the Big Red One, (the proud new nickname correspondents have given the 1st Infantry Division) said it was dug in atop a captured hill, out of drinking water and food, and running low on ammunition.

An air drop was set up to supply these troops, but it was unsuccessful; all parachutes drifted behind enemy lines. Then American planes roared in low to bomb this luckless unit. A tight-lipped headquarters spokesman said such inevitable accidents were the price paid by victorious troops for advancing too swiftly beyond their initial objective.

"The word doesn't reach the air force in time," he commented. "and the planes hit the right coordinates, but it's where the Heinies only used to be. What can we do about it? We pray."

When this story was filed, the battalion had just come under a fierce counterattack.

Lt. Sloan Travis spread out like a disturbed sidewinder, not to make himself appear larger than life and spook a predator, but to get flat as possible, and below the bullets, the whizzing fragments that searched for him.

"Wait!" he shouted at the section of machine guns with him on this misbegotten hilltop. He yelled it for the benefit of Fox Company's riflemen, too. Their platoon leader had been killed by American bombing, leaving Sloan the only brass, forcing him to inherit the command. He didn't want it. "Wait until the mortars lift, then pop up quick because they'll be right behind."

Swoosh—BLAMM!

The Krauts were serious about retaking this high ground, and the U.S. Air Force had unwittingly given them a hand, first by missing the air drop zone, and delivering all the goodies to the enemy, then by their bombing accuracy, the bastards. When the outfit got pulled off line, if ever they did, Sloan had it in mind to find an airstip and beat the shit out of the nearest pilot, unseen of course.

Why hadn't he gone into the then Army Air Corps? Because the pilots weren't handcuff volunteers; they didn't get drafted, but came into the service on their own, junior birdmen looking for glamor and trouble. Which would be okay, if they didn't spend half their time killing GIs and then flying back to safe billets and clean sheets, to cold beer and warm women far, far in the rear.

And to draw extra pay for "hazardous duty."

Swoosh—BLAMM!

Nobody even said thanks to the grimy dogface soldier, much less boosted his pay. Hazardous duty; what the hell was this, the day before the senior prom?

Powdersmoke drifted over his shallow hole in the ground to lie metallic upon his tongue and he wiped muddy sweat from his dusty cheeks and forehead. Unless they got help, this outfit was in bad shape. When the ammo was gone, that would be it, and odds were that the Krauts had no time or inclination for prisoners.

Brrrppp! Brrrppp!

Schmeissers; the Krauts were climbing the slope behind the sweeping fire of their burpguns. Among the ripping noises from the high cyclic rate of fire weapons, Sloan made out the slow, heavier *pops!* of German rifles.

The Fifth Squad's gun opened first: short burst, pause, short burst, as if the gunner was back on the range at Camp Blanding, that cool as he counted off five-round bursts for the 1000-inch E target.

On both Sloan's flanks, the M-1 rifles and carbines opened up, not hysterical, but calm, spaced fire. These men were mainly professionals, aware of their duty and their responsibility to their buddies, their position in the close knit family of the infantry platoon. They would stay here and fight to the last round of ammunition, and that wasn't far off.

Boom!

Grenade; GI, heaved downhill to bounce once and explode, like the infamous Bouncing Betty mines favored by German engineers. The least you could expect as those antipersonnel things were tripped and sprang into the air to go off and spread hot steel fragments, was bad belly wounds or the loss of a leg. Some argued that, like the Castrator boobytrap, the Betty had been designed to blow off a man's balls.

Now, Sloan thought, and lifted to his knees. A German sergeant had just reached the top of the steep slope; he gasped from the climb, and his eyes widened as Sloan popped up from his hole. Sloan gutshot him, and as the man fell, pumped another shot from his M-1 into the rolling body. Other dark helmets bobbed steadily up the hill.

Sloan dropped one and the rest fell back to cover.

Bullets tore at the dirt beside Sloan's knees, and he dropped, too. He could swear that he saw blue smoke puffs there and remembered that the Krauts were said to sometimes use exploding wooden bullets. So much for the Geneva Convention.

Taking off his helmet to make less of a target, he eased one eye over the edge of his hole for a peep. Something moved below, so he angled the M-1 over and spread its remaining five rounds over the area; the clip *pinged!* away and he reloaded; one more clip left.

On his flanks, the friendly fire dwindled, and for the first time since he had been forced into uniform, he thought of his own mortality. Until now being killed happened only to other men, to soldiers run out of luck. He wasn't a soldier, not really; he was a civilian out of place, a writer, a poet—

> . . . I have a rendezous with death
> at some disputed barricade . . .

Oh shit. Alan Seegar had been a poet, and so was Joyce Kilmer. Seegar wrote of death and Kilmer of trees, but both had been killed in that other frigging war, the one to end all frigging wars. Oh shit.

Boom! Boom!

On his right, the grenading flurried, and then stopped. No more frags, but there might be some of the weird rifle grenades left. The guys were loath to fire the yellow finned things; some blew up on the end of the rifle when the trigger was pulled. If only that damned air drop had gotten through with the ammunition. The richest country in the world, the most productive, and it could spare only one screwed-up drop, only a little ammo and a few seriously flawed grenades.

How and why in the name of common sense had the family remained the holy warriors for hundreds of years? So many fuckups, so much bullshit at the higher echelons.

Rrripp—rripp!

Too close; they were on the hill. It was time to haul ass, for the troops to get out and make their way down the hill the best they could. If they could. Krauts were all over the place.

Then a fresh set of M-1s and BARs chorused, a beautiful, thundering roar that rose from the rear and the left flank; help coming in the nick of time. They ought to be cavalry, yellow guidons flying, bugles trumpeting the charge, and John Wayne leading them.

Sloan did his jack-in-the box again, to pump round after round down the enemy held slope while the Krauts were confused by the flank attack.

"Fire! Fire! Pour it on the bastards!"

The M-1's slide locked back, emptied for another clip to be thumbed in, but he had no clips. Sinking back to his knees, he panted for air as the merciless sun hammered him and the acrid taste of burned powder filled his dry mouth. His head jerked around at a noise behind him.

"Lieutenant Travis, I presume?"

Owen squatted there grinning, rifle across his thighs.

Sloan's lips were so dry that his answering grin hurt his

lips. "I never knew how beautiful you are, you crazy son of a bitch."

"Me—I'm pretty, too?" Major Langlois carried a BAR at his hip.

"You're even crazier. The battalion exec doesn't go cowboying off with the posse."

"Hey, now I know that."

Owen said, "Tell us about it later. Right now we have to get the hell off this hill. They're mounting a bigger attack, and there's not enough of us. We'll be back."

Of course; they would come back again and again, for as many times as it took. The old soldiers that didn't make it would leave a legacy for the draftee replacements, and they would always retake the high ground.

Rifle at port, Sloan stumbled down the reverse slope of the hill after Owen Bevale's little band of rescuers.

EYES ONLY, Kill Devil Hill secret file, Aug. 6, 1943: Secretary of State General George C. Marshall called a high level secret meeting here today. Present were Admiral Ernest J. King, chief of naval operations and Air Force Chief of Staff Hap Arnold, Secretary of War Henry L. Stimson and representatives of Winston Churchill who were authorized to speak for him. Generals Preston Belvale and Benjamin Alexander swept the house free of all civilian personnel. Marine armed guards blocked all entrances with orders to allow no one in or out until personally cleared by General Marshall.

Preston Belvale sat in the back of the room and learned things about the big picture battle plans he had not heard before. General Marshall recapped the arguments pro and con for last year's action.

"You recall that five plans were considered," Marshall said. "One—a British-American move against French North Africa; two—an entirely American operation against Morocco; three—combined operations against northern Norway; four—the reinforcement of Egypt and lastly—the reinforcement of Iran. I reluctantly agreed to the first idea, which became Operation Torch. As most of you know, in 1942 I held out for a direct cross-channel invasion designed to drive a dagger into the heart of Germany itself. I can tell you now that such landings will not be mounted this year, either."

Belvale took the note Ben Alexander slid over to him. It read: Churchill argued against crossing the channel so soon, and came up with Sicily instead. I think he's still smarting from the Dieppe raid.

Belvale jotted down his answer: I'm damned glad we didn't try it. Operation Torch cost the Afrika Korps more than a hundred thousand in casualties and PWs, and about a million tons of equipment. Add all that to the defense forces already in place in Normandy, and we'd play hell getting ashore, much less move inland.

Marshall went on. "Joe Stalin wants everything to go his way, and right now. He doesn't consider Africa and Sicily of great importance. Only attacks through France and/or Southern France will please him by pulling pressure off the Russian front."

Alexander leaned close to whisper. "Stalin doesn't consider anyone but Stalin. That whole weird country suffers from extreme paranoia. We bring truckloads of war supplies to Alaska and Iceland airports for quick shipment, supplies that Mother Russia desperately needs, but they won't allow anybody to even peep inside their transport planes. Who is on whose side?"

"Don't give them the stuff," Belvale said. "They've got a hundred thousand troops massed on the China border, and insist upon hoarding them. They're not helping a damned bit against Japan. Let them sweat it out for a while."

"Roosevelt can't see it that way. Good old Joe, he says."

"Good old Joe will gobble up all of Europe, once Germany is whipped."

General Marshall pulled down a map of the Mediterranean area. "Since Mussolini bit the bullet in July, other possibilities are open to us—mass landings on Italy proper, a quick thrust through the Balkans, here and here. Personally, I still favor a cross channel attack and as soon as possible."

One of the Britishers raised his hand and Marshall nodded. The man stood up, and Belvale thought he looked uncomfortable in civvies.

"Sir," he said, "Colonel Kirkland here; the Prime Minister agrees that a channel attack must be made, to bring Germany to its knees. But Mister Churchill feels the landings must be immediately successful. We cannot risk losing the initiative, once the operation is launched."

Henry Stimson cleared his throat. "Colonel, in some quarters here, the feeling is that the British motive is a bit too akin to traditional British imperialism. The thought seems to be that when all of Italy and a broad share of the Balkans is taken, this will allow the Allies—mainly the British—to move into central Europe and stake claims long before the Russians get there."

"Sir—the Prime Minister feels that the same objectives are obtainable by exploiting the Mediterranean theater. He also feels that if the Americans had placed as much emphasis on the Mediterranean as they wished to place on the cross channel operation, the war in Europe would not have been hampered by the shortages of men and material which were husbanded for the channel attack."

Alexander nudged Belvale. "MacArthur ought to be here. He says the same thing every time an LST goes to Eisenhower instead of one more Landing Ship Tank to beef up his island hopping campaign. He squalls whenever he hears of something going to the Brits instead of coming to him. Japan is the enemy, and Hitler only comic opera. The Pacific, first last and always."

"Shh," Belvale whispered. "Marshall's about to fire both barrels."

"Gentlemen," George Marshall said, "I quote from a War Department letter to President Roosevelt: We cannot now rationally hope to be able to cross the channel and

170

come to grips with our German enemy under a British commander.''

Colonel Kirkland's jaw tightened and he sat down.

Marshall went on: ''The shadows of Passchendale and Dunkirk fall too heavily upon the leaders of England. Though they have rendered lip service to the operation, their hearts are not in it, and it will require more independence, faith, and vigor than it is reasonable to expect to find in any British commander. The atmosphere of his government is such that too many obstacles remain to be overcome, and too many side avenues of diversion capable of thwarting such an operation. Therefore the War Department suggests that when Operation Overlord is scheduled, that an American commander be named.''

''Damn,'' Belvale murmured, ''it'll hit the fan now. Montgomery and Patton are already trying to get the jump on each other in Sicily, racing to Salerno and the big headlines, and screw a slow, thorough job.''

''Dunkirk, everybody knows,'' Alexander whispered. ''But Passchendale?''

Barely moving his lips, Belvale said, ''Small town near Ypres in Belgium. You were gassed and in the hospital about then. In 1917 the Brits took it after very heavy losses, and along came the Krauts to take it back.''

Stimson stood up again. ''Reports from the Sicilian campaign are bright; we are advancing on all fronts, although slowly in some areas. Casualties are acceptable. As for the present situation in Europe, I may say that next year will be the earliest opportunity to change it. There will be a top-level meeting of British, American and Chinese chiefs later this year. All concerned will be notified. ''Thank you, gentlemen; that is all.''

Belvale stood back against the wall as the big brass filed out, nodding to those he knew personally. When the last man was gone, he lighted a cigar and thumbnailed his moustache. Ben Alexander coughed and pressed a white handkerchief to his lips.

Belvale said, ''The last report on Penny and her English friend said they passed the first checkpoint off Borneo,

171

where one group of Dyaks collected head money. If their luck holds they might make it to safety, if not to civilization. You heard that Keenan appeared again, not exactly fat and sassy, but indestructible, it seems, and with a reputation as some kind of ghost. Wingate and the Brits are putting him in for a decoration.

"Chad and Owen and the rest of the family are all right for now. Farley's on his way home, with a good chance of recovery."

"Gavin Scott's name appeared on a Swedish Red Cross list of POWS. But not a damned thing on Crusty," Alexander said. "I can use a drink."

CHAPTER 19

Berlin Illustrierie Zeitung—cover illustration SS troops: This is the oath taken by all members of this elite unit since its formation in 1933: I swear to you, Adolf Hitler, as Führer and Reich Chancellor, loyalty and bravery. I vow to you and those you have appointed to command me, obedience unto death. So help me God.

Feldwebel Arno Hindemit tore off the page, crumpled it and carefully wiped himself while squatting. "Such *scheissen;* theirs in the magazine, not mine. My shit is honest. I wish Herr Goebbels would print his propaganda on softer paper."

Hauptmann Franz Witzelei pulled up his trousers and kicked dirt over his leavings. "It is the captured *Ami* rations; our stomachs are not used to such richness."

Arno stuffed the tattered magazine into his field pack and cupped his hands to light a cigarette. "The tobacco is also rich. We thank you for your bounty, *Ami fliegers*. To have their pretty parachutes come down upon us instead of them—ah, it makes a man almost believe that the curse put upon *landsers* may at times be lifted. But then I think—of course; fate holds out the carrot but keeps the club hidden. It will fall upon us when least expected."

"Obedience unto death," Witzelei quoted. "Not so long

173

past, I would have gloried in such a grand sentiment. But where is the mighty *Schutzstaffel,* the fight unto Death's Head regiments now, standing guard in Berlin bunkers? We could use them here and now, in their pretty black uniforms. And what great victories has Goebbels claimed lately?"

"Careful school master; as you have warned me many times, the Gestapo may be listening."

"Fuck the Gestapo; you will not find one of the bastards where the shells are falling."

"Now you speak like a true *landser, hauptmann.* Ah, Herr Goebbels—what is new beyond his latest mistress? Well, this strategic retrograde movement to straighten our lines can be turned into a masterful victory in Sicily. Any ground lost is due to the treachery of the Italians. The little cripple is a mighty talker. Did I ever tell you about the cocksman Goebbels and the beautiful Ann Obra?"

Witzelei buckled his belt. "What would such as you know about a motion picture actress? Come, let us get back to the position before the *Amis* launch another attack."

"One such as me was assigned as a waiter for *Herr* Goebbel's party. A *landser* sergeant ordered to wear a white jacket and pour wine as the *verdammt* Vons strutted about. Generals as thick as sweat on a pig's testicles, and a few junior officers back against the walls. Like Hauptmann Max Schmelling, once the heavyweight boxing champion of the world. Der Max was invited so he would attend with Ann Obra, his beautiful wife."

Witzelei grunted and led the way around the pile of boulders to the command post bunker.

Arno went on, "Goebbels played at being charming with every lady until he thought enough wine had been drunk. Then he cornered Ann Obra and pinched her butt. He should have first looked over his shoulder; Der Max stormed over and knocked the *Reich* minister flat upon his skinny ass. Of course the incident was hushed up and nothing done to Schmelling."

Witzelei climbed down into the hole and adjusted the strap of his helmet. "I wish Goebbels was here to explain away the *Amis* and why they continue to attack."

Arno slid into the hole and checked the clip of his *Schmeisser*. "Troina will soon be lost, and that will mean another retreat to the ocean. While you are wishing, ask that another boat will be there for us."

Field Report, G-3—0840, 6 Aug., 1943: A patrol of the 16th Infantry Regiment has reached Troina. Snipers in town; no armor, and the main body of enemy seen 11 kilometers northeast of Troina.

Field Report, G-3—0950, 6 Aug.—Battalion HQ reports area free of snipers and asks that engineers be sent to clear the heavily damaged town, special attention to be paid to enemy mines.

Field Report, G-2—0600, 7 Aug., 1943: 1st Infantry Division relieved by 9th Infantry Division and assigned II Corps Reserve; many attached units released. The division will remain in bivouac in the vicinity of Troina from this date to 12 August, where rest, rehabilitation and training will be stressed.

Chad Belvale slammed down the phone. "What the hell is wrong with those people? Training, my aching back; there's no wine left in this ragged-ass town; what the Krauts couldn't haul away, they poured out. Yeah, there might be a few starving girls ready to turn tricks for food, but there's no whorehouse as such. No booze and no pussy to ease the strain, but I'll see that my men at least get to sleep as much as they want. And if any rear echelon son of a bitch comes up here and asks about training, I'll have him roped and tied and jeeped up to the Ninth so he can be thrown to the Krauts."

Captain Owen Belvale nodded. "We're promised replacements ASAP. H Company can use some."

Eyeing his son, Chad saw a tired and worn company commander, but a combat soldier you could count on. It made him proud and scared him a little at the same time. Owen had led the rescue party that sprang Fox Company free, something that heavy weapons COs didn't do, if they went by the book. And Major Langlois was no better, damnit. Heroes died young.

He said, "Lieutenant Travis; how's he doing?"

"Couldn't ask for a better platoon leader; he hangs tough. He was on the hill, too."

"Too many officers on that damned hill."

"Are you telling me to stay in the rear?"

Chad shook his head. "I can't do that. I'd like to, but I can't. Just don't push your luck, son."

"Son," Owen said. "You haven't called me that for a long time."

"I think it."

Owen offered a cigarette. "I heard from mom; did you?"

"No." Chad made a project out of lighting their cigarettes with his battered Zippo. There had been no word on Stephanie, either. When combat slowed, the memories came flooding in; London, Scotland; her open laughter, the way she meshed with his every mood. Please stay alive, Stephanie.

Owen said, "Mom set up a riding program for patients at Harmon General Hospital. That's at Longview, Texas. She says it's working out fine."

"Texas, of course. Senator Shelby's back yard."

"Jim Shelby was killed on Guadalcanal. I guess you didn't know that, either."

"She doesn't write to me. I don't expect it."

Kirstin's husband; her other husband. It still irritated him, and that was stupid. Her marriage was no tit-for-tat revenge; Kirstin was an honest woman and wouldn't act that way. She must have loved the man deeply.

"Damn; your mother must have taken that hard. I'm sorry for her."

"Yeah," Owen said, tight-mouthed, and the closeness between them was gone. "She would appreciate that, coming from you. I'll see to my men now."

"Have a detail check for mines. Booby traps—"

"Yes, sir." And Owen was gone.

Damnit; Chad always managed to rub the kid the wrong way, because of the divorce. Part of it was that Owen wasn't a kid, but a good company commander. He didn't have to be told about the booby traps, as if he was some dumb replacement.

But the Krauts were fiendishly clever with explosives. In Africa, they'd flown low behind the lines and dropped pens, whistles, binoculars and the like. Unscrew a pen and it exploded, taking most of your fingers; blow a whistle and lose your face. Binoculars were the worst; they blew out your eyes. Then there were the castrators, Bouncing Bettys and antitank mines; mines set to explode days later to knock out support troops and spread panic. Sometimes they got aid stations or supply dumps.

Planes roared overhead and Chad flinched in reflex. They were American, but he'd been too long under German control of the skies, too familiar with their dive bombing and strafing. The sound of any plane motor pushed his reaction button and made him look for cover.

Chad wondered if he'd ever get over that. He thought that would be when he stood upon the front porch of Kill Devil Hill, grateful for its coolness and the purple scent of wisteria. That could be years from now. Sicily was on the verge of falling, but all of Italy's sharp mountains waited just across the Strait of Messina. An assault landing there would be near suicide for the first waves. Yet a foothold must be made on Europe proper, if only for propaganda purposes. Chad imagined Stalin was putting on the pressure for a second front.

He hoped some other outfit would be tagged for the invasion. After two seaborne landings, luck had to be running out for survivors of the First Division.

Field Report, G-2—8 Aug., 1943: First Engineers removed
on the road and bypasses to Novara, at least 500 "S"
mines and 500 Teller mines. The CO of the 32nd Field
Artillery Battalion states that his unit lost more men because
of mines, in this final phase of the operation than had been
lost throughout the entire campaign to conquer Sicily.

Use of mines became heavier during the final period. Into
the defense and withdrawal from Troina and Randazzo, the
enemy succeeded cleverly in breaking contact by the well
planned siting of mines and demolitions. This points to long
and careful preparations made before the actual fighting had
advanced to these sectors.

All troops are to be cautioned that areas near blown
bridges are heavily sown with antitank and antipersonnel
mines. Stream beds are invariably suspect. Repeat, all
troops are to be warned.

Owen Belvale climbed into the resurrected jeep. Bullet and
shell fragment gouges marked its wounds, but Ordnance
Company had brought it back to life. All glass was gone
from the windshield frame, and the seats were darkly
stained. Standing erect, he thrust his right fist into the air
and pumped it up and down, the signal to his short convoy
to move out. The pull back was coming off piecemeal, unit
by unit moving out as transport was made available.

It was a blessing to ride, after walking and climbing
across this whole miserable island. It was more of a blessing to be heading away from what might have turned into
a staging area. That didn't mean they were home free, because the big brass were buttoned up and saying nothing.
But moving away from Messina was a good sign.

He wanted no part of a thrust at what the press delighted
in calling the "soft underbelly of Europe." Soft, their civilian asses. Italy would be one steep damned mountain after
another, and winter was just around the corner; ice and
mud, freezing rain and too many Krauts to count, all dug

in, their 88s zeroed in on every approach. Any outfit slated for Italy would need a lot of luck.

And the Big Red One? The only word Owen had was that they were headed south to go aboard ship again. Not goddamned Italy, he had asked in the regimental staff meeting, and the only answer he got was his father telling him to be quiet. And the next meeting was for field grade officers only. They might be headed for Italy. He just hoped the hell not, and Colonel Belvale wouldn't tell him one way or the other; by the book Belvale.

Christ; what did it take to get close to his father? Any time his mother was mentioned, the old man clammed up or changed the subject except for a few minutes ago, when he was told of Shelby's death. The divorce and her marriage were facts, and he had brought the divorce on himself. At first Owen had blamed his mother, but he had overheard a conversation between her and Nancy Carlisle. He wouldn't have pictured his father as a swinger. A boozer, yes, but that was in the past.

Dust rolled up when the jeep slowed, and he saw engineers still sweeping the shoulders of the road for mines. So many men lost and more to come. The 16th Infantry Regiment listed five officers and 87 EM killed in action, 39 officers and 357 EM wounded in action. And the kicker was five officers and 128 enlisted men carried as Missing in Action. MIA, bullshit. A few might show up on hospital lists, and a few bodies discovered later, but most of the poor bastards would never be found. They had been blown to unidentified bloody rags or had their foxholes blasted in on them. Some would rot in hidden gulleys and shell holes.

The Sicilian campaign hadn't gone the way of field problems at West Point, not by the numbers in textbooks, but good enough in the long run. Owen would be happier if more Germans had surrendered and less Italians. He'd also be happy if he knew where the hell the outfit was headed.

CHAPTER 20

ASSOCIATED PRESS—Allied Headquarters in North Africa, Aug. 9, 1943: The Allies have carried the land campaign against the Nazis in Italy to the vicinity of Naples.

Naples is a city of almost a million population, and although there is no indication just how close to the city proper the landing or landings were, it is plain that Naples is the objective of the seaborne invasion. Rumors have it that other landings have taken place at Genoa, Pizzo, Geta and Leghorn, but no confirmation is forthcoming.

Allied Headquarters in North Africa—all wire services and individual reporters, 10 Sept., 1943: This is an official announcement: Italy has surrendered unconditionally. All hostilities between that country and the United Nations have ceased. An armistice was signed the same day that Italy was invaded, but the victors reserved the right to withhold announcements until the most favorable moment for the Allies. The armistice terms have been approved by the United States, Britain and Russia.

General Dwight D. Eisenhower, announcing the surrender, promised support to all Italians who help fight the Germans, and reports of partisan guerilla activity are already coming in.

The time and the place would never be better. Lieutenant Gavin Scott checked the terrain against the aerial map he carried in his head, and blinked at the wooden sign leaning beside the road: Rottwell. The PW convoy had entered Germany proper, then; they'd left Austria behind them. Something big must have come off, to make the Jerries hurry along like that. The PWs couldn't know what until they stopped rolling and set up camp. Then the clandestine radio would bring the news up to date as the PWs pieced it together. On the move certain men carried parts of the radio, to make it difficult for the Jerries to find it. But whatever the news, good or bad, Gavin intended to get away.

Rottwell was on the road to Stuttgart, a big city and political seat of the district. The guards had been talking about Stuttgart, brightening as if that would be the end of the line for them. Bouncing on a wooden seat, sardined among too many men, Gavin closed his eyes and pictured the map. Eighty or ninety miles west southwest lay the border of Switzerland and freedom. He couldn't wait much longer; there was no telling how far into Germany they were being taken.

He tasted dust and smelled the unwashed bodies of the Limeys packed around him, the Limeys and one other American lieutenant added to the roster only a few days back. Joe Hillman naturally gravitated toward his own kind, and Gavin made certain that the kid didn't become poisoned by the wait-forever, by-the-book escape committee.

The truck swayed and bumped over a secondary road. Eighty miles or so to neutral Switzerland. The Swiss might intern him, but give him time and he would find a way out. A little more time and he would rub his ruined face into Stephanie Bartlett's pretty mouth. If it cost him every dime of his slice of the family fortune, he meant to find the bitch and make her hurt for laughing at him.

First things first; escape and make it to the border. He held on to wooden slats as the truck slowed. Joe Hillman banged into him and said, "Sorry. I didn't expect the truck to stop."

"No sweat, kid." Gavin whispered the rest: "Stay close; this might be our chance."

The truck stopped. Nobody climbed down until the guards yelled *raus! raus!* Gavin got down slowly and stretched, counting the guards and their positions. They were getting careless, this close to home, bunching up to gossip, some of them putting their backs to the prisoners. Gavin looked over the field and grunted. It was too open, too far from the trucks to the tree line. They would be dropped in seconds if they split for the woods. If only—

Then he heard it, the familiar scream of a diving plane as it arrowed down upon the parked convoy. He glanced up at the silver twin booms of the American P-38 and didn't give a damn that its guns winked deadly red.

"Now!" he said and grabbed Joe Hillman's arm. "Run like hell for the trees."

Everybody scattered for some kind of cover as the bullets *spranged!* into trucks and kicked lines of dirt across the open field. Guards and PWs alike scurried like so many rats, the prisoners yelling son of a bitch at the fighter plane as it pulled out of its dive and clawed for altitude.

Head down and arms pumping, Gavin stretched for the trees, a spot between his shoulders reminding him what a target he made. He didn't look up or around when the plane roared back for another low strafing run, but he blessed the pilot who thought he had stumbled upon a fat Kraut convoy as a target of opportunity. And he hoped the machine pistols of the guards wouldn't touch the guy.

The conifers were thick, their shadows deep and heavily scented with green. Gavin plunged into them, slowing only to avoid low hanging limbs. Joe Hillman pounded behind him and Gavin could hear the kid panting hard. He rounded a worn finger of rock and dropped down into a shallow gulley that had been carved by a narrow stream. Splashing along it, he kept going until it curved the wrong way.

Gasping for air and sweating hard, he went to earth on a slope between two young pines. Hillman dropped beside him. Gavin heard the plane sweep away, followed by an explosion that said one of the trucks blew up. He heard

Schmeissers, too, and wondered if other PWs were making a break or if the Krauts were firing at the plane out of sheer frustration.

"We keep going west by southwest," he said when his heart slowed. "Plenty of mountains between here and Switzerland, and only patches of forest for cover. We'll haul ass now, before they hold head count and miss us. But after today, we travel only by night and hole up during daylight. It's not that far, and if our luck holds out, we'll make it in five or six days."

Five or six days in uniform through enemy country and not speaking the language, and no food, Gavin realized that they would need a hell of a lot of luck.

CIC Pacific Fleet, Pearl Harbor—13 Aug., 1943: Admiral Chester W. Nimitz issued a communiqué today that gave the first details of a raid on Marcus Island, which was also the combat test for the new carrier based fighter, the Grumman F6F, the Hell Cat.

Reports pointed out that the little island, only 1,185 miles from Tokyo, was a surprisingly well fortified air base, but was 90 percent destroyed by bombing and strafing. The Hell Cat fighters splashed 16 Jap Zeros and caught at least 20 on the ground, against 3 planes lost.

Penny Belvale would never get used to the damp tropical heat, to the blazing sun that struck like a great, soggy hammer. A rash irritated her armpits and itched her groin, but she could suffer that and anything else that the jungle and sea could throw at her. She was out of the prison camp and away from that son of a bitch Watanabe. He had lost much face when she escaped, and might take out his embarrassment on the other women. Some day, she thought; some wondrous day when the war was won and she searched him out. Then she would see how shiny and strutting Major Wobbly would be.

Don't do the *seppuku* thing, she breathed; don't commit *hara-kiri;* save that pleasure for me. Stay alive until I find you.

Lying flat beneath a veined and wide-leafed plant, she smelled the fungus, the ancient rot of the primeval jungle, and reached out to touch Stephanie's hand. Fear and suffering, she thought; it developed a bond that drew her closer to another woman than she had thought possible. Leftenant Bartlett was more than a friend, and more than a sister.

Stephanie said, "We're on one of the Natuna Islands, I think. Our guides keep repeating the name. Wee bits of land, too small for the Japs to bother with. Do you understand how these men can navigate so much empty ocean with only a few primitive instruments to steer the bloody canoes?"

"They grew up on the sea," Penny said, "when they weren't out taking heads to shrink."

"Och; you would mention that. No fear, I suppose, so long as your family makes it more profitable to keep ours on our shoulders. Such evil little men, especially the darker ones, the Dayaks."

Penny brushed a leggy green bug from her arm. "Pirates and head hunters; Moros, Malayans and Dayaks. They normally would be at each other's throats, but all of them understand the common denominator—gold. And the Dayaks came a long way to get us; I'd say we're well on the way to their land, to Borneo. Japs will certainly be there, but it's a big island to hide on."

Stephanie sighed and blew down the ragged front of her blouse, then fluttered the material. She was thinner and looked tired and vulnerable, but Penny remembered her killing Sergeant Katana, remembered the bloody knife. When the time of judgment came around, could Penny be as cold? Yes, she told herself, hell yes.

Stephanie said, "What I dinna ken is how your family could arrange our escape, these sea voyages and what must be a complicated system of pay, so that somebody in this mixed bag of cutthroats doesn't try to have it all."

"The same denominator. The Carlisle-Belvales know the

uses of money, the raw power that great wealth can wield. They've avoided using it lightly. In another group that power could be frightening, senators and industrialists bought and sold, for more power, more money. Some old money names have done just that. But the family I married into is military by choice, holy warriors for century after century. Like any good soldiers, they take care of their own, and I'm damned glad they do.''

This time, the insect was furry brown and stung her arm. ''Damn!'' she said, and crushed the bug.

Stephanie drank water from a leather wrapped gourd. ''I left my husband behind Japanese wire. The puir man has no legs and no great family to pay his ransom. If the war goes on much longer, I fear he will die in that sodding camp.''

Touching her hand, Penny said, ''You couldn't help him, and I'm sure he would want to see you free.''

And there's Chad Belvale, she thought, but didn't say it aloud. Maybe he had a hand in getting us out. You love Chad more than you care for your husband; you light up whenever one of us says his name. How far does fair play, stiff upper lip and duty go? It's wartime, Stephanie; nobody promises us a tomorrow, so we ought to make the most of today.

She wished she had someone like Chad to love, a solid man who would love her back. She needed to share her strength and still be able to lean on a man, and not an incomplete man like Farley. Without that, she depended upon the family, upon who she was because of family closeness and tradition.

One of the Dayaks, a scarred and broken-toothed man, brought them breadfruit and a pinkish vegetable she couldn't identify. The fish was only sun cooked, but Penny had learned to eat anything offered her, and Stephanie wasn't far behind. When they finished, Penny tapped the gourd for a mouthful of brackish water.

''The way I see it,'' she said, ''the Malayans will drop off here after they collect their share of the gold. Then we'll sail for Borneo, and if we survive that trip, the Dayaks will leave us to the Moros and the Philippine Islands. But the Japs have taken the Philippines and every other island of any importance. The nearest safety for us is probably Australia—if the little bastards haven't landed there, too."

"Australia?" Stephanie wiped her mouth with the back of her hand. "Bloody hell. That's half the world away."

"I'd say about fourteen hundred miles, as the seagull flies."

"Merciful God!"

"I sure hope so," Penny said.

Special to *The New York Times*—Washington, D.C., Aug. 12, 1943: President Franklin D. Roosevelt hailed the surrender of Italy but warned that the ultimate objectives in this war continue to be Berlin and Tokyo.

"This war does not and must not stop for one single instant," he declared. "Our fighting men know that. Those of them who are moving forward through jungles against lurking Japs—those who are landing at this moment in barges moving through the dawn up the strange enemy coasts—those who are diving their bombs on the target at roof top levels—every one of these men knows that this war is a full-time job."

Crusty Carlisle saw the tattered and faded uniforms before somebody saw him: U.S. Marines wearing utilities.

"Hey, you dumb sons of bitches; knock it off! Do we look like fucking Japs, you trigger-happy jar heads?"

The rifles went quiet. On the beach, Sullivan hugged the sand.

Crusty yelled again. "You bastards hear me?"

A sergeant lifted from the brush. "Shit, they can hear you in Tokyo, big mouth. Who the hell are you?"

"Major General Carlisle, U.S. Army. The guy on the beach is a swabbie, and it's a good thing you guys can't hit a pig in the ass with a plank."

The sergeant muttered, "Jesus Christ—a goddamn general."

Another Marine said, "Has to be a hard ass. For sure it ain't no English speaking Jap."

The sergeant bow-legged slowly toward Crusty, his M-1 at port, bayonet fixed. Crusty moved from the shelter of the tree and showed himself. "Our troopship got torpedoed, some time back; I don't know how long." he said. "Three of us made it this far, but the other kid died. I sure could use some help burying him."

"Goddamn if you ain't two-star brass. You see any Japs, general?" The sergeant's eyes were sunken and his face showed insect bites and about a week's growth of bristle.

"They would have had our asses. Where are we and how do we get out of here?"

"Beats the shit out of me, to both questions. I'm Sergeant Glover, and this squad has been lost ever since we peeled off from the platoon on rafts. We was supposed to drift in behind Jap lines and raise hell. Fucking navy aimed us at the wrong island, I guess. There's some Japs here, but we been ducking them, living on coconuts and fish. We was about to draw a big SOS on the beach, in case we ain't been forgotten. General, you better throw them stars away. Some banzai bastard would give his left nut to pop you."

Crusty nodded. "What about the Japs?"

"Other side of the island; don't know how many, but there can't be a lot. I figure they got some kind of radio relay station, but I wanted to see a way out before we hit them. If they go off the air sudden like, you can bet that a pisspot full of Japs will come looking. It's a small island; I sure hope they didn't hear the shots."

Sullivan came up from the beach, tight mouthed and brushing sand. The other Marines gathered beneath the trees. They stared at Crusty and murmured among themselves. Nine men and the noncom, and Crusty approved the way they immediately set up a defense perimeter, three of them in a half circle to watch the brush. They weren't new to combat.

"Do you still have the rafts?"

"Just one hid out; the other one got tore up on the coral. We buried the pieces so the Japs wouldn't find them."

"What Sullivan was doing when you fired on him."

"Sorry about that, man. We wasn't taking no chances, but I'd especially hate to pop a corpsman."

Sullivan took a deep breath. "You got any wounded?"

"Just sick and sorry, but I feel better having you along."

Crusty said, "If some of you will give me a hand digging a hole—"

Sergeant Glover unshipped an entrenching shovel from his belt. "You got it, general. I never thought to see two-star brass sweating like a fucking boot."

Sullivan spoke again. "Nobody *ever* saw a general like this one. Even the sharks are scared of him. Goddamn; you might be sorry you laid eyes on General Crusty Carlisle."

CHAPTER 21

REUTERS—Melbourne, Australia, Aug. 13, 1943: It is no accident that the Australian Coast Watcher organization was in the right place at the right time. This widespread unit of selfless and daring men was born years before the outbreak of war. This was at a time when to seek funds for military preparations was nothing short of heretical.

As a consequence of World War I settlements, Australia was assigned mandates over the eastern half of New Guinea—Papua—and much of the island screen that now plays such an important role in protecting this country. Heeding Japan's warlike trumpeting early on, a network of coast watchers was established, composed of civil servants, copra plantation managers and volunteer Melanesian natives. These brave men took to the jungles when the Japs overran their lands, and their reports of enemy sea movements are vital to the Allies fighting in this part of the world.

Staff Sgt. Eddie Donnely jammed the heels of his hands against both ears. He had climbed down from the truck filled with replacements and landed too close to a battery of 155mm howitzers. The ground jarred beneath his feet when, almost together, four of the big guns went off, and the sound was a tidal wave that slapped him hard. The 221st FA was at work backing up Eddie's old regiment.

Some twenty yards down a beaten trail, he shuddered in another series of blasts as the 155s fired for effect, and in a moment of echoed silence, asked an artillery lieutenant where the 164th was located. He figured the man to be a junior officer only by the vertical band of white behind his helmet. Insignia of rank disappeared in combat, for snipers looked for bars and stripes. Eddie had tossed his stripes off the fantail of the troopship right after it left Australia, to the wonder of noncoms who had never been in combat.

The lieutenant dug forefingers into his ears and stretched his mouth wide before answering. "Goddamn noise; beats you to death. My old man told me to get in the air corps, but I was scared of heights. What did you—oh, the 164th? Straight up the trail, but it'll be dark soon, and anybody moving around at night gets his ass shot off."

The lieutenant must have carried a lot more weight at one time; his fatigues hung loosely upon his frame and his eyes were sunken.

"Thanks," Eddie said. "I'll chance it."

"Fresh meat is always eager," the lieutenant said. "Damn, you don't even have an atabrine tan and your boondockers aren't rotted through. You'll wish to hell you stayed back here, even with the noise. But there really is no rear area on this miserable island; a fucking Jap behind every tree."

Eddie slung the M-1 on his right shoulder and adjusted the straps of his pack, a full field hump. He would shed the excess weight at the company CP. His fatigue jacket stuck to his back, already sweated through. "I'm not all that fresh. I was hit on the Canal."

"And you let the feather merchants and homesteaders hustle you back here? Then you're flat crazy, real Section 8 material. No hair off my ass, soldier. But I'd swap this bullshit for a Jody suit any time."

(Barracks talk; Jody cadence.)

> I don't know but it's been said
> Jody's had your wife in bed.

I don't know if this is true
But Jody's had your sister too.

Hup—Tup—Three—Four;
Take it on down!

Eddie grinned. "Back home, poor old 4-F Jody has to put up with rationing to get his steaks and gasoline. You don't have to worry about meat stamps here, and you don't have to save up A-coupons for gas to take a Sunday drive—"

WHAM WHAM WHAM WHAM!

The lieutenant flung down his helmet and grabbed his head. He glared at Eddie as his mouth worked. "Son of a bitch! Caught me again."

Eddie moved out smartly from the artillery position to trot up the supply path beaten down by feet only; no tire or armor track marks showed. The line regiments wouldn't be that far off.

He was up, the juices flowing; powder smoke acting on him. Here everything was simple, black and white; live and die. No suits of armor and ancestral banners to frown down upon the interloper in Sandhurst Keep. He wondered about the guys he left behind on Guadalcanal, if their luck held out and they had made it this far. Boof Hardin, happy anywhere, able to laugh off misery and make other men join in; George Griffin, an evilly efficient little bastard; first soldier Burnham, and other men whose voices and faces he remembered long after their names were lost.

Trees wearing snakelike lianas and brush all thorns closed in around him, the high canopy of interlaced branches glooming the narrow trail, and it all came rushing back at him—the jungle, the soggy heat, a palpable odor of tension and fear. A sad wandering of breeze brought with it the unmistakable stench of a corpse bloated beyond the ability of stretched skin to contain the thick black juices— a Jap. A GI rotted differently.

Walking beyond range of the stink, Eddie lit a cigarette. He didn't know anything about the situation up ahead and this might be his last smoke until morning. On his first hitch he had tried quitting smoking; the Texas-Louisiana maneuvers taught him the hard way how far off a glowing spark could be seen. A smartass corporal out of the Indian-head Division made him a two-day prisoner, but not before raising a lump on his head. On the Canal he learned that cigarette smoke could be smelled a long way off on humid air.

Big Mike didn't smoke; he chewed Day's Work or Brown Mule. Eddie had damned near choked, trying to chew and finally realised that girls wouldn't enjoy kissing a guy who chewed tobacco. Big Mike didn't care much about nonprofessional women after the ugly affair with the redheaded bitch. Here his old man would have adapted to jungle warfare as easily as he had to the mountain fighting in North Africa, and as far as he made it in Sicily.

Pulling in smoke, he clenched his jaws. Mike was gone, and Eddie even now couldn't fully believe it. His earliest memories were of craning to look up at a giant in uniform, and how his father was bigger than other daddies on Soapsuds Row, the quarters on post for high ranking noncoms. Mike never grew any smaller over the years, even during the bad time when the major's round-heeled daughter came that close to ruining his career and his life.

It always had been Big Mike and Eddie; the woman who was wife and mother had been a querulous person moving against a faded background, until the stroke that took her away. Despite all the years of army posts, she had never truly been army. Eddie thought now that he should have tried to know her. He didn't think he would have understood her, but he should have tried.

Through habit, he field stripped the cigarette butt and moved on. The old army's widespread buddy network still worked, war or no war. As a favor, bits of personal information had been fed via TWX to General Belvale at Kill Devil Hill, enough to put together a picture of how Big Mike fell. Cancer; a vile and hidden enemy that Mike couldn't fight. It was so like him to go out attacking an enemy he could face.

"Let him be," Eddie said when they asked him about burial. Mike couldn't be brought back in the middle of a war, anyhow. He didn't belong in the Belvale-Carlisle burying grounds, even if he had been family. Mike always shunned civilians, so he couldn't lie easy beside marble tombs and sad concrete angles. Let him be, wherever Graves Registration made cemeteries; he would remain with his own kind.

Behind him, the big guns fell silent, fire mission completed. "Oh shit," Eddie muttered, and unslung his rifle to hurry along and rejoin his old outfit before dark caught him out; before he lost his edge.

It happened; a combat soldier with his mind on anything but survival picked the short odds. Too much thinking about his father and about Gloria, the wife he had left behind at Sandhurst Keep, and he might not get back to her. Would she be better off without him?

One hell of a woman, his Gloria; bright, sweet and sensuous, easy to laugh, so easy to love. But a soldier should never marry; a Regular Army man was already wed to an Olive Drab bitch; she had a hard ass and grew only hind tits, and always handed you the shitty end of the stick, but when she signed on with you, it was for ever and ever, a-fucking-men. The only divorce was if you got bagged and tagged; name on the outside of the mattress cover, name on the inside, the crimp of your dogtag holding between your dead, dry teeth because the crimp was designed for it.

The ground sloped, and the path was more narrow closer to the action. Eddie sensed the sudden coming of darkness natural to this part of the world. Twilight cloaked the jungle for only a few minutes before night slammed down. There—rifle fire ahead, the deep *ka-chung!* of M-1s and the mean whiplash of Jap Arisakas. Not heavy fire as yet, although an occasional grenade added a boom. A feeling out probe, not yet a frenzied attack or a desperate defense. Eddie hurried along.

SPANG!

His head jerked left and down as something axed his

helmet. Reflex threw him down along the same angle; he hit the dirt and rolled. Goddamn sniper this far back and so late in the day that it saved Eddie's head. A Jap behind every tree, the lieutenant said; this one was away the hell up in a tree, considering the line of fire. Lying quiet, Eddie stayed in shadow, only very slowly inching his M-1 around.

Pam! . . . snick-click . . . Pam!

The shots missed him by yards; the Jap was firing blind. Rifle muzzle tilted upward, Eddie searched the tops of coconut trees etched against the lighter sky. On Guadalcanal, Jap snipers roped themselves in the treetops, animal-patient for hours if need be, until they had a shot. The little shits were more animal than human.

Eddie considered; would this tailless monkey give his position away? He probably thought his first shot had been dead on, and the follow-ups were insurance shots. He would be sighting down the long barrel of an Arisaka rifle, a Model 1905 copied from the Kraut Mauser with no improvement. The snicking sound was the bolt action. The rifle would be damned near as long as the Jap was tall and weigh about ten pounds loaded. Too heavy to keep at the shoulder, it had to be rested on a tree limb between potshots.

He waited and the Jap waited. Eddie tasted the sticky night as it blanketed him and the coconut treetops; lost somewhere in the fetid stench of primeval ooze and corpse fertilizer, a rare perfume of jungle flower caressed the air and was as swiftly gone.

Too dark now; he couldn't see the careful son of a bitch, and couldn't be seen by him. Any sniper careful enough to use insurance shots would watch and listen closely. And Eddie could be heard. Easing the bullet-gouged helmet from his head, he spun it up and away down the trail, sent it crashing into a palm trunk.

Pam! Red/yellow muzzle flash piercing the blackness. Eddie zeroed in as it winked out. The Jap worked his bolt: *snick-click.*

Eddie triggered three shots, one shot dead on the flash, one above the sound, one below. No rifle clattered down the palm trunk. Eddie spaced one shot left and one shot right; three rapid ones in the middle. He thumbed another clip into the M-1.

The Arisaka thumped to the earth. The Jap's body hurtled from its hiding place, the tie rope slamming him abruptly against the tree trunk.

". . . *eee-tie* . . . *eee-tie* . . ."

The bastard was still alive, hard hit but alive and there were few things in the world more dangerous than a wounded Jap. How did that oath of the emperor's soldiers go?

> If my arms are broken
> I will kick my enemy.
> If my legs are injured,
> then I will bite him.
> If my teeth loosen,
> I will glare him to death.

"*Eee-tie* . . . *eee-tie* . . ." It was the Jap way of saying I hurt. He had heard its moans and gasps on Guadalcanal. ". . . *eee-tie.*"

Eddie came to his knees, eyes wide and staring hard to make out the wounded sniper. The bastard had lost his rifle, but he could have a Kenju pistol in his hand, or a grenade with the pin pulled and already knocked against his tin helmet to ready the thing.

He would want to die now; he would actively seek death, if only because his sacred weapon had been dishonored. The symbolic Arisaka was as close as the peasant soldier could come to the sword of the samurai. At his training center the recruit was issued that rifle with the whole company drawn up on a parade ground while the commanding officer explained what an honor it bestowed. As his name was called, he came trembling forward, bowed low, accepted the rifle and raised it to his forehead. Then he presented arms with his holy weapon and resumed his place in ranks, one with the legions of the divine Emperor's warriors.

On his feet and crouched, Eddie moved forward. The Jap stirred and tried to wiggle free of his rope harness. Eddie saw him then, a black shadow upside down and hanging about five feet off the jungle floor.

"... *mizzu* ... *mizzu* ..."

Water; he was begging for a drink of water.

Eddie switched ends and drew back his rifle, butt plate now to the front. On the Canal, the Jap that killed Captain Jim Shelby had been silent, had lain in silent ambush for days among a pile of rotting corpses, the dead and stinking bodies of his comrades; just to kill an enemy before he got blown away himself.

"... *eee-tie* ... *mizzu* ... *mizzu* ... *eee-tie* ..."

Without sound, Eddie edged close. What he wanted to do was to let the fucker dangle and take his miserable time dying. But some green kid might come along the trail and lose his life. Maybe the Jap wasn't mortally hit and was faking it.

"Yeah," Eddie said.

"Joe ... Joe ... water."

To the Japs, every GI in the Pacific was named Joe. They practiced to use their limited English in the night, whispering for a light, a cigarette, for water. I'm hit, Joe— Joe, help me.

Anything to pinpoint a GI's foxhole; anything for a chance to kill him.

"... water ... water, Joe ..."

"Fresh out," Eddie said, and smashed the butt of his rifle into the bastard's head—once, twice, and once again as the Jap swung back and forth. Metal clinked against the base of the tree. Squatting, Eddie felt around and found the knife, a U.S. Marine's K-bar.

Tucking it into his belt, he backed across the trail and lay down in the bushes. It was too dark to wander around; any nervous GI could blast him; any alert Jap could nail him. He kept his rifle in both hands. The night was so quiet that he could hear the slow and steady dripping of blood tapping on the Jap's upside down helmet. Eddie would look for his own tin pot after daylight.

He didn't feel any guilt. His lip curled as he thought how pissed the Jap would be when he didn't awaken in ten days surrounded by geisha girls in a soldier's heaven. Nobody with half a brain believed that. His own fucking fault because he believed in the code of Bushido, that duty was heavier than a mountain while death was lighter than a feather. He believed that loyalty and devotion were standard-issue equipment wherever he might find himself. It urged him to make simplicity his aim and avoid frivolity. It informed him that the orders of a superior officer were the same as emanating from the Emperor himself.

And before the bastard left home, he conducted his own funeral.

Know your enemy, the U.S. Army said, but only after the Japs proved they were tougher than an old whore's heart and so goddamn mean, slippery as snakeshit.

"Hey Tojo," Eddie whispered, "did you get to tell yourself good-bye at your funeral?"

The Jap answered . . . drip . . . drip . . . drip.

CHAPTER 22

Drew Pearson Radio Broadcast—From Sources in Messina, Sicily, Aug. 14, delayed: General George Patton berated and slapped a patient in the rear area hospital he was touring recently. He cursed the young soldier, called him a coward, and ordered his doctor to immediately send him to the front. The man was recovering from a severe attack of malaria and acute combat neurosis. His combat record was good and he had already asked to be sent back to his unit.

Doctors fired off a letter to General Eisenhower, who evidently quashed the story. No correspondent has passed it along, until now.

General Patton is a hell-for-leather-armor commander who made history with his tanks in North Africa and Sicily. Personally a crude and often cruel man, he has this time overstepped his authority and should be relieved of his command. Our boys are not stolid SS troopers or humble Japs to be physically mistreated by their officers.

Preston Belvale clicked off the radio and shook his head. Georgie Patton had a penchant for getting into trouble. He had fought with other generals on posts where his tankers were regarded as a sometimes dangerous nuisance. He drove his car like a madman, ignoring posted speed limits and then bullying enlisted Military Police who tried to ticket him. Hell—he was Patton the Great; he designed his own flamboyant uniforms, had his helmet brightly shellacked and sported a pair of pearl-handled 45 pistols. Belvale doubted they had ever been fired. As he recalled, Georgie couldn't hit a bull in the ass with a bass fiddle.

He was ruthless and driving, a field commander par excellence, but he had stepped in it this time. What would Ike do, when he needed the man for the cross-channel invasion that was coming up sooner or later? Patton was the only general who was anywhere near Erwin Rommel's stature in armored combat. That he was also a free wheeling bastard was beside the point until his usefulness was over.

Now all America knew that he had slapped a sick kid, and Ike would have to publicly discipline him, and then hide him somewhere from the press. Some newspapermen had never bought his "Blood and Guts" image, except to quote GIs who said sure, our blood and his guts. Those reporters would be baying after him, and he damned well deserved it.

In Belvale's mind, he had done something far worse, although not as newsworthy. Information had already filtered back about the words Patton had with Terrible Terry Allen and little Teddy Roosevelt near the end of the successful campaign in Sicily, words that caused him to fire two of the best leaders in the army.

Patton was known for his chickenshit insistence that all men wear ties, even in frontline foxholes. He stood with Allen and Roosevelt as weary troops of the 1st Infantry Division slogged by, the outfit that Ike himself had called his Praetorian Guard.

"Crummy," Three star Patton commented. "They have no esprit—look how dirty they are and where the hell are their neckties?"

Two star Allen grunted. "Don't worry about how they look, general; just remember how well they fight. They've done everything asked of them and more. Their neckties— well, I imagine they swapped them to the Arabs, along with their equally useless mattress covers."

One star Teddy Roosevelt gave them his big, wrinkled

grin and leaned on the mortar aiming stake he used as a cane. Reporters made much of that cane, the only kind of arms Roosevelt carried, maybe more so than the gaudy 45s.

For such heresy, Patton had orders cut by Corps G-1 that relieved them both from command of the outfit they'd brought overseas and fought so well throughout two landings and the following tough campaigns. He would replace them in England with a pair of his trained pets. Allen and Roosevelt would be given new jobs leading another division, all newcomers, green troops of unknown quality; it wouldn't be the same for them without the Big Red One. For the first time, Belevale found himself agreeing with mouthy Drew Pearson. Patton ought to have his arrogant ass kicked.

He thumbnailed his moustache and grinned at a new thought. Suppose Patton had laid a hand on some tough soldier like Eddie Donnely? The Articles of War gave every man the right to defend himself, and no doubt Eddie would have knocked Georgie Patton flat on his holy kiester. It wasn't often that a GI had a chance to flatten a three star general and get away with it. If it had been Big Mike—the older, calmer soldier, seasoned in two wars and more duty oriented than his son—Mike might have caught Patton's wrist and surreptitiously squeezed some common sense into the general, or calmly broken a couple of his fingers.

Belevale sighed; Big Mike had seemed immortal. So many of the old breed were vanishing, their luck running out in their second war. He lit a cigar.

Of course, anybody who belted a general wouldn't get off scot free, despite the Articles of War. Legally nothing could be done to him; covertly he would catch concentrated hell in Fort Whistlestop, Kansas, or Camp Igloo, Alaska, until he understood that things would never get better and took himself out of the army. Belevale wasn't sure that Eddie Donnely would quit under all the pressure his commanders could apply. The boy was just that stubborn, just that much army and Gloria would back him against all injustice, all threats: she would suffer the slings and arrows forever if need be. Gloria was that kind of woman and Donnely was lucky she loved him.

Belvale sat behind his desk in the Hill's war room and rubbed his gimpy leg. In such an instance, to see that justice prevailed, the family might have to interfere, pressure he didn't like to use. He muttered, "I'm glad he wasn't one of ours."

"Sir?" Joann Belvale looked up from her files.

A steady girl, he thought; she had taken her father's death much better than her mother had handled it. To help her grief and out of duty to the family, Joann practically lived in the war room, answering phones and sorting TWXes, bringing the situation maps up to date. Dan Belvale would have expected no less of his daughter.

And of his wife? Adria withdrew into some deep, hurting corner of herself when Dan was officially listed as KIA. She had not yet come out of her sorrow, keeping much to herself, taking long walks in the deep, silent woods behind the Hill. Adria had reeled under a double blow, losing both her son and her husband to the enemy; reeled but did not break.

And for once, Minerva did the right thing and held her peace.

Texas wasn't the only place good for men and horses but hell on women. Kill Devil Hill and Sandhurst Keep created their own kind of fire and brimstone. Women born into the family and those who married into it were often forced by grief and loneliness to become better soldiers than their men. Some of them turned bitter and blamed the family. If anything happened to Eddie Donnely, even knowing the reasons for shipping him out, Gloria would never forgive the man who ordered him back overseas: Preston Belvale.

"Thinking out loud," Belvale said. "The Patton mess."

"I heard that some of the war correspondents are miffed at Drew Pearson." She brushed a wisp of russet hair from her smooth forehead. "It seems they had a gentleman's agreement to release no word on the incident, and then somebody leaked the news to Pearson. Is any man so important to the war that he can do whatever he pleases and not be punished? Is General Patton that important?"

"In his way; Ike will need him before long. The Germans are no doubt keeping a close watch on where Patton is sent, because that's probably where we will strike from next. Maybe Ike should have openly sent him into Italy, but that's Mark Clark's show and he never got along with Georgie. Damned few people do. But he is good at his work, Joann; he's damned good. Eisenhower will make a show of punishing him, and then keep him out of sight for a while."

"Not fair," Joann said.

"The army," Belvale said and moved to stare at the Pacific situation map. So many islands large and small; MacArthur screaming for more men, landing craft, air power and armor, more of everything he needed to defeat the Japs. His long winded protests pointed at favoritism, the ETO more important than the Pacific. But the thing that rankled MacArthur most was that Ike had once been a major on his staff, and that Eisenhower was being considered as important as his former commander.

Long past, Churchill had convinced Roosevelt that the primary threat was posed by the Nazis in Fortress Europe. Now that Mussolini had fallen, more power should be thrown against a tottering Hitler. The Russians were not only holding, but were steadily pushing the Germans back. Hirohito could wait, Churchill said, and once Europe was reclaimed, the Allies would be in condition to throw everything they had at Japan and sink those damned islands.

Belvale looked closely at the map. Soldiers and Marines bleeding to take one miserable atoll after another didn't think their campaigns were second rate. They were told that the engineers would follow and build airstrips as fast as possible, thus bringing Japanese positions and warships into better range of bombers and fighters. In time the island campaigns would place Flying Fortresses over Tokyo itself, bringing heavy firebomb raids to decimate wood-and-paper shacks, to destroy ships, docks and factories and incidentally kill Japanese.

Jimmy Doolittle had done a hell of a job, hitting Japan

with a few B-24 bombers from what the president called "Shangri-La," in actuality an aircraft carrier. But that raid had been a gesture for civilian morale, a big surprise for warlord Tojo, and a sign that America was capable of striking back.

The Pacific area had already eaten Major Dan Belvale and chewed up Lieutenant Farley Belvale, spitting out a hollow shell of the boy. It had brought down Senator/Captain Jim Shelby, perhaps the family's strongest supporter in Congress.

And Crusty Carlisle; how he missed that old warrior; how difficult it was to believe him dead. Now Staff Sergeant Eddie Donnely was out there, his father's death bitter in his throat. Closing his eyes for a second, Belvale murmured, "Good luck, boy."

An entrance bell tinkled and when he looked around, he saw that Gloria had come into the War Room to lend a hand. Bending over a desk top, her head was close to Joann's, their shining hair like two lovely flowers. Hell on women was right he thought, even these strong ones.

AGENCE FRANCE PRESSE—Southwest Pacific, on the Trail to Numa-Numa, Aug. 15, 1943: At about 2000 hours last night, a number of fanatic Japanese crept up to the tight perimeter of the 164th Regiment of the Americal Division and attempted to infiltrate into its center. This first try was beaten off by alert riflemen, as were the next two attacks thrown at the dug-in infantrymen for the next two hours or better.

When dawn broke today, 36 enemy dead were found outside the perimeter. Evidence was found that the bodies of other dead or wounded had been dragged down the slope. In addition, scouts reported finding 10 fresh graves in the area, indicating that at least that many more had been killed in almost around-the-clock attacks that gained the Japanese no ground.

Eddie Donnely shared the foxhole with Boof Hardin, now a sergeant and one of the few guys left who remembered Eddie. The hole was more a vertical rifle pit than a long, shallow dig. Boof had worked like hell, building this hole. He was thinner, and despite his deep-dyed atabrine tan, at times shaking when the malaria hit. Boof had hung on to his sense of humor.

"Funniest thing I ever saw," he said, "was your sad-sack ass coming down the trail. Man, I thought you'd be on a California beach telling war stories and holding as much tit as you could get in each hand. But yonder you came just like you had sense enough to pour piss out of a boot. How come you ain't?" He worked a spoon at a can of rations Eddie had brought. "Man oh man—I ain't seen a can of meat and beans since we came ashore. Meat and vegetable hash, meat and vegetable stew can't nobody tell which is which, and the rear echelon always steals the meat and beans. Appreciate your business, old son."

"Why aren't you getting that malaria treated back in an aid station.? I saw medic tents setting up on the beach."

"Pill rollers won't let me bring my herd of anopheles mosquitoes; them little bastards depend on me to feed them. Besides, the medics are scared I'll breathe on them; look here at the patches on my skin; pinta, they call it, kind of like leprosy. My hair's full of trichosporosis—whatever the hell that is, and a Mississippi mule'd have trouble walking with the dhobie itch between my toes."

Boof Hardin tilted his head and checked the treetops. "Hell, buddy; every swinging dick in this fucking zoo has malaria. Yours will come back real quick, if the Japs don't salt you down first."

Swinging his head slowly again, he said, "You make out one of them up in the trees? I could of sworn I heard some scuffling up there after the firefight and just before daylight. Every time I think I know all the tricks them bucktoothed bastards have, they come up with something new."

Eddie stared, looking for the early morning sun to wink off a bit of metal, searching high, serrated folds of dark palm leaves for clashing colors, for a thing nature hated—

a distinctive right angle. "Don't see anything. Is this jungle any different from the Canal? Maybe you heard a monkey or one of those big rats."

Stepping down from the fire step Boof said, "I never figured out which trees are poison, never mind all the bugs and snakes."

The oil of the Kamaday tree, Eddie thought; if it entered your body forget medics and pray; the bark of the Abuab and the sap of the Dalit were as deadly. The black gum of the Ligas only swelled you up and agonized your flesh, while the milky white sap of the Buta-buta caused total blindness. The army gave you the nomenclature of poisonous flora, but when a Jap shot at you, you'd dive into the closest tree and take your chances.

"At least," Boof said, sitting in the muddy bottom of the hole and accepting a cigarette from Eddie, "here we ain't got that goofy bird that barks like a big dog or the one that sounds like some eight-ball banging two rifle stocks together. That one scared the shit out of me every time. Hey—how many replacements came up with you?"

"Started out by myself, but I counted six or eight milling around back at the CP."

Boof inhaled smoke and let it dribble out. "Cigarette tastes funny when it ain't mildewed. Six or eight? Hell, we need sixty or eighty."

Eddie balanced his rifle on the lip of the hole and looked left and right. "Two recruits in the left flank hole. There should be old timers one on one."

"Like I said, not that many survivors left. Guy catches a million dollar wound, he don't come back on his own. Everybody ain't crazy as you."

Sprang! The bullet kicked dirt at the hole next door.

Boof grunted. "Shit; they left snipers. That's what I heard last night."

Eddie peered through the battle sights of his M-1 and searched the tree tops; nothing. The bastards were masters of camouflage.

One of the replacements yelled, "I see him!" And fired four quick shots.

Arms and legs flailing, a body crashed through the branches and thumped into a screen of brush beyond the perimeter.

Eddie frowned. Both kids next door leaped out of their hole and ran toward the body.

"Wait!" Eddie shouted. "Wait, goddamnit!"

The Jap rifle fired twice more—*bam!bam!*—and this time no ricochet sounded. The replacements went down, one on his face, one spun back into the hole.

"Dummy," Eddie grated. "A fucking decoy." Putting his shots in a tight circle, he emptied a clip into a suspect tree.

Beside him, Boof Hardin's fire chopped bits of bark and leaves lower in the branches.

Screaming, the Jap hurtled from his hiding place, still holding to his long Arisaka rifle. He kicked on the jungle floor, and Eddie put two into him from a fresh clip.

"Poor dumb shits," Boof said. "Didn't get their cherries broke good. I wonder if one of them wears size 9 shoes. Mine rotted through last week."

NORTH AMERICAN NEWS ALLIANCE—Somewhere in the Solomon Islands, Aug. 22, 1943: On Arundel Island American troops making a recon sweep discovered today that the Japs, having lost approximately 600 men in defense, sneaked their surviving men out and abandoned the island. Sources here presume they were moved by submarines.

So it was on Sagekarasa and the neighboring islets. U.S. Intelligence reports contend that Japanese troops are being evacuated at night from the Central Solomons and moved by sea to concentrate in the southern islands.

Crusty Carlisle lay at ease in the shelter covered by taro leaves long and wide. The heat and rest made his arthritis no problem. He figured it was about ten days since he'd swum ashore with another soldier and a navy corpsman.

They buried the soldier, the gutsy kid who did his damnedest to live and then died apologizing because he never got the chance to fight the Japanese. Crusty fingered the single dogtag tucked safely in his pocket. Its mate had been placed between Woodall's teeth for a someday identification. The boy deserved a better grave than the shallow hole where he lay; after the war Crusty would see to that.

Their landing on this nameless atoll brought a squad of stranded U.S. Marines to light. Now everybody was equally lost. Maybe the Japs on the other end of the island were just as confused; maybe they were a permanent post, a signal unit that kept a watch on the sea and sky. Reports by radio on Allied ship and plane movements would be greatly valued by the Nip swabbies who ran the Tokyo Express down the sea lanes known as The Slot.

They might be taking a lesson from the British and Australian coast watchers, the civilian planters and missionaries who volunteered to stay behind when the Nips overran one island after another, butchering all Europeans and enslaving the natives. The watchers' early warnings had helped the navy and ground troops to keep Guadalcanal and Tulagi free of Jap airfields.

Closing his eyes, he tried to remember details of the high brass briefings he had attended aboard ship. That was about it: Tokyo Express, Iron Bottom Bay, The Slot—and Washing Machine Charlie, the lone bomber whose nightly runs over Guadalcanal disturbed the sleep of the troops and little else.

He looked up at the overlapping leaf roof that protected him and Sullivan and a stumpy, ornery jar head named Jessup from rain and Jap sighting from the air. In three other lean-tos, the rest of the Marines hid out and slept and bitched about the navy putting them ashore on the wrong fucking beach.

Whatever the Jap bastards were up to on this island, they had lived too long. They probably had a boat or a motor barge tucked under cover at their beach. It would be a way to get off the island and back into the mainstream of the war. Besides, he was tiring of bitter tasting mussels, bony little fish caught at night and cooked over small daytime fires, and the ever present coconuts. When he made it out of here, he never wanted to see another banana. Kee-rist; he didn't know which was worse, green bananas boiled in a helmet filled with salt water, or cooked black on a stick as if they were hot dogs.

He didn't bitch aloud, for he knew how lucky they were to feed off the land. There was papaya and taro, stringy yams, pau pau and tapioca. He was grateful for them and thought that the Japs were, too. They didn't have to cruise all over the island for food to supplement their field rations, and so this end of the island was relatively safe.

Crusty's Marines—and who the hell would ever dream that he would get mixed in with the fucking Marines?—had set up shop about 100 yards from the beach, dug the grave and their foxholes, then pieced together their huts of taro and banana leaves lashed over a loose framework of thin tree branches. They also were creative with the remains of the ship's raft, exulting in the fish hooks and line from its emergency pocket, stringing bits of metal for warning alarms, using the bright orange outer material as ground sheets in the huts where it couldn't be spotted from the air. And possibly the best find of all, a little spring of fresh water.

Crusty sat up. Sergeant Glover had two Marines with him, scouting the Jap positions and strength. They were due back before dark; at night, no troops could just glide through the brush without bringing fire on themselves, much less Marines who didn't seem to give a good goddamn how much noise they made.

"Hey diddle, diddle—right up the middle," he murmured. That was how they operated, head on. It often cost too many casualties, but he had to admit it got the job done. Too, they took care of their own; they brought out their wounded, and if at all possible, their dead.

The army was more practical and less concerned about its wounded. Some clown in the War Department had decided that down the line it took four men to care for one wounded man. And even if only one soldier stopped to help his buddy, that pulled two men out of action instead of one. Multiply by—say a dozen—casualties and their helpers, and a company size attack was in trouble. Crusty remembered orders that had come over the teletypes at the Hill, orders that were passed to all units: any man who is not a medic and stops to assist the wounded will be court martialed.

"Horseshit," he said. "Screw that cut and dried horseshit. Standing by your buddy is what makes the difference between good troops and boy scouts."

The navy corpsman looked up from his work with a needle, patching his worn dungarees. "What now, general?"

"I say we've been here too long, and we've stretched our luck about as far as it will go. Those Japs must be real eight-balls for not running a few patrols, at least around the beach if not through the jungle. It's just not natural for the little bastards to relax like that."

"We'll know pretty soon," Sullivan said, "when the gunny gets back. Hell, general, if we had us some hula girls, we could wait out the war right here. No sirloin steaks or chocolate malts, but we don't get bombed or shot up, either."

Crusty sat up and drank water from a halved coconut shell. "Another week or so in these same uniforms, and we'll all be bare-assed nudists. That ought to scare the shit out of anybody come looking for us. Kee-rist; I never saw so many ugly bastards in one place."

Sullivan bit off thread. "You think anybody will come looking for us? Hell, general; the Marines have been here longer than us, and I don't see the fleet out there."

"Be happy the Japs haven't come looking."

"So we'll go looking for them."

Scratching behind a knee where a sand flea had got to him, Crusty grunted. "That's what we get paid for, son— looking for trouble and kicking the shit out of the troublemakers."

Back from the spring on the first of a twice a day water run, Jessup leaned into the shelter and said, "Gunny's coming home."

Sergeant Glover unslung his rifle and sat down cross-legged. Sweat drenched his utilities and dripped from his hairy face. He emptied two shells of water, and then reached into a top pocket. "Shit! I keep forgetting I been out of smokes for a week. That's okay; the fucking Japs got cigarettes. We smelled tobacco smoke, and I damn near went into their camp to get me some."

"How does it look, sergeant?"

Glover licked his lips. "Radio layout, like we figured, general; antennas and gas engine power. One big tent; some leaf shacks. Couldn't make out but two machine guns; no vehicles. Piss-poor security; bastards fishing out in the open. Same area, they wade out knee deep to shit. Japs; go figure."

Crusty nodded. "How about a barge?"

Scratching under one arm Glover said, "Uh-uh; they must of come in on the civilian boat they got anchored in the cove. One sail and an engine."

"How many of them?"

Glover grinned, showing a gap in his teeth that looked natural with his broken nose. "I make it enough to go around. Ain't sure because they kept going in and out the tent; round 'em off at twenty."

"Tomorrow okay?"

"Ain't this a bitch? Can't get used to a two star general asking *me* anything. Yeah, if we slip out of here at night and take plenty of time to get into position before daylight."

A ship and a coast watching radio station; twenty or more well armed Japs against ten rifles and two unarmed supernumeraries.

"We go," Crusty said. "Pity the poor fucking Japs."

CHAPTER 23

REUTERS—London, Sept. 13, 1943: An upcoming meeting of the four leading powers of the United Nations at Moscow will seek agreement for unconditional surrender of Axis countries. Sources in London and Washington said that the Big Four will also plan to work together after the war to guarantee world peace.

RED STAR—Moscow, Sept 13, 1943: The Russian army went on to capture the town of Perekop and smash through to Armyansk, cutting off the Germans in the Crimea from retreat by land. The enemy suffered great losses in men and equipment.

INS—Washington, D.C., Sept. 14, 1943: The Ways and Means committee today voted to raise the rate on first class, out of town, mail to 4¢ an ounce and fixed the price of air mail at 8¢ as compared to the present 6¢. The tax on entertainment admissions was set at 2¢.

Gavin Scott chewed a sour grass stem to ease the ache in his belly. He lay tucked into low lying branches of a gnarled cedar. Three feet away, Lieutenant Joe Hillman hid his fetal curve in a deadfall of dry limbs.

It had taken them five agonized days to reach this final ridge that looked down upon the border of Switzerland. Not that there were markers trumpeting the fact, but Gavin had watched Jerry patrols use a beaten path this side of a frosted valley. The valley must be Switzerland; it meant freedom and getting back behind the guns of a P-38.

His gut rumbled and he swallowed the chewed grass. They'd had nothing to eat for two days, not since they uncovered a crock of olives in an abandoned mountain shack, greenish black olives and a loaf of scummed bread so hard it had to be soaked before they could gnaw off a bite.

Gavin had figured that they would have been in Berne by now, or wherever the Swiss interned fugitive soldiers of whatever side. He hadn't figured on so damned many patrols criss-crossing the area. He hadn't thought on such icy cold, a killing cold that numbed them through dangerous, too-bright nights of shining moon when they were afraid to travel far.

Joe Hillman had worn brown dress shoes when his B-24 bomber was shot down on a low level mission. He had neglected to don the fleece lined flying boots that kept Gavin's feet warm. Now he paid the price in frostbitten toes. If the Jerries got close to their trail, Joe wouldn't be able to run for shit.

Fixing his eyes on the valley, Gavin fumbled for more grass and chewed down upon a sliver of cedar. It was bitter; he spat. "Shit!"

Joe Hillman hissed it: "Another patrol? Are they looking for us, you think?"

"How the hell would I know? Nothing in sight right now, but I say we sweat it out here until dark."

"Yeah—okay—sorry, man."

Damned whistling it was okay. Gavin was running this show, sorry that he let the goofy bastard come along. He'd thought the kid might be some help scrounging food and water, or keeping Jerries off their back. Fat chance; he was a whining burden that got heavier day by day.

About eighty miles they had come, slinking past occupied farm houses like stray dogs, forced to huddle together for a little warmth and shivering through the long nights and hungry, always hungry. Now only about two hundred yards separated them from freedom, from coffee and a hot meal.

"How about that goddamn Escape Committee?"

All the stuffy, by-the-book Limeys were stuck deep into Germany by now, if Allied planes hadn't chopped the unmarked POW convoy to bits. And here was their bloody nuisance, Lieutenant Scott, not far from getting another fighter plane and becoming the hottest ace in the ETO, maybe in the whole world, if he didn't run out of war before the world knew what he could do.

Catnapping through the afternoon, he swallowed what saliva he could work up and heard Joe Hillman's thin groans. Then it was dusk, and with the twilight came the cold. Gavin inched from his hiding place and stood up, rubbing his stiff lower back and aching knees in turn.

"Scott—you see anything? Jesus—hell of a time just getting to my knees—oh Jesus, maybe I'll lose my toes; they turned black."

Gavin listened to the rising wind, to the few evergreens rustling their branches; he tasted ice riding the dark, and didn't hear a patrol.

"Crawl if you have to," he hissed. "We have to go right now."

"Yeah—okay, man; I can do it. I can make it—off in the wild blue yonder, huh?"

"Keep it quiet."

Hunkered low, he eased down the weedy slope, ten yards, twenty. The valley was a pool of blackness; this side of it was open, with very little cover. He could make out the lighter strip that was the path worn by hobnail boots. Behind him Joe Hillman bumped some good sized rocks; they clattered down the hill like beats on a fucking kettle drum.

Then the kid yipped in pain, and even though he smothered it, the sound carried a long way.

"Shit, Hillman! Hurry up! A patrol's on the way."

He wasn't shitting; off at nine o'clock low, a flashlight winked; a Jerry stumbled and cursed. Gavin threw himself across the sentry path and rolled into the valley, scraping his hands and the scarred side of his face.

"Hillman—"

The flashlights multiplied, their beams swinging this way; a German shouted a guttural command; helmets banged together.

"Scott—Scott—my goddamn feet—oh Jesus—"

"Give up," Gavin called and spun to hurry down the valley. The Jerries would damned sure rake Swiss territory with fire, if they thought anybody was making it out of the great Third Reich.

"Oh Jesus!"

Moving as quick and quiet as he could in the dark, Gavin silently thanked the kid for pulling attention away from him.

"Wer bist du? Hand hoch!"

"Surrender—I surrender—"

"Fier! Fier!"

Machine pistols ripped and ripped again.

Gavin looked back to see the flash of red fireflies. Then he turned a finger of the Swiss hill and put it between himself and the Jerry squad. He wasn't exactly home free, but he had a good start.

CHAPTER 24

REUTERS—London, Sept. 15, 1943: Benito Mussolini, liberated from mountaintop captivity by his own carabinieri in a daring raid by German paratroopers, is now no more than a puppet manipulated by Hitler.

Italy is in chaos since its surrender, see-sawing among Germans, Allied forces and Italians fighting on both sides. Mussolini today proclaimed the "Italian Social Republic" and formed a new government with authority over part of the peninsula occupied by the Germans. However, Italy had to yield Trieste, Istria and the Trentino-Alto Adige to direct administration by the Germans.

Meanwhile, the people of Naples have risen against the Nazis who have plundered shops, taken over public transport and rounded up thousands of citizens to be shipped to forced labor camps. Sniping from rooftops has harassed the Germans. Desperate Italians attacked and burned eight German tanks, blocking entry to the city's main square. The uprising continues.

Feldwebel Arno Hindemit pulled in his head as a bullet kicked bits of glass over the far end of the shop floor. He didn't try to find the sniper. He was in an exceptionally good mood and didn't want to break it just yet.

"We must be thankful that fools tend to fire blind. In my

215

gratitude I will allow the wonderful panzers to seek out the sniper, or perhaps the *Schutzstaffel* will see it as their holy duty. Unless, of course, he comes in here and tries to take back this food. Then I will shoot him ten times and beat him over the head with my *Schmeisser*. What food! Italians are poor soldiers, granted; but they are marvelous cooks. This dried sausage is the best I have tasted, and look, *mein hauptmann*—a beautiful golden cheese, an entire cheese to be shared by us alone."

Sitting low behind a splintered counter, Captain Franz Witzelei stretched his legs across the dirty tiled floor. "And the bounty of wine. My sergeant, I decorate you with the order of the grand nose, with swords. Only you could have smelled out the *italienische* secret cache, hidden as it was in a false wall."

"I will wear it above my Iron Cross. It is more valuable." Arno sliced a thick piece of salami and another chunk of pepperoni; then he passed both sausages over to the captain. Before biting into the meat, he sniffed its spiced richness with deep appreciation. An eternity, he thought; a thousand years since he had tasted decent food. Beyond the first few weeks in North Africa, those weeks of loose bowels brought on by gorging on plump dates, Malaga wine, olives and sweet blood oranges, there had been little extra to eat.

"Die Panzerhahrer," he said. "They will fuck it up as they did in Tunisia. We must walk behind while they ride so as to arrive first and skim the cream. Remember how they stole the Arab chickens without considering that the *landsers* would appreciate a few eggs? Here in Naples, if they were not such *angsthasen* as to climb out of their iron boxes, the cowards would have robbed us of this special dinner."

Eyes closed, Witzelei slowly chewed meat. "Think what big targets the panzers make. There was not much to enjoy in Sicily. Not only is it a miserably poor and rocky island, but the damned *Amis* gave us no time to breathe, much less to go foraging. A short campaign for them, *nein?* The only good thing for us is being unattached; no colonel knows who we are or where we are supposed to be. Sample the cheese, my friend. Ahh, it must have been produced for the gods.''

"Then the gods are Italian. These days Germany worships only one, and he sets a damned poor table.''

Outside on the street, a rifle fired. It was answered by a long burst from a heavy machine gun.

"Verdammt angsthasen," Arno muttered around a delicious mouthful of cheese. "One shot from a crazy Italian, and the *panzer grenadiere* fire a hundred bullets in return. They waste ammunition because they do not have to carry every round upon their aching backs; and if they burn out the gun barrels, what does it matter? Such *dummkopfe;* such dumb bastards, and when the *Ami* tanks come to town, ours will discover pressing business to the north.''

He took a long swallow of sour red wine and sighed. In the middle of a partisan uprising, here they were nice and dry, warm, and reasonably safe. Filling his stomach and warming it with wine put him at peace with the world around him, including snipers.

It was seven years since he had first put on the uniform, and for five of those years he had been at war. Once he had been proud; now he was only tired. What was a born soldier to do? Unlike many others, he had not been forced into uniform. He believed in duty and honor, as his father had believed, and his father before him, not in emperors, the Kaiser or *Führer,* but in the army itself.

Once it had been an honorable profession, even though the Prussian Vons always got in the way. But that was before Hitler, before crazy *"Adi"* and *Mein Kampf* and *judenrein.* There had been a girl with pigtails dipped in midnight, a girl whose laughter overflowed as she played girl games. She was strong and quick enough to also play boy games. No child asked what church she attended.

In 1938, when Arno was home on his first leave from the army, not a child any more and seeking Sarah's laughter again, the brightness of her who was no child either, he found the yellow star painted upon her door and she was gone; the homes along the remembered street were *juden-*

rein—cleansed of Jews. That night he got falling down drunk for the first time.

Like any reasonable man, Arno thought the Austrian corporal would fade away. He had not, and one step at a time, bit by bit, it became too late to change out of the uniform; too late for anything but war.

He sighed. This day was too rare to dim with memories. He said, "In France, *hauptmann*, you would have considered putting me on report for criticizing the *Führerprinzip*."

Drinking from his own wine bottle, Witzelei tilted back his dented, smoke-blackened helmet. "In Poland, I would have considered having you shot. Easy victories are intoxicating."

Arno chuckled and rubbed his stubbled chin. "Then I would not be around to cover your schoolmaster ass when the hangover began."

"Eat, great nose and the savior of educated asses; drink while there is time. I do not think we can remain long in Naples and those mountains to the north will be damned high and damned cold."

Arno munched. If you looked at it one way, they were lucky. Warsaw to Paris to Dunkirk; to Bizerte and Palermo, they had been together while keeping their arms and legs intact. They had escaped capture in Tunisia and Sicily as the beaten *Wehrmacht* fell apart around them, as so many of their comrades also went down.

Had they been scooped up by the *Amis* or the Tommies, there would be no more mountains to defend, no more dreams of fantastic secret weapons that, once unleashed in the name of Goebbels, would immediately destroy the Allies and win the war. *Die scheiss;* propaganda did not win wars, nor panzers nor *Luftwaffe;* wars were won only by *landsers* slogging over enemy ground. It was a stipulation of the curse. Even twisted Goebbels himself, who walked *hinke-tatsch, hinke-tatsch,* bouncing his bad foot, must know by now that victories were not won in retreat. But he would not announce it to the country.

A "strategic withdrawal" was even now straightening the

lines in Russia; Africa and three hundred thousand men were lost, dead or captured in the last struggle of the Afrika Korps. Sicily had been overrun in a matter of weeks, and the *Ami* landings in Italy proper had been successful. It would have been easy to give up to the Americans, and it was still an option.

"But," Witzelei said, as if Arno had spoken aloud, "we would not enjoy food and wine in a prison camp. I too have thought of surrender."

Savoring a great bite of golden cheese, Arno said, "We have lived in each other's skin for too long. I do not know if I care to have an officer reading my mind."

The next explosion was big, a mighty thunderclap that dusted them with plaster shaken from the ceiling of the shop; shards of glass tinkled. A ball of acrid smoke tried to ruin the flavor of the cheese, and failed.

Witzelei drank wine. "I was never an officer as *Adi* and the bastardly SS defines them. I have always been a schoolmaster playing at officer. The longer this *verdammt* war continues, the more schoolmaster shows through."

Corking his wine bottle, Arno stuffed it into his jacket and slung his machine pistol. "If the *hauptmann* who reads minds will be so kind as to carry the food? That was a panzer's ammunition exploding. Our brave Italian allies have managed to blow up a German tank. The street will be blocked, and the *Schutzstaffel* will look about to fix the blame on *landsers* who did not do their duty."

Arno stood up. The fucked up SS and the twice fucked Gestapo could place no hold upon them that would make them continue fighting. The SS units were hard pressed trying to clear roadblocks and drawing their depleted ranks tighter. And the Gestapo—those turds did not come up to the front. It wasn't sausage and wine that kept him and the *hauptmann* going, that pushed them to their limits. It certainly was not blind faith in Adolf Hitler. There was honor left in simply doing the job. Arno had little left but his word. There was a residue of honor, if only in a few soldiers and civilians that circumstances turned into good soldiers.

But Witzelei was vulnerable; he had a wife and baby daughter in Berlin. A lifetime soldier could not afford such tender chains; he would think on them when survival should be the only thing on his mind.

"It is always so." Witzelei packed his pockets with cheese and salami. "The *Schutzstaffel* have become more policemen than front line soldiers. I begin to believe in your theory of the infantry being forever cursed."

"Even officers can learn, given time," Arno said.

CHAPTER 25

ASSOCIATED PRESS—New York, N.Y. Sept. 16, 1943: Times Square's incandescent tiara, hidden in the dimout chest for the past 16 months, burst into about 40 percent of its pre-war brilliance last night as lighting restrictions were eased. It wore all its jewels except the giant spectaculars. From twilight through ten p.m. marquees, store and hotel signs blinked, quivered and chased their tails as they had before Pearl Harbor. Unmasked traffic signs loomed inordinately large to eyes unaccustomed to their full power.

This was the impenetrable blackness of the grave, darkness without end. Penny Belvale's eyes ached as she tried to pierce the sweaty jungle night. Flat on her belly, she held her breath and Stephanie's hand tightened on hers.

Every small sound magnified itself, man sounds, because the nightbirds, the lizards and locusts, the rats, serpents and other things that fed in the dark fell silent until men had passed them by. Where a man walked, however quiet to his own ears, a puddle of utter silence circled around him. When he moved on, the cacaphony of wild things again grew. Penny learned that in the time since they had fled the prison camp. How long had they worked their way through jungles and bobbed in their boat—weeks, months? An eternity of blistering sun and nights of terror.

The men sailed the strange boat day or night with an uncanny sense of direction, putting ashore when they had to have food and water. This clump of jungle was off a little strip of beach; Borneo, land of head hunters. But she feared the modern, more efficient killers. She was almost certain that the muted movement so close ahead was troops on a night patrol. That meant their little band had blundered too near a big Japanese base. If some native greedy for reward had reported their landing, the Japs were a search party, far more dangerous.

The Dyaks and Moros had gone to earth at the first alien sounds, the first hint of trouble. Those instincts had helped to keep their band alive and undiscovered so far. Easing out her breath and drawing in humid air that was heavy with rot and mold, Penny prayed that their luck would hold.

Never much of a churchgoer, she wished she knew more than: now I lay me down, our Father Who art in heaven, and the rest of: yea, though I walk through the valley of shadow. Somebody had listened those nights when she lay beneath Hideo Watanabe's thrusting body with her eyes squeezed tight and her teeth locked so hard that her jaws hurt. Somebody heard her silent cry of rage when Watanabe slapped her for some act inconsequential to a civilized man. She was beyond his reach now, free of the prison camp, and with Stephanie by her side. Whether it was God or General Belvale who had brought them this far, maybe the protection could take them the rest of the way home.

She would throw herself onto a Jap bayonet rather than be returned to the wire, rather than be spread one more time upon Watanabe's *futon*. He had lost much face by her escape, and would see that she paid for his humiliation. After he had hurt her physically and mentally, he would have her executed. Stephanie couldn't go back, either; she had knifed the man who mistreated her.

A twig cracked; a man grunted and metal rattled, a noise totally alien to the jungle. Oh god! The Japs were right on top of them.

HYAHH!

The shriek axed through her, snapped her into a tense

ball as a gun went off with a sudden bright flare and another man yelped. Stephanie's hand jerked away; wild noise exploded the night and ripped the jungle. Penny gasped as a heavy weight slammed across her. She threw her hands across her face and felt a helmet. Jap! Hooking her nails at a face she could not see, ripping her knees into a yielding body, she fought to roll from beneath him.

And warm blood spurted down upon her.

Choking back the scream that clawed her throat, she heaved the limp body off her. She choked back sickness, too. Sticky blood pumped from the Jap's neck chopped almost through by a kriss or a barong, the wicked knives of her guards. The fight roared all around her—gunshots and grunts, screams of agony.

Stephanie—where was Stephanie?

"Penny!"

There, a confused shape sharply defined against a muzzle blast red and yellow, a growling man shape entwined with Stephanie, rolling this way. "Help me—"

Both hands raking out and down, Penny found the rifle slippery with blood, closed upon it as Stephanie and her Jap battled erect to their knees. Dark, so damned dark; she clamped the rifle in her right hand and felt out with the other. A shirt stiff with sweat, a leather strap; smell of fish oil; not Stephanie.

Desperate, terrified that she would get the wrong one in the dark, Penny poked with the bayonet point. The Jap yelled. Penny clutched the greasy rifle with both hands and drove the bayonet in with all her strength. The Jap fell away, his weight snatching the rifle from her.

Startling by its suddenness, the jungle went quiet but for the ragged gasps of men sucking for air and dim sounds Penny couldn't identify. She flinched as Stephanie's arms came around her.

"Whist, lass—it was that close, but it's all right now. You gave me back my life."

"What—how many Japs—where—"

"All four down in split seconds. Our escort is that deadly quick and canny with the knives. The bastard that tried me must have had eyes like a cat. He ducked under and caught me, but you sent him to his bloody ancestors."

"Bloody," Penny breathed and trembled her hands out to wipe them on a uniform she couldn't see, on the body of the man she had killed and didn't want to see.

"Sit quietly. They're stripping the bodies for anything we can use. I think we must hurry; too bad the Japs got off shots. Their sodding mates will be along soon."

Softly from behind, a hand touched Penny's shoulder. She whirled about on her knees.

"*Njonja . . . mem . . .*" one of their guards said. "Missy—do good, missy."

Wishing that her stomach would settle, Penny said, "All this time and you never let us know you speak English."

"In camp, you *tiedor* . . . sleep with goddamn Jap. Other *njonja* kill goddamn Jap in camp, but not know you same same good. Now you *berperang* . . . fight good, kill goddamn Jap. Now we speak you name *ajam dadoe* . . . same same good fight rooster. Speak friend more better than gold."

Stephanie said, "That's a sort of Malay-pidgin, used sometimes as far as Singapore. He's right about one thing; a friend like you is better than gold. Right about goddamn Japs, too."

Penny clenched her teeth against the hysterical laughter that threatened to shatter the night and her stability. Killing a man wasn't a damned bit funny and she thought she was going to be sick.

REUTERS—London, Sept. 16, 1943: Downing Street officials were cautiously optimistic today that this city's stubborn courage has outlasted the enemy's Blitz from the air, and that for all serious intent, the long and costly Battle of Britain is over.

Today German air losses are running about eight to one of ours. In the past only a few desperate RAF pilots could rise to meet fleets of Luftwaffe bombers determined to rain death and destruction upon English cities. Despite severe attacks by enemy fighters flying cover, the RAF concentrated upon shooting down the high level bombers, offering their machines and their lives to protect the people below.

Now a horde of angry Spitfires darken the skies at the first air raid warnings, and an Air Vice Marshal who asked that his name not be used said that Hitler made a fatal strategic error by ordering the bombing of civilian population centers instead of concentrating upon wiping out our airdromes.

In tribute to the gallant men of the Royal Air Force, Prime Minister Winston Churchill said it best: "Never in history have so many owed so much to so few."

Chad Belvale always froze when any plane thundered overhead. He hadn't been in England long enough for his reflexes to change. After so long in Tunisia where the *Luftwaffe* dominated the air, and Sicily where the Krauts sometimes owned the skies, he might never get over the reflexes that shrilled take cover! take cover!

Catching a glimpse of a low flying Spitfire, he let out his breath, and moved slowly across the rear courtyard of the manor house where officers of the second battalion were billeted. Another infantry division occupied the Big Red One's former home at Tidworth Barracks, and here were no barracks as such for the outfit as it was brought up to strength by replacements fresh from the States.

This had not been a military area, this green and gentle countryside around the little town of Bridgeport, no Tidworth Barracks or Salisbury Plains, England's answer to Fort Benning, Georgia. He corrected himself; not a twin, for there the infamous Phenix City crouched just across the river in Alabama. It was the meanest town in the country, where drunk GIs were fined according to rank and hustled every way from gambling and dime a dance halls to Ma Beechie's cribs where hookers would lift everything but the brass buttons off the uniform.

Often they gave something back: diseases that bought the luckless soldier 30 days on a locked ward while he was treated with sulfa drugs. If he was really a loser, he got to writhe daily in an Iron Lung thing where hot water jacked his temperature to 104 degrees or so.

To top off his misery, the days he spent on treatment were unpaid "bad time," to be made up at the end of his hitch.

Still, that was better than ending up in the Chatahooche river with your throat cut. That happened when a soldier hung around Phenix City too long. The river more than divided Alabama and Georgia. It separated civilization from barbarism.

Chad breathed deep and tasted salted fog that carried the coming bite of winter. Far better to mark time here where you could usually get warm and dry off, than exist in a frozen foxhole.

Bridgeport had no crap tables, no cribs and only a few little pubs whose allowances of whiskey and beer did not last long. Now some 18,000 men and all their equipment, the rolling stock, artillery and Cannon Company's half-tracks, were dispersed throughout the district, and many of the troops lived with civilians in their requisitioned homes. It was not the greatest blessing for the families in many cases, but extra or smuggled GI food and PX purchases of rationed items long gone from local store shelves made the intrusion more bearable for others.

American soldiers placed in close proximity with British lassies were bound to become involved. The longer such a situation lasted, the more requests for permission to be married would cross Chad's desk, and the more British fathers would demand audiences with the commanding officer of the bloody Yanks who impregnated their darling daughters. Some husbands-to-be would cooperate; some would be difficult to convince.

Chad thought there must be many more thousands of troops scattered about England in the same fashion, a great military buildup that was being hidden from enemy eyes in the sky. The next Allied landing was shaping up as the biggest armada in history and the attack potentially the most dangerous. Both sides knew that the channel jump would have to be made; the question was when and where. This cool Fall morning marked almost a year since this outfit had gone ashore at Arzew, Algeria for their baptism of fire. Then came Sicily. Was France next? Norway? Would a landing in northern Italy take the pressure off Mark Clark's 5th Army troops battling dug-in Germans for every foot of the mountainous terrain?

The British were going all out to fool the Krauts with imitation trucks, tanks, artillery, antiaircraft pieces, to-scale inflatable rubber models that looked amazingly like the real thing from the air. These were maneuvered back and forth around the east coast ports, under just enough careless cover to convince the Krauts who read the air photographs that they were kosher.

He glanced down at worn slate flagstones that had been carefully laid by artisans in centuries past, then up at an old vine as thick as his wrist, dogged greenery that had worked tendrils into plaster covered stones on its way to the roof. It was like England itself, ancient, steady and determined. A popular war song chanted "There'll always be an England," and he thought that was probably right. Helpless civilians had taken a terrible beating during the Blitz, and only their bulldog courage kept them going; by God and the guts of the RAF, Limey land survived.

Grinning, he could imagine what Johnny Merriman would say to that concept. The Britisher had fought beside him during the rough early days in a Europe overrun by the German *blitzkreig* to the miracle evacuation at Dunkirk. He had lost a hand in the ill conceived Dieppe raid and showed up in Algeria brandishing his iron hook, a wild dispatch rider on a speeding motorcycle. Merriman blamed the RAF for everything from no close ground support to spreading stories that English girls could avoid being knocked up if they screwed in the vertical position. But even Johnny Merriman would have to credit his air force for beating back Hermann Goering's bombers.

Weak sun blotted away the last wisps of night fog and Chad tucked deeper into his field jacket, hands balled into the pockets. To him, England was Leftenant Stephanie Bartlett, and Scotland was her at home on the heathered moors and its blue lochs. Even before the regiment left North Africa crowded into the Liberty ship USS *Thurston,* he realized that returning to Great Britain would shake him up. He could not enter the Underground again without meeting her ghost in the shelter of air raids past.

After the troop training schedules had been laid out, he would travel to London and pull as many strings as he had to. As soon as he touched base at the Hill to catch up on long delayed family news, such as the whereabouts of Farley and Keenan, then he would seek other news.

Stephanie and Penny; what had been heard of them since the fall of Singapore to the Japanese? Damnit; pretty Penny shouldn't have been there, but there was some excuse for her landing there to rescue women and children. Penny was a stand-up woman, more of the family than the man she had married, his son Farley. If there was any way for her to tough it out, she would outlast anything the Japs threw at her.

Stephanie could have remained in England but for the interference of a Provost general who couldn't get at Chad any other way for the "scandal" created when London newspapers pointed out that Chad and Stephanie were married, but not to each other. The bastard had gotten her shipped to Singapore when it was on the verge of being overrun.

"I warned the pompous son of a bitch," Chad said to the country estate, to the chill, damp air. "I'll have his fat ass served up on toast."

Maybe he wouldn't want to hear the news; any POW might die at the hands of the Japs. They believed anyone who chose capture over death was not worthy of honor, and Japan had not signed the Geneva Convention.

Oh, you strutting little bastards; keep back enough samurai swords to gut yourselves bloody with honor, because after we win this war we're going to hang every son of a bitch who had a hand in starting it.

Stephanie, the light and laughter of dawn and sundown; the pixie meant to live in a fairy ring and dance to the silver music of moonlight. Such a deep and freely giving woman, she had a core of strength and honor equal to that of any samurai. He prayed it would carry her through.

If she died in a Jap PW camp, he would personally pull the hangman's rope and string up the camp commander.

"You might have loved honor a little less," he murmured in paraphrase, "and loved me a little more."

But she would not have been Stephanie, she had not turned her back on the unloved husband caught up in the sad and futile defense of the crown colony of Singapore. She would do her duty to her country and her wedding ring.

Looking up at a narrow second floor window, Chad noticed a glint of sunlight against the pale blond head of a junior officer passing behind the panes. It reminded him of Kirstin and he frowned. It was unnatural to think of his lover and his ex-wife at the same time. Kirstin was also strong and independent. He wished he could have been there to offer some kind of comfort when she received the War Department telegram informing her that Senator Jim Shelby had been killed; Captain Shelby, that was. It was easier for Chad to think of the man's rank than to remember him as Kirstin's husband and her as a widow.

The thought of other telegrams nudged at him, notifications that very well might carry the names of Owen or Farley or Chad Belvale. He only now remembered that Kirstin was still the beneficiary of his GI insurance and listed as his next of kin. She would need all her strength if the telegrams piled up on her . . . *The War Department deeply regrets to inform you* . . .

That was a distinct possibility. No member of the family had to be told that casualties came with the territory; they always had and ever would. Like the Spartans, the Belvales and Carlisles returned carrying their shields or being carried upon them.

Special to *The New York Times*—Washington, Sept. 16, 1943: President Roosevelt, as commander in chief of the Armed Forces, today ordered Secretary of the Interior Harold L. Ickes to take immediate possession of the nation's coal mines. The fourth wartime strike of 530,000 union members of the CIO headed by John L. Lewis began at midnight last night.

"Coal must be mined," declared the president. "The enemy does not wait."

He told the miners that the government is offering them a fair contract and they have no right in wartime to refuse to work under it. He also authorized the use of troops to keep the mines in production.

Willie H. Jordan, a defiant coal miner in West Virginia said, "Go ahead, bring in soldier boys; they'll find out you can't mine coal with bayonets."

To which wounded infantry sergeant Edward W. Barker of New York City, hospitalized since the battle of Sicily, replied: "No coal means a slowdown in ammo shipments; it means mortar and artillery shells will be rationed when they are badly needed. Maybe I can't mine coal with my bayonet, but I can sure as hell use it to make the stupid S.O.B.'s dig for me."

Corporal Morgan was another returnee; once wounded, he had made his way back into action. He was towheaded, chunky and his fair skin peeled easily. He suffered more than the average doggie sweating it out on Bougainville, but you'd never know it, Eddie Donnely thought. Morgan had soldiered with another outfit on Guadalcanal, and said it didn't make a constipated shit to him where he went, as long as he could keep on killing Japs.

Eddie sat with Boof Hardin at the platoon CP, a full twenty yards behind the lines. Their newly arrived platoon leader was in conference at company headquarters, since no real action was underway.

"I just hope," Hardin said, "that nobody else gets a wild hair up his ass and sends us out in broad daylight to find a prisoner."

Fatigue top off, Eddie exposed his fiery heat rash to the baking sun. That way it healed better than any powders and potions that the medics didn't have, anyway. "Morgan volunteered; he's got Didyk and Carico with him; he volunteered them, too."

"Lord protect me from heroes. If he gets killed, guess who gets the shitty end of the stick next."

"I don't think he's looking for a medal. There's something a little weird about the guy, but it might be that he's mightily pissed at the Japanese Empire for his own reasons."

Hardin sifted lemonade powder into his canteen cup, stirred the water with a grubby finger, tasted it and made a face. "I'm mightily pissed at the Japs, too. But I ain't out in the brush looking to snatch one out of his spider hole. You know well as me that them little shits don't take kindly to being roped and tied. If our cherry brass wants me to bring him a live Jap, I might just get lost for about three days."

"And you might just not get lost. I know you."

Taking another pull at his lemonade, Hardin hawked and spat. "Only because the brush is full of goddamn snakes. I ain't ever been friendly with no goddamn snakes. You remember that sniper we popped the other day? Bucktoothed bastard could of eaten corn on the cob through a chicken wire fence. You remember what he had stuffed in his shirt? A goddamn snake all peeled and almost dried. He meant to eat the goddamn thing. Scared me bad enough to shit a squealing worm."

Eddie smiled. "Can't be much worse than that crappy lemonade."

"This stuff don't have a backbone and all them little rib bones and it never wiggled out of my canteen cup. Anyhow, it damn near kills the taste of them purification tablets."

Peering into the near fringe of jungle, Eddie cocked his

head to listen, then pulled his rifle close. "First Squad is on the line there, right? Somebody is stirring around."

Casually, Boof Hardin caressed the stock of the BAR he had lately taken to using. He watched the jungle until men came out of it. "Damned if the Three Musketeers ain't caught them about ninety pounds of prisoner. And damned if Morgan ain't toting him like a baby. Didyk and Carico are looking at him like he lost his feeble mind."

Eddie tensed and glanced over his shoulder. "And here comes our brand new second john with that Nisei interpreter from regiment. Can't wait to question Morgan's prize and make some brownie points at battalion. I can't remember his name, can you?"

Hardin licked lemonade from his forefinger before pointing it at the Nisei. "Uh-uh. It took me a month to remember Sergeant Yoshikawa yonder. He's got the most dangerous job in this outfit. If I looked like him, you couldn't get me within a mile of any GI with a loaded weapon."

"Put him down, corporal," the lieutenant said. "Sergeant, find out where the main body of his unit is."

One eyebrow lifting, Yoshikawa winked at Eddie. "You got it, sir. He probably won't say a word, though."

Morgan lowered the prisoner gently upon the ground. The Japs' hair had grown some since his head was last shaved; he was gaunt and shaking with malaria. His uniform was worn through in places and his callused feet were bare below the standard wrap leggings. Yoshikawa rattled something in Japanese that the prisoner didn't answer. Louder, the nisei repeated the question. The prisoner squatted with his scrawny ass only inches off the ground and looked blank.

Corporal Morgan patted his red, peeling face with a dirty kerchief. "Hold on a minute, sarge. I caught him and busted him just once. I didn't beat the shit out of him, so maybe I can convince him."

He unscrewed the top of his canteen and offered water to the Jap. The slant eyes widened for a moment, then the

Jap ducked his head in a bow and took a long drink from the canteen.

"Good, ain't it?" Morgan said.

The interpreter spoke again; the PW didn't answer.

"Here," Morgan said, lighting a cigarette and giving it to the Jap.

Hardin whispered, "Short as cigarettes are around here, that proves Morgan is bucking for a Section 8."

Drawing deeply of the smoke, the prisoner bowed again and still refused to say a word.

The lieutenant snapped, "Haul him to battalion; he'll talk there. He's in shock at being pampered."

"If you say it, sir." Sergeant Yoshikawa shrugged.

"Stubborn, ain't he?' Morgan said.

Then he pushed the muzzle of his rifle to the Jap's head and pulled the trigger. Blood, brains and chunks of stubbled bone leaped from the exit wound.

"Goddamn!" the lieutenant yelled. "You—you carried him out of the jungle, you gave him water and a smoke—then you killed him!"

Bending low, Morgan retrieved the cigarette smoldering between the Jap's fingers and put it between his own lips. "Son of a bitch died happy, didn't he?"

Eddie looked at Boof Hardin sitting with his mouth hanging open. The lieutenant swallowed and Eddie could see the effort it took for him to bluster. "Corporal, we wanted that prisoner for information—"

"Wasn't getting any." Morgan took a long drag on the butt. "You don't like it, sir—send me to the fucking front."

CHAPTER 26

UNITED PRESS—On the Eastern Front, Sept. 16, 1943: General Petrov's troops have captured the ruins of Novorossiysk. A large part of the German army has managed to reach the Crimea, ending its venture into the Caucasus.

REUTERS—Headquarters, South West Pacific Command, Sept. 16, 1943: Their supplies from air and sea cut off by Allied blockades, Japanese on Lae—estimated at 7,500 plus remnants of the Salamua garrison, decimated in earlier fighting, retired to the northwest last night. Australians of the 7th and 9th Divisions converged on the abandoned site and occupied it.

ASSOCIATED PRESS—With the 5th Army in Italy, Sept. 16, 1943: Forward units of the American 5th Army and the British 8th Army joined up near Vallo di Lucania. Field Marshal Kesselring, commanding the southern group of German armies, began to withdraw toward the "Gustav Line" along the Garigliano River and the Sangro River.

Captain Owen Belvale thought that, given enough time, he might get used to English 'arf-and-'arf beer, unappetizingly dark, warm and flat. Then again, why should he want to? When the division was here before, he had become a sort of anglophile. He liked the British for many things: their hangtough attitude, their caring just under the veneer of careful politeness. He might have found what their women were like, if he'd had time. The pre-Africa training schedule was a bitch, and he'd had his ashes hauled professionally just twice—once during a hurried weekend in London, and again in nearby Andover. It was quick release and no promises, and who ever said good-bye to a hooker.

Fighting Joe Hooker of the Grand Army of the Republic never said good-bye to the camp followers who trailed his troops through the Civil War. He thought it normal enough. Other commanders spoke of Hooker's women. Soon the name was simply hookers, immortalizing Joe Hooker while the other commanders were long forgotten.

Would the ancient Bevales, the lord and lady Belvales of the castle, frown on whoring? He doubted it; each of the Crusades had kept the men far off and long away. All those small wars between when the family hired out its swords also made for extended separations. So pliant women must have been in high favor, or those not fast enough on their feet.

And what of the ladies left behind? Chastity belts might not have presented much of a challenge to a locksmith and new kids could be hidden with the peasants or added to the household staff.

This time while he was in England, barring the invasion coming due in the middle of winter, he hoped to seek out the original lands of the Carlisles and the Belvales. History had it that the estates had been side by side. Maybe there would be ivy covered ruins to prowl. From a tumble of dark and damp stones maybe curious ghosts would whisper to him of lances and war banners and forgotten glories. He wouldn't find them here in Southampton, and the trip might give him something to discuss with his father some day.

He drank and realized that British beer hadn't improved a damned bit during his absence. He had never been considered a drinking man, but the small pub's smug warmth was appreciated. Going off by himself had been a necessary move, too. Excepting Sloan Travis, who had caught officer of the guard just as Owen took this public relations detail to Southampton, he didn't much bum around with company grade officers of the regiment.

He'd done that a couple of times, and the nights ended the same way; war stories that brought on drunken tears and puking in the loo. The real brutality of the war had receded when the troop ships left Sicily behind; he'd as soon keep it back there. It was enough to know that more heavy fighting was in his immediate future; dwelling on the past blood letting was morbid. Soldiers died; the family laid no claim to immortality.

And he couldn't have invited his father to come pub crawling. Light colonels drank with other field grade officers, or with full birds, not junior officers. If Owen had asked, his father would probably have come along, once he got over the surprise. Although the family lived somewhat by the Articles of War, it sidestepped them when necessary.

But after the first how-are-you and did-you-hear-about-back-home, he just wouldn't know what the hell to say to his old man; he never had known. If they scratched a personal surface, it was like peeling scabs off unhealed wounds. Then they cut each other up, adding new wounds. The war had made some fleeting changes between them, mostly for the better, but away from military subjects, the tension showed.

No stickler for regulations either, Owen would have shared the evening with his enlisted men, but they sped off as soon as their gear was locked safe away at the British trucking company where they were billeted. From the first night, when they had latched on to local service women, they found their own interests.

Owen treated himself to a smoke, not a mildewed Phillip Morris, but an honest to God Lucky Strike, even if it didn't come out of the familiar green pack. He held the white pack and peered at the message below the red bullseye: Lucky Strike Green has gone to war, whatever the hell that meant; was it something in the metallic ink that was needed to kill Krauts? Issue it directly to the troops.

The fresh butts proved again that Corporal Weintraub was the best hustler in the outfit. Real chocolate, not the tooth-breaking D ration bar, was gold; Weintraub had plenty in his footlocker. The Brits hadn't seen oranges in many months; Weintraub's footlocker smelled like Florida at the harvest. Cigarettes, cigars, pipe tobacco—see Weintraub. He didn't peddle goodies to H Company GIs; he gave them away. For him, Owen figured, the fun was in the doing, not in the keeping.

Civilians were a different matter, and even then it was trade and not sell. He had screwed British service women for a mile around, and before the Southampton detail, was working his way through the ladies of the NAFFI—Navy, Army and Air Force Institute, England's wordy answer to the PX and Red Cross.

Weintraub had a contact at battalion and another at regiment. He knew of this special duty assignment before Owen did, and asked to go along. Owen and six EM he picked were to demonstrate American weapons and the fabulous jeep at Southampton's sports center. As a public relations move, it couldn't have been better. They became the first American soldiers the city had seen, and it was like an assignment in Eden. The English couldn't do enough for them; and according to the troops, neither could the lonely English women—cheerio; knock you up in the morning.

Sipping beer, he smiled. A few days returned to Limey land and he was falling into British speech patterns—loo for latrine, pub for bar, Jerry for German; lorry and chemist. Protective coloration? No Englishman would take him for a native, in or out of uniform. A soldier's need to belong, then; to find a little bit of stability in his rootless world; to be accepted, even if only for this night.

> There's a troopship just leaving Bombay
> bound for old Blighty shore,
> heavily laden with time expired men
> bound for the land they adore.

He recognized the tune. After a few beers—this stuff or pretty good cold French brew, Tommies of the British First Army in North Africa were apt to sing it and GIs to learn the words. He remembered the Foreign Legionnaires trying to sing along, and their habit of adding cherry syrup to their glasses of beer. What the hell; some Mexicans livened their *cerveza* with squirts of hot sauce.

Owen looked around. This pub, the Brickmaker's Arms, had a battered piano tucked into the far corner, where different English uniforms swirled around a few gray civilians. He leaned away from the bar to focus on the piano player, a small woman radiant under a wealth of hair that shone not quite red and not quite brown. The color was close to that of his mother's Morgan horses readied for a show, curried and brushed so the summer coats shimmered and glistened in the sun. Her eyes, when he could catch a glimpse of them, seemed to be an intriguing blue-green. He had never seen eyes quite that shade before. Maybe the half-and-half was stronger than he'd thought.

> Now there's many a lad just doing his time,
> and many a twerp signing on,
> but there'll be no promotion
> this side of the ocean,
> so cheer up, me lads, bless them all.

The song had been born in the days of the *pukka sahib*, the road to Mandalay, Gunga Din and Inja's sunny clime. It was chanted by Tommy Atkins putting it all behind him. Owen lit another cigarette and would bet there'd be no far flung posts of empire after this war. This one spent too many men and too much money. And that white man's burden was changing fast, as the restless colonies stirred. A shame in a way; the sun at last setting on the empire and its pageantry.

Still, bless them all. Owen drained his glass. "Barkeep, another one, please, and a double of something stronger."

He might as well tie one on; have one for Big Mike Donnely, and bless the young troopers of H Company buried in Sicily, bless those left behind in Algeria and Tunisia. They had not worn the Crusader's cross, and they hadn't believed their mission was holy. When the 16th waded ashore in Arzew its men were by far Regular Army, the professionals. To them it was only a job tougher than they had seen before. It was what they were paid for. It was why the eagle shit on payday. They deserved more than holes scraped in alien ground. His brother should have a Purple Heart for the battle rattle that pulled him out of combat.

And surely a blessing was due the regiment's unlucky son of a bitch who had been killed on Salisbury Plains during a road march. The Stuka buzzed low with its guns snapping—one recon plane on its way back home; one lousy Kraut with nothing better to do than strafe the road. He had scored the first casualty of World War II on the Big Red One.

Heavenly Father, did You extend a welcoming hand to those men first to fall in World War I? In case You forgot, their names were remembered on honor rolls in 16th Infantry dayrooms.

Usually on the wall behind the pool table.

"Gin is all I have; sorry, captain," the barkeep said; the publican, if Owen continued his word collecting. "Rationing, Yank."

"Okay, gin."

Bless them all, bless them all,
the long and the short and the tall.
Bless all the sergeants, the doubly old ones;
bless all the corporals, and their bleeding sons,
for we're saying good-bye to them all.

The gin smoked its way to his stomach. Cheer up, Owen; there must be something to boozing it up; everybody did it, even his old man. Owen chased the warm gin with warm beer. Maybe especially his old man, a long time ago in those between-war years, the peacetime years when you prepared for the next war. Yes, Colonel Belvale drank now, but he never got sloppy, on or off duty. Not even when he got the news about Farley, or Major Dan Belvale being KIA.

Owen remembered lying awake in the bedroom shared with his brother, in the married officers quarters on post. He heard the short, sharp clashes between his parents. Mostly the edge was in his mother's voice, and back then he blamed her for not seeing the many facets of soldiering. Certainly she knew beforehand about the alternating tension and boredom that was standard in peacetime. She should have been prepared to accept the long separations, for didn't she understand that the family ladies were expected to wait in the castles? Couldn't she see and comfort the fear of not measuring up to those tattered battle flags in the great hall? Soldiers got drunk on payday; it was tradition. There were a lot of traditions, but the chastity belt had gone the way of the war axe and the spiked mace.

Now there was divorce.

. . . the long and the short and the tall . . .

"Another of the same, Mister Publican."

The piano went silent in the corner and the singing faded. Owen downed the double shot of gin and his throat constricted; cigarette smoke floated thick and he coughed.

"Not that used to strong drink? Odd for a Yank, wouldn't you say?"

Her eyes were blue with green flecks; no—green with blue flecks, and he still couldn't be certain about her hair, worn loose to her shoulders, call it chestnut or call it sorrel, it held the glow of tiny lights. Her gray wool dress was cut so simply that it called attention to every curve of her small, neat body. At first look she could be a schoolgirl; look again and she was the teacher and you were sorry you hadn't done your homework. You could volunteer to clean the erasers after school, just to keep looking at her.

She wore no jewelry and didn't need it. Her only makeup was a damp touch of lipstick on a soft and mobile mouth. Anything more would spoil the effect.

Muffling another spasm in his handkerchief, he shook his head. "Not for this one."

"It might be the drink," she said. "Wartime gin is a bit raw. It mixes better with tonic rather than beer."

She had a voice like rich desserts, smooth with a hint of fullness, a promise of satiety to come. There was a whisper of huskiness behind the words, and maybe he was just reading the echo of her music into it.

"I was listening," he said, to apologize for not going to hover around the piano with the other uniforms. "You play well. Will you have a drink of raw wartime gin—with tonic?"

Her laugh was husky, too; just enough. "My playing is only adequate for pub patrons on the verge of sloshing, and since gin is the only liquor left in supply, thank you."

She was Helene Lyons; she said cheers, Captain Owen Belvale, and lifted her glass to him. Sipping her drink, she fended off other admirers who approached her bearing drinks and cigarettes and hope in their eyes. She did it in a way that made each man feel he was special, that her smile promised him, and him alone, a wondrous slice of the future.

Feeling the gin, reeling from her nearness, he said it kind of blurred: "You do that very well; the brush off—lots of practice, I guess."

Up this close, the scent of her was lightly spiced, fragile in the wisps of cigarette smoke, but insistent. The warm radiation of her knees was only inches from his, and her breasts moved gently, timed to long, slow breaths.

Owen had seen it before, the pink and white complexion so clear and so dear to some lucky English girls. Helene's skin was like that, but translucent, its underglow beckoning a touch to prove the silken depths existed.

"Not that much, Yank. The war and gin and the pub; men not certain of tomorrow. Any comfort, any woman will do. And the Blitz taught the women they could also stop short of tomorrow."

Oddly, she was the girl in fifth grade who sometimes loaned pencils and didn't always turn aside if he stared in class. And she was also one of the snow queens bussed and chaperoned to military school dances, unattainable, but lied about in barracks after Taps.

Owen lit her cigarette and sensed a bit more—the townie girl of Flirtation Walk at the academy, bearing her townie hopes of marriage after graduation, a sweetness tempted and possibly offered in careful portions. He breathed Helene's scent and felt an undercurrent that was none of the above, but a quiet pulsing all her own. There was this powerful sexual thing. He wasn't afraid of submerging who and what he was. This woman or any other could be only a passing excitement. Being a sensible man and determined not to inherit his father's problems, he took the advice of old soldiers and married the army. Damned right; until death do us part.

He couldn't continue staring into her eyes; she might read too much in his. She was the most beautiful woman he had ever seen, and close up, such loveliness was unsettling. It was like having Lana Turner or Betty Grable on your lap. You fantasized about movie stars but if one of them crawled into your sack, you wouldn't know what to say or do at first. Weintraub would put it as not knowing whether to shit or go blind. Owen forced himself to stare down into his glass. The publican refilled it and hers, too.

His lips were only a bit numb. "I went into a public house to get a pint of beer . . . the publican he ups and says . . ."

She picked it up. ". . . we serve no redcoats here. Shall I be a girl behind the bar and laugh and giggle fit to die?"

Draining his glass, Owen said, "Practicing my English-English; publican and lorry and loo; boiled sweets and like that. I don't know how Kipling got wedged in there. I felt I had to say something, anything to hold your attention."

"Why?"

"So I wouldn't appear idiotic. So you wouldn't leave me for the first piano to come along."

Helene laughed, no girlish titter, but a full and happy sound that showed her wet white teeth, perfectly formed and sharp little teeth. Then she said, "You're my first Yank. Am I your first well met English woman?"

He hesitated. "Yes and no; not quite."

She laughed again. "Ah yes—London and Piccadilly Circus. What is it you Yanks call the ladies of the evening— Piccadilly commandos?"

He had never been so ill at ease with a woman. Looking away, he was still compelled to glance back at every fleeting movement of her face, drawn by her eyes and the richness of her mouth, the tantalizing flick of her pink tongue.

He said, "GIs are nothing if not inventive."

"Gee-aye?"

"Government issue; general issue; applied to the soldier himself it's a fairly recent and loose term. I think it started with garbage cans—they're galvanized iron, and then it was applied to everything else. There's GI soap and a GI party, which means Friday night scrubbing, mopping and polishing the barracks for Saturday morning inspection. It can mean a hardnose sergeant or an officer who does things by the book. I'm babbling."

"Keep it up, please; you have such a nice voice."

Owen could barely feel his lips. He said to himself, don't be drunk. Not now; don't get drunk. "And you don't wear a uniform or a wedding ring."

Oh, brilliant.

Helene didn't seem to mind. She told him of her job in a defense industry and no, she had never been married. Once engaged to a pilot officer shot down over France.

"Sorry," Owen said, lying through his teeth.

She was in mourning and angry at once, she said; she meant to do her share in the war. She went that straight to work in an ammunition plant, even before women were being drafted into the services.

"You must have loved him very much." He could have chewed his tongue off.

Her lashes lay thick upon her cheeks as she stared into her drink. "I thought so; now I am not that certain. We've been at war for these four long years, and war changes everything and everyone."

Lifting her face, she looked directly into his eyes before he could glance away. "I thought I was in love with my pilot officer; he was that handsome, so thoughtful and dependable. He was so bloody proper he was boring. I realize that I was not in love, but in heat."

Owen swallowed. "In heat."

"We had never done it, you see. When he was declared killed in action, I fucked the first passable lad of the RAF. Symbolic, would you say?"

Even if Owen could talk, he didn't know what to say.

CHAPTER 27

TOP SECRET, General Preston Belvale, Eyes Only—the Solomon Islands, Sept. 16, 1943: Fighting continues on Arundel Island and the nearby islet of Sagekarasa with intensive artillery activity. At a conference of Allied commanders at Port Morseby in New Guinea, General MacArthur maintains that it is necessary to establish a beachhead on Bougainville as quickly as possible and build up a large base there. This would give the Allies control of the whole Southwest Pacific and enable them to break out toward the Central Pacific.

Kirstin Belvale-Shelby longed the young stallion, flicking the line and trailing the long whip behind his hocks whenever he thought of turning into the circle or breaking gait. He moved well at the trot, not paddling or winging or reaching out to float like an Arabian. He produced that rolling forefoot motion inherent to Morgans of good bloodlines. He would be blue ribbon show stock once he got over his youthful foolishness and settled down to work. He hadn't stood to a mare yet, but had plenty of it on his mind. A three year old filly in the back stalls was in full heat. Humans could smell nothing, but horses picked up the ready odor a mile away.

From his seat on the top rail of the training ring Gregorio Venegas said, "Ah, the young ones, eh *señora*? They are proud and fierce in their independence and the world has nothing to teach them."

Kirstin glanced sharply at her ranch foreman. Was he critical of her liaison with the boy from the hospital? She refused to call it anything else. His deeply wrinkled face showed only a mahogany sunburn. She looked back to the stallion. "George Bernard Shaw said that youth is wasted on the young."

"Ah, *es verdad*. But I would be twenty again, so that I might waste my youth at a dead run; never would I walk or trot. I would even sleep standing up, so I would be ready to run at a moment's notice. I think I would never marry."

"And if you became wind broke and spavined?" She watched the horse.

Pushing back his battered straw hat with a broad thumb, Gregorio said, "Ah—but I would have had my time of freedom; no hobbles; to have worn no spade bit, or even a halter, not lived in a stall and certainly never touched with the spur."

"I have never used a spade bit or cruel spurs—like the Mexican rowel."

Gregorio scratched his cheek. "Of course the *señora*—"

"Tries to remember that *mañana* always comes; for the old old ones as well as for the young."

The horse loafed and she snapped the longe line.

He changed the unsaid subject. "Manuel does well at the riding school when you return to the ranch?"

"You know very well that Manny is a fine hand with horses, and with people as well."

From the corner of her eye, she saw the look of distaste at the gringo use of his son's name. It served him right. Sliding off the rail, he watched her longe the horse a bit longer. Then he said, "This one will over reach if he is not careful. The hind feet will strike the heels of the forefeet."

It was rare when Gregorio didn't have the last word. He climbed down and walked quickly to the house. Kirstin smiled as she drew in the smell of the ring's fresh sawdust and flared her nostrils for the sharp perfume of horse sweat. The stallion's trot had dropped to a slow jog that would delight quarter horse owners. An unnatural gait, it was not good for a Morgan.

"Supy," she called, "I control this line and that means I control you."

Chasley Superman bowed his neck, the long mane flowing, his tail arched as he broke into a canter to prove he didn't have to pay attention if he didn't want to.

"The hell you say! Trot, Supy—*trot!*" She popped him beneath the chin with the metal snap hooked into the halter. It demonstrated his limits and didn't really hurt him.

Small pointy ears flicking back and forth, he got the message and settled into a steady two-beat rhythm on his diagonals.

"Good boy," she called, "good boy."

If only handling the men in her life was like this training; some know-how and a lot of patience. She didn't want control or to be controlled, just a working partnership. She had tried patience with Chad Belvale. He hadn't let up on his drinking, and finding him in bed with that slut was too much.

She'd been lucky to meet Jim Shelby, to share a little time with him. Her military experience hadn't convinced him not to accept an army commission. Not to try to measure up to the Belvales and Carlisles, he said; it's war and I wouldn't feel right not going.

For Christsakes, she had come back, does it have to be infantry?

So he died, in one of the army's many ways. At least it was the short form, spelled out with bullets, as with Walton Belvale and Dan Belvale, the son and the father. They were family; they were bred to be soldiers and to die for God and country, and more to the point, for the faded banners in the great halls of Kill Devil Hill and Sandhurst Keep.

"God, Jim—you never had the time to become a line soldier. You—"

The horse angled his head at her and dropped into a walk.

"Ho, Supy. Ho—that's it; just stand ho."

Oh yes, the army had many ways to create a blank file. As with Farley, gentle Farley shut off in his mind from horrors he had seen and could not accept. Owen's defenses would not allow such outside penetration. Owen was more like his father. And Chad would remain Chad Belvale, drunk or sober to the goddamn sword born. He wasn't fighting right now, just marking time in England, Preston Belvale said. He could pull strings and fly to Hawaii to be with his son. Travel would be easy for him, a field grade officer with high connections in Washington.

She could picture him shaking his head and saying things about being fair and if none of his soldiers could go home on leave, neither would he. Why didn't he at least send Owen? Answer: the same stupid reasons.

"Walk," she called to Chasley Superman, and frowned to be comparing man and horse. The stallion was born to the purple, a champion-to-be from a long line of champions. It would be a sin for him to turn into a backyard horse, to get pulled and pushed and whipped for reasons he would not fathom. But he had limitations, and by God, so did Chad.

"All right, damnit—not you, Supy; not you."

When Nancy Carlise had called from Hawaii and told her that Farley was safe there, but shouldn't have visitors for a while, she'd wanted to fly out right away if only to hold her son's hand. She would have used every contact to wrangle a priorty. She didn't owe a damned thing to the great hall.

"Ho!" she told the horse. "Stand ho."

She was thankful that Nancy Carlisle was there at Tripler General to nurse Farley back to health, to give him special attention when Farley came out of the combat fatigue. Kirstin refused to think *if*. In the last war they had called it shell shock, and some of the kids who rode her horses at Harmon General joked about battle rattle. It wasn't funny and these days medicine had new ways to treat it.

Farley would be all right; nobody was shooting at him and he was safe.

"Owen," she breathed. Owen had to stop measuring himself against his father. Struggling to come out of Chad's long shadow, he might take too many chances. Chad, he's your son, too; take care of him for me.

And take care of yourself.

She didn't know how long Gregorio had been standing at the gate, but she was glad he was there. "Cool him out for me, please. I—I have to go back to Longview."

His worn and lived-in face showed understanding. *"Con Dios, señora."*

"With God, Gregorio; and thank you."

Leaning against the fence as the horse was led away, she realized that she could no longer avoid doing something about Harlan Edgerton. He was sweet and thoughtful and adoring and half her age. That don't matter; he said. But it did.

As badly as he had been wounded, left hand gone and his right leg blown off, he wouldn't have to return to the war. After he was comfortable with the prosthetics, there would be an honorable discharge and a lifetime pension. It would not make up for the loss of the boy who had asked no more from life than to farm the land that had been in his family for three generations.

Now he would try to make it. A short time ago he had balanced on the lip of the abyss, half a man thinking on suicide. Her riding program had given him some confidence and she convinced him he was still a man by taking him to bed.

All right; it had done something for her, too. She hadn't planned to seduce Harlan; it sort of happened, and it was a good and natural thing to do. It was good for her to be warmed and freely giving in bed. Lovemaking was a rebirth, a denial of death as permanent, an affirmation of life. But she had affirmed it more than once, and when Harlan asked her to marry him, she fled to the ranch.

Now she had to go back.

Honolulu Star Bulletin via AP—Sept. 16, 1943: Today the first Allied aircraft touched down on the newly built strip on Vella Lavella.

In New Guinea, Japanese planes attacked Allied ships carrying supplies to the Finshafen bridgehead, but with only moderate success.

The Australian 20th Brigade broke through Japanese lines on the Bumi River, north of the bridgehead.

Dawn eased shadow gray out of black night, and pink tendrils of dawn crawled up out of the gray. Kee-rist; it had been the longest night in Crusty's life. That included those spent at sea on a balky raft with hungry sharks circling. Sharks were here, too, fucking Japs that were more deadly and less merciful for their short step up the ladder of evolution.

His command, all eleven of them, had wormed this close to the Japanese perimeter yesterday afternoon. Then they buttoned up for the night and prayed no sentry would stumble over them. Nobody dared to slap at insects and the mosquitoes fattened through the night. As the sky lightened, Crusty sat hunched next to Sullivan, the navy corpsman. Carefully, he massaged his shoulders, silently damning the arthritis that stiffened them during the night. He would feel better if they had weapons better than the K-bar knives loaned them by the Marines. There just weren't enough rifles to go around, and he sure as hell didn't want to take one from dead hands.

This close to the Jap camp and the beach, the jungle thinned and a beaten path pointed the way to the fresh water spring in a coconut grove. Taking the point, Sergeant Glover had come upon it and posted a man there to do in the next water carrier that came along.

"And do it quiet," he had ordered. "Stick him or bust him with your rifle butt or twist his slope head off with your hands. Just don't let me or the Japs hear a gunshot.

And when *you* hear the firefight start, angle off to your right front and nail any asshole that runs out the back.''

The other Marines spent the tense night in a half circle in the treeline above the Jap camp and the sandy beach. Two men were set to target the entry to the radio shack; two more positioned to zero in on the machine gun. The gun, protected from the night dampness by a canvas cover, was dug in to rake the bay and the boat bobbing at a log dock.

Evidently the Jap commander thought he was safe from attack by land. Crusty grinned; on a small scale, this would be the fall of Singapore over again. The Limeys had cemented their big guns to repel an enemy fleet, because the jungle at their backs was "impassable."

It was light now, and the other machine gun wasn't in sight; that worried Glover and Crusty both. Nothing to do but sweat it out, they decided. Crusty admitted that he couldn't have positioned the men better. Glover was good at his job.

Scanning the area below, Crusty looked hard at the boat bobbing gently in the calm and shielded bay—ketch, lugger or schooner. A boat was a boat, a fucking ship or whatever. No matter the nomenclature, it was small and not to be trusted. Look at what happened to the troop ship.

Boats were like the army mule. Legend held that a mule would be good to you all the days of his life, just to get a clear shot at you at the end. This boat looked ratty, its paint flaking, tired of going island to island and now to be captured by the Japs.

Crusty concentrated on the camp area, the radio shack and three smaller huts, all the standard leaf huts. A wisp of smoke curled from shack #2; the cook fire. A Jap came shirtless and weaponless from the main shack and bowlegged down to the rough dock of palm logs lashed together. Halfway to the boat he dropped his pants and squatted.

Sullivan whispered, "Little bastard taking his morning shit."

Crusty whispered back: "He'll never get to wipe his ass."

Rifle across his shoulders and his hands hooked over it like a tired soldier of any country, a Jap sentry walked slowly across the beach. Two came out of the cookhouse and strolled toward the machine gun.

"Fire!" yelled Glover.

Ka-chug! Ka-chug! went the M-1s. *Ka-chug! Ka-chug!*

Still clinging to his Arisaka, the Jap sentry staggered and fell. The machine gunners didn't lift the cover of the Nambu, chopped down in their tracks.

On the dock, the early riser twisted as bullets swept him into the sea, bare ass shining and his pants around his ankles.

Brrtt-pop-pop-pop!

The other gun, emplaced in good camouflage at the far side of the camp; a Marine in the open, running for it. Spurts of sand kicked around him as he spun and went down.

Japs leaped from the radio shack, dropping to kneel and fire into the tree line. One stood erect, samurai sword in one hand, a pistol in the other; an officer. Marines dropped him across the bodies of his riflemen. Japs ran every which way, ants scattering from a kicked nest. All the little bastards were sworn to die for their god-emperor who promised that in ten days they would rise in heaven.

That concept was okay with the Marines; they helped the Japs on their way with 30 caliber bullets.

Behind the radio shack, the machine gun fired a long burst; in its echo, a Marine shouted curses.

"Kee-rist," Crusty said. "Enough bigod waiting. Rifles aplenty out there for us. Come on, sonny."

"Holy shit," Sullivan said.

Out of the trees with gunsmoke sharp around him, Crusty snatched up the dead officer's pistol and ducked into the radio shack. A chunky Jap was seated at the transmitter, screaming into the microphone. He dropped it and whirled with a pistol in his hand.

Crusty beat him to the punch—one in the chest, one

more as insurance because Crusty didn't trust the striking power of the pissant pistol. An issue 45 would have knocked the Jap ass over tea kettle and ended it. This one slid off the wooden crate he'd been using as a chair and melted over onto his back.

"Good," Crusty grunted. "You didn't bleed all over the radio."

CHAPTER 28

REUTERS—Somewhere in China, Sept. 28, 1943: General "Vinegar Joe" Stilwell today announced a new military program for China, indeed, for the entire China/Burma/India theater. He spoke for the re-establishment, with American aid, of 60 divisions of the Chinese Nationalist Army.

Relations between the American commander and Generalissimo Chiang Kai-shek, never smooth, have at least calmed for the moment as the men work in accord toward their mutual goal, defeating the Japanese.

Nights like this had no business being out by themselves. It was soft but not swarming with danger and insects. It was warm but not sticky, and the air carried the sweetness of frangipani blossom, and gardenia, not the rot of jungle and the many things that died in it. Up off the beach somebody sprinkled the jeweled notes of a slow guitar on the sea breeze. Coming down to his usual be-alone place on the unspoiled sand, he had seen the orange lights and the golden lights partially covered or dimmed as a concession to a loose brownout instead of the complete blackout that the navy wanted.

Keenan Carlisle agreed with the islanders on that score. The Japs knew how to find Pearl Harbor without a guide of street lights; they could always home in on that Honolulu radio station again, as they'd done on that December 7th. All the scurrying around by the starched admirals and golfing generals now would never make up for the idiotic mistakes they had made in one of the great military fuckups of all time. It was right up there with the Charge of the Light Brigade and Custer's last stand.

The hell with them and their clean and spit polished play-soldiering. He stretched on the blanket and made himself one with the night. It was a trick he'd learned traveling through the jungles of other lands, a means of survival. You didn't hide tense in the night; you became the night. You did not move, no matter what insect or reptile wandered your body. You pulled the plug, disconnected the brain so that no quiver of your mind touched another man's sensitive aura. Your heightened senses spread out around you, a web of warning to alert you to any threat, so that you were neither asleep nor awake, but in stasis, made one with the dark.

On this peacetime kind of beach he could not unlock his body's warning system; at least, not all the way because his mind knew he was safe, no matter what. He heard the little waves murmur and followed the guitar music. Watching the moonlight paint his legs, he thought that Chang Yen Ling would capture the glory of such a night in a new poem.

Looking toward the horizon and into the sea, Keenan saw her walk a silvered path across the water. She moved strongly and with her own kind of grace, this woman of the people; so beautiful, this selfless healer of wounds. This was another kind of change, subliminal, brought on by lights and music and clean sheets, the trappings of civilization.

This night he could watch her image glide across the waves and dissolve in the moonlight without him again and again reliving that time of the blood and the feeding sharks of another bay in another part of the world. That much of him had been healed. It didn't mean that the *yonsei* would not return to stalk the night and leave a string of headless

Jap corpses behind. All the dead goddamned Japs in the world couldn't balance the loss of Chang Yen Ling.

And Nancy? She still wore his name and of course he cared for her. Before Yen Ling, he would have said he loved her. Cared for and loved were not the same. Both women had a place in his life, but not the same place.

He could think straight now. The next step was to heal the body; he would rebuild his strength and return to China where the Japs were thickest and where he knew something of the land. On the phone to Kill Devil Hill, he'd told General Belvale that. Your choice, the general said; if Crusty could be here, he would never have doubted your decision. You are family, so I don't question your choice, either. Just don't push yourself too hard.

Keenan, Belvale had added then, see what you can do for Farley. He doesn't have to feel guilty. His breakdown wasn't a betrayal of his country or his troops. I'm sure you agree that every man jack of us has a breaking point. Some reach it earlier than others. Between you and Nancy, the boy ought to clear his head soon. I've told her that I'll bring him home whenever *she* says he's ready. The opinions of the other pill rollers don't count.

Amen, old man, Keenan whispered to the ocean, to the soft wind blowing, and to the memory of Chang Yen Ling. And for Charles Crusty Carlisle, each of them one of a kind. Amen.

. . . Warning . . .

It was faint, a sound masked by the easy rolling of the gentle surf, so thin an alien noise that he wasn't sure he had heard anything at all. It was behind him, a little crunch of sand. Keenan tensed as it came again, closer. Another second, he thought; one more footfall.

. . . Warning! . . .

There it was.

Rolling, he caught an ankle and jerked it to him, bringing the intruder down hard. Keenan came to his knees with a fluid motion that the *yonsei* would approve. In an extension of the same movement, his free hand poised to crush the windpipe.

"Keenan!" She froze him in place with the single word, his name hissed up at him. Good lord, he had come that near to killing nurse Susie Lokomaikai. Shaken, he leaned back and away from her. The soft night and the moonglow; his return to civilization to take his place with the men and boys who didn't wear the thousand-yard stare in their sunken eyes—that sure sign of too much combat come too close. All of it had lulled him, had helped to grow a new skin for him. But it was so fragile that a shallow scratch peeled it away when his survival button was pushed.

"I'm really sorry, Susie. I didn't know—are you hurt?"

Sitting up, she palmed sand from her hair and then shook it with both hands. "Only my pride; my fault, major. By now I ought to know better than to ease up on a combat soldier without *hookani*—making some kind noise. You scared me so bad I sound like a beach boy."

"It was reflex—the jungles, the Japs. I might have killed you. Maybe I should see the shrink that Nancy—that, that my—oh hell; that nurse Carlisle has talked about."

"I already know you one time married to her; okay by me. But more better you don't see the shrink. Man, that *haole* got problems his own. No damage for me, and more better—hey! I didn't break this jar of *okulihao*. Good pineapple bootleg is hard to find. That other stuff make your hair fall out."

Keenan said, "You followed me from the hospital? Nancy and the shrink sent you, right?"

"I sent myself, man; and don't holler on me. That'll bring on an attack of pidgin nobody can follow, even me. I followed you before, in case you fell out on the street. I never had the nerve to come this close before. Which is how come I brought the booze. If you check, you'll find it's two drinks short. I needed them. Oh, never mind saying thanks; it's all part of our friendly nurses' service."

Up close, the moonlight playing over her face, Susie might have been that other woman wanting to be loved, on a stony beach in China. Susie's hair—that rich midnight cascade of the Oriental woman, spilling to her bare shoulders, exotically scented, a white flower tucked over her ear.

He resisted the look of her, the scent of her. You're out of uniform, lieutenant. No civilian clothes in wartime, remember?"

"This *okulihao* don't give a good goddamn about regulations. Us natives drink it straight from the jar; no sissy glasses for us." She twisted the top of the jar and passed it to him.

The whiskey was colorless, and its bouquet a bit sugary. Without holding the jar to a light, he would guess that the whiskey would be as clear as the home made corn whiskey back in the Virginia hills. Sitting beside Susie on his blanket, he took a long swallow.

"H-holy shit!" It was liquid fire burning down to explode in his stomach.

She laughed, the sound of silver temple bells; the sound of a lover's wind tiptoeing through a mandarin's garden. Tilting the Mason jar, she took a generous pull of pineapple whiskey.

"Whoo! This stuff make you spit in Mister King Kong's eye; give him much *kakaha;* maybe even whip his hairy ass."

He laughed. Susie was easy to laugh with. During her shifts on the ward, she usually brought a new joke for him; if not, her bubbly humor and bright smile were just as good for lighting up a ward of broken men. She was young, smart and beautiful; what could she want of him? Maybe she wasn't kidding about following him to see that he didn't crap out and lower the curve for the ward's success rate. But here she was, bearing a jar of skyrocket fuel.

She said, "I see them come and go, the young men and the old soldiers. Sometimes they get well all the way through. Some get well in the body but not the head." Sighing, she had another drink.

He took the jar. "Which one am I, girl?"

Leaning back on her elbows, she stretched her legs beside his, not quite touching and he thought he could feel a vibration. "I'm not a girl; I'm a woman. I think no doctor can reach inside and fix where you hurt. I think you have to heal that part by yourself. You're much different now than the day you were carried in on a litter. You'll grow stronger day by day, and one morning you'll go right back to the war, and damn what the doctors say. Or what I say."

His second drink of *okulihao* went down smoother. He said, "You've been talking to Nancy. Most times she knew what I was thinking before I did. Even though she's here, the rest of Nancy and me seems far off and not all that real. So much of what I called important back then, in that other world, doesn't mean much now. I wonder which is the real world, out there in the jungles, or here."

When she tilted her head away from him, black-black hair sheeted the near side of her face. "Yes, we talked, your wife and me. Ex-wife isn't all that ex. Both of you carry the imprint of what you had before, man; good or bad. She was straight with me, honest with me, I think. She told me about your rich and powerful family and that she asked for the divorce, not you."

"But why did you—"

"You *puniu?* So dizzy? I'm here to make love with you. I'm not afraid of your grand family. I am the granddaughter of kings; the blood of Kamehameha himself runs in my veins. The right place and the right time. Here and now."

"Girl—woman, you—"

"At ease, major. You talk too much."

Her mouth was soft, tasting of flowers and the flavor of sunwarmed peaches. Little minnow flicks of her tongue, gentle tappings of her teeth; her mumu magically falling apart so the moonbeams highlighted her silken skin and kissed the dark hollows. She drew him down to her, cushioning him with her breasts and slowly rolling her hips while helping him out of his clothes.

She was more than youth and more than beautiful. So smooth she was, so supple and warm, a maker of rhythms slow and deep or staccato beats that locked him into her. At first she was Chang Yen Ling, the tasting come back and the dream returned. Rocking with her, he closed his eyes and willed her to be his lost love. And then the lines blurred, breaking the overlay of one woman upon another. Then his need, stripped of all subterfuge, and his held-in loneliness concentrated on the only woman in the world and she was called Susie.

NORTH AMERICAN NEWS ALLIANCE, feature to follow—With the Allied armies in Italy, Sept. 30, 1943: Furious engagements continue in Naples between the insurgents and German troops. Finally, after the Germans again used tanks, a truce was arranged by both sides to take effect at 0700 this morning.

It did not hold. Heavy fighting continues, and General Mark Clark's 5th Army headquarters announced that the Allies are at the gates in the southern part of the city.

In an aside, the general's aide commented that if the Italians had fought as well with the Germans as they did against them, the Allies might still be in Sicily or even Tunisia.

An Italian soldier who escaped the city and was taken prisoner explained: "We never hated the Americans. It did not take long to hate Germans, but we could do nothing about it. Now we can."

UNITED PRESS—Allied Headquarters, Solomon Islands, Sept. 30, 1943: Last night the Tokyo Express completed the evacuation of some 9400 men from Kolombangara. US naval and air forces intervened, but to little or no effect.

Eddie Donnely remained on one knee, rifle at the ready. The arm hung on a thorn bush, along with bits of singed uniform. Close by was the burned pit where the mortar had exploded. The 81mm shell must have hit the Jap on the head and blown him to pieces. His buddies had hauled off the mangled corpse as they often did to hide their losses, but they missed the severed arm.

If they had seen it, they would have at least stripped it of the two wrist watches. Hanging there, the thing was obscene; the bloody end facing out, the watches glittering in a shaft of sunlight that penetrated the jungle ceiling.

"They have to be American watches," Corporal Morgan grunted. "According to what we can see of that uniform, the son of a bitch wasn't an officer and the peasants never own watches unless they take them off GIs. And maybe the GIs weren't dead yet. Dirty sons of bitches."

Boof Hardin said, "Some Jap will wear *your* watch, if you don't keep your big ass down."

"No fucking way, man. No goddamn slant eye ever lived that can put old Morgan down."

"They hit you before," Eddie said.

"Lucked out."

Eddie scanned the brush left and right. "The Tokyo Express was busy last night. The captain thinks the Japs are pulling out."

Boof lay flat with his BAR. "Their ships didn't shell us much, like usual. Maybe they did haul ass, which won't make me a bit mad. My asshole been puckered so long it may not open much. I'll keep on dropping them little round pills like sheep shit."

Still erect, Morgan moved toward the severed arm.

"Watch it," Eddie said.

"You see any Japs?"

"Like the Apaches and Comanches, when you don't see them, that's when they're dangerous."

"You watch them John Wayne movies in the hospital? Shit—he damned near had me believing that one Gyrene can whip a dozen Japs or a hundred fucking Indians. Ain't no feathers stuck up a Jap's ass. Ain't no John Wayne here, neither."

Morgan slung his M-1 and leaned close to the arm to peer at the watches. "Hey—told you they're American; one's a Bulova." He lifted the arm off the bush.

And blew away most of his face.

CHAPTER 29

REUTERS—London, Sept. 30, 1943: The largest air raids of the year hit this city last night with high explosives, delayed action bombs, fire bombs and navy mines. Fire fighting teams have been hard at it since the beginning, and have saved many of the row houses in the heaviest hit neighborhoods. The Royal Navy is sweeping the Thames for the mines and disposal units have pulled the teeth of several time bombs. Casualties have been reported in the Royal Engineer disposal units by new type detonators. All members of such teams are volunteers.

Brigadier Foxworth was most congenial, and Chad didn't know which had done the most to make him that effusive, the case of rare, aged Scotch, the Cuban cigars or the invoking of Preston Belvale's name. Possibly any or all of them.

"And how is Brigadier Belvale these days? He was a wonder in your AEF, in the first war. A wonder I say."

"He says the same thing about you, sir. But grandfather wears three stars now—a lieutenant general, sir."

Foxworth poured drinks for them and drank his off in a swallow. "Three stars, you say? Three stars. Your grandfather, yes."

"He wondered if you might be interested in a short tour

in Washington. Sir, grandfather realizes how important you are here, but we do require a man of the general's stature as liaison. Rations and quarters pay, although a house will be held in your name."

The whiskey spread more redness across Foxworth's veined face and thick neck. Chad refilled the man's glass and waited.

Foxworth said, through a haze of fragrant blue smoke, "If I could be posted to Washington, I suppose I would be expected to be at hand to brief gentleman in your House of Lords. The Senate, it's called? Washington, yes."

"They will benefit much through your experience and wisdom, sir." Chad damned near choked on that one. Then he said, "Sir, there may be a minor snag. I understand that a colonel from your provost section has applied for the post through our embassy. I don't know how the information got out so early. A diplomatic leak, I suppose; the colonel is probably close with some minor attaché, for him to be approved so fast. But why worry? Of course, he should immediately step aside for your appointment, brigadier."

Foxworth coughed around a drag on his cigar. "A colonel? Colonel, you say. Pushing himself like that; friends in high places, and the orders already approved?"

Chad poured the general another drink. "Sir, I don't think you should worry. Surely a man of your rank—"

"Pushy; a toadying move, political, I say; damned politics." He emptied his glass.

"If the general agrees, there may be a way. A shortage of officers in so many theaters—"

"Yes, shortage; blank files to be filled. Job to be done away from any sort of politics, far from London. Far, I say—Wingate continues to beg for replacements, and although his ragtag group of Chindits is hardly military, I think service with it will do the colonel good. Teach him how the other half lives, yes. So it will be the China-Burma-India theater."

"Good choice, sir, the CBI. That duty assignment for Colonel Hodgkins-Smythe—"

Chad needed the shot of Scotch that he had been holding

for quite a while. He hated this bullshit maneuvering, but it was better than using the family's wealth as a bribe or a club. He had threatehed "Colonel Blimp" with the club, when Hodgkins-Smythe got involved because of what the British army considered bad publicity regarding Stephanie and Chad. All they'd done was save a hurt kid's life during a bombing raid. It hit the fan when he and Stephanie were identified in newspapers as married, but not to each other. Stephanie's husband being stationed at Singapore and under seige didn't help matters. The Brits got sticky about liaisons like that. Too many wives of English soldiers were playing footsies with Americans.

Colonel Blimp showed up to escort Chad to Heathrow airport. Chad's travel orders had been sneaked through by the family's longtime enemy, General Skelton. There was no time to get them changed then and there. And the Brits tried to hide Leftenant Stephanie Bartlett from him. That failing, the bastards had been warned not to ship her overseas. So they sent her to the hottest spot in the Pacific, an outpost about to fall to the Japanese—Singapore. It was better for her to die beside her husband than to live in sin. Okay, Colonel Hodgkins-Smythe, you pompous son of a bitch, enjoy your new post in the jungles. Since Wingate has no use at all for a provost colonel, he'll sweat that lard off your ass in a line outfit.

Cheers, you bastard; you might be bullet proof.

ASSOCIATED PRESS—With General Mark Clark's Fifth Army in Italy, Oct. 4, 1943: In the U.S. VI Corps sector, while the 3rd Division on the left of the line makes for the Volturno River, the 34th and 45th Divisions move by separate routes toward Benevento, an important road junction.

During the night Allied Commandos landed near Teremoli, seizing the harbor and the town, and the British 78th Division linked up with them.

Chad Belvale's excuse for being in Italy was that the big wheels in London headquarters wanted an unbiased opinion on the front and why movement was so slow. He was already tired of stacked arms and just marking time, so he talked to some people on both sides of the Atlantic and became an official headhunter. The Big Red One was in a long training phase for guess what invasion to come. Major Lucien Langlois, as the battalion exec, could run things as well as Chad, maybe better; the Cajun was a hard task master and harder on himself. Second Battalion of the 16th Infantry would be ready to jump the English Channel when the orders came down, if that was tomorrow or next week. The only directive Chad left was to walk hell out of men and officers, because even a few weeks in garrison stole the legs of the infantry.

The big jump wouldn't come off this winter, but sometime in the spring or summer, when the channel weather was supposed be better. Chad would have to see it; the big ditch was better known for sudden squalls and rainstorms. In general the Channel weather was just vicious. General Eisenhower would have to pick the day and the hour. Chad didn't envy him the task. Once his orders sent the invasion armada from its several ports there could be no recall, and if the water was too rough and the ceiling too thick for close fighter support, and a major pounding from the navy gunships, the largest fleet in world history could screw up royally. Casualties would be heavy even before they managed to get ashore at Pas de Calais or Normandy, or possibly southern France. Thank God the spread of good landing sites was wide, too wide for the Krauts to beef up defense troops in all probable areas.

As the Italian landings had been? From his canvas side seat in the cargo compartment of the C-47, Naples was a reminder of antiquity and the burning of Rome without a Nero fiddling, unless you could count Mussolini hauling his spaghetti ass out of town. Chad had been relieved to find that the smoke was bigger than the fire, and that a good part of the smoke was fueled by knocked-out Kraut tanks and smoldering ships in the harbor. He tapped his driver on the shoulder and the jeep pulled over.

"Real mess, ain't it, colonel? Our bombers caught a shit-pot of boats all drawed up at them docks yonder." The driver took time to roll a smoke of Bull Durham, closing the tobacco sack with a pull of his teeth on the tag and drawstring. For sure a down home boy, Chad thought.

Ships tilted crazily, some lifted and jammed into warehouse skeletons of blackened iron, some burned at their docks, a few sunk with only their stacks or masts showing above water. They were all merchant ships, as far as he could tell, but that was okay; they had carried equipment and supplies for Fascists and Nazis. Now disgusted ex-Fascists had attacked the tanks and sniped Germans retreating from the American 5th Army. The combat action was to the north now, and according to SHEAF G-2 in London, the outlook for fighting through the mountains appeared grim, and much yet depended upon whether the Germans would go along with declaring Rome an open city. It would be a damned shame to wreck the Eternal City, while trying to steer clear of the Vatican. Maybe there were enough Catholics left in the Kraut army.

"Okay, driver. Let's see if we can find Mark Clark's headquarters."

"My name's Holcomb, sir; Private Sammy Holcomb. Reckon I can get us to headquarters even if they moved it again."

The jeep passed on through the oily smell, the fried black smell of burning things, its driver dodging obstacles in the road—bomb craters and fallen walls that engineer bulldozers had partially shoved to one side. A dangling power line swung back and forth, sparking as it touched metal.

"Somebody'll sure as hell get stung on that," Holcomb said, twisting the wheel. "Probably one of them hungry ass I-talians. Just hope it ain't one of them kids. Goddamn, you ought to see them poor little bastards; big old eyes watching you scrape out your mess kit. You just plain got to save something to put in their cans. They don't never eat it there; they take it home so their folks can share it. Goddamn war's hardest on younguns."

The jeep jerked right and slewed as the driver avoided wreckage. "Sorry—sir."

"No need; you missed it."

"Ain't sorry about that; when I get riled up, I plumb forget to say sir or colonel."

"No need for that, either. I agree with you about the kids. The war isn't their fault, and it helps to remember who started the thing. How do you feel about fighting in the north?"

"You asking a private, a jeep driving yardbird? Goddamn, colonel."

"The yardbirds do the fighting, don't they?

"For certain sure, but I never figured to hear no high brass admit it. Them mountains are going to be a bastard to get through, because them goddamn Krauts ain't going to lay down and just let us do-si-do in. I hear some of them brass assholes—begging the colonel's pardon, sir—I hear them assholes go on about sunny Italy and how the Krauts is hightailing it for home and everybody might be home for Christmas. Bullshit; I talked to some of them line outfit doggies coming back all boogered up. They said them mountains get higher and meaner as you go. They said the Krauts is digging in and bringing up more fucking tanks, and about a million of them goddamn 88s. They ain't about to give up nary a foot of land without a fight."

Lurching, the jeep angled around a pothole that could have been made by a mortar round, it was that neatly rounded and charred.

Holcomb said, "So if you're wondering how come a jeep jockey is interested in the fighting and not protecting his soft, safe job away back here, I done put in to go back to my old outfit in the Red Bull Division, the 34th. After I got hit and when I come back from the hospital, they give me this goddamn jeep. I swony, if they don't give me a transfer, I'm going over the hill, going north bigod and fuck this rear echelon shit. Oh hell, I done it again; no military courtesy like they say. Sorry, sir."

"No need, son," Chad said. "When we get to headquarters, I'll see to it that you get that transfer, quick as you want."

"Sir—yes sir; goddamn, sir. You're my kind of officer, sir."

Chad smiled. "And you're my kind of soldier, Private Sammy Holcomb."

CHAPTER 30

UNITED PRESS—Somewhere in Italy, Oct. 12, 1943: The American 5th Army jumped off in a major attack on the Volturno Line. German positions on the other side of the river are extremely strong and in depth. As yet there are no reports of gain or casualties.

REUTERS—London, SHEAF headquarters, Oct. 12, 1943: Today 357 bombers of the American 8th Air Force blackened the skies in a massive attack on Bremen and Vegesack. Reports and aerial photographs deem the raid a major success, but the bomber fleet incurred heavy losses.

Scott Travis turned another card that wouldn't play on his solitaire layout. He had never seen the game played against the house in Vegas, but talk about it abounded: you paid 52 bucks for the deck; the house paid you five bucks for every card in the ace piles above the seven card layout. If Scott had been playing in Vegas, he would owe better than 800 dollars.

"Shit," he said. *"Scheisse, merde!"* And kicked over the wooden crate he used for a table.

Internment by the goddamn Swiss was boring. He'd read the three books the library had in English; they were boring, too. He couldn't believe that one of them was the life story of a raghead, a guy named Ibn Saud who kicked the shit out of a bunch of other ragheads and united his country. The only good part was when Ibn Saud got shot in the inner thigh and a rumor ran through his tribe that he wasn't a man any more. To quash the story, he sent to the nearest town for a virgin and balled her all night, sending out the bloody marriage rag for proof. Scott liked that.

Some of that Arab *cous-cous* would be okay about now, if they kept their dirty fingers out of the pot. Here the food was heavy on fish, potatoes and cheese. It was far better than the stuff the Jerries fed, but not even as good as American air corps rations. And these imitation civilian clothes, for the Limeys, a handful of French who'd been sweating it out here for years, for some Jerry deserters, and a few American bomber crews; the suits and sweaters all the same, drab and floppy. When he first came, officials took his uniform, right down to the warm flying boots.

Being behind the wire again was bad; a prison stockade by any other name was a pain in the ass. The BBC in London kept the camp informed on the war, and on all fronts, the Jerries were going downhill; the Japs, too, but not as fast. The war might be over before he got out of here; no more kills in the air, no publicity for a nickel and dime hero who was barely an ace.

The squarehead Swiss had reported him to their Red Cross, and by now the family knew he was locked up safe here. Who would get him out? Damn it, wasn't that the great family creed—duty, honor, country? He didn't give a shit how much it cost, just so he got back to the war. He had made it this far on his own; if the great family didn't give him a hand, and ASAP, he'd get the rest of the way.

One squarehead Red Cross guy wasn't all that unyielding, and Scott was working on him. Twenty, twenty-five thousand would buy a lot of fish. The guy was softening, and getting the money to Switzerland should be a snap. The gnomes of Zurich took their bite to keep bank deposits secret, and a private number would release them. No sweat there, and the goddamn bureaucrat ought to get on the stick before long.

Here he had too much time to think, to mull over the rights and wrongs done to him. Stephanie's put down outranked the other wrongs, rankled deeper and came to the top of his mind when he wasn't busy, when he wasn't flying and making his record, adding to his score. Back in England the bitch had laughed at him—laughed!—after he screwed her in the back seat of a taxi. It wasn't a rape, either. She had wanted it as much as he did, maybe more. But she laughed, goddamn her. Leftenant Stephanie Bartlett had a payoff coming and she'd get it; just as soon as he got out of this barbed wire hotel for internees. She was no virgin bride, but he could come up with something and send out her bloody drawers. He would get out; he would.

INS—New Britain, Oct. 12, 1943: The US 5th Air Force, with new fields on Munda and Barakoma, began a big strategic offensive yesterday. Spokesmen said the entire Bismarck Archipelago could now be neutralized, and especially the big Japanese naval base at Rabul, hit yesterday by 349 aircraft, the first of many strikes to come.

This raid sank four transports and a patrol boat, and damaged three destroyers, three submarines, one tanker and one auxiliary craft. The Jap headquarters were taken completely by surprise.

Nancy Belvale had never done it in the open, had never made love with the sunlight as the only cover. Just for a moment, she wanted to hide, to call it off. But Fitz was so beautiful, all brown and sungold and cute little midnight curlings of pubic hair. The rest of his body was without hair, sleek and smoothly muscled.

"It's okay to be scared," said Sgt. Fitzgerald Kaole Di-Gama. "But I don't think anybody will show up way out here. And if they did, they probably wouldn't turn us in for fraternizing. This is Oahu; live and let live."

The air was washed by the bright blue sea and dusted with some kind of flowery scent. Lying on her side, stretched upon the hospital blanket, she stroked his chest and her fingertips tingled. "It's not that, Fitz. I just feel kind of funny."

"Because your *kanaka,* your man, is in the hospital. His shadow stretches this far?"

She tasted his warm skin. "No."

Keenan's presence here really didn't disturb her, and when she considered it, his memory hadn't for a long time. Of course she was glad he had been found alive—again. And she sincerely hoped that his luck would last, that he would put away the painful specter of the Chinese woman he loved. Keenan held that dark shade close, speaking of her only in his earlier delerium.

"No," she repeated. "I'm new to making love like this, in a coconut grove beside the ocean."

"It's a good way, the way of my people for hundreds of years; my Hawaiian people, that is. I figure my Irish blood would think too cold and rainy, and the Portugese part too moral; all those black robes. I stay with the Hawaiian me, as much as I can."

"Then I will, too."

His hands roamed her softly, petting and finger walking her taut skin until the core of her melted and she relaxed, giving herself up to the bronze kisses of the sun, to the gentle explorations of his lips. He kissed her all over, making her tremble, and came back to her mouth which applauded him hungrily, lips and tongue and teeth; her mouth which drank of his spiced breath.

"You are a *malle* woman, calm as an inner lagoon, quiet and gentle."

"Not always," she whispered, and lifted herself above him, over him, to poise for a delicious moment before guiding him into her body.

Still he would not hurry, and as she straddled him and her hair fell forward to gauze across his face, Nancy knew there would never be another first time, not like this. She did not want it to end.

NANA, feature to follow—Melbourne, Australia, Oct. 12, 1943: A heroic network of Coast Watchers has done yeoman duty from radio outposts hidden deep in jungles and atop high Pacific island mountains. Since the outbreak of hostilities, these brave lookouts have reported on all Japanese movements by air and sea. Their sightings have warned Allied ships to be ready, and for planes to take to the air and protect airfields slated to be bombed by the enemy.

Their primitive camps must be moved often so Japanese radio finders cannot pin down the locations. Mostly Australians, and a few clergymen who remained with their flocks, they know the territory intimately. In many cases they are aided by loyal natives.

Even so, some of these selfless men have been captured and beheaded, along with their native helpers.

Crusty Carlisle wished they hadn't shot up the radio when his Marines shot up the Japs. The men tried to fix it, but all they got was static from time to time. The good thing was how they packed it off and managed to get the boat around to the other side of the island without running aground. They camouflaged the boat in a green-scum lagoon and the Jap search party didn't find it, or anything else. The Marines bitched about dragging Japs off into the bush and digging their graves. When the search party showed up to check on the radio silence, they found more silence and a deeper silence. There was no food, no weapons, and not even a set of footprints. The base was empty and ghostly, as if a giant hand had reached down and eliminated everything but the buildings.

From a safe vantage point Crusty had watched the Japs so apeshit trying to find out what happened to their outpost.

They stayed for just two days, and then took off in the motor launch that had brought them. All of them were jittery, looking over their shoulders and scared to penetrate the jungle to any depth, so the search was hit and miss. You could see them sweating out some bloodthirsty jungle spook, and how happy they were to put the island behind them.

Emptying and making the camp mysterious had been Sergeant Glover's idea. Crusty had it in mind to ambush the Japs, but if only one lucky bastard made it back to the launch and a radio, word would flash back to home base, wherever that was. Then a bigger, less nervous force would be sent to comb the atoll thoroughly. It was better this way, staying under cover so an occasional snoop plane marked with the flaming asshole never saw anything amiss on the atoll.

It nagged at Crusty that a strong recon force hadn't already come for another sweep. The little bastards were known to write off an outpost and never think twice, but this setup had to have been reasonably important. And some ranking officer wouldn't buy the ghost story.

"Gunny," he said to the Marine sergeant, "my instinct tells me—no, yells at me—to haul ass off this island. We sat it out for too long already, trying to get a fix on our people. I feel a whole shitpot of Japs coming on."

Sergeant Glover nodded. "My sentiments exactly, general. Just in case, we been storing fresh water aboard the ship like you said; coconuts, papayas, taro and all that's left of the Jap chow; we even dried some fish."

"We got anybody who knows how to sail that ship?"

"Corporal Tefft, the guy who steered it around the point when we hid it. Remember, a Jap bullet creased him across the ass? Says he used to sail a little on a lake in Oregon."

Crusty scratched where sand fleas had been feeding on him. His was a tough old hide, impervious to the heat rash that irritated some of the men. "Beats a poke in the eye with a sharp stick. This ocean ain't a calm lake. But if Tefft doesn't capsize the ship, and as long as you have that prismatic compass, we ought to point in the right direction. Everybody's all rested up and getting hog fat, so it's time we get back to the war anyhow. Let's police up any sign that we've been here at all, brush the sand and shag ass."

"Like the corpsman said, nobody ever saw a general like you. Shit, any kind of brass taking suggestions from a grunt would be a miracle."

Crusty put a finger to his hairy lips. "Shh; everybody will find out how I got to be a general, by listening to good advice from the ranks."

The Japs had plenty of gas to run the dynamo that fed their radio, and an extra supply for the ship's rusty one-lunger engine. It was more evidence that the base had been of some importance.

Palm leaf brushing carefully behind him as he backed, the navy corpsman said, "I guess most of us been sun-burned enough that we'll look like Nips from the air. A couple of them dinky uniforms might help in case a Zero buzzes us; anybody on deck goes into the gook squat and waves. We stick the meatball flag on the stern. The Nips painted over the real name of the ship and put some squiggles of their own on it."

Crusty took a drink of coconut milk and brushed his mouth; all this face hair was good for keeping mosquitos off, but an irritant. That reminded him. "Pretty good, Sullivan, but anybody on deck has to shave; the Japs don't sprout much hair. And never mind bitching about no razors. I hear the Marine K-bar knife can do anything. Sullivan, are you sure you haven't messed around with sailboats? You could give Tefft a hand."

"Uh-uh, general; deep water scares the hell out of me. I damned near went ape in that raft."

Standing up, Crusty plugged his coconut. "You did all right when you had to. I guess you have to again. We can't stay here and we have to be pretty damned lucky to remain afloat, much less find our way home. Ain't I a cheerful old bastard?"

SECRET to Kill Devil Hill, scrambled, Code 3—The Italian Front, Oct. 13, 1943: Torrential rains have turned the Volturno line into a quagmire, bogging down tanks and trucks, making any large troop movement extremely difficult. German units defending the positions have been identified as the 15th Armored Division, the Hermann Goering Panzer Division and the 3rd Division, making up General Hans Hube's XIV Armored Corps. Resistance to 5th Army probes has been intense.

Preston Belvale rubbed his game leg and sat looking at the war map. It appeared as though Mark Clark was about to get his tail in a crack. Rains like that meant low ceilings and little or no direct air support. American casualties would be high and reported only in dribbles, so as not to shake up the homefront. Certain representatives and senators would have to be contacted to help in smoothing over any shock from casualty lists. Army induction centers would be told to cut corners in training time so that replacements filled the gaps. These would be the Hill's priorities.

"Important, general?" Gloria Carlisle-Donnely stood before his desk with a sheaf of yellow TWXes in hand. Technically she was not yet cleared for Secret communiqués. He made a mental note to look into the delay.

"Nothing on the Pacific. From the ETO, the first proof that Roosevelt listened too long to Stalin and his insistence on a Second Front right away. Stalin said he considered Sicily only a diversion and hammered away on the need to take pressure off the Eastern Front. Tired and ill, our president allowed himself to be conned, and in Italy we're making the first payment on that contract. Nothing to do about it now."

Belvale sniffed the length of a new cigar. "We weren't ready for a channel crossing, either; I'd say we still aren't. We're fighting on two fronts; no matter how long it is, the Russians just have one, and the supply problems are German. Our defense industries are working around the clock, but we still come up with a spot shortage of landing craft or planes or tanks.''

"Or men." Gloria's face was tight.

He bit the end off his cigar. "No news, so Eddie is all right. You'll be the first to know, even if he's only wounded.''

She bit her lips. "Only wounded."

"Dear, Eddie Donnely would have gone back on his own.''

"Like grandfather."

Belvale lighted his cigar, giving himself time. "Yes, just like Crusty. Like Big Mike Donnely and the nameless kids falling in Italy as we speak. It's what the family does, what it is; you know that.''

"Yes, I know. I know and I don't like it any more." She stalked away, her back stiff and straight.

Joann Belvale waited before approaching him. "She's worried about Eddie, of course, and that she might be pregnant. But there's nothing definite yet. Do you have a list of people you want me to call about that Secret TWX?''

"Thanks for reminding me. In a minute, my dear." Sinking back in his chair, he drew a thumbnail across his moustache. The women, he thought; the family was hell on them, but they always came through; they toughed it out. Only the first report on pretty Penny and the English woman had come in, after the first payment in gold had been picked up. They were out of the PW camp and should be a goodly way across the Pacific.

The family luck had been running bad of late; maybe it would change.

CHAPTER 31

REUTERS—New Guinea, Oct. 14: A captured enemy document has enabled the Australian 9th Division to take the necessary steps to repulse a series of fierce counter-attacks launched by the Japanese. These branched out from the strongpoint of Sattelberg, which overlooks Finschafen.

INS—Washington, D.C., Oct. 14: While a bill authorizing a navy equivalent of the WAC, called WAVES, was before the House, Rep. Beverly M. Vincent (D-Kentucky) affirmed the Southern view of womanhood.

"They are God's creatures," he said, "made close to the angels."

He scoffed at the theory that the WAVES would release male personnel for sea duty, saying that the girls would be more interested "in putting on lipstick and looking in mirrors" than doing any work. He criticized spending the $200 needed to uniform each recruit and pounced on the navy's suggestion that some WAVES would be used in the culinary services.

"Why, bless you, don't you know they're not going to spend $200 to dress up a girl and then put her in the kitchen?"

Penny threw up.

Cocking his head, the chief Dyak turned and stopped the column.

"The h-heat." Penny fought the good fight, locking her teeth until the sickness pried them open and the greenish yellow fluid fountained out. It was the heat, the muggy, suffocating heat that blanketed the jungles of Borneo. If it wasn't the heat, then it was being forced to breathe the rotting stench. A sick sweat channeled her cheeks. Maybe something in the bad food was just catching up.

Stephanie wet a hankie from her canteen and handed it down. It cooled Penny's feverish skin a bit, only a bit. "I'll be all right."

"Sure you will. Here, take a drink."

It could be the brackish water, or just being off her feet for a bit, but the seasick feeling was departing slowly. "Sorry," she said to Stephanie and to the Dyak. He stood in a patch of sunlight coming weakly through the thick green canopy. Bengis was a squat and ugly little man whose lines of lumpy blue tattoos didn't help his face. He was more comfortable now on his home ground. His three men squatted whenever forward movement stopped, going so still that insects crawled their faces without notice. Penny noticed how their black marble eyes never stopped searching the brush, constantly flicking here and there. She had the feeling that, if they had long ears, those also would be reading the jungle around them, moving back and forth the way an alert horse used them.

"Missy number one okay?"

"Yes, Bengis; thank you. I'm ready to go on."

He more or less smiled, showing canine teeth filed sharp. "Missy know what mean, my name?"

There was only a faint rumble in her stomach now. "No, I'm sorry."

"Mean my heart is hard; mean me man like eat blood."

Rising carefully, Penny kicked dirt over the mess she had made. "I think you are hardhearted when you must be; but inside you are a gentle man."

One of the other Dyaks snorted, and Bengis frowned

briefly at him. Then he said to Penny. "You fix goddamn Jap number one good. You baby my village; god man come, make *kawin, nikah.*"

"What? I don't understand."

"*Kawin, nikah.*" Then a thrusting of his lips left no doubt what he meant. Stephanie said, "I think you just had a proposal, but it could be simply a propostion."

Penny stared at the man. "Baby? What baby? Do you mean you want a baby from me?"

"Missy have baby now."

No, no, no. She tried to remember her last period. It was the heat and the stench, the terrible food; she was worn down from the long sea voyages, the sweaty, killing marches. Since she killed that Jap, she hadn't felt just right.

A Jap baby, oh God; Watanabe's baby, oh God.

She threw up again.

UNITED PRESS—Detroit, Mich., Oct. 15, 1943: As manpower becomes scarce, there are few worries about whether women can do the job. Even the conservative Ford Motor Company, which in all its history has employed women only in clerical jobs, now has a work force of 40 percent women in its Willow Run plant.

Kirstin tried to soften the blow. Gently and without lingering, she kissed Harlan Edgerton good-bye, only a brushing across lips she had savored, when tasting forbidden excitement and youth.

"Harlan, it's wonderful that you asked me to marry you. It's the highest compliment that a woman can receive, especially an old widow lady."

He started to protest and she hushed him with her fingertips. "You know I have sons older than you—"

Harlan kissed her fingers. "It don't make a difference to me. If you feel like you can't put up with living with a cripple—"

"Harlan, Harlan; we proved there's nothing for you to worry about. You're a whole lot of man—a very young man forced to grow up too quickly."

The pinkish fingers of his left hand were slightly cupped and couldn't move; it was his dress prosthetic. For actual usage, a network of straps operated a metal clamp. He had worked hard to control its opening and closing. The right leg was more difficult for him; putting weight on the stump was painful and would remain so through several fittings and until the time when his skin callused over the end. It would take even more time for him to stop feeling the sharp aches in knees and toes, the ghost pain so real because the nerve endings continued to send signals from long gone extremities.

"I can grow up some more." He held out his good hand. "Kirstin, I love you. I love you so much."

She pressed both hands against her belly. "I believe you do; you believe it, too. Damn it, Harlan. I never meant for us to go this far. I saw a sad and bitter man wasting himself because—because he was afraid he couldn't make love. Now you know you can."

"You never cared for me? I was just a handy experiment and you'll pick another crip to work on?"

She faced him fully, faced the hurt in his blue eyes. "No; I'm not a caseworker, and not even a Doughnut Dolly. You helped me as much as I helped you. My terrible loneliness finally eased. So I think I'll stay home for a while. The ranch hands can keep the riding program going until I can decide what to do with the rest of my life."

Again he reached out and this time took her hand. "Reckon I'll never forget you."

"Please don't."

Quickly then, so he would not see her cry, she hurried past the portable stalls and didn't stop to talk with the ranch hands. She didn't know what else to say to anyone. It had all been covered, but there was a need to peel away more layers of skin, to expose a hurt that might never heal.

If she could have done that with Chad Belvale, if Chad

knew how to be honest with her, maybe they would still be married.

Special to *The New York Times*—Washington, D.C., Oct. 15, 1943: The Third London Protocol was signed here today. It extends American aid to the USSR until June 30th, 1944.

The United States will provide the Soviet Union with 2,700,000 tons of supplies through Russian ports on the Pacific and a further 2,400,000 tons through the Persian Gulf.

Owen Belvale lay warm in the feather bed, his entire body smiling. He picked up outside sounds from force of habit. He listened to the city noises of Southampton, always the survivor, the infantryman, even with Helene Lyons softly pulsing beside him. She could make any man lose his senses, common or extraordinary. He hadn't been intimately involved with that many women, but he realized that this one was exceptional, the kind of woman who had become great courtesans of history. He had often wondered why thrones had fallen and business empires rocked because of one woman. Now he knew. It was as if she peeled back his skin and got inside with him to discover needs deeply hidden, even from himself.

He listened to the ebb and flow of her breath, then heard an outside noise, an extended whine, its tenor rising and falling. Propping upon one elbow, he lighted cigarettes for them both. Some part of her remained inside him for she murmured, "Barrage balloons, luv. Wind makes that sound playing upon the cables. It is a bit ghostly, until you become used to it."

Close against him, her body was childlike in size, small and neat, but a woman grown in the feeling of its hills and hollows, not in the fiery depths still bubbling within her. He said, "Is Jerry still trying to blitz the shipyard and docks?"

I think I love you, woman.

It didn't happen like this: man meets beautiful woman—no, soldier meets beautiful woman in foreign land, which was quite a different thing; she lets him take her to bed on the first date—no, she practically leads him to her own bed. Whatever, Owen had never been affected like this. It was as if their bodies had never been used before, as if sex was brand new and had been waiting through childhood and through puberty for this magic moment to be released.

"Major air raids are rare. The Blitz is about finished, I should hope." Helene snugged her mouth into the base of his throat and tickled the words against his skin. "These days it's one or two planes, usually; nuisance raids by the dive bombers, or spy flights to discover what dear old Blighty is up to now."

I love you, woman.

Maybe he was pushed off balance by her directness. Helene said fuck as easily as she said hello, and not for shock value. It wasn't overused, and coming from her, somehow it didn't sound coarse, just honest. Owen had no experience with a woman who told him what she liked in bed and guided him through each step. This didn't make him feel less a man; it excited him, turned him to more giving than taking. And when she dedicated herself to him, the pleasure was so intense it was painful. He understood what Hemingway meant in *For Whom the Bell Tolls;* the earth could move.

He would feel like a fool saying it aloud. He wanted to talk with her, and not to her, but that would take practice. Playing social games was so much a part of life, at least in the States. A woman's refusal to play them was rare and unsettling.

Fair Helene, whose face launched a thousand ships.

Good lord; now he was going more literary. Careful that the bell doesn't toll for thee. He couldn't afford to lose this woman by doing or saying something stupid. Not now. Not ever.

UNITED PRESS—The Italian Front, Oct. 15, 1943: The US Third and 34th Divisions continue to advance towards Dragoni. After taking Roccaromana, the two units of American VI Corps prepared for the decisive attack to capture Dragoni and the bridges over the Volturno beyond it.

(ADD LATE COPY) Units of the US 34th—Red Bull—Division, opened the attack on Dragoni at dawn October 16, only to find that the Germans withdrew during the night. Engineers are clearing the roads and buildings of mines that the Germans always leave behind them to slow pursuit.

Three vehicles ahead, a heavy explosion hurled a jeep and its passengers into the air. Men screamed into the echoed smoke and swirling dirt.

"Medic—Medic!"

Chad Belvale clamped his nose and blew hard to clear his ears. They opened just in time to hear the three-quarter truck four vehicles behind his jeep get blown all to hell. It must have been a bigger mine; chunks of metal and ripped, smoldering blankets rained down on Chad and his driver, Sammy Holcomb. A combat boot bounced on the hood, a foot still in it and seeping bright blood.

"Holy shit," Holcomb said. He dropped the windshield and used his M-1 to poke the boot off. "Poor son of a bitch. Either one of them mines could of got us. Them fucking Krauts are getting cute again. Bet they were wooden box mines with plastic timers; so many pushes before they go off, and the mine detectors couldn't pick them up. Goddamn; I'm scared to move and scared to stay; shit or go blind. How about you, colonel?"

"I stay scared, son. It helps to keep me alive."

"Reckon we have to sit it out right here. Can't drive around because the fucking Krauts always mine the shoulders of the roads. It ain't raining for a change. Okay if I leave the windshield down? We got a pretty good piss cutter up front."

An upright iron post had been welded to the front bumper and well braced. Back in Africa word spread swiftly through all units, after some jeep drivers and their front seat passengers literally lost their heads to piano wires stretched across the roads at night. Piss cutters sprang into being, made to slice the wires before the wires sliced anyone else.

Jeep floorboards were almost all thick with sandbags, to offer some protection against mines. If for no other reason, they were a psychological comfort.

Chad offered Holcomb a cigarette and snapped his Zippo at it. Holcomb drew smoke. "Can't get used to a bigod colonel lighting my cigarette."

"If I'm not busy, why shouldn't I? Maybe next time, you'll light mine.

"And I don't mind a bit, colonel."

Carefully, medics picked their way beside the convoy, leaning into the Dodge fenders to stay off the edge of the road. They headed up the line to see if anybody was left to patch up. Smoke rode the warm air, carrying the unforgettable odors of cooked flesh and blistered metal, of burned powder. Powder, not cordite; not since World War I had cordite been used. It was a catchall word, like shrapnel, another misnomer. In the days of Blackjack Pershing it was a flying shotgun shell crammed with steel balls. Maybe the word was easier to remember than fragments. A weapon by any other name killed you just as dead.

Holcomb said, "Did you read about the big booby trap the goddamn Krauts left in the Naples post office? *Stars & Stripes* said the damned thing went off a week after we took the town—a whole week; so it could booger up more folks; never mind they're mostly civilians, women and little kids. Goddamn Krauts got something to answer for."

"This war, I think something will be done. It's been too bloody for forgive and forget."

"Yeah; if the guys that start wars had to fight them, there probably wouldn't be no wars."

No chance of that, Chad thought. But if the impossible should happen, what of the family, of the long line of warriors reaching far back in time? They were bred to conflict—ride forth and carry the cross, spread the message. It would be a wonderful world when the warrior was not needed. Until then, there were battles to be won.

CHAPTER 32

ASSOCIATED PRESS—Headquarters, the Italian Front, Oct. 20, 1943: During the night, a battalion of the 78th Division (British, 8th Army) crossed the Trigno River. This was the first time the 8th Army has been in action since General Montgomery reorganized the sector.

Units of the US 34th Division attacked Sant'Angelo D'Alife, but were hurled back.

UNITED PRESS—Somewhere in the South Pacific, Oct. 20, 1943: A battalion of American paratroopers jumped today at Voza, in Choiseul Island, southeast of Bougainville. The minimum objective is a diversionary attack, and the maximum, to establish a base for a full scale landing against Bougainville.

The enemy boat nosed around a low lying finger of coral and brush. It didn't come fast, but about anything that swam or floated could overhaul *Crusty's Flying Fuck,* the latest name for the fishing boat drafted into the Jap navy, and the Jap boat that had joined the United States Marines. The new name was painted small beyond the Jap squiggle writing. One group of Marines had wanted to use the entire phrase; take a flying fuck at a rolling doughnut. They were barely outvoted.

And Tefft, the central Oregon deep water sailor, stayed lucky at the wheel, following a rough daylight course set by Sergeant Glover's compass. They were exposed to spotter planes, surface vessels and submarines. There would be less chance of being seen if they moved only by night, and a better chance of getting lost just following nature's star chart.

They had relied heavily on by guess and bigod, and now the guess had slipped. Crusty hoped the bigod line didn't return a busy signal. It would be a bitch to get nailed now. Everybody on this tub had long been carried MIA; the boys got a kick out of dreaming up returned-from-the-dead acts when they got home. Now, who knew?

He watched the Jap boat grow bigger, sharing another nameless bay in yet another islet where nobody was home. There was no fresh water here and no food beyond sand crabs. You had to be flat bellied and hollow to try one of those stinkers. Crusty had planned to anchor for the night and start out again in the morning. He got a bad feeling that the oncoming boat signalled another island not far off, a Jap held island.

It wasn't much of a patrol boat, just another converted coastal runner, but a Nambu heavy machine gun mounted in the bow and the fried egg flag blowing on the stern turned it military, made it dangerous.

Wait—there was another gun forward, a strangeness of shaping but somehow familiar. The thing had a long nose pointed through a shield. Oh hell yes; it was an American 37mm antitank gun, no doubt picked up by the Japs when Corregidor fell. A split-trail, wheeled weapon not of much real use against armor, it could raise hell with this old scow.

Flattened on the deck, Crusty lined up the binoculars that had been come by courtesy of a Jap officer gone missing with his troops on Spook Island.

"I count eight Japs," he said. "Could be more below. You two short and ugly bastards check on your diapers and head rags. They've probably got glasses on us, too. You'll sucker the peanuts in close until we can get at them. Tell you what—that string of fish we caught this morning:

keep squatted as much as you can and hold up the fish, offer them to the Japs.

"Remember to show a lot of teeth and bow. Keep those rifles hidden until you have to use them. When you do, take out anybody close to those guns. When it hits the fan, we come up out of the hold and pour it to them."

He backed on his belly to the hatch. "The main thing is to hit them hard and fast, before they can get a radio message out. If they can bring a real gunship down on us, or just one lousy plane, we will all buy the farm."

One of the men said, "Buy the farm? Jesus; my grandpa said that all the time. I wonder how old this general is."

Standing on the ladder, Crusty lifted his head. "Your grandpa alive, peanut?"

"Ahh—yessir, last time I heard."

"Think on that."

In the dark and steamy hold that stank of fish oils and man sweat, Crusty gave the word; the skinny, according to Marine jargon. Then he said, "Glover, since there are only two portholes on each side, I'd appreciate it if you and the next best rifleman use the ones on the left side—"

"Port side, general."

"Whatever; what the hell do you call the porthole on the other side—the right hole? I always figured one of those had hair on it."

They laughed and he said to Glover: "Even if you can't get a direct sight on the machine gun or the antitank weapon, keep the bastards away as best you can, rake that bow. If the Japs get either of those guns going, our collective tit is in the wringer. The rest of you fuckups follow me when I pop out of the hatch, and come shooting, because this is the Crotch's specialty—hey, diddle, diddle, right up the middle. Just try to hit something."

As he climbed the ladder, the arthritis reminded him that his shoulders were still no bargain. At the top he pulled his M-1 toward him and heard somebody say, "Damn! I think that old bastard is Chesty Puller in disguise."

And another voice: "I'd give him at least even money if

somebody roped their dicks together and threw them over a barbed wire fence to fight it out."

"You think either of them can even *find* their dicks?"

Yet another voice: "They got them big, hairy balls; they don't need no dicks. If they want to, they can piss out their ears."

Crusty grinned and eased his shoulders out of the hatch. When troops made jokes at an upcoming firefight, they were all right; they didn't convince themselves of impending death. On the other hand, a tight silence pulled tension to the snapping point.

The Jap boat was closing, not fast, but narrowing the gap of water. He couldn't see anyone at the bow guns. He glanced at the "natives" who might be overacting the part. One kid waved the string of fish, their bellies flashing silver in the low sun. The other guy's bow was a shade extreme, since he stayed upon his hands and knees to wave his head up and down. They were burned dark and were scroungy enough to be natives or Japs, but their rifles waited, oily and cared for, out of the enemy's sight.

The labored *putt-putt* of the other engine wheezed louder since the *Flying Fuck*'s engine had been shut down in anticipation of the night harbor, its rusty anchor dropped. Maybe the Jap CO had the same idea. Crusty drew a deep breath as one double-ugly Jap moved toward the bow; only one so far, and that little bastard belonged to Crusty Carlisle. He was already dead and just wasn't smart enough to know it.

Gone tense, Crusty forced his neck muscles to soften and controlled his breath. He lay the rifle on the deck and wished the ship's rails—gunwales?—whatever, were lower. When he had to move, he'd better be quick popping onto the deck. Another little bastard followed the first one to the bow guns. Two more Japs came out of the hold; that made ten turds, alike as a string of sausages going bad. Maybe there were others downstairs—below, dammit. The Marines were fucking up his vocabulary.

Yes, goddamn; the Japs had a radio aboard; the strung antenna glinted high between the two short masts. Radio:

messages; if the Japs had come back to the old island, Spook Island wiped clean for a thorough search, they would have broadcast the description of the ship gone missing. What made that seem far fetched was the raggedy trawler coming to check them out. A gunboat with information would have blown them to pieces by now, *sayonara,* the kiss off and no questions asked.

Oiy . . . oiy! . . . hey!

Head and shoulders out of the hatch, Crusty wrapped a hasty sling around his left arm and cradled the M-1. The two Japs at the guns lounged there, leaning on the shield of the 37mm and grinning.

. . . Oiy! Oiy! . . .

The sunburned Marines were putting on a show, waving the string of fish and bowing like mechanical apes all wound up.

Old joke: what do you get when you cross a Marine with an ape?

A retarded ape.

The Japs at the rail yelled something else, a sharp, command yell.

Crusty hurtled out onto the deck, making room for those behind him. He went to one knee, in the best firing range tradition.

Old joke: Yeah, and what do you get when you cross a Marine with your sister?

The clap.

"Fire! Fire!"

He took out the pair at the guns. The "natives" opened at the other deck as Japs sprang away in all directions. Marines leaped from the hold, firing as they touched down, firing in mid-air. Splinters and chips jumped upward from the Jap deck as fire team Glover blasted up through the gun positions. They caught a Jap diving at the Nambu and knocked him over the side.

The deck house—Crusty hammered a Jap trying to get inside. Others fell; eight, ten? How many, oh lord, how many?

Beats me, son; I always had trouble with math; remember that thing with 666?

Pumping shots at the deck house until the empty clip *spanged!* out, Crusty roared at his people to board; they were close enough.

"Tear up that radio!"

He thumbed a fresh clip into the rifle and lifted the heel of his hand to let the bolt snap forward. Gunfire raged around him as Marines threw themselves at the other ship. One kid bought it partway, butted the hull bloody and curled limp in the water as the ships rocked together and blotted him out forever.

Acceptable casualties, somebody's money-making ass. There would always be casualties, but you didn't write them off as if they were a sand table problem at the Academy. What you did was try to make the dying worthwhile.

The ships bumped again, harder this time, about flipping him over the side. Swaying erect, he caught his balance just as the firing ceased and that sudden, eerie silence fell, that strange silence that sometimes descends upon battlefields.

"General—" It was one of the sunburned Marines, sticking his dark head out of the bullet-ripped deck house.

"Yes, son?"

"Two down in here, and I don't think they got off a signal; big radio is shot all to hell."

"Thank you, son." How often he called them son; they were his sons, every one. He was proud when they did the job right, and it hurt to lose them.

Sergeant Glover patted a rag at a bullet gouge on his cheek. "What now, general?"

Carefully, Crusty stepped onto the Jap deck. "If I weren't here, as the ranking noncom, what would you do?"

The gunny peered at the sun. "It'll be dark soon, so I wouldn't get out of here tonight, but before good light in the morning. So first we feed the Japs to the fish, lash this tub to the *Fuck* to halfway hide it from the air and sea. Cast off and sink the bitch before daylight, after stripping her for what we can use."

"Both guns?"

"Yeah; mount them in the bow, the way they got here. If we get spotted, seeing the guns will confuse them for a while, make them think it's their own tub."

Crusty put on the safety and propped his M-1 against the mast. "Solid planning, sergeant; do it. Save the Jap flag for camouflage."

"You got it, general."

Bending, Crusty took hold of a dead Jap's ankles.

"Hey, general—take a break; we'll do it."

Crusty grunted and dragged the corpse to the far rail. It went over the side with barely a splash.

"Son, I don't know how it is in the old Corps, but with us old doggies, we clean up as we mess up. Besides, I don't mind policing up the area for garbage."

Glover flipped a salute. "Asses and elbows, general; asses and elbows."

CHAPTER 33

INS—Moscow, Oct. 24, 1943: The Moscow Conference between the foreign ministers of the Soviet Union, Great Britain and the United States ended here today. The principle of unconditional surrender for Germany was confirmed.

Also approved were the first steps in founding an international organization for the preservation of peace.

A consultive European commission was chosen and scheduled for London, to study post-war problems which will arise after Germany surrenders.

SECRET to Kill Devil Hill, scrambled, Code 1A—Oct. 24, 1943: The Treasury Islands assault group, part of Rear Admiral Wilkinson's Task Force 31 sailed for its objective today.

US Vice Admiral Spruance issued his first plan for Operation Galvanic, the invasion of the Gilbert Islands.

On New Guinea, the Japanese had no more replacements to throw into their recent attack and withdrew to their strong point at Sattelberg.

REUTERS—On the Italian Front, Oct. 25, 1943—A much rumored "ghost brigade" surfaced with a bang here today. Very much flesh and blood, the Free Polish Brigade fought up two steep mountain ridges under intense fire and broke the German defensive line near Monte Massico and Monte Santa Croce.

The presence of the Free Poles, all eager volunteers, has been held a military secret for some time. Sources at 5th Army headquarters said the unit was pieced together from refugees who had escaped to England and trained there under cover.

Regimental Commander Col. Jerzy Prasniewski said, "The Germans were surprised to have us knock upon their door. They did not invite us in, and did not remain to welcome us."

The last time Chad Belvale shook hands with this man was more than four years ago, on a too-busy, too-bloody beach called Dunkirk. A chance meeting there confirmed his nephew's death in Warsaw. Lt. Walton Belvale was the first of the family to be lost in this war, and had soldiered beside this man as a U.S. Army observer. The tactics and term of *blitzkreig* had just broken upon a stunned world and Walt fell before America was technically at war.

"Colonel Prasniewski."

"Ah, major, the world has turned many times. Oh—I see now it is Colonel Belvale. Congratulations. I am aware of only one Free Polish general as yet, but no matter. The pleasure of action makes up for rank and titles."

The colonel might have stepped fresh out of a Hollywood movie set. Everything about him fairly shouted aristocrat and swashbuckler, but Chad knew Prasniewski to be real and larger than life. It was good that in this modern, often impersonal war there was room left for soldiers like him. It was good that he had survived this long.

Prasniewski now wore the dirt-drab battle dress of the Brits; he had appeared more dashing in his own uniform, when he had worn the eye catching white and gold of the Polish Cavalry, moustached and carrying a dress sword. He was the only man that Chad knew who could have worn a flamboyant cloak. He still had the moustache, waxed to its sharp ends, but the sword had turned into a swagger stick.

"Orderly," he said, and through the newly made wreckage of another era and other wars, came the colonel's batman.

"Tea, sir?"

"Thank you; and you, colonel? Tea or coffee? My troops have not yet—how do you say?—liberated any wine or anisette."

"Thanks; tea will be fine."

Steamy tea meant England and Stephanie Bartlett. It was foggy mornings in the heathered hills of Scotland and Stephanie snugged warm in the feather bed. Hang in, darling. Stay alive and come back to me.

They sat on stone pillars chopped off ragged by artillery. The war rolled on by them and slid downhill to set itself for another mean climb under fire, perhaps the worst the 5th Army had faced so far. Battered Polish soldiers lay resting in the sun or sat leaning against cracked walls of this little town of Cassino. They all wore the far, far stare of the combat man, that blank, hurt look and a thing more; these men were glad to be here, and they clung to their pride. Every step to the north was a step closer to home for them.

Across the cobbled street and beneath a reasonably whole roof, an aid station was set up. Along the bullet-chipped wall of a onetime cafe, the dead lay, some upon canvas litters, some placed side by side on the stones. It didn't matter what uniform they wore; they were neighbors now.

Prasniewski said, "These men have had an opportunity to fight back, and so they may hold up their heads once again. They remember the destruction, the murder and pillaging of Poland.

"Some are alive to recount the battle of the Warsaw ghetto, how those desperate Jews, down to the smallest child, fought to the death. The German armor and artillery, the flame throwers and machine guns did not immediately overwhelm the defenders. With so few arms and such great hearts they held out against all the Germans could do."

The tea arrived upon a gleaming silver service, milk, sugar and lemon on the side.

Smiling, Prasniewski poured. "We must apologize for the lack of sugar cakes. Corporal Janik has had little time to reconnoiter."

Chad laughed and sniffed deeply of the steam. Hot tea, damnit; not the iced tea of Virginia, mint sprig and lemon slice and a dusting of powdered sugar around the rim.

That sort of tea was seated on the front porch of Kill Devil Hill, quiet there behind the purple waterfalls of wisteria. It had been Kirstin, too.

"My son has such an orderly, who is also his radio operator. Could wars be fought without such talents?"

"Not comfortably." Prasniewski crossed one glistening boot over the other and sipped tea. "Your son is an officer, such as Lieutenant Belvale? I believe he was your nephew?"

"My son is a captain in my battalion. He commands a heavy weapons company." Chad took sugar and lemon for his tea. Then he said, "Another son was—wounded in the Pacific. We have lost others."

Slowly, the colonel drank tea. When Chad offered a cigarette, he accepted with the suggestion of a bow, and said: "I think it is always so, to be part of a family which sees warfare as its duty and its goal. I think I am the last of my line to do this; the others—"

Spreading the fingers of his left hand, he said, "Well then; we would have had it no other way. May your bloodline continue for as long as it would wish. Know that Lieutenant Belvale was a good soldier."

Chad spun the wheel of his scratched and dented Zippo and lighted Prasniewski's cigarette. A slow wind rose, a bit chill now, and carrying the stench of combat, the burned and broken things, blood and pieces of a wall that men had pissed against for a hundred years.

"Maybe none of us gets to choose a life path. We do what we can, I suppose, or what we must do."

Prasniewski brightened. "But of course. You are here to—observe, as you did in France? As your nephew did? Back in London, I drew a careful map of where the lieutenant fell. When we return, I shall be certain that you receive a copy."

"I'll stay awhile with the Polish Brigade, if that's all right. My own unit is just marking time in England, training for its third amphibious operation."

The orderly appeared from behind a tumble of smoking ruins, a dark green bottle in each hand.

"Anisette," Prasniewski said.

"Liberated by Corporal Janik."

Janik showed silver-capped teeth. "Welcome, colonel, and welcome again."

Prasniewski held a bottle to the light. "I suppose a good orderly is difficult to find these days, one who frees the enemy's dried sausage as well as his potables."

And the first of the *nebelwerfer* barrages shrieked in, too close to be random fire.

WHAM-WHAM-WHAM!!
WHAM-WHAM-WHAM!!

Prasniewski blew rock dust from the anisette bottle. "Unless there is a misfire, they always arrive in sixes, fired from a great, clumsy packet of 15-centimeter tubes. A wheeled packet of course, so they can run off to another position before counter battery fire can be laid upon them."

"We saw a few of them in Tunisia."

"Ah, yes; forgive me; I enjoy practicing English and the American language. There are a few major differences."

Corporal Janik brushed the second bottle carefully before presenting it to Chad. He seemed as unconcerned about danger as his colonel.

"Your health," Chad said and damned near choked on the licorice tasting stuff when the next *nebelwerfer* fire forced the Polish infantry to scatter for cover.

The very air always stank in a close combat zone, acrid gunsmoke, the sizzle of wood and cloth burning in the aftermath. Chad's ears rang and he spat to clear his mouth of the taste.

"*Our* health," Prasniewski said. "Yours and mine and Sergeant-to-be-Janik's. Excellent anisette, sergeant. Please share it."

And to Chad, he said, "Look far out at about eleven o'clock high, very high. That monstrous pile of stone atop the mountain is a famous monastery. The Boche are using it as an observation post, so that we will be naked to their eyes, day after day. Monte Cassino; they think we will not bomb such a holy place."

Swallowing another drink, Chad said, "They're probably right. Damn, this is going to be a long war."

BLACK STAR—Eastern Front in the Crimea, Oct. 25, 1943: Russian troops have isolated German forces by capturing Armynsk at the base of the peninsula. They have also landed more troops at Kerch.

Meanwhile, Berlin propaganda claims their armies made heavy counter-attacks in the Krivoy Rog area, and as usual, count them as "great successes."

SECRET, EYES ONLY, to Kill Devil Hill, scrambled, Code 2B—Solomon Islands, Nov. 1, 1943: At 0730 hours this date, Task Force 31 put the 3rd Marine Division and a special detachment of army troops ashore in the area of Cape Torokina (Empress Augusta Bay) on the central southern coast of Bougainville.

Task Force 39 and carrier planes from Task Force 38 bombed the airfields on Buka Island. Although many Japanese aircraft are unserviceable, the enemy managed to field a number of planes which damaged a few American transports and a destroyer. Some 104 Japanese fighters struck the convoy and landing parties, at a heavy cost to *them* of 100 fighters and 16 bombers.

Eddie Donnely lifted slowly to one knee and mopped sweat from his forehead. The air was thick and muggy, lying heavy in the lungs; it was like trying to breath under water. To the east, sporadic small arms fire sounded as the Marines made the first solid contact with what had to be disorganized resistance. He hoped that the Japs would soon recover from their shock and fall into their defensive pattern. That's why his detachment was here, anticipating the reaction and setting up for it. Here on the high ground, he had a good view of Empress Augusta Bay and a fair spread of the beach.

Lieutenant Stasio rose whispering beside him, a chunky, growly man. "I'd feel better if we'd had time to dig in."

"We were lucky to get the job done in time."

Stasio held a cigarette between his lips but didn't light it. "Does G-2 ever know what it's doing?"

"The only game in town, lieutenant. It looks good on paper. The local Japs have been pulling back off the beaches to miss getting beat up by our ships. No resistance until they slip back to the landing and either jump on us while we're hauling stuff ashore, or sweep inland in the rear of the main force."

Boof Hardin crawled to them. "Could be they're up against the Marines and ain't coming back. I sure hate to waste all them mines, and there's a couple of booby traps that are downright beautiful."

Raising the binoculars, Eddie checked the bay. "Okay so far. G-2 thought not much would happen at sea until late tonight. Then the Japs will bring in reinforcements or use their big guns on us. Hardin—"

"We got the ship-to-shore radio set up and working five by five. You want to do commo? When you reckon them little bastards to sneak back here? I feel kind of bare-ass if I don't have me a foxhole."

"Yeah," Lieutenant Stasio said.

"Send the radio up for me. We stay quiet in the bush until and if the Japs come down. If they have scouts out, they'll pick us up if we're digging in or just moving around.

Pass the word to take turns sleeping, and nobody lights a cigarette. Anything to add, lieutenant?''

"No, damnit; regiment threw me into this operation because I happened to be passing. Hell, I had my orders cut; I'm supposed to be on my way to Melbourne for special training. I don't know shit from Shinola.''

Boof chuckled. "Boy, did you take a wrong turn. Sarge, I'm gone.''

Eddie watched him move into deeper cover, handling the BAR as if it were a belly gun; Boof Hardin was a big and powerful guy.

He said to Stasio, "You saw the stuff we planted; enough to blow off the ass end of this island and scatter a bunch of Japs halfway to Tokyo. The boxes placed around the area look as if it was abandoned in a hurry; the Japs ought to buy that, since they've got the only heroes in this war.

"If they don't come by land, then it's two if by sea. They want to feed in more troops and hang on to this island. This is the best landing site for miles, according to Recon pictures we've been getting from the navy fliers. Either way, we have a weenie roast.''

"It all sounds too damned easy and I ought to be in Melbourne. Here comes the radio. I'll take up the prone position for now. Blow reveille if the Japs don't buy any of this and come busting up here to screw me out of my trip to Australia.''

"What kind of special training, lieutenant?''

"Demolition; we're supposed to check out a lot of new firecrackers.''

Eddie grinned. "Somebody figured you to ace this job, using up the old stuff.''

"Fuck them," Stasio said. "Fuck them and feed them beans.''

(Barracks talk: Tell it to Jesus; the chaplain's on pass.)

Inland, the sounds of the firefight faded away. The heat and the quiet settled heavily upon Eddie, and from time to time he came close to nodding off. Sleep was easy; sleep was real, a clean white sheet against the dark. Nothing moved through the afternoon, and by evening the C-rations had been eaten and the cans buried. Drinking water ran low, but nobody bitched about the lack of action, and they needed the rest.

Gloria, Eddie thought, Gloria and Sandhurst Keep, fire and ice and what the hell did he think he was doing, marrying into her high brass family? She was a whole lot of woman, and goddamnit, she was army—RA all the way.

Inside his head he said: Big Mike, did I screw up her life? You never married after Ma died, and you didn't love her in the first place. You let that shiny bitch from Officer's Row twist your guts.

Or maybe you knew all along that a soldier ought to be a soldier and nothing more—no husband, no daddy. The fucking army has to be your life and your wife, and no divorce.

(Barracks talk, Cash Street in the Canal zone: no mama, no papa, no Uncle Sam . . . Get out of here, you little bastard.)

Stasio did his time on the radio, and the night eased quietly by; night birds set up a gossip line, and monkeys chattered high in the canopy. The jungle sounds were good news; if the Japs came sniffing back, a puddle of silence would grow before and after them as all night things hushed at their passing.

Eddie's watch face showed its fluorescent numerals at 0139 when radio traffic suddenly picked up, crackling into his ear phones. It said that the Japanese 8th Fleet, commanded by Rear Admiral Sentaro Omori, was heading for Bougainville.

Hauling fresh troops or just gearing up to hammer Empress August Bay with those huge shells? Eddie strained to hear every report through the static that came and went. He heard nothing important until 0230, when a flash told him that the U.S. Task Force 39, made up of the light cruisers *Montpelier, Cleveland, Columbia* and *Denver,* was steaming north with its screen of eight destroyers to protect the bay.

Minutes later the destroyers fired the first torpedoes against the enemy squadron, and an excited swabbie on open radio called out that a Nip destroyer just rammed the Nip cruiser *Sendai*. A salvo from the friendlies caught the *Sendai* again as Eddie peered out to sea. All he could see of the sea battle was those flashes on the horizon so like heat lightning.

Fascinated, Eddie picked up the same excited sailor laughing his ass off about Omori's flagship, the heavy cruiser *Myoko,* and the destroyer *Hatsukaze* colliding. Flares broke high in the sky and Jap planes came in to score hits on the *Denver,* but didn't stop her. Another set of white flares broke over this end of the bay, and Eddie shut down his radio.

Lieutenant Stasio touched Eddie's shoulder and whispered. "Our bird dogs didn't come late for a change?"

"Kicking Jap navy ass. Tojo won't be putting reinforcements ashore."

A parachute flare floated zigzag nearer the beach.

"What do you know," Eddie murmured, "G-2 was on the stick this time. Can you make out Japs infiltrating onto our beach?"

"Barely," Stasio hissed. "Should I wake the troops?"

"They're wide awake. I hope that flare holds long enough to pull more of the little bastards onto the beach. If I count down—"

There was no need to push the plunger from the high ground. Some greedy Jap had gone for the booby-trapped food. The curved beach leaped into the air with a thunderous roar, one explosion feeding into the next one.

"Banzai," Eddie said.

CHAPTER 34

REUTERS—The Italian Front, Nov. 3, 1943: In the British X Corps sector, patrols from the 7th Armored Division and 476th Division reached the Garigliano River. The 8th Indian Division attacked repeatedly against the German 16th Armored Division.

The operations were supported not only by a tremendous barrage from field guns, but also by effective saturation shelling by warships cruising along the Adriatic coast.

He could not see. *Gott im himmel,* he had gone blind.

Arno Hindemit's ears roared and he tasted blood. With shaking hands, he felt over his face and found only split lips. Carefully, his fingers probed over cheekbones and forehead; *Gott, Gott*—not his eyes.

Nothing. The blast still echoed in his ears, and if he had a choice, let him remain deaf, so long as he could see, even a little bit.

Yes, there was light. Maybe all would clear up when his head stopped spinning. Never had he felt anything like the concussion from the huge navy shells. They must be the size of *lastkraftwagens* as big as trucks. A few of them would flatten an entire town. Here they were overkill, anything to make a simple landser's day miserable.

Spitting blood, he strained his eyes wide, forcing them

to see, commanding them to focus. Slowly, they did. He made out a great, smoking hole where the machine gun section had been.

ZUU-ZUU-ZUU—a deadly steam engine hurtling through the agonized sky.

His body reacted without conscious direction, twisting him into a ball, every muscle crying *enug! enug!*—enough.

But this huge shell passed over, and the others that followed, steam locomotives thundering. The *Amis* were lifting the barrage and walking it farther inland. Pity the poor bastards that would die there; without guilt, he was grateful that the shells were not falling here.

His ears popped. The captain; Witzelei—*scheissen!* There he lay in that awful flat position of the dead or badly wounded, blood oozing out of his ears.

Coming first to his knees, Arno struggled upright and wobbled over to Hauptmann Witzelei. Dizzy, he stopped to find the pulse in Witzelei's throat. Yes, he lived; for this moment, he lived.

Arno flinched at the explosions of mortar shells and the maddened bee buzzing and whining of mid-range automatic weapons fire. That was the reason the naval shelling had moved along. The *Amis* were coming.

He took the captain's wrists and pulled to lift Witzelei limply across his shoulders. Panting, he plodded around the great shell hole and moved downhill, feet braced wide on the muddy slope. If Witzelei didn't lose too much blood, they might make it.

Schiessen; this long at war and he had forgotten to pick up his machine pistol.

An omen?

Lt. Gen. Preston Belvale stared at the telephone he held. Halfway around the world the word had been passed, by drums and runners, by radio signals and phone lines: Penny Belvale and Leftenant Stephanie Bartlett had made it to Borneo, which he had hoped and in general expected. He should be able to get them the rest of the way home.

Just now, he had been ordered to report to the War Department. Before any of the family could think of a break, something big was coming up.

MAJ. GEN. CHARLES CARLISLE: There's a hell of a lot of ocean between here and wherever the wind is taking us. The motor quit days ago, and we're still in Jap waters.

CAPT. GAVIN SCOTT: What do you know? Suddenly I have a numbered account in Zurich, more than enough to pay my way out. When my pet squarehead notified the family that I'm alive and interned here through the Swiss Red Cross, an extra note went along. Not much more of this neutrality crap, and I'll be flying again. I'll find Stephanie Bartlett, too.

KIRSTIN BELVALE-SHELBY: It took awhile for me to get back to the horse program, and I won't allow myself to become so involved with any patient again. I'm not sorry it happened with Harlan Edgerton. When Chad called to give me news about the boys, our boys, it was almost as if we haven't been apart for so long. Almost.

TECH. SGT. EDDIE DONNELY: It's one damned island after another. Only the names change, only the faces change as luck runs out for the older guys and the replacements come in. I'm having trouble concentrating; I think about Gloria too much. What's next for the troops? How many islands do we bypass before we can get on with the war? The Philippines, I figure; they're next.

MAJ. KEENAN CARLISLE: Susie Lokomaikai is beautiful; Susie is so much like Chang Yen Ling, kind and giving and very strong. She will understand when I have to go back into combat. I am still *yonsei,* and there are Jap heads to be taken.

NANCY CARLISLE: I don't know if I'm in love with Fitz. I love being with him, and so far there's no awkwardness about Keenan. To me, Keenan often talks of returning to his hate mission, killing Japanese. He doesn't know that Susie is mostly Japanese.

PENNY BELVALE: I'll do anything to lose this baby, this hated thing growing inside me. And I will stay alive, whatever it takes, so I can go back and find Hideo Watanabe and kill him. Stephanie will help me.

LT. SLOAN TRAVIS: The outfit is balanced upon a knife edge. If we don't get off the dime and make the big landing, we'll go stale. Listen to me—damn; I'm still a civilian at heart. I just sound like Regular Army. And speaking of which, Owen Belvale doesn't, any more. He's an inch or two from real trouble, because of that frigging woman.

LT. COL. CHAD BELVALE: The observation post at Monte Cassino is killing us day by day and nobody higher up will order it bombed. The Polish Brigade is thinking about taking the monastery in a frontal attack. That's suicidal, but these soldiers will climb that mountain through hell and high water. I'd like to stay with them and their larger than life colonel, but I've been ordered to get the hell back to my own outfit. The big one is coming up, but if the Krauts stop us at the water, this war will go on forever.

LOOK FOR BOOK 4 OF

THE
MEN AT ARMS
SERIES

ALLIED IN VICTORY

At Bougainville in the Solomon Islands, the Japanese are dug in to the end, and Major Keenan Carlisle pays the price when he is captured by the enemy. General Preston Belvale goes to England to help prepare for the top-secret invasion of France, while Colonel Chad Belvale fights with the courageous Free Poles through the gory battle for Cassino, and Captain Owen Belvale gets in over his head with a beautiful woman.

Secrecy, planning and courage are of the essence. But the Belvales and Carlisles are caught up in their own desperate struggles. Penny Belvale and Leftenant Stephanie Bartlett survive a Japanese attack that kills all but one man of their Burmese rescue team, while General Crusty Carlisle leads his Marines to safety.

The war is entering its crucial hour. On Normandy beaches and in Hiroshima, conflagration awaits . . .

CON SELLERS

MEN AT ARMS

The saga of two legendary military families fully involved in the global inferno of World War II.

"Compelling...A rich and dramatic series about two great American military dynasties and their epic battles in World War II."—W.E.B. Griffin

MEN AT ARMS I: THE GATHERING STORM
September 1991

MEN AT ARMS II: THE FLAMES OF WAR
December 1991

MEN AT ARMS III: THE WORLD ABLAZE
March 1992

MEN AT ARMS IV: ALLIED IN VICTORY
June 1992

**Available in Paperback
from Pocket Books
Beginning September 1991**

POCKET
B O O K S

415

THE BEST MEN'S FICTION COMES FROM POCKET BOOKS

- [ ] BIG TIME Marcel Montecino .... 70971-2/$5.99
- [ ] BOOMER Charles D. Taylor .... 74330-9/$5.50
- [ ] BRIGHT STAR Harold Coyle .... 68543-0/$5.95
- [ ] BROTHERS IN BATTLE Con Sellers .... 65254-0/$4.95
- [ ] THE CROSSKILLER Marcel Montecino .... 67894-9/$5.99
- [ ] DEEP STING Charles D. Taylor .... 67631-8/$4.95
- [ ] FLIGHT OF THE INTRUDER Stephen Coonts ..70960-7/$5.95
- [ ] MEN AT ARMS #1
      THE GATHERING STORM Con Sellers .... 66765-3/$4.95
- [ ] MEN AT ARMS #2
      FLAMES OF WAR Con Sellers .... 66766-1/$5.99
- [ ] RAISE THE RED DAWN Bart Davis .... 69663-7/$4.95
- [ ] RED ARMY Ralph Peters.................................... 67669-5/$5.50
- [ ] SWORD POINT Harold Coyle .... 73712-0/$5.99
- [ ] 38 NORTH YANKEE Ed Ruggero .... 70022-7/$5.95
- [ ] A TIME OF WAR Michael Peterson ...70126-6/$5.95
- [ ] UNDER SIEGE Stephen Coonts ....74294-9/$5.95
- [ ] THE WAR IN 2020 Ralph Peters ....75172-7/$5.99

Simon & Schuster Mail Order Dept. MEN
200 Old Tappan Rd., Old Tappan, N.J. 07675

POCKET BOOKS

Please send me the books I have checked above. I am enclosing $_____ (please add 75¢ to cover postage and handling for each order. Please add appropriate local sales tax). Send check or money order—no cash or C.O.D.'s please. Allow up to six weeks for delivery. For purchases over $10.00 you may use VISA: card number, expiration date and customer signature must be included.

Name _____

Address _____

City _____ State/Zip _____

VISA Card No. _____ Exp. Date _____

Signature _____ 213-01

"This is the best first novel I have ever read."
—Tom Clancy

NORTH SAR

GERRY CARROLL

A Novel of Navy Combat in Vietnam

In this searingly realistic novel, one of the most decorated naval aviators since Vietnam brings us the dramatic story of attack bomber pilots and helicopter pilots flying combat *Search and Rescue* (SAR) — in the Navy's air war against North Vietnam.

Available in Hardcover from Pocket Books

POCKET
BOOKS

449-1